THE GABRIEL HOUNDS

By the same author

AIRS ABOVE THE GROUND

THIS ROUGH MAGIC

THE MOON-SPINNERS

THE IVY TREE

MY BROTHER MICHAEL

NINE COACHES WAITING

THUNDER ON THE RIGHT

WILDFIRE AT MIDNIGHT

MADAM, WILL YOU TALK?

The
GABRIEL HOUNDS

———⋯⦵⋯———

by Mary Stewart

———⋯⦵⋯———

M. S. MILL CO., INC.

NEW YORK

distributed by William Morrow & Company, Inc.

FOR
HELEN KING

AUTHOR'S NOTE

This story is freely based on the accounts of the life of the Lady Hester Stanhope. I have tried to shorten my references as much as possible, but for those who are interested, the list of books on page 84 will act as a guide and also an acknowledgment of my main sources. My debt to Doughty's *Travels in Arabia Deserta*, and also to Robin Fedden's marvellous *Syria and Lebanon* (John Murray) will be more than obvious.

One other word may perhaps be necessary. In a story of this sort it is inevitable that officials are mentioned by office, if not by name. Any references to Government bodies, Cabinet Ministers, frontier officials, etc., are made purely for the purposes of this story, and do not refer to any actual holders of these offices, living or dead. Moreover, though the Adonis Valley certainly exists, the Nahr el-Sal'q—with the village and the palace of Dar Ibrahim—does not.

I should also like to thank all those friends, from Edinburgh to Damascus, who have given me so much generous help.

M. S.

Chapter One

————◦◦◦————

No vain discourse shalt thou hear therein:
Therein shall be a gushing fountain;
Therein shall be raised couches,
And goblets ready placed,
And cushions laid in order,
And carpets spread forth.

—THE KORAN: Sura LXXXVII

I MET HIM in the street called Straight.

I had come out of the dark shop doorway into the dazzle of the Damascus sun, my arms full of silks. I didn't see anything at first, because the sun was right in my eyes and he was in shadow, just where the Straight Street becomes a dim tunnel under its high corrugated iron roof.

The souk was crowded. Someone stopped in front of me to take a photograph. A crowd of youths went by, eyeing me and calling comments in Arabic, punctuated by "Miss" and " 'Allo" and "Good-bye." A small grey donkey pattered past under a load of vegetables three times its own width. A taxi shaved me so near that I took a half step back into the shop doorway and the shopkeeper, at my elbow, put out a protective hand for his rolls of silk. The taxi swerved, horn blaring,

9

past the donkey, parted a tight group of ragged children the way a ship parts water, and aimed without any slackening of speed at the bottleneck where the street narrowed sharply between jutting rows of stalls.

It was then that I saw him. He had been standing, head bent, in front of a jeweler's stall, turning over some small gilt trinket in his hand. At the blast of the taxi's horn he glanced up, and stepped quickly out of the way. The step took him from black shadow full into the sun's glare, and, with a queer jerk of the heart, I saw who it was. I had known he was in this part of the world, and I suppose it was no odder to meet him in the middle of Damascus than anywhere else, but I stood there in the sunlight gazing, I suppose rather blankly, at the averted profile, four years strange to me, yet so immediately familiar, and somehow so inevitably here.

The taxi vanished into the black tunnel of the main souk with a jarring of gears and another yell of its horn. Between us the dirty hot street was empty. One of the rolls of silk slipped from my hands, and I grabbed for it, to catch it in a cascade of crimson just before it reached the filthy ground. The movement and the blinding colour must have caught his attention, for he turned, and our eyes met. I saw them widen, then he dropped the gilt object back on the jeweler's stall, and, ignoring the stream of bad American which the man was shouting after him, crossed the street towards me. The years rolled back more swiftly even than the crimson silk as he said, with exactly the same intonation with which a small boy had daily greeted his even smaller worshipper:

"Oh, hullo! It's you!"

I wasn't a small girl any more, I was twenty-two, and this was only my cousin Charles, whom of course I didn't worship any more. For some reason it seemed important to make this clear. I tried to echo his tone, but only managed to achieve a sort of idiotic deadpan calm. "Hullo. How nice to see you. How you've grown!"

"Haven't I just, and I shave nearly every week now." He grinned at me, and suddenly it wasn't the small boy any more. "Christy love, thank goodness I've found you! What in the world are you doing here?"

"Didn't you know I was in Damascus?"

"I knew you were coming, but I couldn't find out when. I meant, what are you doing on your own? I thought you were here with a package tour?"

"Oh, I am," I said, "I just got kind of detached. Did Mummy tell you about it?"

"She told my mother, who passed it on to me, but nobody seemed very clear what you were doing or just when you'd be here, or even where you'd be staying. You might have known I'd want to catch up with you. Don't you ever give anyone your address?"

"I thought I had."

"You did tell your mother a hotel, but it was the wrong one. When I rang them up they told me your group had gone to Jerusalem, and when I telephoned there they referred me back to Damascus. You cover your tracks well, young Christy."

"I'm sorry," I said, "if I'd known there was a chance of meeting you before Beirut . . . Our itinerary was changed, that's all, something to do with the flight bookings, so we're doing the tour back to front, and they had to alter the Damascus hotel. Oh, blast, and we leave for Beirut tomorrow! We've been here three days now. Have you been here all the time?"

"Only since yesterday. The man I have to see in Damascus isn't coming home till Saturday, but when I was told you'd be about due to arrive here, I came straight up. As you say, blast. Look, perhaps it's a good thing they've turned your tour arsy-versy—you needn't go tomorrow, surely? I've got to wait here till the weekend, myself, so why don't you cut loose from your group and we'll do Damascus together and then go

on to Beirut? You're not bound to stay with them, are you?"
He looked down at me, raising his brows. "What on earth are
you doing in a package tour, anyway? I wouldn't have
thought it was exactly your thing."

"I suppose not, but I got a sudden yen to see this part of
the world, and I didn't know a thing about it, and they make
it so easy—they do everything about bookings and things, and
there's a courier who speaks Arabic and knows the score. I
couldn't very well come on my own, could I?"

"I don't see why not. And don't look at me with those
great big helpless eyes, either. If any female was ever entirely
capable of looking after herself, it's you."

"Oh, sure, Black Belt of the nth degree, that's me." I
regarded him with pleasure. "Oh, Charles, believe it or not,
it's marvelous to see you! Thank goodness your mother
caught up with you and told you I'd be here! It'd have been
lovely to have some time here with you, but it can't be
helped. I'd planned to wait around in Beirut after the rest of
my group goes home on Saturday, so I'll stick to that, I think.
Have you had a good trip? A sort of Grand Tour, wasn't it,
with Robbie?"

"Sort of. Seeing the world and brushing up my Arabic
before doing some real work in Beirut. Oh, it all went like a
bomb . . . We drove down through France and shipped the
car to Tangier and then ambled along through North
Africa. Robbie had to go home from Cairo, so I came on
alone. It was in Cairo I got Mother's letter saying you were
coming on this trip of yours, so I came straight up, hoping
we'd coincide."

"Did you say you had to see someone here? Business?"

"Partly. Look, what are we standing here for? This place
smells, and any minute now we'll be mown down by one of
these donkeys. Come and have some tea."

"Love to, but where do you propose to find tea in the
middle of Damascus?"

"In my little pad, which is the nearest thing to the Azem Palace you ever saw." He grinned. "I'm not at a hotel, I'm staying with a man I knew at Oxford, Ben Sifara, I don't know whether you ever heard your father mention the name? Ben's father's a bit of a V.I.P. in Damascus—knows everyone and owns a bit of everything, has a brother banking in Beirut and a brother-in-law in the Cabinet—Minister of the Interior, no less. The family's what they call a 'good family' over here, which in Syria just means stinking rich."

"Nice going. At that rate we'd be well up in the stud book."

"Well, aren't we?" My cousin was crisply ironic. I knew what he meant. My own family of merchant bankers had been stinking rich for three generations, and it was surprising how many people were willing to overlook the very mixed, not to say plain bastard blood that pumped through the Mansel veins.

I laughed. "I suppose he's a business contact of Daddy and Uncle Chas?"

"Yes. Ben made me promise to look him up if ever I was in Syria, and Father was keen for me to make contact, so here I am."

"Big deal. Well, I'd love to come. Just wait a moment till I get my silk." I considered the brilliant mass in my arms. "The only thing is, which?"

"I'm not wild keen on either, if you want the truth." My cousin lifted a fold, felt it, frowned at it, and let it fall. "Nice texture, but the red's rather fierce, isn't it? People'd post letters in you. And the blue . . .? Not, but not, for you, my love. It doesn't suit me, and I like my girls to tone."

I regarded him coldly. "And just for that I'll buy them both and have them made up in stripes. Horizontal. No, I do rather see what you mean. They looked all right in the shop."

"Since they keep it pitch dark in there, they would."

"Well, fair enough, I wanted it for a dressing gown. Perhaps in a dim light . . . ? I mean, the pattern's rather nice and Eastern . . . ?"

"No."

"The sickening thing about you," I said tartly, "is that you're sometimes right. What were you buying for yourself along Woolworth Alley, if it comes to that? A ring for Emily?"

"A jewel for my love, certainly. A blue bead for my car."

"A blue bead for your—? A *blue bead* for your car? Now this I really do not believe!"

He laughed. "Didn't you know? Blue beads ward off the Evil Eye. All the camels and donkeys wear them, so why not the car? They sometimes have rather fetching turquoise ones. Never mind now, I can get one any time. Do you really want some silk? Have a heart, anything you get at home will be just as good, and you won't have the trouble of carrying it."

The shopkeeper, who was just behind me, and whose presence we had both completely forgotten, here said with justifiable bitterness: "We do all right till you come. The lady had very good taste."

"I'm sure she had," said my cousin, "but you can't expect me to stand for a dressing gown in pillar-box red or budgie blue. If you've anything else more suitable perhaps you'll show it to us."

The man's expression lightened to pleased comprehension, and, as he took in my cousin's obviously expensive clothes, anticipation. "I understand. Forgive, sir. You are the lady's husband."

"Not yet," said Charles. "Come on, Christy, let's go in and buy it, and then get out of this and go where we can talk. My car's in the square at the end of the street. Where is your party, by the way?"

"I don't know, I lost them. We'd been through the Great Mosque, and then we were all trailing in a sort of croc through the souks and I stopped to look at the stalls, and then they'd sort of gone."

"And you let them go? Won't they start combing the souks with bloodhounds when they find you're missing?"

"Probably." I gathered up the silks and turned to the shop doorway. "Charles, if there was some really luscious off-white—"

"Seriously, hadn't you better telephone the hotel?"

I shrugged. "I doubt if they'll even miss me before dinner. They're used to me wandering off by now."

"Still the same spoiled little madam I love?"

"I just don't like crowds. Anyway, look who's talking! Daddy always said you were spoiled rotten yourself, and it's true, so help me."

"But yes. Dear Uncle Chris," said my cousin placidly, following me into the black cave of the shop.

In the end I did buy white, some lovely heavy off-white brocade which, not much to my surprise, Charles seemed to conjure from some dim shelf which the shopkeeper hadn't previously shown me. Moreover, it was cheaper than anything I had yet seen. Nor did it come as much of a surprise to hear Charles talking to the shopkeeper and his assistant in a slowish but what seemed to be passably fluent Arabic. He might (as my parents had often told one another in my hearing) be 'spoiled rotten,' but nobody had ever denied that he had considerable intelligence when he chose to use it—which was (as they insisted) about once a month, and then entirely in his own interests.

When we had reached the square, followed by the shop boy carrying the silk, Charles's car was instantly recognizable—not by its make or colour, neither of which could be seen, but by the six-deep crowd of small boys who stood round it. On investigation it proved to be a white Porsche 911 S. And because I loved my cousin and knew my stuff, I promptly gave him his cue.

"What a little beauty! How do you like her?"

He told me. He opened the bonnet and showed me. He almost stripped her down to demonstrate to me. The small boys loved it. They crowded in, twelve deep now, open-mouthed and staring, and probably taking in rather more than I did of the MacPherson struts and lower wishbones, compression ratios and torques and telescopic dampers . . . I let the loverlike phrases roll over me and watched my cousin's face and hands and remembered all the other times—the electric train set, the kestrel's egg, the first wristwatch, the bicycle . . .

He straightened up, hauled a couple of boys backwards out of the engine and shut the bonnet, paid off the two biggest who had presumably been on guard for him, and gave the shop boy a tip that startled him into fervent speech. We drove off.

"What's he saying?"

"Just 'thank you'. In other words, 'The blessing of Allah be upon you, your children, and your children's children.'" The car threaded its competent way out of the packed square, and turned down a narrow rutted street with every telescopic damper working overtime. "This means you, more or less. I hope we're still engaged?"

"*Faute de mieux,* I suppose we are. But I seem to remember that you broke it off yourself, and in writing, when you met that blonde female—what was her name, the model? The one that looked like a Belsen case."

"Samantha? She was very chic."

"Oh, sure. They have to look that anyway, don't they, so that they can wear all that far-out clobber standing up to their knees in the sea, or stable straw, or empty Coke bottles or something. What happened to Samantha?"

"Probably met her just fate, but not with me."

"Well, that was ages ago—just after the last time we met.

No one else in my way? You can't tell me you've been going straight for four years?"

"Are you joking?" He changed down, turned sharp left and accelerated down another filthy little alley with a total width of about a yard and a half. "But actually, yes. Virtually, if you get me."

"I get you. What happened to Emily?"

"Who the devil's Emily?"

"Wasn't it Emily? Last year. I'm sure Mummy said Emily—or was it Myrtle? The names you pick."

"I can't see that any of them are worse than Christabel."

I laughed. "You have a point there."

"As far as I'm concerned," said my cousin, "we're still pledged as from the cradle. The lovely lolly is still in the family, and Great-Great-Grandfather Rosenbaum, on whom be peace, can stop whirling in his whited sepulchre as from now, so—"

"Mind that puppy!"

"It's all right, I saw it—at least, the Porsche did. So that's settled. *Also gut!*"

"You take a lot for granted, don't you? Just because I stayed faithful all my teens, even when you had spots."

"A fat lot of chance you had to be anything else," said my cousin. "You were as fat as a seal puppy yourself. I must say you've improved." A sideways look, summarily brotherly, with rather less sexual appraisement than a dog-show judge. "In fact, you're rather gorgeous, coz, and I like that dress. Well, blight my hopes if you must. Is there someone?"

I grinned. "Watch it, love, or you'll find it's for real, and you'll be selling your car to buy a diamond."

"Suits me," he said lightly. "And here we are."

The Porsche slowed down and turned at right angles out of the street into a small unappetizing courtyard, where the sun struck blindly down into the dust, and two cats slept on a stack of battered petrol cans. In one corner was a wedge of indigo shade, and into this, with an elegant economy of effort, he drove the car and parked it.

"Front entrance, Damascus style. Looks like nothing on earth, doesn't it? Come in."

It didn't look at first as if the courtyard could be the entrance to anything. It was boxed, stiflingly, by its high, blind walls, and smelt of hens and stale urine. But at one side a big archway was forbiddingly blocked by a door whose warped timbers still held, in the massive wrought handle and hinges, a hint of some ancient splendour. Charles opened the door on a black passageway, which gave at the other end on an arch of light. We went through.

The light came from a second courtyard, this time an oblong about the size of a tennis court, with pointed Moorish arches on three sides holding a shady cloister, and on the fourth, at the end of the court, a raised platform or dais behind a triple arch, which made a kind of stage or small inner room. The back and sides of this dais were furnished with wide bench seats set against the wall, and I recognized the 'divan' or place where men of the East meet and talk. Even in modern Eastern houses today the sitting rooms are often arranged like this, traditionally, with chairs and sofas backed against the wall on three sides of the room. Low tables stood in front of the couches. In the middle of the court a fountain played; the floor was tiled with blue and white, and the miniature colonnade was jeweled and glittering with mosaics in blue and green and gilt. A turtle dove crooned somewhere, orange trees stood here and there in tubs, and where the fountain splashed I caught the gleam of a gold fin. The court was very cool, and smelt of orange blossom.

"Come into the divan," said Charles. "Yes, it's rather lovely, isn't it? There's something very satisfying about Arab building, I always think—all poetry and passion and romance, but elegant with it. Like their literature, if it comes to that.

18

But you ought to see the furniture; my bedroom's done up with the rejects from Bluebeard's chamber."

"I know what you mean, I saw some choice pieces in those homey little rooms in the Azem Palace—all inlaid with mother-of-pearl like smallpox, or else pure Victorian and made of arthritic bamboos. But oh, Charles, the rugs! Look at those . . . and that blue one on the couch . . . am I really allowed to sit on it?"

"Go right ahead. I think Ben'll be in soon, but meanwhile as he keeps telling me, his house is mine, so what would you like? Tea?"

"I think I'd rather have coffee. What do you do, clap your hands and summon the eunuchs?"

"More or less." On the quite hideous inlaid table in front of me, there was a little brass bell. He picked this up and rang it, then prowled restlessly—he had always been restless—down the steps of the divan as far as the fountain, waiting. I sat down on the beautiful blue rug, leaned against the cushions, and watched him

No, he hadn't changed. As children, we were always supposed to be very much alike, Charles and I; in fact when we were small, people had taken us for twins. This had always infuriated Charles, who in those days had been aggressively masculine, but to me, dumbly worshipping my clever cousin as only a small girl can, it had been a delight. As we grew up the resemblance had, of course, faded. There were still the basic similarities, the dark hair, high Slav cheekbones, slightly aquiline nose, grey eyes and spare build. Now he was some inches taller than I, and he had broadened, but had seemingly reacted from the aggressive masculinity of adolescence towards a sort of carefully casual elegance which somehow suited him, and oddly enough was no less male. He had on his North African travels acquired a fine tan, and this made his eyes look lighter than my own, though this may only have been in contrast to the black lashes which were (in

Nature's unfair way) longer and thicker than mine. Be that as it may, Charles's eyes were beautiful, dark grey and thickly fringed. Occasionally still, I thought, the resemblance between us must be striking; a turn of the head, a trick of the voice, a movement. What we certainly had in common was the 'spoiled' quality that we were so quick to recognize in one another; a flippant cleverness that could become waspish, an arrogance that did not spring from any pride of achievement but was, I am afraid, the result of having too much too young; a fiercely self-conscious rejecting of any personal ties (including those of our families) which we called independence, but which was really an almost morbid fear of possessiveness; and something we called sensitivity, which probably only meant that our skins were too thin for our own comfort.

Perhaps I should explain here that the relationship between Charles and myself was at once closer and more distant than that between ordinary cousins. For one thing, we were not first, but second cousins, with nothing nearer than a great-grandfather in common; for the other, we had been brought up together almost from birth, certainly from the time when memory starts. I couldn't remember a time when I had not shared everything with my cousin Charles.

His father, Henry Mansel, had been the senior member of our—the English—branch of the family, the other male members being his cousins, the twin brothers Charles and Christopher. Christopher, the junior twin, was my father. Charles had no children, so when Henry Mansel and his wife met with a fatal sailing accident only a few months after the birth of their son Charles, my uncle took the baby to bring up as his own. Remembering no others, young Charles and I had of course always regarded his adoptive parents as his own, and I believe it came as a considerable shock to my cousin to be reminded on approaching his majority that he would eventually take precedence of his 'father' in the family's private corridors of power. A marked family likeness helped to close the ranks. Henry Mansel had strongly resembled his cousins, and they—our 'fathers', as we thought of them—were identical twins who had been, almost up to the time they were married, both inseparable and indistinguishable. They had, in fact, married on the same day, having chosen girls who bore no relation to one another, but who—as one could see still— had been of much the same physical type. Happily, the two Mrs. Mansels liked one another immensely—happily because, when Henry's death left vacant the family house in Kent and Charles took it over, his brother built one for himself within a mile of it. So Charles's adopted son and Christopher's daughter had been brought up together until four years ago, when Christopher had exported his family—Mummy and myself—to Los Angeles, from which earthly paradise we had occasionally escaped to stay at Charles's home, our own house being let for the duration. But my visits there had never coincided with my cousin's. In the intervals of Oxford he had spent his time abroad, enjoying himself doing what he called 'looking around', and indulging the flair for languages which was part of our heritage from a mongrel ancestry, and which young Charles intended to turn to account when he went into one of the family's Continental banks. I had not flown so high. I had brought nothing home from Los Angeles except an American flair for dressing, an accent which I lost as soon as I reasonably could, and three years' experience of the frenetic world of American commercial television, where I had served a wild apprenticeship as producer's assistant in a small company calling itself Sunshine Television Incorporated—this apparently in blissful ignorance of the fact that like most companies it was normally referred to by its initials, *S. T. Inc.*

Now here we were again, my cousin and I, and back without effort on the same terms. It was not that we had been, like our fathers, inseparable—that wasn't possible. What had held us so easily together was, paradoxically enough, a sort of mutual rejection. We had each recognized in the other a refusal to be claimed, and respected this. This had made tolerable—and even funny—the thin-worn family joke about our engagement, and the 'convenient marriage' which would weld Charles back into place without legal awkwardness, and keep the cash in hand in the best dynastic tradition. We never knew—were never allowed to know— whether the idea of the match was anything more than a joke. I had heard my father insisting that the family characteristics were bad enough singly, but squared they would be lethal, whereupon Uncle Charles would retort that since my mother was partly Irish, and Charles's had been half-Austrian, half-Russian, and his paternal grandmother French, the stock would be strong enough to stand a match a good deal closer than that between second cousins. We also had a Polish Jew, a Dane and a German among our assorted great-grandparents, and counted ourselves English, which was fair enough.

To Charles and myself, familiar from early childhood with this light-hearted, dynastic match-making, the subject had little interest. It had occurred to neither of us, in actual fact, that we could be the object of one another's sexual stirrings. Reckoning ourselves as much proof against each other as brother and sister, we had watched with equal amusement and derision each other's first romantic adventures.

The affairs were brief, and inevitable. Sooner or later the girl would start assuming a claim on Charles, and be dropped without trace. Or, somehow, my own pinup would lose his gloss, Charles would say something less than forgivable about him, I would retort furiously, then laugh and agree, and life would be whole once more.

And our respective parents bore with us lovingly through it all, took off the leading strings, gave us the money, listened to what mattered and forgot the rest, possibly because they wanted freedom from us as urgently as we thought we wanted freedom from them. The result was that we went back to them at intervals like homing bees, and we were happy. Perhaps they saw more clearly than could Charles and I, the basic security in our lives which made his restlessness and my indecisiveness nothing more than the taking of soundings outside the harbour. Perhaps they could even see, through it all, the end that would come.

But here we were at the beginning. A young Arab in white had brought in a tray holding an elaborately chased copper urn and two small blue cups which he set on the table in front of me. He said something to Charles, and went out. My cousin came quickly up the steps of the divan and sat down beside me.

"He says Ben won't be in just yet, not till evening. Go on, you pour."

"Is his mother away, too?"

"His mother's dead. His father's sister runs the place for them, but she lives retired, as they say. No, *not* a harem, so don't look so curious and hopeful; she merely has a long siesta and won't come out till dinner time. Smoke?"

"Not now. I don't much, as a matter of fact, only now and again for effect, rather silly. Good heavens, what are those? Hashish or something?"

"No, absolutely harmless, Egyptian. They do look awful, don't they? Well now, tell me what you've been doing."

He accepted the cup of strong black coffee from me and curled back on the silk-covered seat, waiting expectantly.

Four years of gossip is a lot to catch up on, and we had never been letter writers. I suppose more than an hour had gone by, and the sun had moved over to leave half the court in shadow before my cousin stretched, stubbed out another Egyptian cigarette and said: "Look, what's all this about sticking with your group? Won't you change your mind and cut loose now? Stay till Sunday, and I'll drive you up—the Barada Valley's lovely, and there's a good road."

"Thanks all the same, but I'd better stay with them. We're doing that run by car in any case, and having a look at Baalbek on the way."

"I'd take you there."

"It would be smashing, but it's all fixed, and as a matter of fact I've packed, and you know there's all that silly business with visas here. Mine's dated tomorrow, and there's this business of a group passport, and there was such a hooha anyway about my staying behind after the group leaves for England on Saturday that I can't face it all over again. I think I'll just go."

"All right, then, I'll see you in Beirut. Where are you staying?"

"I thought I'd move to the Phoenicia once I'm on my own."

"I'll join you there. Book in for me, will you? I'll telephone you before I leave Damascus. What had you planned to do with the extra time, apart—I suppose—from going up to Dar Ibrahim?"

"Dar Ibrahim?" I repeated blankly.

"Great-Aunt Harriet's place. That's its name, surely you knew? It's on the Nahr Ibrahim, the Adonis River."

"I—yes, I suppose I knew, but I'd forgotten. Goodness, Great-Aunt Harriet . . . I never thought . . . Is it near Beirut, then?"

"About thirty miles away, along the coast road to Byblos and then inland into the mountains, up towards the source of the Adonis. The road runs up the ridge on the north side of the valley, and somewhere between Tourzaya and Qartaba there's a tributary river called the Nahr el-Sal'q that goes tumbling down to meet the Adonis. Dar Ibrahim's in the middle of the valley, where the rivers meet."

"Have you ever been there?"

"No, but I'm planning to. D'you really mean you hadn't thought about it?"

"Not a flicker of a thought. I'd certainly intended to go up the Adonis Valley and see the source where the cascade is, and the temple of Whoever-it-is, and the place where Venus and Adonis met—in fact I was thinking of hiring a car for the trip on Sunday, after the group go . . . But to be honest I'd forgotten all about Aunt H. I hardly even remember her, you know; we were in Los Angeles when she was home last, and before that it was—heavens, it must be all of fifteen years! And Mummy never said a thing about this place of hers—Dar Ibrahim, was that the name?—but that's probably only because her geography's about on a par with mine and she'd never realized Beirut was so near." I put down my cup. "Right in the Adonis Valley? Well, I might go with you, at that, if only to see the place and tell Daddy what it was like. I'm sure he'd think there was hope for me yet if I told him I'd trekked up there to put some flowers on the old dear's grave."

"She'd probably kick you in the teeth if you tried," said Charles. "She's very much alive. You really are a teeny bit out of touch, aren't you?"

I stared. "Alive? Aunt H? Now who's out of touch? She died just after New Year."

He laughed. "Not she. If you're thinking about the Last Will and Testament, that's nothing to go by, in the last few years she's sent them round about once every six months. Didn't Uncle Chris get the famous letter renouncing her British nationality and finally cutting everyone off with sixpence? Everyone except me, that is." He grinned. "And I was to have the Gabriel Hounds and her copy of the Koran because I showed signs of taking a 'reasonable interest in the real civilizations of the world'. That was because I was learning Arabic. In some ways," added my cousin thoughtfully, "she must still be very innocent if she thinks Mansel and Mansel takes an interest in anything whatever except for the basest of all possible reasons."

"Look, come off it, you're kidding me."

"About the Wills and so on? Indeed I'm not. She renounced us in beautiful round early-Victorian terms—her letters were period pieces, you know—the family, Britain, God, the lot. Well, perhaps not God exactly, but she was going to turn Mohammedan, and would we please send out a reliable English stonemason to build a private cemetery where she could rest for ever in the peace of Allah among her beloved dogs, and would we also inform the Editor of *The Times* that the paper of the overseas edition was too thin to allow her to do the crossword puzzle properly, and she would like it changed."

"You can't be serious."

"As an owl," said my cousin. "I swear to every word."

"And what in the world are the Gabriel Hounds?"

"Don't you remember them? I suppose you don't."

"I seem to remember the phrase, that's all. Wasn't it something in a story?"

"A legend in that book we had called 'North-Country Tales', or some such title. The Gabriel Hounds are supposed to be a pack of hounds that run with Death, and when someone's going to die you hear them howling over the house at night. I've an idea myself that the idea must have come from the wild geese—have you heard them? They sound like a pack of hounds in full cry overhead, and the old name for them used to be 'gabble ratchet'. I've sometimes wondered if the 'Gabriel' doesn't come from 'gabble', because after all Gabriel wasn't the angel of death . . ." He glanced across. "You shivered. Are you cold?"

"No. One of them gabbling over my grave, I expect. What have they to do with Great-Aunt Harriet?"

"Nothing, really, except that she had a pair of china dogs I lusted after, and I christened them the Gabriel Hounds because they were like the illustrations in the book."

"A pair of—oh, no, really, you must be out of your tiny

mind. That's schizophrenia, or is it skitso? Nobody in this world can want to own a white Porsche with one hand and a pair of china dogs with the other! I don't believe it."

He laughed. "Real china, Christy love, Chinese china . . . They're Ming as ever was, and probably museum pieces. Heaven knows what they're worth now, but since I had the good taste to fall flat in love with them at the age of six, and Great-Aunt Harriet with even better taste fell flat in love with me at the same time, she promised them to me. And stark raving bonkers though she undoubtedly is now, she seems to have remembered." He made a restless movement. "Oh, don't you see, it doesn't really matter about the dogs, they make a good excuse, that's all."

"For going to see her?"

"Yes."

"Taking your family responsibilities on your head at last?" I said it derisively, but he didn't laugh or disclaim, as I had expected. He gave me an odd, slanting look from under the long lashes, but said merely: "I don't want to pass up the chance. It sounds such a damned intriguing setup."

"Well, of course I'll go with you, out of sheer roaring curiosity, and let's hope she does remember you, because I'm darned sure she won't remember me. She must be at least a hundred."

"Not a day over eighty, I swear, and active with it by all accounts. She's a local legend, goes galloping about the countryside on horseback with a gaggle of hounds and shoots whatever there is to shoot for her own dinner."

"Gabble, you mean. I remember that about her, who could forget? When she stayed with us that time she brought eight King Charles spaniels."

"It's Tibetan terriers now, and salukis—Persian greyhounds, the dogs the Arab princes used for hunting. Oh, she's gone the limit, I gather—turned Arab herself, male at that, dresses like an Emir, smokes a hubble-bubble, never sees anybody except at night, and lives in this dirty great palace—"

"Palace?" I said startled. "Who does she think she is? Lady Hester Stanhope?"

"Exactly that. Models herself on the story, one gathers. Even calls herself Lady Harriet, and, as you and I well know, we've had a lot of queer things in the family, but never a Lady." He stared, not flatteringly. "What do you know about Lady Hester Stanhope?"

"Didn't I tell you? When we spent last Christmas at your house they put me in your room, and I read some of your books. You've an awful lot about the Middle East. Have you really read all that Arabian poetry and stuff? And the Koran?"

"All through."

"Well, you might say it was your library that gave me the idea of seeing this part of the world in the first place. We always did go for the same things, didn't we—or maybe you'd say I tagged along where you went . . . ? I'd always had vaguely romantic ideas about Petra and Damascus and Palmyra, but never thought about really coming here; then I saw the advert for this package tour, so I thought I'd join up, find my way about, then stay on after they'd gone and take my time filling in a few extras. One of them was Djoun, Lady Hester Stanhope's place."

"It's a ruin now."

"I know, but I still thought I'd like to see it. She was quite a girl, wasn't she? I read everything you had about her, and nice snappy reading it was, compared with some of those tomes of yours. I had flu just after Christmas and was stuck indoors for a fortnight, and Mummy hadn't time to rake round the bookshops for something more my weight."

He grinned, undeceived. "Don't work so hard at not being clever. I'm not one of your muscle-bound blonds."

"Neither you are," I said.

Our eyes met. There was a tiny silence, in which the fountain sounded oddly loud. Then my cousin got up and reached a hand. "Come and see the water lilies now the sun's gone. They shut while you watch."

I followed him down into the now coolly shadowed court. The lilies were pale blue, held on stiff stems a few inches above the water, where their glossy leaves overlapped the still surface like tiles of jade. Gold fins winked here and there below them, and a gold bee sipped water at a leaf's edge. A powder-blue petal shut, and another, till one by one the lilies were turbaned up, stiff and quiet for the night. Another late bee, almost caught by a folding flower, wrestled his way angrily out of the petals, and shot off like a bullet.

I watched half absently, my mind still busy with the recent fragments of information Charles had flung at me, the intriguing picture of the eccentric old lady who had dropped so long ago out of family reality into family legend. The picture Charles had just given me of her blurred and blended in the imagination with the vivid mental pictures I had built up during that Christmas period of enforced reading. It was true that I had found some of Charles's books heavy going, but the accounts of the eccentric Lady Hester had been extremely readable, not to say racy.

She had gone out to the Middle East in the early eighteen hundreds, an Earl's daughter in the days when rank counted for almost everything, a masculine peremptory woman who, as Pitt's niece, was also accustomed to political consequence. After traveling round in considerable state with a retinue which included lover, slaves, and attendant physician, she had decided to settle in Syria (as it then was) and eventually purchased for herself a mountain-top fortress near Djoun, not far from Sidon. There she had lived in Eastern state, dressing as a Turkish Emir, and ruling her household of servants, Albanian guards, Negro slaves, companions, grooms, and personal doctor with a rod of iron and at times, literally, a whip. Her fortress, perched on a hot bare hilltop, was described by a contemporary as 'an enchanted palace', and was a world in itself of courtyards, corridors as complex as a Chinese puzzle, walled gardens approached by winding stairs, secret exits cut in the rock where the Lady's spies came and went, the whole exotic with murmuring fountains and luxuriant gardens. It was a deliberate re-creation of an Arabian Nights' wonderland with all the fantastic properties of Eastern fairy-tale solidly at hand. Roses and jasmine, mute black slaves and nightingales, camels and sacred cats and Arab horses, she had them all. Fearless, utterly selfish, arrogant and eccentric, and growing with the years beyond eccentricity into megalomania, she meddled in local politics, defied the local Emirs, and placed herself—with some success—above the law. She finally seems to have believed in her own mystical destiny as Queen of the East who would one day ride crowned into Jerusalem at the side of the new Messiah.

The end came as it comes to the determined *puissante et solitaire*—she died alone, old and destitute, her fortune spent, her fortress rotting around her, her servants robbing and neglecting her. But she left—along with her debts—a legend that persists to this day.

It was certainly intriguing to think that it might be persisting in one form in the person of my own Great-Aunt Harriet. From what I knew of the lady, I thought she would (apart from the rank) fit into the role quite well. She had wealth, considerable personality and some scholarship, and had traveled widely and with a retinue which, though not quite as impressive as Lady Hester Stanhope's in 1820, had created quite as much stir and trouble a hundred years later. She had married an archaeologist, Ernest Boyd, and thereafter accompanied him on all his working journeys, hanging over and (it must be confessed) superintending his 'digs' from Cambodia to the Euphrates Valley. After his death she gave up active work and returned to England, but continued to take a deep interest in the Middle East, and financed one or two expeditions that stirred her fancy. Two years of England's weather had been enough. She had said good-bye to the family (this was the last visit that I remembered) and gone off to the Lebanon, where she had bought her hilltop refuge and settled down (she told us) to write a book.

From this fastness she had made one sortie, four years ago, just after my side of the family had gone to Los Angeles. She had come, she said, to settle her affairs—which meant removing her considerable assets to the Lebanon—pick up a mate for her revolting (Charles said) Tibetan terrier Delilah, and shake the mud of England off her skirts for good. This was the last I had heard. Whether she had in fact written anything at all during her fifteen years' exile nobody had any idea, except for the occasional remakes of her Will, which the family read with pleasure and then disregarded. We could get along as well without Great-Aunt Harriet as it appeared she could without us. There was of course no resentment on either side; my great-aunt merely personified in herself the family's genius for detachment.

So I still regarded my cousin doubtfully. "You think she'll see you?"

"Oh, she'll see me," he said calmly. "My mother was always pretty sarcastic about Great-Aunt Harriet's penchant for young men, but I see no reason why we shouldn't trade on it. And if I tell her I've come to demand my rights, viz. the Gabriel Hounds, it'll appeal to her; she was always a tough egg who liked people who stuck out for their dues. If I can get to Beirut by Sunday evening, what do you say we make a date of it together for Monday?"

"I'm on. It sounds intriguing, if I thought one could believe a word of it."

"Sober truth—or as near sober truth as you'll ever get in this country," promised my cousin. "Don't you know what they say about it? That it's a country where anything can happen, a 'country of prodigies . . .'" He quoted softly: " 'The men inhabiting this country of prodigies—those men of rocks and deserts—whose imagination is higher coloured and yet more cloudy than the horizon of their sands and their seas, act according to the word of Mahomet and Lady Hester Stanhope. They require commerce with the stars, with prophecies, miracles and the second sight of genius.' "

"What's that?"

"Lamartine."

"Makes it sound as if even Great-Aunt Harriet might be normal. I can hardly wait. But I'll have to go now." I glanced at my watch. "Heavens, yes, it's dinner time."

"I'm sure Ben would want you to stay. He'll be in any minute. Can't you?"

"I'd like to, but we've an early start tomorrow, and I've things to do." I stooped to retrieve my handbag. "And you're going to drive me home, dear boy, and no mistake. I'm not venturing through the dark streets of Damascus for you or anybody—even if I could find the way which I probably can't. Unless you simply lend me the Porsche?"

"There are some risks I will take," said my cousin, "and some I won't. I'll drive you back. Come along."

We crossed the court quietly together. Someone—the Arab boy, probably—must have brought a lamp in and set it in a niche near the door. It was an Aladdin lamp of some silvery metal which was probably in daylight hideous; but in the dusk, and holding the small orange buds of flame, it looked quite beautiful. The deep blue oblong of sky above the open court was pricking already with brilliant stars. No ugly diffusion of city lights spoiled the deep velvet of that sky; even hanging as it was above the glittering and crowded richness of the Damascus oasis, it spoke of the desert and the vast empty silences beyond the last palm tree. The courtyard itself was quiet. The far murmur of city traffic, no louder than the humming in a shell, made a background to this still quiet, where the only sound was the trickle of the fountain. The well in the desert. A fish moved below the surface, and the flick of gold, caught by the lamp, seemed to underscore the beauty of the living water. One could almost hear the fish moving. A bird settled itself crooningly to sleep above the arcade in a rustle of leaves.

"A turtle dove, do you hear it?" Charles's voice, quiet as it was, made me jump. "The poets say she calls all the time for her lover—'*Yusuf, Yusuf,*' till her voice breaks in a sob. I'll ring you Saturday evening then, at the Phoenicia, to tell you when I'm coming."

"I'll be waiting. I only hope that after all this we get our Arabian Nights' entertainment at Dar Ibrahim. Oh, *you* probably will, fascinating creature that you are, but is there the faintest reason why she should want to see me?"

"She'll be delighted to see you," said my cousin generously. "Damn it, I was even quite pleased to see you myself."

"You must be slipping, paying me compliments like that," I said, preceding him to the doorway.

Chapter Two

———————◦◦◦◦◦◦———————

Adonis
Who lives away in Lebanon,
In stony Lebanon, where blooms
His red anemone.

           —JAMES ELROY FLECKER: *Santorin*

I SUPPOSE I had assumed Charles to be exaggerating the Dar Ibrahim 'legend', but it seemed he was right. I found it quite easy to get news of my eccentric relative in Beirut. In fact, even had I never heard of her, she would have been brought to my notice.

It happened on Saturday, the day the group left for London, and I moved myself to the Phoenicia Hotel to plan my brief independence and wait for Charles. On what was left of the Saturday I wanted to get my hair done and do some shopping; then on Sunday I planned to hire a car and driver to take me exploring up into the Lebanon range to the source of the Adonis River.

It was when I approached the desk clerk in the hotel, to ask him to lay on a chauffeur-driven car for this trip, that I came across my great-aunt.

The clerk entered into my plans with enthusiasm, almost managing to conceal his private thoughts about the inexplicable whims of tourists. If a young woman was eager to incur the expense of a car and driver to go up and look at a few dirty villages and a waterfall, then of course he would help her . . . and (I could see the expert assessment of my clothes, my room number, and my probable bill) the more expensive the car, the better.

"And I understand," I added, "that right up at the Adonis Source there's the ruins of an old Roman temple, and another smaller one not too far away, that I might visit."

"Yes?" said the clerk, then hurriedly changing his intonation. "Yes, of course, temples." He wrote something, passing the buck with some relief. "I will tell the driver to include them in the itinerary."

"Please do. What do we do about lunch?"

Now this, it seemed, was talking. He brightened immediately. There was the famous summer hotel—I had heard of it, no doubt?—where I could get an excellent meal, and with music. Oh, yes, there was music in every room, continuous music, taped round the clock, in case the mountain silence got you down. And a swimming pool. And tennis. "And then, of course, if you make a slight detour on your way back you'll be able to see Dar Ibrahim."

He misunderstood the surprise on my face, and explained quickly: "You have not heard of this? Oh, Dar Ibrahim's a palace where an English lady lives, a very old lady who used to be famous, and she bought this palace when it was falling into ruin and filled it with beautiful things and planted the gardens again, and in the old days famous people would go up to stay with her, and it was possible to see over some parts of the palace, just as today you can see Beit ed-Din and the Crusader Castles. But now, alas . . . she is old now, and they say a little—" he made an eloquent face and touched his forehead. "The place is shut up now, and she sees no one, and she never leaves the palace. But I have heard what a wonderful place it used to be, and I have myself seen her riding out with her servants . . . but that is all changed, she is old, and it is a long time since anyone has seen her."

"How long?"

He spread his hands. "Six months, a year, I cannot say."

"But she's still there?"

"Certainly. I believe I heard talk of a companion, but this may be rumour. I think there are still two or three servants with her, and once a month supplies are sent from Beirut up to Sal'q—that's the nearest village—and taken across by mule."

"Isn't there a road?"

"No. The road goes along the ridge above the valley, and to get to Dar Ibrahim from the village one must walk, or go by mule." He smiled. "I wasn't suggesting you should do this, because of course it's not worth it now, you can't get in. I was only recommending the view. It's very fine. In any case, Dar Ibrahim looks all the better from a distance."

I said, trying it out: "Actually, I had heard of the place. I think I know some relatives of hers in England, of the old lady's. I'd thought of trying to see her. I'd wondered if perhaps I might write her a note and ask if I could visit her." Something—I'm not quite sure what—forbade me to explain to the clerk my own relationship with his local legend.

He shook his head doubtfully, but with a gleam of curiosity in his eyes which told me that my reticence had probably been wise, "I suppose you could try, but when she would get it, or when you would get an answer . . . There is a porter at the gate—" he shrugged—"but they say he lets no one through at all. He takes in the supplies and pays for them, and if there are letters, or if she has written letters, they are handed over at that time. But for a long time now she has received no one—no one, that is, except the doctor."

"The doctor? Is she ill?"

"Oh, no, not now. I believe I did hear of something last

year—about six months ago, in the autumn, and the doctor going up each day. But she recovered, and now is well enough."

She had certainly been well enough, I reflected, to draft another snappy Last Will and Testament at Christmas. "A doctor from Beirut, was this?"

"Yes, an English doctor."

"Do you know his name?" I added, rather apologetically: "If I can't see her, I might get news of her from him."

The clerk could not remember the doctor's name, but he promised to find out for me, and indeed the next time I passed the desk he had it ready, a Dr Henry Grafton with an address somewhere near Martyrs' Square. I thanked him, and went back upstairs to my room, where I picked up the telephone directory and looked up Grafton, H. L.

The number was there. After a little trouble I managed to get it, and a man's voice answered in Arabic, but when we had sorted ourselves out through his excellent French into his even better English, he had to disappoint me. No, Dr Grafton was not here, Dr Grafton had left Beirut some time back. Yes, for good. If he could help me . . . ?

"I was just making some inquiries about a relation of mine," I said, "a Mrs Boyd. I understand she was a patient of Dr Grafton's a few months back when he was in Beirut. I wonder—is she perhaps now on your list? The thing is—"

"Mrs Boyd?" The voice was puzzled. "We don't have anyone of that name, I'm afraid. What's the address?"

"She lives outside Beirut, at a place called Dar Ibrahim. I believe it's near a village called Sal'q."

"Dar Ibrahim?" The voice quickened. "Do you mean the Lady Harriet?"

"Why, yes, I—I suppose I do," I said, feeling rather foolish. "I—I'd forgotten . . . yes, of course, the Lady Harriet."

"As far as I know she's fine," said the voice, "but she's certainly not my patient. In the normal way I would have attended her after Grafton left, but she wrote to tell me she had made other arrangements." Some undercurrent, perhaps of amusement, in the smooth voice made me want to ask what these were, but this was hardly possible. Probably (I thought) a letter renouncing the world, the English, and the medical profession, or at least another Last Will and Testament. "May I know who is calling?" asked the voice.

"Lady Harriet's great-niece. My name is Christabel Mansel. I'm here in the Lebanon on holiday, and I—none of us has heard from my great-aunt for some time; in fact, I'd got the idea she was dead. But then I heard she was still alive, and someone at the hotel here—I'm staying at the Phoenicia —told me Dr Grafton had attended her, so I thought I'd ring him up to find out anything I could. You say he's left Beirut. Is he still in the Lebanon? Would it be possible to get in touch with him?"

"I'm afraid not. He went back to London."

"I see. Well, thanks very much, I might try to look her up myself."

There was a slight pause at the other end. Then the voice said, carefully expressionless: "One gathers she lives very much retired."

"Yes," I said, "I understood so. But anyway, thank you for your help. Good-bye."

"Good-bye," said the voice.

I found myself grinning as I put the receiver down. What was implicit in the pleasant voice was, unmistakably, the Arabic equivalent for 'and the best of British luck'.

Charles rang up that evening to say that Ben's father had been delayed, so he himself couldn't get up before Sunday evening at the earliest, and might not manage even that. "But in the name of all the gods at once," he finished impressively, "I'll be with you on Monday, or perish in the attempt."

"Don't ask for it," I said, "at least not till you've bought your blue bead. You told me this was a country where anything could happen."

I didn't mention my own inquiries about Great-Aunt Harriet, or that I was beginning to develop quite a lively sense of curiosity about the eccentric recluse of Dar Ibrahim.

* * *

The desk clerk had certainly done his best to get me a nice expensive trip. The car was a vast American affair with fins, air-conditioning, blue beads to ward off the Evil Eye, and hanging in the window a text from the Koran which said: "Place your reliance on God."

It also had an altimeter. This I didn't quite believe in until the driver, a lively sharp-faced young man called Hamid, told me we would be going from sea level to about eight thousand feet in one fell swoop, since the Adonis Source was right up in the High Lebanon. I settled down beside him in the front of the car, and watched the altimeter with fascinated amusement as we turned away from the coast at Byblos, and began to climb.

Hamid had underestimated the number of fell swoops that were required. At first the road was reasonable, and bored its way upwards through villages and terraced fields, where the carefully spaced apple trees stood knee-deep in growing crops, and dark-eyed children played among the hens in the dust. But after a while the road shook itself clear of the little green settlements to climb more steeply through the last belt of cultivation before the flocks claimed the stony earth. Here still in every sheltered corner a neat terraced wall dammed in some carefully banked soil, and fruit trees were in meagre bloom. On the more exposed terraces the thin green blades of some grain were growing, almost smothered by the sheets of spring flowers that grew everywhere, at the roadside, in the terraced walls, in the very seams of the rocks. Hamid stopped the car with smiling good nature and let me explore them with rapture; orchids, pale cyclamens, a huge flax-blue geranium, the scarlet-petalled Persian tulip, and the red anemone that flowers for Adonis.

Presently we were out of the cultivation and running along switchback ridges where grey shrubs clung to the rock, and the only flower was the yellow broom. The air was crystal clear, and in wonderful contrast to the heavy air of the coast. Now and again we saw a flock of the Eastern-looking sheep, cream or honey-coloured or spatchcocked with black, moving with drooping ears and heads carried low as if always looking for food. Glossy black goats grazed with them, and each flock bunched closely round its shepherd, a solitary figure standing wrapped in his burnous, arms crossed over his stick, watching gravely as we went by.

The road climbed. The altimeter needle moved steadily to the right. The air grew piercingly fresh. The yellow broom dropped below us, and at the verges of the narrow way tufts of grey thin leaves hunched among the stones. The car swerved terrifyingly round bends with rocks threatening to scrape the offside wing, and on the other side a sheer abyss where crows and ravens tilted and croaked below us.

Then suddenly there was space on both sides. We were running along the hogsback of a dizzyingly exposed ridge with, to the left, a prospect of white rock and blue distance and crest on crest of wooded mountain to the sea; and deep down on our right, ice-green, flashing and hiding and flashing again as it rushed and curled down its great forested gorge, ran the Nahr Ibrahim, the Adonis River.

And presently, dipping through rocky gorges which here and there trapped the sun and allowed thin apple trees to blossom with their feet deep in the red anemones, we came to the Adonis Source itself.

The source of the Adonis River has been magic, time out of mind. To the primitive people of a thirsty land, the sight of the white torrent bursting straight out of its roaring black cave half up a massive, sun-baked cliff, suggested God knows what gods and demons and power and terror. It certainly suggested fertility . . . the river carries life with it for thirty water-seamed mountain miles. And where the water bursts from the rock the corrie is suddenly green, and full of trees and flowering bushes, and the red anemone grows along the torrent side.

So here, treading on the ghostly heels of Isis and Ishtar and Astarte and the Great Mother herself who was Demeter and Dia and Cybele of the Towers, came Aphrodite to fall in love with the Syrian shepherd Adonis, and lie with him among the flowers. And here the wild boar killed him, and where his blood splashed, anemones grew, and to this day every spring the waters of the Adonis run red right down to the sea. Now the corrie is empty except for the black goats sleeping in the sun on the ruined floor of Aphrodite's temple, and against the roar of the torrent the drowsy stirrings of the goat bells come sharp and clear. The rags that flutter from the sacred tree are tied there as petitions to the last and latest Lady of the place, Mary.

Even without the legends, it would have been breathtaking. With them, the scene of white water and blazing rock, massive ruins, and bright flowers blowing in the wind from the fall, was something out of this world. And as we turned eventually out of the corrie onto the track—it could hardly have been called a road—that would take us home by a different route, the scene had its final touch of Eastern fantasy.

A little way beyond and out of sight of the Adonis corrie, a few Arab houses straggled along the water-side. A path, a white scratch on the rock, climbed out of this at an angle to the road. And up this path, going easily, went a chestnut Arab horse, the white burnous of its rider filled out by the motion like a sail, the scarlet and silver of the bridle winking in the sun. At the horse's heels cantered two beautiful dogs, fawn-coloured greyhounds with long silky hair, the saluki hounds which were used by the princes of the East for hunting gazelle.

A curve of the road hid them, and all at once it was time for lunch.

We saw the rider again, on our way down the other side of the valley. We had spent more than an hour over lunch, and the horseman must have used paths which cut off a thousand difficult corners that a car had to take. As we picked our way between the potholes into some tiny settlement in a lost high valley where the snow lay not very far above us, I saw the rider below, walking his horse down a barely visible path that took him thigh-deep through a field of sunflowers. The dogs were invisible below the thick, heart-shaped leaves. Then they raced ahead of him out onto a lower curve of the road, the horse breaking into a canter behind them. So clear was the air that I could hear the jingling of bridle bells above the thud of hoofs in the dust.

The squat peeling houses of the village crowded in on the car and hid him from view.

*   *   *

We stopped in the village to buy oranges.

This was Hamid's idea. We could have bought them at one of the dozens of stalls on the way out of Beirut, but these, he said, would be something special, straight from the tree and warm with the sun and ripe, divinely ripe.

"And I shall buy them for you as a present," he said, drawing the car to a halt in the shade of a mulberry tree and coming round to open the door for me.

The village was poor, that was obvious; the houses were nothing more than shacks patched with mud brick, but they were screened with vines, and each one squatted among its laborious terraces of fruit and grain. Some of the Goddess's fertility had spilled over into the place, for all its height. It must be sheltered from the worst of the winds, and there would be no lack of moisture as the snow melted. The carefully trapped water stood deep-green in square cisterns under the bare silver poplars, and the village—just a handful of houses in a natural amphitheater sheltered from the wind —was full of fruit blossom, not only the enchanting glossy trees heavy with the waxy flowers and fruit of oranges and lemons, but the snow of pears and the sharp pink of almond, and everywhere the blush-pink of the apple, the staple fruit of the Lebanon.

The sun was hot. A small crowd of staring children had gathered round the car; they were very small and rather engaging, with their thick black hair and enormous dark eyes and thumb-sucking curiosity. The place seemed dead, with the afternoon deadness. No one was in the fields; if there was a café it was only some dark room in one of the cottages; and I saw no women. Apart from the children, the skinny hens scratching, and a miserable-looking donkey with rope sores, the only creature moving was an old man who sat in the sun smoking a pipe. He could, indeed, hardly be said to be moving. He seemed to be smoking almost in his sleep, and his eyes turned up slowly and half blind to Hamid as the latter greeted him and asked him a question in Arabic, presumably who would sell us the fruit that hung still on the lovely trees.

The old man waited a full half minute while the question wound its way through his brain, then he removed the pipe from his mouth, turned his head through a full three degrees, spat revoltingly into the dust, and mumbled something to himself. Then his eyes resumed their myopic staring at vacancy, and the pipe went back into his mouth.

Hamid grinned at me, shrugged, and said: "I won't be a moment," and vanished into a dark doorway.

I wandered across the street, the children following. At the edge of the road was a six-foot retaining wall holding up, it seemed, the entire plateau on which the village was built. Below this were the terraced fields where I had seen the rider on the chestnut horse. The sunflowers were too tall and too thickly planted to allow the lovely profusion of flowers that I had seen in the lower reaches of the hills, but there were wild irises at the foot of the wall, and a blue flower like a small lily, and like shining drops of blood among the sunflower roots I could see the red anemones.

I climbed down. The children climbed down, too. I helped them, bodily lifting down the last one, a half-naked atom of perhaps three, probably with scabies. I dusted my hands off on my slacks and hunted for flowers.

The children helped. A big-eyed boy in a grubby vest and nothing else yanked out a handful of pinks for me, and little Scabies came up with a dandelion or two. There was a great deal of conversation, Arabic and English and (from Scabies) stone-age grunts, and we all understood one another very well. The clearest thing about the business was that I was expected to hand over something substantial in return for the company and the flowers.

"A shilling," said Hamid from above me, sounding amused.

I looked up. He was standing at the edge of the road. "Are you sure? It seems very little. There's six of them."

"It's quite enough."

It seemed he was right. The children grabbed the coins, and melted up and over the wall faster than they had come down and with no assistance whatever, except for Scabies, who was heaved over the last lap by Hamid, dusted off, and sent on his way with a clap over the bare buttocks. Hamid turned back to me.

"Can you manage it? Some of the stones aren't too steady."

"I won't bother. I'll just walk down and meet you on the road as you drive down. Did you get the oranges?"

"Yes. All right, then, don't hurry, I'll wait for you below."

The path where I had seen the rider was a dry and well-worn right of way some eighteen inches wide, going down at a slant through the sunflowers and descending by three or four stony gaps in the terracing. The huge flowers, heavy-headed, were turned away from me, facing south, and the path was a narrow chasm between head-high plants. I saw now that they were planted a yard or so apart, and between them some other plant with glaucous green leaves and plumes of brownish flowers fought its way up with mallow and cornflowers and a dozen other things towards the light. Where the horse had brushed through, the leaves hung bruised and crumpled, and above the honey-smell of the sunflowers there was the clean, musky smell of deadnettle.

I made my way down towards the road. At the gap in the wall leading down to the last terrace the sunflowers gave way to a more familiar crop of corn, and standing sentinel where the crops divided was a fig tree, its buds just bursting into young green. Its silver boughs held the buds up against the bright sky with an enchanting grace, and against the rough-cast of its stem some wild vinelike plant clung, with flowers as red as the anemones. I stopped to pick one. The vine was tough, and a hank of it pulled away from the trunk, uncovering something that lay below. On the bleached silver of the exposed stem, scrawled in red, was the sketch of a running dog. The drawing was crude but lively; the thing was unmistakably a long-haired greyhound with a plumed tail. A saluki.

It is surely common experience that when once something has been brought to your attention it crops up again and again, often with an alarming appearance of coincidence or even fate. It certainly seemed as if, once Charles had mentioned them, the creatures were going to haunt me through the Lebanon, but there was after all nothing so very odd about it; one might say that in England it is possible to be haunted by poodles. I went down to the road.

Hamid was sitting on a low wall at the edge of the road

beside the car, smoking. He got up quickly, but I waved him down. "Don't bother. Finish your cigarette, do."

"Would you like an orange?"

"I'd love one. Thanks. Oh, aren't they gorgeous? You're quite right, we don't get them like this at home . . . Hamid, why do they grow sunflowers?"

"For oil. They make a very good cooking oil, almost as good as olive oil, and now the Government has built a factory to make margarine with it also, and offers a good price for the crop. It's part of an official campaign to stop the growing of hemp."

"Hemp? That's hashish, isn't it?—marihuana? Good heavens! Does it grow up here?"

"Oh, yes. Have you never seen it? I believe you grow the same plant in England, to make rope, but only in hot countries does it bear the drug. In past time there has always been a lot of it grown up in these hills—it's the right climate for it, and there are still places where the inspectors don't go."

"Inspectors?"

He nodded. "Government officials. They're very anxious now to get the growing of these drugs under control. A certain amount is grown legally, you understand, for medical use, and for every stage of its growth and handling you must have a license and be subjected to strict controls, but it's always been easy enough for the peasants in these wild parts to grow more than they declare, or to harvest the crops before the inspectors come. Now the penalties have been made stricter than ever, but there are still some who try to get past the law." He lifted his shoulders. "What would you? It pays, and there are always men who will take the big risks for the big money." He dropped his cigarette into the road and trod the butt into the dust. "You saw the old man up there, the one I spoke to?"

"Yes."

"He was smoking it."

"But can he . . . ? I mean—"

"How can they stop him?"

I stared. "Do you mean it's grown right here?"

He smiled. "There was some growing beside his house, among the potatoes."

"I wouldn't know it if I saw it," I said. "What's it look like?"

"A tall plant, greyish colour, not very pretty. The drug comes from the flowers. These are brownish, a spike like soft feathers."

I had been carefully depositing my orange peel out of sight behind the wall where we sat. Now I sat bolt upright. "There was something like that growing under the sunflowers!"

"So?" he said indifferently. "It will be gone before the inspectors get here. Shall we go?" He opened the car door for me.

All in all it had been a strange and heady sort of day. And things seemed to be going my way. It seemed the inevitable climax to it that as I got into the car I should say with decision:

"You said you'd show me Dar Ibrahim on the way home. If there's time, I think I'd like to call there today. Would you mind?"

* * *

At about four o'clock we slid round a steep bend and into the village of Sal'q. Hamid stopped the car beside a low wall beyond which the land dropped clear away to give another of those staggering views of the Adonis Valley.

"There," he said.

I looked where he pointed. Here the valley was wide, with the river, magnificent and flowing swiftly, cutting a way down for itself between dense banks of trees. From somewhere to our left, beyond the little village mosque, fell the

47

tributary river to meet the Adonis in the valley at the bottom. Between the two streams a highish, wedge-shaped tongue of land thrust out like a high-prowed ship down the valley's center, and on its tip, like a crown on the crag above the meeting waters, sprawled the palace, a seemingly vast collection of buildings running back from the edge of the promontory to spread over a fair area of the plateau. Towards the rear of the building the ground fell away sharply in a small escarpment shelving down to the level of the plateau, and here the palace wall rose straight out of the rock. Near the top I could see windows, a row of ornate arches looking out towards the village, but apart from these, except for a few small openings that seemed to be little more than ventilators, the walls were windowless, blank and white in the sun. Towards the back of the palace the green of sizable trees showed inside the walls. Outside, stretching back towards the roots of the mountains that divided the gorges of the Adonis and its tributary, the plateau stretched open and stony and barren as the valley of dry bones.

There seemed to be no way to get there except down a rocky track along the side of the tributary stream.

This Hamid was explaining. "And you have to cross the water at the bottom," he said. "There is a ford with shallow water, but sometimes in the spring, you understand, when there has been rain, it can be very deep and fast, and floods over the stepping stones. But it will be all right today. You really wish to go? Then I will come with you to show you the way."

It did not seem to me that it would be very easy to miss the way. I could see the path as far as the bottom of the hill, and—I am very long-sighted—I could even see the ford from where I stood. There must have been a stone bridge there at one time, for the ruined piles were unmistakable. And no doubt beyond that the track up to the palace would be equally unmistakable.

I looked at Hamid in his immaculately pressed dark city trousers and equally immaculate shirt.

"That's very good of you, but there's no need for you to bother, you know. I can hardly miss the way. If you'd rather stay here with the car, and perhaps find something to drink in the village, some coffee, perhaps, if there's a café . . . ?" I looked round me at the singularly unpromising gaggle of huts which was the village of Sal'q.

He grinned. "There is, but with all gratitude, I shall not try it today. I will certainly come down with you. It's a long way for a lady to go alone, and besides, I believe that the porter there speaks nothing but Arabic. You would perhaps find it a little difficult to make yourself sufficiently understood?"

"Oh, lord, yes, I suppose so. Well, thanks very much, I'd be terribly grateful if you'd come. It looks a pretty tough walk, I must say. I wish we had wings."

He locked the car, and dropped the key into his pocket. "Along here."

The path led round the wall of the mosque, past the little graveyard with its curious Moslem stones; the slender pillars with their stone turbans which indicated the graves of men, the lotus-carved steles for the women. The whitewashed minaret stood prettily against the pale hot sky. Past the crumbling corner of the graveyard wall the track suddenly turned downhill in steep zigzags, treacherous with loose stones. The sun was heeling over from its zenith, but still beat fiercely on this side of the valley. Soon we had gone below the lowest of the village terraces, where the hillside was too steep and too stony for anything, even vines, to grow. Some bluff of hot rock hid the stream from us, so that no sound of it came to our ears. The silence was intense. The whole width of the valley seemed to be filled with the same hot, dry silence.

Round a steep turn in the path we disturbed a herd of

goats, black and brown with long silky hair, flop ears, huge horns and sleepy, wicked yellow eyes. They had been grazing on heaven knows what on that barren slope, and now slept in the sun. There were about thirty of them, their narrow clever faces—watching us with calculation and without a hint of fear—giving the impression somehow not that this was a herd of animals owned by men, but that we were walking through a colony of creatures who lived here by right. When one of them got leisurely to its feet and strolled into the middle of the path, I didn't argue with it. I got off the path and walked round it. It didn't even turn its head.

I had been right about the old bridge. The tributary (Hamid told me it was called the Nahr el-Sal'q) was not wide compared to the Adonis, but at this time of year there was fully twenty feet of it to cross, swiftly sliding water, shallow in places over white pebbles, in others tumbling with foam over split boulders, or whirling deeper in a hard dark green in pools which must have been breast deep. At the far side the water was bounded by a low cliff, perhaps five feet high, from which the bridge had originally sprung. The foundations could be seen deep in the clear water. On the side where we stood there was little left but a pile of large squared stones, some of which had been removed and roughly arranged in the water to make stepping stones about a yard apart.

"There was an old bridge here once, a Roman bridge, they say," said Hamid. "These are still the old stones. Can you manage it?"

He took my hand to help me across, then led the way straight for the foot of the cliff, where I saw a path curling its way up through tangles of wild fig and yellow broom towards the head of the promontory.

It was a steep climb but not difficult, obviously practicable for mules or even horses. We saw no sign of life other than the lizards, and the kestrels which circled above the cliff.

There was no sound except that of the water running below us, and the scrape of our steps, and our breathing.

As we came out eventually at the top of the crag and saw the eyeless walls of the palace in front of us, I had the oddest feeling that the building was completely dead and deserted, that this was almost a place outside life. It seemed impossible that anyone should live there, least of all anyone I had known. No one, surely, who had ever been a part of my own extraordinary but vital family could shut themselves away here in this bone-white graveyard of a place . . .

As I paused to get my breath, eyeing the scoured pale walls, the locked gate of bronze, I found myself remembering the last time I had seen Great-Aunt Harriet. It was a dim childhood's memory . . . The orchard at home, at windfall time, and one of those soft gusty September winds with the leaves swirling, and the apples thudding into the damp turf. The sky was full of afternoon clouds and the rooks wheeling to go home. I remembered Great-Aunt Harriet's voice cawing like a rook with laughter at something Charles had said . . .

"There used to be a bell beside the door. You tell me what you want me to say, and if the old chap isn't asleep, we might get him to take a message," said Hamid cheerfully, leading the way across the dusty rock towards the gate.

Chapter Three

————◦≫≪◦————

This batter'd Caravanserai . . .
                —E. FITZGERALD: *The Rubáiyát of*
                Omar Khayyám of Náishápúr

THE MAIN GATE—double leaves of studded bronze under an elaborately carved arch—was at first sight vastly impressive, but as one approached it could be seen that the heavy knocker had vanished from its hinge and that the carving had been fretted almost to nothing by the wind. The walls, high and blind, showed here and there the remains of some coloured decoration, ghostly patterns and mosaics and broken marble plastered over and painted a pale ocher colour which had baked white with the strong sunlight. There was a bell pull to the right-hand side of the gate.

Hamid tugged the handle. Distinctly, in the silence, we could hear the creak of the wires as they strained, foot by rusty foot, to pull the bell. Seconds later, with a squeak and jangle of springs, it clanged hollowly just inside the gate. As the echo ran humming down the bronze a dog barked somewhere. After that, again, there was silence.

Hamid had just raised his hand again to the bell when we

heard footsteps. Hardly footsteps; just the whispering shuffle of slippers on a dusty floor, then the sound of hands fumbling at the other side of the gate. It was no surprise to hear the heavy sound of bolts being dragged back, or that, when the gate began to open, it creaked ominously.

I caught Hamid's eye, and saw in it the same bright anticipation as was no doubt in my own. After such a build-up, whoever opened the gate to us could hardly fail to be an anticlimax.

But he wasn't. He was better than all expectation. One tall leaf of bronze creaked slowly open on a passage that seemed, in contrast to the sunlight where we stood, to be quite dark. In the cautious crack that had opened we could see a thin bent figure robed in white. For one mad moment—such had been the Hitchcock lead-in to his appearance—I thought the man had no face; then I saw that he was dark, almost black, and against the blackness of the passage behind him only his white robes showed up.

He peered out into the light, an oldish man, stoop-shouldered, his skin wrinkled like a prune under the folds of the kaffiyeh, or Arab headdress. His eyes, red-rimmed and puckered against the light, had a greyish look about them which spoke of cataract. He blinked, mouthed something at Hamid which I took to be Arabic, and started to shut the gate.

"One moment. Wait." Hamid was past me into the gap with one quick stride, and had a tough young shoulder against the gate. He had already told me what he intended to say. The quick-fire Arabic sounded urgent. "This is no ordinary visitor, but one of your Lady's family, whom you cannot turn from the door. Listen."

The old man paused uncertainly, and Hamid went on. "My name is Hamid Khalil, from Beirut, and I have driven this young lady up to see your mistress. Now, we know your Lady receives no visitors, but this young lady is English, and she is the daughter of the Lady's brother's son. So you must go and see your Lady and tell her that Miss Christy Mansel has come from England to see her—Miss Christy Mansel, bearing greetings from all the Lady's relatives in England."

The porter was staring, stupidly, almost as if he had not heard. I began to wonder if he were deaf. Then I saw he was looking at me, and that in the opaque eyes a sort of curiosity was stirring. But he shook his head, and again from his lips came those strangled sounds which I realized now were the struggles of someone with a severe speech impediment.

Hamid shrugged at me, expressively. "They didn't tell us the half, did they? 'No communication with outside' is right—this man's all but dumb. However, I don't think he's deaf, so I dare say he has some way of taking messages. There's no need yet for despair."

"That wasn't quite what I was feeling."

He laughed and turned back to the old man, who, gobbling and muttering under his breath, had been making vague attempts to shut the door against the younger man's determined shoulder and (by now) foot. Hamid raised his voice and spoke again, sharply. Even without his subsequent translation to me, the gist of what he said was obvious.

"Look, stop playing about with the gate, we're not going away until you've taken the message to your mistress, or sent someone who can talk to us . . . That's better! Now, have you got it? Miss Christy Mansel, daughter of her brother's son, has come from England to see her, even just for a few moments. Is that clear? Now go and give the message."

There was no doubt that the old man could hear. Open curiosity showed now in the face that shot forward on its stringy neck to stare at me, but he still made no attempt to go, or to invite us in. He shook his head violently, mouthing at Hamid and holding on to the edge of the gate with what looked like a mixture of obstinacy and apprehension.

I intervened, half uneasy, half repelled: "Look, Hamid, perhaps we shouldn't . . . I mean, forcing our way in like this . . . He's obviously had his orders, and he looks scared to death at having to disobey them. Perhaps if I just write a note—"

"If we go away now you'll never get in. It's not your great-aunt he's scared of. As far as I can make out he's saying something about a doctor. 'The doctor says no one is to go in'."

"The *doctor?*"

"Don't worry," he said quickly, "I may be wrong, I can hardly make him out, but I thought that's what he said. Wait a minute . . ."

Another spate of Arabic, and again the horrible stammering syllables from the old man. Flakes of spittle had appeared at the corners of his mouth, and he shook his head violently, and even partially loosed his panic hold of the door to flap his hands at us like someone driving hens.

"Please—" I said.

Hamid silenced the old man with a snapped word and gesture. "Yes?"

"Hamid," I said decisively, "This settles it, I insist on getting in. If I can't see my great-aunt, I'll see the doctor, if he's here. If he isn't, then someone must write his name and address down for me, and I'll go and see him straight away. Tell him that. Tell him I insist. And if you like you can tell him that my family can make quite a bit of trouble if anything should happen to my great-aunt, and the family not be allowed to know about it." I added: "And for pity's sake if there's anyone at all in the place who *can* talk to us, we want to see them, and fast."

"I'll tell him."

How he did actually express my demands I have no idea, but after a further few minutes or so of wrangling, the porter, filmed eyes turned up hideously to heaven and palms thrown up to disclaim all responsibility, pulled open the door at last and let us through.

Hamid gave the ghost of a wink at me as he stood back to let me pass him. "I told him you were exhausted with the walk from Sal'q and refused to wait outside in the sun. If we'd once let him shut the door I doubt if we'd ever have heard from him again."

"I'm sure we wouldn't. For goodness' sake come with me, won't you? I mean, something tells me I may not be welcome."

"I wouldn't leave you for worlds," said Hamid comfortably, taking me by the elbow to steer me into the cool darkness. "I only hope that you find all is well with the Lady . . . and I may easily have been mistaken in what that old dervish was trying to say. Well, at least we are inside . . . That alone is something to tell my children's children."

Behind us the gate creaked shut, and there were the ominous sounds of the bolts being replaced. As my eyes adjusted themselves to the dimness I saw that we were not actually in a passage, but in a high barrel-roofed tunnel about fifteen feet along which ended in another heavy door. To either side of the tunnel was a smaller door. One of these was open, and in the dim light of a slit window in the inner wall I saw an ancient truckle-bed covered with tumbled blankets. The porter's lodge, no doubt; perhaps originally a guardroom. The door opposite this was shut and padlocked.

The old man opened the door at the tunnel's end, letting in a shaft of bright light. We followed him into a big courtyard.

This would be the outer court of the original palace, the *midan*, where the Emir's people would gather with gifts or petitions, and where his troops would show off their horsemanship with games and mock fights, or ride in to dismount after battle or the hunt. Under the archways on three sides were buildings which must have been stables and harness rooms and perhaps quarters for soldiers; on the fourth, to our left as we entered, was a high wall beyond which I saw a glimpse of green. In its heyday, with the bustle of servants and the tramp of horses and rattle of arms, it would have been an impressive place. Now it was quiet and empty, but the scuffed dust showed recent evidence of beasts, and the place smelled of horses.

The porter did not pause here, but led us right-handed across the *midan* and in under the arcade, through another door which gave on a darkened passage. Through this his white robes shuffled dimly ahead. Vaguely I glimpsed passages going off to left and right, and doors, some of them open on rooms where it was too dark to see anything; but in one of these some kind of skylight shed a glimmer on sacks and boxes and a stack of broken chairs. The passage took three right-angled turns through this labyrinth before it led us out into another courtyard, this time small, and little more than a light-well lined with arched grilles, and one blind wall against which was piled a stack of timber. As we passed I saw out of the corner of my eye a streak of movement which, when I looked sharply that way, had ceased. Nothing. But I knew it had been a rat.

Another corridor; more doors, some of them open and giving on dilapidated and dirty rooms. The whole place had the air of something deserted long since, and lived in only by rats and mice and spiders. Not a floor but was filthy, with gaps in the ornamental tiling; the wall mosaics were dim and battered, the window grilles broken, the lintels cracked. A heavy, dusty silence slept over everything like a grey blanket. I remember that as we passed some crumbling wall a rusty nail fell from its socket with a clink that made me jump, and the rustle of plaster falling after it sounded like a puff of wind in dry leaves.

It was a far cry from the 'enchanted palace' that imagination—more powerful than reason—had led me to expect. I began to wonder with tightening nerves what I should find at the end of this quest. 'Stark raving bonkers' had been Charles's verdict, and had seemed, as he delivered it, no more than faintly comic; but here, following the shuffling guide along yet another corridor with its dim and dwindling prospect of warped and gaping doors, its uneven floorings, its smell of years-old decay, I began, quite fervently, to wish I had not come. The thought of coming face to face with the combination of helplessness, senility, and perhaps sickness, which must live at the center of all this decay like a spider in the middle of an old dusty cobweb, could fill me with nothing but dismay.

Suddenly we were out into another courtyard. I had completely lost my bearings by this time, but from the fact that beyond the roofs on the far side I could see crests of feathery green, I guessed we were somewhere towards the back of the palace.

This court was about fifty feet square, and at one time must have been as ornamental as the one where Charles and I had talked in Damascus; but now, like all else, it had fallen into disrepair. In its better days it had been floored with marble, with blue tiled arcades and pretty pillars and a pool at the center. At the foot of each pillar stood a carved marble trough for flowering plants. These were still full of soil, but now held only grass and some tightly clenched, greyish-looking buds. There was one spindly tamarisk hanging over the broken coping of the pool. Somewhere, a cicada purred gently. Grey thistles grew in the gaps of the pavement, and the pool was dry.

Under the arcade to one side was the usual deep alcove in the shadow where, up a single step, was the dais with seats on three sides. I would have distrusted any cushion that this place might produce, but I need not have worried; the seats were of unpadded marble. Here the porter indicated that we should sit, then, with another grotesque bout of yammering directed at Hamid, he turned and went. Silence came back, broken only by the churring of the cicada.

"Smoke?" asked Hamid, producing cigarettes. He lit mine for me and then wandered back into the sunlight of the courtyard, where he squatted down with his back against a pillar, absently narrowing his eyes against the brilliant sky where the trees beyond the wall waved their green feathers.

"If she does not receive you, what will you do?"

"Go away, I suppose, once I've seen the doctor."

He turned his head. "I am sorry. You are distressed."

I hesitated. "Not really. I hardly know her, and I'm pretty sure she won't remember me. She spent most of her time out East till her husband died, and after that she only lived in England for about two years—that was when I was very small. She left fifteen years ago, for good, when I was seven. I haven't seen her since the time she came to say good-bye. I'd hardly be surprised if she just sent a message back now to say she can't even remember my name. That is, if the dervish gets it right . . . I wonder if he can give a message at all? As a noncommunicator he just about wins, wouldn't you say? He ought to be at the Royal Court."

"But surely your Queen would not—? Ah, here he is," said Hamid, rising, "and praise be to Allah, he has brought someone with him."

The 'someone' was a young man, a European, tall and thin and carelessly dressed, with light hair bleached to fair by the sun, and grey eyes. He had the slightly confused air of someone startled awake from sleep, and I suddenly remembered Great-Aunt Harriet's alleged nocturnal habits. Perhaps the staff slept during daylight? He paused for a moment in the shadow before dismissing the porter with a gesture, then came forward into the sun. I saw him wince as if its fierce light worried him, as he approached slowly and with apparent reluctance over the broken pavement. He looked about twenty-four.

His voice was friendly enough, and what was more, English. "Good afternoon. I'm afraid I didn't get your name. I gather from Jassim that you have an urgent message for Lady Harriet? Perhaps you could give your message to me?"

"You're English? Oh, good." I stood up. "It's not exactly a message. My name's Mansel, Christy Mansel, and Mrs Boyd—'Lady Harriet'—is my great-aunt. I'm in Beirut on holiday, and someone told me that my great-aunt was still living up here at Dar Ibrahim, so I came up to see her. I'm sure my people at home will be very glad to have news of her, so if she'll spare me even a few minutes, I'd be very pleased."

He looked surprised, and, I thought, guarded. "A great-niece? Christy, did you say? She never mentioned anyone of that name to me."

"Should she have?" My voice was perhaps a little tart. "And you, Mr—er . . . ? I take it you live here?"

"Yes. My name's Lethman, John Lethman. I—you might say I look after your great-aunt."

"You mean you're the doctor?"

I must have sounded abrupt and surprised, because he looked rather taken aback. "I beg your pardon?"

"I'm sorry, it was only because I suppose you look—I mean, I expected somebody older. The porter told my driver that 'the doctor' wouldn't allow anyone to see my great-aunt, that's how I knew you were here. If he did mean you, that is?"

"I suppose he did . . ." He pressed the heel of his hand to his brow, shook his head sharply as if to wake himself up, and gave me the flash of an embarrassed smile. His eyes still looked blurred and unfocussed. They were grey, with wide, myopic-looking pupils. "I'm sorry, I'm still a bit stupid, I was asleep."

"Oh, goodness, I do apologize. When one's madly sight-seeing all day one tends to forget the siesta habit . . . *I'm* sorry, Mr. Lethman. It was just that when the porter said 'the doctor' was here I began to think my great-aunt must be ill. I mean—if you have to live here . . . ?"

"Look," he said, "we'd better clear this up. I'm not a doctor really, unless you like to count half a course in psychological medicine—" A quick look. "And don't let that worry you, either, because I'm certainly not here in *that* capacity! Your great-aunt's pretty fit, and all I actually do is keep an eye on the Arab servants and see to things generally, and provide her with a bit of company and conversation. I don't 'have' to live here at all in the sense you mean. All that happened was that I came here—to the Lebanon—to do some research for a paper I wanted to write, and I was marooned up here one day, driven to ground by one of the flash storms they have occasionally, and your great-aunt took me in, and somehow one thing led to another, and I stayed." His smile had something tentative about it, but oddly disarming, so that I thought I could supply the missing bits of the story quite easily. He added: "If you can think of a better place to write in, just tell me."

I could think of a million better places to write in, among them almost any room almost anywhere within daily reach of people, but I didn't say so. I asked: "How long have you been here?"

"Nearly a year. I came last July."

"I see. Well, it's a relief to know she's all right. So I'll be able to see her?"

He hesitated, apparently on the brink of saying something, then gave that odd little shake of the head again, and ran his hand back over his brow, almost as if he were smoothing away some physical discomfort like a headache. I saw Hamid watching him curiously.

"Look," I said, "if you've something to tell me, go ahead. But let's sit down, shall we?"

He followed me into the shade of the divan, and we sat down. I laced my fingers round one knee and turned to

61

regard him. He still looked uncomfortable, though not in the physical sense; his long body looked relaxed enough, and his hands were slack on his knees. But there was a tight knot of worry between his brows.

"How long since you heard from your great-aunt?" he asked at length.

"If you mean how long since I myself did, I never have. In fact I only remember seeing her about three times in my life, and the last time was when I was about seven, but my family hears from her now and again. There was a letter last year some time—just before Christmas, I think it was. She certainly wrote as if she were fairly fit and in her right—that is, fairly fit. But it didn't bother much with news."

I got the idea that he knew what I meant, but he didn't smile. He was frowning down at his hands. "I only asked because—" A pause, then he looked up suddenly. "Miss Mansel, how much do you and your family know about the way she lives here?"

"I suppose we know very little, except the obvious things, that she's perhaps getting a bit more eccentric as she gets older, and that she's made her life out here for so long that it isn't very likely she'll ever want to move and come home again. You'll have gathered that our family's never been very strong on family ties and all that, and of course lately Great-Aunt Harriet's had this thing about cutting all her ties with England home and beauty—that's almost all her letters have been about, when she wrote at all. Don't think the family minded, they didn't. What she does is her own affair. But since I came out here I've heard a bit more about her, and I gather that now it's a pretty far-out kind of eccentricity . . . I mean, all this Lady Hester Stanhope imitation. Is it really true? Does she really live like that? Mr Lethman, she isn't really bats, is she?"

"No, oh no," he said quickly. He was looking immensely relieved. "I wondered if you knew about that. It wouldn't be very easy to start explaining from scratch, but if you know the Stanhope story it makes it relatively simple. I won't say your great-aunt deliberately set out to be a modern 'Lady of the Lebanon', but when she first settled here at Dar Ibrahim she did keep a bit of state, and various people made the comparison to her, and then she discovered that the old Stanhope legend was still very much alive among the country Arabs, and she herself got a good deal of benefit from it in the way of service and influence and—you know, the various by-products of celebrity. It was the locals who started calling her 'Lady Harriet', and it simply stuck. Your great-aunt was amused at first, I gather, and then she discovered it suited her to be a 'character', and in the way these things have, it gradually grew beyond the point where it could be stopped, and certainly beyond the point where she could treat it as a joke, even to herself. I don't know if you can understand this?"

"I think so," I said. "She couldn't detach herself any more, so she simply went with it."

"That's it. Nor did she want to detach herself. She'd lived out here for so long, and in a way she'd made it her country, and in a curious way I believe she feels she has a kind of right to the legend." He smiled, the first smile of genuine amusement. "If you want the truth I think she has a fair amount in common with her original. Well, she simply settled down to enjoy it, and got a great deal of pleasure from the more picturesque details—riding out with the hounds and hawks, for instance, letting Dar Ibrahim be used again as a halt for caravans on their way from High Lebanon and Antilebanon to the sea, and receiving the occasional 'distinguished traveler'—mostly archaeologists, I believe, who'd known her husband and his work. She even meddled a bit with politics, and for sometime now she's been threatening—though I think it's only window dressing myself—to turn Muslim." He paused. "And then of course when I turned up out of the blue she was delighted. I was to be the 'resident physician' who has such a large part in the Stanhope story . . . you know that Lady Hester Stanhope kept her own doctor with her at Djoun? Well, when our 'Lady Harriet' took me in, and found I'd been half way to a medical degree, it suited her down to the ground. So I get a courtesy title which impresses the Arab servants, and what I actually do is provide your great-aunt with company and conversation. I need hardly add that if she did need medical attention I'd get it from Beirut."

"Who does she have now that Dr Grafton's gone?"

"Dr Grafton?" He sounded quite blank, and I looked at him in surprise.

"Yes, don't you know him? Surely, if he attended her six months ago you must have been here."

"Oh, yes, I was, I was only wondering how you knew the name."

"Someone at the hotel who told me about Dar Ibrahim said my aunt had been ill last autumn, so I got them to find out who her doctor was, and rang him up to ask about her. I was told then that he'd left Beirut. Who does she have now?"

"She hasn't needed anyone since then, I'm glad to say. She's got a bit of a thing now about the Beirut doctors, but I've no doubt that if it's necessary I'll make her see the light." He smiled. "Don't worry . . . I really do look after her quite well, you know, and I run the place for her as far as one can. And if you're thinking about the general four-star-hotel atmosphere you've seen up to now, let me tell you that there are five courtyards, two gardens, three Turkish baths, a mosque, stabling for fifty horses and twelve camels, several miles of corridors including a secret passage or two, and as for mere rooms, I've never managed to count them. I use radar to get from the Prince's Court to the Seraglio."

I laughed: "I'm sorry, was I looking at the dust on the floor? Don't you have slaves to go with the décor?"

"Only myself and three others—Jassim the porter, a girl called Halide, and Halide's brother Nasirulla, who lives in the village and comes over during the day. Actually we manage quite well, because the old lady herself lives very simply now. I may tell you that her part of the palace is a bit better kept than this. Halide's a good girl, and looks after your aunt pretty well. You really have no need to worry about her."

"Did I say I was worrying? I didn't mean to throw you on the defensive like this. What have I said? I'm sure Aunt Harriet's having a whale of a time being Lady of the Lebanon, and I'm glad you're here to look after her. All I want is to see her for five minutes so's I can tell my people all about it."

Another of those pauses. Here we were, I thought; back to Square One.

He shifted on the hard seat, and glanced sideways at me.

"Yes, well, that's rather it, don't you see? The point is, we've standing orders to stall everybody off, and—" his gaze dropped again to his hands—"anything she's ever said to me about her family didn't lead me to think she'd make an exception there."

I grinned. "Fair enough, I'm not blaming you, or her either. But can't we let her decide for herself? I take it she doesn't know I'm here yet? Or will Jassim have got that across to her?"

"He hasn't seen her yet, he came straight to me. As a matter of fact, he gets more across than you'd think, but he didn't get your name. I wasn't sure who you were myself, till I spoke to you. I admit he isn't so hot as a messenger—you might call him one of your aunt's charities, like me—but he's pretty useful as a staller-off at the gate, and we can't get anyone much to stay here nowadays. There isn't much money, you know."

There was something about the way he said this, looking at me steadily with those curiously unfocussed eyes. I noticed that the whites were bloodshot, and he looked as if he didn't get enough sleep, but he seemed relaxed enough now, his long spare frame slack on the marble seat as if this were thick with silk cushions and Persian rugs. He was dressed in grey light-weight trousers and a blue beach shirt, neither of them expensive, but he wore on his wrist a really magnificent gold watch, bought no doubt in Beirut. I found myself remembering what Charles had said about Great-Aunt Harriet's penchant for young men, and some other corner of my mind came up with the phrase 'undue influence'. But this I ignored; it was after all irrelevant. If Aunt H could get a young man to run her ramshackle palace for her and give her the kind of company she liked, so much the better. Especially if it was true that there was very little money left. I wondered just how true this was, and if Mr Lethman looked on the sudden irruption of a relative as a threat to his own position vis-à-vis the 'Lady Harriet'. In which case my good-looking cousin Charles might be even less welcome than I. I decided not to mention Charles till I saw Aunt H herself.

John Lethman was saying: "Jassim wouldn't have been able to see your aunt yet, in any case. She usually sleeps a good deal during the day. She's a nightbird, you know, like her original. So if you could wait a little longer, then I can go and ask her about it? Halide usually goes in to wake her at about six."

"Of course I'll wait," I said. "That is, if you don't mind, Hamid?"

"Not at all," said Hamid without moving.

There was a slight pause. Lethman glanced from Hamid to me and back, then consulted his watch. "Well, that's fine, it won't be long now, and we'll see." Another pause. He cleared his throat. "I suppose I ought to warn you . . . Of course I'll do all I can, but I can't guarantee anything. She's old, and sometimes forgetful, and—well, let's call it 'difficult'. And some days are worse than others."

"And today's been a bad one?"

He made a rueful mouth. "Not too good."

"Well, if she really doesn't feel up to seeing me, then that's that, isn't it? But tell her I'll come back any time she says, when she's feeling better. I'm in Beirut till at least mid-week, and I could stay on. I was going to ring up soon to tell my people what I was planning, and it'd be rather nice if I could give them news of her. In fact, Daddy might just be ringing up himself this evening."

" 'This evening'? Hadn't you understood? I meant it literally when I said she was a nightbird. She usually seems to wake up and be at her best at something between ten and midnight, and after that she's quite often up all night. If she receives anyone at all, that's when she sees them."

"Good heavens, she does play it for real, doesn't she? Do you mean that if I'm to see her, I've got to stay here all night?"

"Until pretty late, at all events. Could you?"

"I could, but I can hardly keep my driver here until the early hours of the morning. Could you put me up? Have you a room?" I meant 'a room that's fit to sleep in', so the question wasn't as absurd as it might have sounded. Mr Lethman seemed to be considering the question on its merits. There was a short pause, then he said, agreeably enough:

"We could certainly find you one."

I looked across at Hamid. "Do you mind? We can see what my great-aunt has to say, and if I do have to wait and see her later on, would you go back without me? You could call at the hotel and tell them I'm having to stay up here for the night, and—are you free tomorrow?"

"For you, yes."

"You're very good," I said gratefully, "thank you. In that case, could you come for me again in the morning? Wait in the village, don't bother to come right across as far as the gate."

"I will certainly come to the gate," said Hamid. "Don't you worry about that. But I don't much like going away now and leaving you here."

"I'll be all right. And I simply must see my great-aunt."

"Of course you must, this I understand. I am sorry, I know it's none of my affair, but surely it could be arranged that she could see you for a few minutes now, and then I could take you back to your hotel."

Beside me, Mr Lethman straightened suddenly. His voice held a weariness and exasperation that was quite obviously genuine. "Look, I'm sorry about all this. I'm not making this difficult just for fun, you know, in fact I'm hating the position I seem to have got myself into, having to stall you off when you must think I've no standing in the matter at all—"

"I wasn't exactly thinking that," I said, "and you have got standing, haven't you? I mean, this is her home, and if she's asked you to live here, there it is, and no arguments. Even if you're not officially her doctor, I suppose you could call yourself her steward or something."

"Malvolio in person, yellow stockings, cross garters, and all." A flick of feeling in his voice that I didn't like, gone as soon as heard. He followed it with another of those disarming smiles. "But you see the situation's hardly normal in any way at all. I suppose I've got used to it, and in any case this is a damned queer country where one learns to accept almost anything, but I realize this place must seem pretty weird to anyone like yourself coming into it for the first time. It did to me when she first received me. She uses what were the Emir's rooms—the Prince's Court, we call it—and an old State Divan is her bedroom. It's kept pitch dark most of the time. The Stanhope woman did the same out of vanity. I don't know what your great-aunt's motive is, certainly not that, possibly just imitation; but I remember when I was taken along there at midnight the first time I wondered what sort of loony-bin I'd landed into. And lately she's taken to—" He stopped, and seemed to be examining the tip of one shoe with great attention. "How well do you remember your great-aunt?"

"Not really at all. My impression is that she was tall and dark and had piercing black eyes and wore black, things that flew round her like the White Queen's shawl. She did have a shawl, and she used to pin it with a diamond pin. I remember Mummy saying that her diamonds were filthy. That struck me as funny, I don't know why."

"Diamonds? I'm afraid they must have gone long since. I never saw any." He sounded regretful, I thought. "Actually she's not so very tall, though I suppose she'd seem so to a child. And as for her clothes now, they're part of the legend, too."

"Oh, I know, she dresses like an Eastern male. Well, why not?" I unclasped my hands from my knees and straightened a trousered leg. "I dress like a European one, after all."

"I wasn't fooled," said Mr Lethman, with the first really human glimmer he had shown. The worried look had lightened a little. He got to his feet. "Well, I'll go and see what the score is. I'll certainly try to persuade her to see you straight away. It's possible she may, and welcome you with open arms, but if she won't, we can make arrangements for you to stay the night. All right?"

"All right."

"That's fine, then. I'll let you know the worst."

He smiled perfunctorily and left us.

I went over to the pool and sat down on the coping beside Hamid.

"Did you hear all that?"

"Most of it," said Hamid. "What you might call a funny setup, eh? Smoke?"

"Not just now, thanks. I don't very often, actually."

"He does."

"How d'you mean?"

"Hashish."

I stared. "No? Does he? How do you know?"

He lifted his shoulders. "His eyes, didn't you notice? And other signs—one gets to know them. He'd been smoking when we came."

"Then that's why he was so sleepy and other-worldly! He said he'd been asleep, and let me think it was just a siesta. I thought he'd probably been up part of the night with my great-aunt. Smoking! No wonder he resented being interrupted!"

"I don't suppose he was resenting you. The smoke can make you relaxed and easy-going, and not know what you're doing. He was finding it hard to think. I smoke it myself sometimes; everybody does in the Lebanon."

"Do you?"

He smiled. "Not when I'm driving, don't worry. And not much, me; I've too much sense, and it's dangerous. It affects different people different ways, and by the time you've found what it does to you, sometimes it is too late. Did you hear him say he was writing a book? If he stays here and smokes *marjoun,* he will never write it. He will think for years that he has only to start tomorrow, and it will be the best book ever written . . . but he will never start. This is what the *marjoun* does; it gives you visions and takes away the will to translate them. He will end up like that old man, coughing in the sun and dreaming dreams . . . What will you do if he comes back to say the old lady won't see you at all?"

"I don't quite know."

"I'll tell you what I should do. If he says she will not see you, tell him that you wish to hear this from the old lady herself. If he will not allow this, then tell him that you can only accept such an order from a real doctor, and that you wish a doctor from Beirut to see her straight away. Oh, you can do this very pleasantly. Ask him which doctor he recommends, and what time tomorrow will be convenient. Then you tell me, and I bring you."

There wasn't much expression in his voice, but I stared at him. "What are you suggesting?"

"Nothing." He shrugged again. "Seems to me that things must go very much as he orders them here, and we only have his word for it that there is no money left. She was—I repeat was—a very rich old lady."

"But the family don't care about—" I stopped. It was patently no use explaining to Hamid that nobody wanted Great-Aunt Harriet to do anything with her own money except have a good time on her own terms. Anyway, there were other considerations here than money. I said, slowly: "If it's true that she's perfectly fit, I'd say she can probably take care of herself, and I'm also pretty sure she wouldn't thank me for interfering. All I want is to know that she is still 'hale and hearty', and that being so she can dispose of her filthy old diamonds any way she pleases. He's probably right that she's done it already."

"Very likely." I didn't know whether Hamid's dry tone meant that he was thinking of the economies obviously practiced in the place, or of John Lethman's gold wristwatch. He added: "I do not suggest anything, me, but I have a very unpleasant nature."

"So have I. And if he really is smoking marihuana—hashish, that is—" I took a breath. "That settles it, I shall insist, whatever he says. I'm terribly sorry to have kept you hanging about like this, you've been very patient."

"You are paying for my car for the day, and for my time. How I spend the time is no matter, and it saves petrol to sit in the sun and smoke."

I laughed. "You've got something there. And you're right, I must see her. If necessary I shall play hell and insist."

"There's no need."

I jumped. I hadn't heard Mr Lethman come back, but he was there, with Jassim behind him, coming quickly along the shaded side of the arcade, and looking as if he'd been hurrying. Or, I thought, as if he'd had a slightly dicey interview. At least he looked wide awake now, even brisk.

"She'll see me?"

"Yes, she'll see you, but I'm afraid it'll have to be later tonight." He made an apologetic gesture. "I'm sorry, I did try to persuade her, but I told you, it's not a good day, so I didn't like to press it. She's had a touch of bronchial asthma lately, nothing to worry about, but it sometimes prevents her from sleeping. She won't hear of calling the doctor, and since we still had the prescription from last autumn—it was the same trouble then—I didn't overrule her. In a way it's the remedy that's the trouble, rather than the disease. She finds it depressive. To tell you the truth, the idea of a visit from you cheered her up a good deal."

"That's wonderful. I promise not to tire her."

"Have you made arrangements with your driver? I'll fix you up with a room now, before I go back to your great-aunt."

"It's all settled. Hamid's coming back for me tomorrow."

"Fine," he said, as if he meant it. "Well, if you'll come with me, Jassim will show your driver the way back to the gate."

As I said good-bye to Hamid, I thought I saw Jassim looking at me rather longingly, as if he would have liked to throw me out, too. But he eventually shuffled off into the shadows, and Hamid, with a final cheerful wave to me, went after him.

Mr Lethman led me the other way, towards the rear of the buildings.

"So she didn't take much persuading after all?" I said.

"None at all," he admitted, "once she'd grasped who you

were. To be honest she couldn't remember much about you, but she's very keen to see you now."

"I had a feeling she might be. Sheer roaring curiosity, I suppose."

He glanced down with what looked like surprise. "Well . . . yes, you could say so. Don't you mind?"

"Why should I? The motive doesn't matter as long as the result's all right. She's seeing me, isn't she? Anyway, it's only fair. What d'you imagine *my* main motive is for visiting Dar Ibrahim?"

"I—yes, of course." He sounded disconcerted.

"What's the matter? For goodness' sake, does that shock you?"

"No. But . . . you're a very unusual girl, aren't you?"

"Because I insist on my own way, or because I don't think relations are obliged to be fond of one another whether they like it or not? It's not unusual, it's only that most people won't admit it." I laughed. "Oh yes, I like to go my own way, but I recognize other people's right to do the same thing. It's about the only thing in my favour."

"What if their way isn't the same as yours?"

"Oh, if I feel really strongly about anything, it's full steam ahead and damn the torpedoes, but I'm open to argument. Where are you going to put me?"

"In the Seraglio."

"Well, that's putting me in my place, isn't it? Under lock and key?"

"Just about. At least, all the windows are barred." He smiled down at me, suddenly charming. "It's only because it's the best end of the palace, I assure you . . . We may be grudging hosts, but once we've had to give in, we do the thing properly. First-class accommodation, to make up for lack of welcome. Did you know that the Lady Hester Stanhope graded her guests according to status? I believe the third class used to get a pretty rough night."

"She would. It's nice of you to top-grade me when I'm giving you all this trouble."

"Heavens, it's no trouble. Actually I'm delighted you're staying—your great-aunt isn't the only one who likes company . . . I'm simply relieved she took it this way and I didn't have to quarrel with you. I'm certain your visit will do her a world of good—in fact, I can't help thinking it would be nice if she took a sudden shine to you and pressed you to stay for a few weeks, then *you* can sit and read the Koran to her at three in the morning, and give me a night off."

"Is that what you do?"

"It has been known. Shall I suggest it to her? How long can you spare?"

"I'll let you know in the morning."

He laughed, and pushed open a wooden gate that hung a bit crooked under a weed-grown arch.

"In here," he said, and ushered me past him.

Chapter Four

————— ❧ —————

And still a Garden by the Water blows . . .
               —E. FITZGERALD: *The Rubáiyát of*
                   Omar Khayyám

"OH!" I said, and stood still.

John Lethman shut the gate behind him, and came to my elbow. "Do you like it?"

"*Like* it!" I drew a breath. "What did it use to be?"

"Oh, just the Seraglio Garden. I'm afraid it's terribly neglected."

It was, of course, but this was a large part of its beauty. After the prospects of sun-baked stone and dusty ruin that had been assaulting my eyes all afternoon, the riot of green and flowers and the shimmer of cool water was wonderful.

It followed the now familiar pattern of the courtyards, a paved space decorated with flowers and bushes, with a pool at the center, surrounded by shaded arcades out of which opened the various rooms and offices. But this place was huge. Apparently the Seraglio rooms and garden filled the whole width of the palace, stretching well back over the flat surface of the plateau. On three sides of this vast space ran the arches of the long colonnades, throwing their pattern of sun and shadow over the doorways of what had been the women's apartments. On the fourth side—to the north—the colonnade marched with the outer wall where a row of delicate arches looked out across the Nahr el-Sal'q towards the village and the distant snows of the High Lebanon. High though these windows were, they were heavily barred with lattices so close that a hand could hardly have been thrust through them.

Within this frame of columns, long ago, some expert had laid out a big formal garden, and had somehow led water down from some high spring to feed the trees and flowers and fill the pool—no ornamental pond this time, but a wide stretch of water, almost a lake, which held at its center a small island crowned with a grove of trees. On this, at the heart of the green grove, I saw the glint of gilded tiles—the roof of a miniature building like an exotic summerhouse or folly; a Persian-style kiosk, with an onion dome, decorative pillars and latticed arches and shallow, broken steps.

There had once been a bridge across to the island, a slender, pretty affair; but now halfway over a broken gap yawned, some six feet wide. The lake itself was paved thickly with lily leaves, and at the edge the irises had spread into dense battalions of spears. All round the brink went a wide paved walk where ferns and briars thrust up the cracked marble slabs. From the shingled roofs of the arcades and down between the pillars jasmine and purple bougainvillea and roses hung festooned like cobwebs, and every cornice was white with birds' droppings and fully inhabited by doves calling *'Yusuf, Yusuf'*, like mad things. The contrast between the formal design of oblong lake, graceful arches and elegant kiosk, and the riotous natural growth that had invaded them, was excitingly attractive. It was like a formal Persian painting gone wild.

"Not a weed out of place," I said. "It's gorgeous! And to think I was always sorry for those poor women. Well, that settles it, Mr Lethman, I'll move in tomorrow for a long, long stay. How long can you do with me?"

"Wait till you've seen your room before you commit yourself," he said, leading the way.

The room was midway along the south side of the garden. It was a plain square room, with a highish ceiling and chequered marble floor and patterned mosaic on the walls in panels of blue and gilt framing texts of Arabic writing. Unlike the other rooms I had seen so far, this one was clean, and well lighted by a triple window which looked straight out over the Adonis Gorge. The window was barred, but not so heavily as those which gave on the plateau. And for obvious reasons: the outer wall of the Seraglio apparently rose straight from the edge of the rock above the river.

"The bedroom's next door," said Mr Lethman, "and the bathroom's the one after that. When I say 'bathroom', of course, I mean the whole works, a hammam—steam rooms, cold rooms, massage rooms, the lot." He grinned. "But guess what, no steam."

"Any hot?"

"You can't be serious? But there is running water, straight off the snow, and it's all yours." The smile faded, and he looked at me a little doubtfully. "You know, it's terribly brave of you to stay. We're not geared for this kind of thing."

"I'm enjoying it," I said truthfully.

"I suppose whatever else it is, this end of the place must seem like a slice of real Eastern romance? Heaven knows I hope you can keep your illusions . . . I'm afraid the bedroom's not ready yet. I'll send Halide along to fix it up in a minute, and bring you some towels. Is there anything else you'll want?"

"Only a toothbrush, and I don't suppose the hammam runs to that. Don't look so worried, I was only joking. I'll do very well for one night, if supper could possibly include an apple? I hope Great-Aunt Harriet's régime does run to supper?"

He laughed. "Have a heart. What's more, you'll be glad to hear that Halide doesn't feed me on your great-aunt's diet! I'll have to leave you now, I'm afraid." He glanced at his watch. "You'd like a drink, I'm sure. I'll send one straight away. It'll soon be too dark for you to explore much, but go where you like—except for the Prince's rooms, of course, and either Halide or I will be there to fend you off if you lose your way."

"Thanks, but I'll just stay here. The garden's lovely."

"Then I'll be back to join you in about half an hour, and we'll eat."

When he had gone I sat down on the divan cushions, looking out over the gorge where the last of the light netted the tips of the trees with gold. Below, the shadows deepened through purple to black. It would soon be dark. I realized suddenly that I was tired, and hoped that when Halide came with the drink it wouldn't be the conventional Arab welcome of arak.

It wasn't, and it wasn't brought by Halide, but by a stocky young Arab who was presumably the brother, Nasirulla. He was dressed like Jassim in white robes, and came in silently with a tray which held a lighted lamp, two glasses, and a bottle of the golden wine of the Bk'aa. This is a lovely wine, light and dryish and about the best that Lebanon produces, and he couldn't have brought anything I'd sooner have had at that moment. I began to think kindly of Mr John Lethman.

When I spoke to Nasirulla he eyed me sidelong, shook his head, and said something in Arabic. Then he set the lamp in a niche near the door, sketched a salaam, and went out.

*   *   *

With the coming of the lamp the darkness, as it always does, seemed to fall quickly. Only minutes after Nasirulla had left me the blue sky beyond the windows dimmed to blackness, and by seven o'clock it was quite dark.

I sat curled on the window seat, sipping the golden wine, and wondering what the night would bring.

It was very quiet. The night sky was like black velvet spangled with big stars, and, as if it had indeed been a velvet curtain, all sound seemed to be cut off, even the faintest murmuring of the river below my window. In the garden the doves had fallen silent and not even a breath of air stirred the feathery trees. Through the open door I could smell jasmine and roses, and some other strongly scented flowers, and below those exotic scents, as a sort of reminding undertone, the sweetish stagnant smell of the pool.

Mr Lethman came back at about a quarter to eight, and with him Nasirulla with the supper tray. There was soup, scalding hot in a big thermos jug, and dish of *shawarma*—mutton flavoured with vinegar, lemon, onion and cardamom seeds and grilled on a long spit. With this came a bowl of salad, a dish of pale butter and half a goats' milk cheese, a pile of unleavened bread and some apples and another bottle of wine. Nasirulla put this down on the low table, said something to Mr Lethman, and then left us.

I said: "If you call this living simply, count me in."

He laughed. "I told you Halide fed me extra on the side. By the way, Nasirulla says she's on her way to do your room now."

"I'm giving you a lot of trouble. I mean, bringing the tray all this way for one thing. Where d'you usually eat?"

"Here, quite often." He added apologetically: "You'll probably find out, so I may as well tell you, these are my rooms. No, listen, please . . . I was going to sleep over the other side tonight anyway, so you're not to think you've put us to any trouble at all."

"Not put you to—? Mr Lethman, I don't know what to say! Turning you out of your room!"

But he cut short my protestations by serving the soup and handing me mine in an eared round mug along with some Arab bread, then refilling my wineglass. It seemed almost as if he were bent on making amends for his earlier reluctance to let me in; or as if, once the Lady Harriet had accepted me, traditional Arab hospitality must have its way, and there was literally not enough that he and the Arab servants could do to make my stay a comfortable one. Any connection between my lively host and the harassed, sleep- or smoke-bemused young man of the afternoon seemed purely coincidental. He seemed to be laying himself out to entertain me, and we chatted pleasantly throughout the meal.

He knew a fair amount about the history of the place, and was very entertaining about what he called the Lady's 'cut-price court' of Dar Ibrahim, but I noticed that he said very little about Great-Aunt Harriet herself, and behind his reserve I thought I could sense respect and liking for her. Whatever else he mocked, and however much she might invite it, he did not mock his patroness, and I liked him the better for it. He was certainly interested in everything I could tell him about the family. The only thing I refrained deliberately from mentioning was Charles's presence in Syria, and the fact that he, too, was planning a visit. I intended to find a good moment to tell Great-Aunt Harriet myself that he wanted to see her, and so by-pass all the difficulties of persuasion at second-hand. Not that, if Charles was right, any persuasion would be needed. If she had agreed so readily to see me, whom she would hardly remember, then her favourite Charles was practically in already.

Halide brought coffee at nine o'clock, with the information that Nasirulla had gone back to the village, and that my room was ready.

She was not much like her brother in appearance, being younger and slimly built. She was a dark-skinned Arab, walnut rather than olive, with huge dark eyes, slim neck and delicate hands. Her dress was of bronze-green silk, a rich-looking material and a sophisticated colour; her eyes were outlined with black in a way London would have recognized; and under the thin silk she wore, unless I was mistaken, a French—a very French—half-cup bra. Like a great many Arab women she wore her bank account on her wrists, which jingled with thin gold bracelets. No simple Arab maiden this one, and—if I was any judge—wasting no sweetness on the desert air. As she told Mr Lethman (in English) about the room, she looked me over in her turn, and the message passed, clear from female to female in any language from Eskimo to Aborigine: "Not that he'd look at you, the mess you look in those trousers, but keep off my patch, will you, or I'll make you sorry."

Then, with the black eyes modestly lowered, she was saying to John Lethman, in her pretty, softly accented English: "When you have finished your coffee, the Lady would like to see you again."

She went out, leaving the door open. I watched her slim graceful figure vanish into the shadows of the arcade, beyond the small light cast by the lamp; but I thought she hadn't gone very far. In a moment or two I knew that I was right: where the waters of the lake reflected a faint greyness from the star-filled sky I saw a movement. She was waiting among the bushes by the water's edge, probably watching us through the open door.

John Lethman made no move to shut it. Since he was obviously anxious to finish his coffee and answer the summons, I hurried with mine, too.

Soon he got to his feet. "I'm afraid I'll have to leave you now, but I'll come back as soon as she lets me, and take you across. Now, are you sure you'll be all right here?"

"Why not? Don't worry about me, I'll be fine. I'll find a book."

"Of course, take anything you want. You can turn the

lamp up quite easily if it's not bright enough; Halide'll show you how."

He turned his head sharply as a bell jangled somewhere deep in the buildings, sounding very loud in the hushed night. And from somewhere nearer, startled off by the violent and prolonged pealing of the bell, came the sudden furious baying of dogs. Big dogs, by the sound of them, inside the building, and quite near.

"What on earth's happened?" I demanded, startled.

"Just your great-aunt getting impatient. I'll have to go, I'm sorry. I'll be back to fetch you as soon as I can."

"But those dogs?"

"Oh, that's nothing, they always make that hellish noise when the bell goes. Don't worry about them, I'll shut them up before I come back for you."

" 'Shut them up?' You mean they're loose about the place? They sound dangerous."

"Well, they're our watchdogs, they have to be. But they're only turned loose at night, and they can't get into the Seraglio if you keep the main door shut. You'll be quite safe." He flashed me a sudden smile. "Not to worry, it's not your night for being eaten alive—at least, not by the dogs."

He went. I heard the wooden gate shut behind him, and a few moments later his voice calling to the dogs. The baying stopped, and silence came back. In it I saw Halide, glimmering in the doorway in her green silk.

"If you will come this way, I will show you your room."

She had lit another lamp for me in the bedroom, and set it on a shelf near the bed.

This room was a twin of the other, but seemed bigger, as it contained no furniture but a narrow iron-framed bed, a flimsy-looking bamboo chair, and a hideous chest of drawers painted black, which held a rather beautiful lacquered looking glass and a battered old tin box with metal clasps labeled *S.S. Yangtse Maid*. The floor was bare and so were the window seats on the dais. The bed was made up with Irish linen, yellowish and not very well ironed, and the red honeycomb quilt covered what looked like the hardest and healthiest mattress in the world.

I didn't think somehow that this was Halide's patch; there would have to be a good deal more Eastern glamour about any affair of hers. Was that what John Lethman had meant by 'sleeping on the other side'?

However, it wasn't this thought which made me say: "I've turned Mr Lethman out, haven't I? Where will he sleep?"

A shrug, not quite insolent. "There are plenty of rooms." When I didn't answer she glanced at me, perhaps a bit uneasily, and added with an attempt at civility dragged up with obvious difficulty: "He is with the Lady often at night. He'll maybe sleep in the morning."

"Oh, well, perhaps I haven't upset things as much as I thought." I smiled at her. "But I'm afraid it's giving you a lot of trouble, changing the rooms round twice."

She didn't make the usual disclaimer, but this may only have been because her English wasn't good enough for polite skirmishing.

"You have seen the bathroom?"

"Yes, thanks. Is the water drinkable?"

"Yes, but there was water on the supper tray. I will leave that. If there is nothing else—?"

"I don't think so, thank you. It all looks very nice, and I'm sure I shall be comfortable. Oh, would you show me how to turn the lamp higher, please? Mr Lethman said I might look at his books while I was waiting."

Back in the other room she obliged, lifting the lamp down and setting it on the table among the books. I thanked her, and examined them while she began to stack the used dishes on the tray. She said nothing more, but I saw how she watched me, and it wasn't imagination to read a wary hostility into those quick sidelong glances. Irritated now, and wishing she would finish her job and go, I concentrated on selecting a book. As light reading for whiling away an hour or two they were hardly promising. An Arabic grammar, a few books on Syria and the Lebanon which I had already read during my convalescence in Charles's room, and a collection which might be said to represent John Lethman's homework—some volumes (also familiar to me) about the original Lady of the Lebanon: Joan Haslip and Roundell and Silk Buckingham and the three old volumes of Dr Meryon's diary about his redoubtable patroness. I looked at the flyleaves. As I thought, they were Great-Aunt Harriet's own copies, presumably lent to her latter-day 'Dr Meryon' for his close study . . . I skipped along the row. T. E. Lawrence's *Crusader Castles,* Guillaume's *Islam,* the Everyman *Koran,* Kinglake's *Eothen* . . . all Aunt Harriet's. No medical textbooks, which were presumably too bulky to carry on field work. The only things which carried his own name were—interestingly enough—Huxley's *The Mind Changers,* Frazer's *Golden Bough,* and a newish paperbound copy of Théophile Gautier's *Le Club des Hachachiens.* No novels except Dostoievsky's *The Brothers Karamazov* and Margery Allingham's *The Tiger in the Smoke.*

The last volume in the row was De Quincey. I turned the pages idly while Halide stacked the dishes rather loudly on the tray.

> The opium-eater loses none of his moral sensibilities, or aspirations: he wishes and longs, as earnestly as ever, to realise what he believes possible, and feels to be exacted by duty; but his intellectual apprehension of what is possible infinitely outruns his power, not of execution only, but even of power to attempt. He lies under the weight of incubus and nightmare . . .

Plus ça change, plus c'est la même chose. It was exactly what Hamid had said. I put the opium nightmare back as Halide lifted the tray and went with it to the door.

"I'll shut it for you," I said, moving to do so, but she paused in the doorway and turned.

"You are really the daughter of the Lady's brother's son?"

I worked it out while she stared at me across the dishes.

"Yes."

"Your father is also here in the Lebanon?"

"No."

"He is dead?"

"No," I said, surprised. "Why?"

"Then you travel alone?"

"Why not?"

She ignored this, too. She was intent on some line of her own which I couldn't follow, but which was obviously intensely important to her.

"You—you stay here long?"

Curiosity made me less than truthful. "As long as she'll let me," I said, watching her.

She said quickly: "She is not well. You will have to go in the morning."

I raised my brows. "That's for her to say, surely?" I added, with innocence concealing a flicker of malice: "But of course in a place this size I needn't be in her way. Mr Lethman asked me to stay as long as I liked."

The black eyes flared, whether in alarm or anger it was impossible to say. "But that is not possible! He—"

Jangling, imperative, and sounding very bad-tempered, Great-Aunt Harriet's bell shattered the silence once more. Further away, but still obviously at large, the watchdogs bayed. The girl started, so violently that the things on the tray clashed and rattled.

"Saved by the bell," I said. "You were saying?"

"No. No. I must go!" Then, almost fiercely, as I made a move to follow and open the main gate for her: "Leave it! I can manage, I can manage!"

The gate shut behind her. I stared thoughtfully after her.

85

Saved by the bell, indeed. I thought I could add the score. Whether or not John Lethman had a stake in Great-Aunt Harriet, I was sure that Halide had a stake in John Lethman. And I wasn't sure how that added up for Great-Aunt Harriet. I went back to the bookshelf.

It would be nice to be able to record that I was the kind of person who would pick up the Dostoievsky or the Huxley or even *The Golden Bough* and curl up with it for a glorious evening's read. But when eventually Mr Lethman came for me as he had promised, he found me a few chapters into *The Tiger in the Smoke,* and half wishing I had chosen something less exciting for a night in the deserted wing of a ruined palace.

He was armed, not with an oil lamp, but with an enormous and very powerful electric torch.

"Ready?" he asked.

He led me back to the courtyard where Hamid and I had waited, but there we turned right, away from the main gate, the way I had seen him go to Great-Aunt Harriet. The place was vast, far bigger even than I had imagined. We seemed to walk for ever up corridors, round corners, up steps, down steps, and across at least two more small courts, in the first of which a trickle of water showed that all the wells had not dried. As we traversed the second I heard, from behind a closed door, a scratching sound followed by a deep whining yelp that made me jump.

"It's all right, I told you I'd shut them up." He shone the torch momentarily towards the door, and in the gap at its foot I saw the gleam of a dog's damp nose snuffling at the air. "Sofi! Star! Quiet there! Watch your step, Miss Mansel, the threshold's broken here. This is the Prince's Garden."

I don't know quite what I had expected, something at least as grand as the Seraglio Garden, but in fact the Prince's Garden was very small. The air was heavy with the scent of jasmine, and I caught a glimpse in the torchlight of a low wall which might contain a pool, but the garden seemed to be little more than an oblong yard with one or two troughs of flowers and some small symmetrical trees in tubs. John Lethman shone the torch straight down on the cracked slabs of the footway, but he could have saved himself the trouble, for, from an open doorway about half-way along the side of the garden, light was spilling out between two small tubbed trees. It was only the dim orange light from a lamp like the one in my own room, but in the heavy darkness it seemed very bright.

He paused in the doorway to stand aside for me. His voice sounded different all at once, tight, wary, deferential.

"I've brought Miss Mansel, Lady Harriet."

I went past him into the room.

Chapter Five

———◦∞◦———

There came
A tongue of light, a fit of flame;
And Christabel saw the lady's eye,
And nothing else saw she thereby . . .
—S. T. COLERIDGE: *Christabel*

THE PRINCE'S DIVAN was enormous, and in it prevailed what I can only call a luxurious squalor. The floor was of coloured marble strewn here and there with Persian rugs, all very dirty; the walls were patterned with intricate mosaics, each panel framing in fretted stone a recess which must once have held a statue or lamp, but which was now empty except for an accumulation of rubbish—cartons, papers, books, medicine bottles, candle stubs. In the center of the floor the fountain had been roughly boarded over and now did duty as a table where stood a large tray of greyish silver holding a pile of plates and the remains of a recent meal. Beside this, on the floor, was an empty bowl labeled DOG. A chest of drawers in shiny mahogany, covered with more bottles and pillboxes, stood against the wall. One or two shabby kitchen chairs and a big thronelike affair in red Chinese lacquer completed the furniture of the lower end of the room. Dust lay everywhere.

A wide archway of delicately chiseled stone framing three shallow steps divided the lower from the upper section of the divan. Set right back in one corner of the upper rooom or dais was a huge bed, which at one time must have been a luxurious affair with legs shaped like dragons' claws, a high carved headboard, and hanging from the ceiling above it some sort of gilt device resembling a bird, which was supposed to have held bed drapes in its talons. Now one wing of the bird was broken, the gilt was flaked and dirty, and from the claws hung only a couple of rubbed velvet curtains which could have been any shade from dark red to black, and which sagged in big loops down on either side of the bedhead, almost concealing with their heavy swags of shadow the figure which reclined there in a welter of rugs and blankets.

The light which had flowed so generously out on the flagway of the garden hardly penetrated into the upper corners of the room. It came from an old-fashioned oil lamp standing among the supper dishes, and as I passed it, approaching the bed, my shadow seemed to leap monstrously ahead of me, then teeter up the steps of the dais to add another layer of darkness to the grotesque obscurity in the corner.

For grotesque it certainly was. I had expected to find Great-Aunt Harriet very different from a child's far-back recollections of her, but not quite so outlandish as this. As I had told John Lethman, I had retained merely a dim memory of a tallish hook-nosed woman with greying hair and snapping black eyes who argued fiercely with my father, bullied my mother over the garden, and had a habit of bestowing sudden and exotic gifts on me and Charles, in the intervals of ignoring us completely. Even had she been dressed as she was fifteen years before, I should not have known her. John Lethman had warned me that she would have shrunk, and this was so; and though I thought I would have recognized the jutting nose and black eyes which peered at me from the shadows of the bed curtains, nothing—not even Lethman's warnings—had prepared me for the sheer outlandishness of the figure which sat there like a Buddha cocooned in coloured silks and gesturing with one large pale hand for me to come nearer.

If I had not known who it was, I should have taken her for some fantastically robed Eastern male. She was wearing some kind of bedgown of natural silk, and over this a loose coat in scarlet velvet with gold facings, and over this again an enormous cashmere shawl; but these draperies—in spite of the soft and even luxurious materials—had a distinctly masculine air. Her skin had a sallow pallor and her lips were bloodless and sunken, but the black eyes and well-marked brows gave life to the fullish, oval face, and showed none of the fading signs of old age. She had daubed powder lavishly and carelessly, and some of it had spilled over the scarlet velvet. Above this curiously epicene face she had twined a towering turban of white, which, slipping a little to one side, exposed what for a shocked moment I took to be a bald skull; then I realized that she must have shaved her head. This, if she habitually wore the thick turban, was only to be expected, but it was somehow the final touch of grotesqueness.

One thing I would have known her by; the ring on her left hand. This was unequivocally as big and as bright as I remembered from my childhood. I remembered, too, how impressed Charles and I had been by the way my mother and father spoke of the ring. It was a cabochon-cut Burma ruby, the size of a thumbnail, and had even in those days been immensely valuable. It had been the gift of some princeling in Baghdad, and she wore it always on her big, capable and rather mannish hands. The ruby flashed in the lamplight as, wheezing a little, she beckoned me closer.

I didn't know whether I would be expected to kiss her. The idea was somehow repellent, but another glitter from the ruby, indicating a stool near the foot of the bed, halted me thankfully.

"Hullo, Aunt Harriet, how are you?"

"Well, Christy?" The voice, little more than a whisper, had a strained, asthmatic breathiness, but the black eyes were live enough, and curious. "Sit down and let me look at you. H-m. Yes. You always were a pretty little thing. Quite a beauty now, aren't you? Not married yet?"

"No."

"Then it's high time you were."

"Have a heart, I'm only twenty-two!"

"Is that all? One forgets. John tells me I forget things all the time. I'd forgotten you, did he tell you that?"

"He said it was quite likely."

"He would. He's always trying to make out that I'm getting senile." She darted a look at John Lethman, who had followed me up the steps and was standing at the foot of the bed. He watched her steadily, and I thought uneasily. The sharp gaze came back to me. "And if I did forget you, it'd be hardly surprising. How long since I saw you?"

"Fifteen years."

"Hm. Yes. It must be. Well, now I come to look at you I suppose I would have known you. You've a look of your father. How is he?"

"Oh, he's fine, thank you."

"Sends his dear love, I suppose?"

The tone, still sharp, was wantonly provocative. I regarded her calmly.

"If he knew I was here, I'm sure he'd send his regards."

"Hm." She sat back abruptly in her corner against the pile of pillows, retreating into her cocoon of draperies with the little settling motions of a broody hen spreading herself down onto eggs. I thought the monosyllable was not unappreciative. "And the rest of 'em?"

"All well. They'll be terribly pleased when they hear I've managed to see you, and found you well."

"No doubt." No one could have called the dry whisper senile. "An attentive family the Mansels, wouldn't you say? Well?" And again, when I didn't speak: "Well, girl?"

I sat up straighter on my stool. It was very uncomfortable. "I don't know what you want me to say, Aunt Harriet. If you think we should have come to see you before, you could always have asked us, couldn't you? As it is, you know quite well you've been sending us all to the devil, solo and chorus, about twice a year for fifteen years. And if you'll forgive my saying so, I wasn't exactly welcomed with open arms today!" I added crisply: "In any case, you're a Mansel, too. You can't tell me my people don't write to you just as often as you write to them, even if it's only to thank you for the latest edition of your Will!"

The black eyes glittered. "My Will? Ha! So that's it! Come to collect, have you?"

"Well, I'd have a job, since you're still alive, wouldn't I?" I grinned at her. "And it's a heck of a long way to come for sixpence . . . But if you like you can give me my sixpence here and now, and I won't bother you again."

I couldn't see her expression, just the eyes, shadowed under brows and turban, watching me from the pillows. I caught a glance from John Lethman, half amused, I thought, and half apprehensive, as she stirred suddenly, plucking at the coverings. "I could have died out here for all they'd have cared. Any of them."

"Look—" I said, then stopped. Charles had implied that she liked to be outfaced, and certainly up to now I had had the impression that she was trying to needle me. But the Great-Aunt Harriet that I had remembered wouldn't have talked like that, not even to provoke a retort. Fifteen years seems a lifetime to the young: perhaps at the other end it's a lifetime, too. I ought to be feeling, not discomfort and irritation, but compassion.

I said quickly: "Aunt Harriet, look, please don't talk like that! You must know quite well that if there was anything you wanted—anything you needed—you've only got to let Daddy know, or Uncle Chas, or any of us! My family's been in America for four years, you know that, and I suppose we're a bit out of touch, but in any case it was always Uncle Chas you wrote to, and I understood from him—I mean, I thought you'd always made it so very clear that you wanted to stay out here, live on your own terms . . ." I made a vague, wide gesture that took in the neglected room and beyond it the dark confines of the sleeping palace. "You must surely know that if there was anything—if you were ill—if you really did want someone to come here, or needed help of some kind—"

Deep in its shadowed corner the bundle on the bed was so still that I faltered. The lamp had been burning low, but now some trick of the draught or unevenness of the wick sent up a tongue of light, and I saw the quick glitter of her eyes. It wasn't pathos at all. The instinct that was forbidding me to feel compassion had been right.

"Aunt H!" I said roundly. "Are you sending me up? I mean, you're just teasing, aren't you? You must know you're talking nonsense!"

"Hm. Nonsense, is it? Meaning that I have got a devoted family?"

"Well, heavens, you know what families are! I don't suppose ours is any different from any other! You must know quite well you could cut us all off with sixpence till you're blue in the face, but we're still your family!"

"Hear that, John?"

He was looking, I thought, acutely uncomfortable. He opened his mouth to say something, but I cut across it:

"You know quite well what I mean! Just that if you needed anything, or anything happened to you—well, London to Beirut only takes six hours, and someone would be here and raising the place before you even knew you wanted them. Daddy always says that's what a family is, it's just collective insurance; as long as you're alive and well it just goes ticking along and takes no notice, but let anything go wrong, and the company moves in. I mean, look at my Uncle Chas when his cousin Henry died! Daddy says they never gave it a second thought, just took it for granted. Heavens, I do what I like, and nobody stops me going where I want to, but I know quite well that if I was in the least spot of trouble and got on the phone to Daddy, he'd be here in three seconds!" I looked up at John Lethman, hesitated, then added decisively: "And don't start teasing Mr Lethman as well. It doesn't matter what you say to me, but I might as well make something else clear here and now, even if I may be speaking out of turn . . . Everybody'll be as pleased as Punch that he's here with you, so you'd better be nice to him, because the longer he stays the better! For goodness' sake, we're not neglecting you—we're just letting you get on with it the way you want to, and you seem to be making a pretty good job of it, if you ask me!"

She was laughing openly now, the cocoon heaving to the wheezing breaths. The big hand went up, and the ruby flashed. "All right, child, all right, I was teasing you! A fighter, aren't you? I always did like a fighter. No, I don't make it easy for people to get in to see me; I've had too much trouble that way, and say what you like, I'm getting old. You were very insistent, weren't you? If you're so full of this 'live and let live' of yours, why did you come?"

I grinned. "You'd be annoyed if I said it was family feeling. Call it curiosity."

"What had you heard to make you so curious?"

"What had I heard? You must be joking! I suppose you're so used to living in a place like this and hedging yourself with legends like a—well, like a—"

"Superannuated Sleeping Beauty?"

I laughed. "Bang on! I mean, yes, if you like to put it that way! But seriously, you're a celebrity, you know that! Everybody talks about you. You're one of the sights of the Lebanon. Even if I'd been no relation I'd have been told all about you and urged to come and look at Dar Ibrahim; so when I realized I had a copper-bottomed excuse to call to see you, and even bulldoze my way into the palace—well, boiling oil might have stopped me, but nothing much short of that."

"Make a note of that, John; boiling oil is what we need. Hm, you're a Mansel to your claw tips, aren't you? So everybody talks about me, do they? Who's 'everybody'?"

"Oh, this was just someone in the hotel in Beirut. I was planning a trip—"

"Hotel? Who were you chattering about me to in a hotel in Beirut?" She made it sound as if it were a brothel in Cairo.

"Not exactly chattering. It was the desk clerk, as it happens. I was planning a trip up to the Adonis Source at Afka, and he told me I'd be passing near Dar Ibrahim, and—"

"Which hotel?"

"The Phoenicia."

"It's new since you were in Beirut," put in John Lethman. It was the first time he had spoken. He still seemed ill at ease. "It's the big one I told you about, on the harbour."

"The what? Phoenicia? All right, go on, what were they saying about me in this hotel?"

"Nothing much, really," I said. "The desk clerk didn't know I was a relation of yours, he was just telling me this was an interesting place, and he said I might as well get my driver to come back by Sal'q and stop so that I could get a view of the palace. Then I told him I knew your family—I still didn't tell him who I was—and asked how you were and if he'd heard anything about you."

"And what did he tell you?"

"Only that as far as he knew you were perfectly all right, but that you hadn't been outside the palace for quite a time, and he told me you'd been ill a short while back, and had a doctor from Beirut—"

"He knew that?"

"Well, heavens, it was probably in all the papers! You're one of the local legends, after all! Didn't Mr Lethman tell you, I rang the doctor's house up to try to get news of you—"

"Yes, yes, yes, he told me. A lot of use that would have been. The man was a fool. A good thing he's gone, a very good thing . . . Much better now, much better." The shawl had slipped; she pulled at it with a sort of flouncing irritation, suddenly pettish, and I heard her muttering to herself what sounded like "Ringing up about me," and "Chattering about me in hotels," in a whisper which was all at once not dry and sharp at all, but vague and blurred. Her head shook, so that the turban was dislodged even further, exposing a little more of that shaved scalp.

I looked away, repelled, and trying not to show it. But wherever I looked was a reminder of a slovenly eccentricity; even the clutter of medicine bottles on the chest was dusty, and dust gritted under my shoes as I shifted my feet on the floor. The room, big as it was, felt stuffy, and my skin prickled. I found myself suddenly longing to escape into fresh air.

"Christy . . . Christy . . ." The wheezing mutter jerked my attention back to her. "Stupid name for a girl. What's it short for?"

"Christabel. It was the nearest they could get to Christopher."

"Oh." She plucked at the covers again. I got the sharp impression that the eyes watching me from the shadows were by no means forgetful; that this was a game she played when it suited her. The impression wasn't pleasant. "What were we talking about?"

I pulled myself together. "The doctor. Dr Grafton."

"I was not ill; the man was a fool. There's nothing wrong with my chest, nothing at all . . . In any case, he's left the Lebanon. Wasn't there some chatter about him, too, John? Some scandal? Didn't he go back to London?"

"I believe so," said Lethman.

I said: "They told me so when I rang up. They didn't say anything else about him."

"Hm," she said, and all the dry malice was back in her voice. "Probably put his plate up in Wimpole Street by now and making a fortune."

"I never heard any scandal, but it's true he's gone. They say his practice went to a very good man." John Lethman gave me a quick, speaking look, and then leaned forward. "Now don't you think you should have a rest, Lady Harriet? It's time for your tablets, so if you'll allow me, I'll ring for Halide, and see Miss Mansel back myself—"

"No," said Great-Aunt Harriet uncompromisingly.

"But, Lady Harriet—"

"I tell you, boy, stop fussing. I won't take the tablets yet, they make me sleepy. You know I don't like taking them. I'm not tired at all, and I'm enjoying the gel's visit. Stay where you are, child, and talk to me. Entertain me. Tell me where you've been and what you've been doing. How long have you been in Beirut?"

"Only since Friday evening. Actually, I came with a package tour . . ."

I started to tell her about the trip, making it as amusing as I could. I wouldn't be sorry when the interview was over, but the old lady seemed back on the beam now, and I had no intention of letting John Lethman, on whatever excuse, winkle me out of the presence chamber until I had, so to speak, introduced Charles. He wouldn't want to miss this bizarre setup, and he wouldn't be likely to be put off by what I had to tell him. I wondered in passing why she hadn't spoken of him herself, but I would soon discover that, and it was up to my cousin to fight his own way in past the opposition if he wished to.

So I kept clear of his name, and talked away about Petra and Palmyra and Jerash, while Great-Aunt Harriet listened and commented, apparently well entertained, and John Lethman waited in silence, fidgeting nervily with the bed-curtains, and with his head turning from one to the other of us like someone at a Wimbledon final.

I was in the middle of describing Palmyra when she startled me suddenly by reaching out a hand and yanking at a bellpull which hung among the curtains of the bed. The building echoed to the familiar clanging peal, and then to the noise of the baying hounds.

I stopped talking, but she said almost snappily: "Go on. At least you can talk. Did you visit the hillside tombs?"

"Heavens, yes, there was a conducted tour, we had to. I suppose that's not the right thing to say to an archaeologist, but one tomb looks very like another to me, I'm afraid."

"True enough. What happened to the party?"

"They went back to London on Saturday morning."

"So you're on your own now? Is that suitable?"

I laughed. "Why not? I can look after myself. And as a matter of fact—"

"Not much doubt of that. Where's that stupid girl?"

She snapped it suddenly at John Lethman, who jumped. "Halide? She can't be far away. If it's your pills, I can—"

"Not my pills. I told you I'll not take them yet. I want my pipe."

"But, Lady Harriet—"

"Ah, there you are! Where the devil were you?"

Halide came quickly across the lower part of the room. She could not have been far away when the bell rang, but she breathed fast and shallow as if she had been running. Her face was sallow, and she looked scared. She didn't spare me a glance as she crossed the floor and mounted the steps towards the bed.

"You rang?"

"Of course I rang," said Great-Aunt Harriet irritably. "I want my pipe."

Halide looked uncertainly from her to John Lethman and back again, and the old woman made one of those flouncing impatient movements in the bed and barked: "Well? Well?"

"Get it for her, please," said Lethman.

The girl threw another scared glance at the bed, and scurried down the steps to the dressing chest. I looked after her with a touch of surprise. Nothing so far had led me to think that she would be easily frightened, and it wasn't easy to see how my great-aunt could frighten her, short of the methods used by Lady Hester Stanhope, who kept a whip and club by her bed to use on her slaves, and who when service was poor had treated them all—her doctor included—to a purge she called the Black Draught, forcibly administered. I looked at the 'Lady Harriet'. She was sitting hunched like some peculiar Eastern jinnee in her welter of silks and blankets, and might, I thought, inspire nervousness, but not fear. But then something caught my eye on the wall above the bed. There were two sets of pegs in the wall, half hidden by the bed-curtains, and across one of these lay a stick, and across the other a rifle. I blinked at these in disbelief. There were surely, in the mid-twentieth century, limits to what could be done even here . . . ?

I really must get out of here soon. I must be more tired than I had thought. Or perhaps the strange food at supper . . . ? As I pulled myself together to go on with my story, I heard Great-Aunt Harriet saying, perfectly pleasantly: "Just a small pipe, my dear. And I'll have the amber mouthpiece."

The girl, hurrying with clumsy fingers, pulled open a drawer and took out a wooden box which appeared to hold tobacco and mouthpiece. These she brought to the bed, and fitted the mouthpiece to the tube of the apparatus that the Arabs called the nargileh, or hubble-bubble pipe. As she passed out of Great-Aunt Harriet's view behind the bed-curtains I saw her throw a quick inquiring glance at John Lethman, and receive a rather irritable nod. This, then, was the cause of her nervousness; she was in the familiar, awk-ward position of the servant being bidden by one master to do what she knew the other would disapprove.

Lethman said in my ear: "I can't offer you a cigarette, I'm afraid, she won't allow anyone else to smoke in here. In any case she only approves of herbal tobacco. I'm afraid it smells vile."

"It doesn't matter, I don't want one."

"What are you muttering about?" asked Great-Aunt Har-riet sharply, peering. "All right, Halide, it's going very well." Then, to me: "Well, go on, entertain me. What did you do in Damascus? Tramped round the Great Mosque, I suppose, like a lot of gapeseeds."

"Exactly like gapeseeds, Aunt Harriet."

"Are you laughing at me, gel?"

"Well, it's such a gorgeous word. What are they?"

"God knows. Probably aren't any any more. The world isn't what it used to be." She sucked at the pipe. "Did you like Damascus?"

"So-so. I didn't have enough time to myself. But something rather nice happened there, I ran into Charles."

"Charles?" Her voice was sharp, and I thought I saw Halide and John Lethman look at one another again, quickly. "Here?" asked Great-Aunt Harriet. "What's this, a family convention? What the devil's my nephew Charles doing in Damascus?"

"Oh, not Uncle Chas," I said quickly, "I meant Charles, my cousin—my 'twin'. He's on holiday over here, too. He was to have come up with me to see you, but he probably won't be in Lebanon till tomorrow, and I'm afraid I stole a march on him. As a matter of fact it was he who sent me to see you in the first place; he's terribly keen to come himself, and I'd probably never have dared to barge in like this if he hadn't put me up to it."

There was silence. The pipe bubbled, rather sickeningly, and she blinked at me through the smoke. The air was acrid, and stuffier than ever, and I felt waves of heat coursing over my skin. I pulled myself upright on my stool.

"You—you do remember Charles, Aunt Harriet? You'll not have forgotten him even if you *had* forgotten me—he was always your favourite."

"Of course I haven't forgotten him. How could I? A handsome boy. I always liked handsome boys."

I smiled. "I used to be jealous, let me tell you! D'you remember that time—the last time I saw you—when you came to stay, and you brought the parrot and all the dogs, and you gave me an ivory fan, and you gave Charles the incense burner and the joss-sticks, and he set the summerhouse on fire, and Daddy was so furious he said he was going to send him home, only you said if he went you'd go too because the rest of the family were as dull as ditchwater, and anything Charles did shone like a bad deed in an insipid world? I only remember that because it's a sort of family quotation now."

"Yes, I remember. The way time goes. Sometimes fast, sometimes slow . . . and the things one remembers . . . and the things one forgets. A handsome boy . . . yes, yes." She smoked for a while in silence, nodding as if to herself, then relinquished the mouthpiece of the pipe to Halide without looking at her. The black eyes lifted again and fixed on me. "You're like him."

"I suppose I am. Not really any more, now we're both grown up . . . though I suppose you remember him fairly recently. Something must persist. We've the same colouring."

"Very like him." It was as if she hadn't heard me. She was

still nodding to herself, the black eyes veiled and absent, her hands unsteady with her shawl.

"Lady Harriet," said John Lethman, abruptly. "I really must insist you take your tablets now, and rest for a little. Miss Mansel—"

"Of course," I said, getting to my feet, "if Great-Aunt Harriet will tell me what I'm to say to Charles?"

"You may give him my regards." The whisper was harsh as the rustle of dry leaves.

"But—" I regarded her a little blankly. "Don't you want to see him? He'll be in Beirut at the Phoenicia with me, probably tomorrow. May he come up to see you? If it'd be less bother, he could come up tomorrow evening after dinner and wait till you're ready to receive him? He has his own car; he wouldn't need to stay, like me. I'd love to come with him myself and see you again, but if two people are too many—"

"No."

"You mean we can both come? Oh, that's marvelous! Then—"

"I mean I won't receive him. No. I have received you, and it's been a pleasure, but this is enough. You may take what news you have of me to my nephews Charles and Christopher, and be satisfied with that."

As I opened my mouth she lifted her hand and added, more kindly: "All this must be strange to you, but I'm an old woman and I have chosen my way of life, and it seems to me that the only good thing that age brings is the right to be as arbitrary as one wants, and to live as one wishes as long as one can afford it. However outlandish and uncomfortable you may think it is here, it suits me, and you can tell them at home that I'm perfectly well, and quite content with my way of life and the privacy I bought when I bought these high walls and that dumb fool at the gate and what service Halide chooses to offer. So we'll have no more protestations."

"But he'll be desperately disappointed! And what's more, he'll be furious with me because I've taken his turn with you, so to speak. You were rather his favourite relative, you know. And as a matter of fact, I think it was rather important for him to see you. I don't know whether you knew, but there's a plan under way for opening a branch of the bank in Beirut, and Charles'll probably work there—at least for a time—so while he's out here now I know he wants to make all the contacts—"

"No."

"Aunt Harriet—"

"I have spoken," she said, rather splendidly, with a flashing gesture of the ruby which was meant to obliterate me, and did.

I gave up. "All right, I'll tell him. He'll be glad I found you so well. Is there anything you'd like us to send you from England? Any books, for instance?"

"I can get all I want, thank you, child. Now I'm tired and you may go. Take my messages to your people, but don't think I want a spate of letters, because I don't. I shan't answer 'em. When I'm dead John will let you know. No, you needn't kiss me. You're a pretty child and I've enjoyed your visit, so now go."

"I've enjoyed it, too. Thank you for letting me come. Good night, Aunt Harriet."

"Good night. John, you'll come straight back here when you've seen her to her room. Halide! Is that stupid girl going to take all night with those pills? Oh, there you are. Now don't forget what I've said, John, come straight back here."

"Of course," agreed Mr Lethman, sounding relieved. He already had me half-way towards the door.

For a final parting, it had the strange note of casualness which seemed exactly right. I paused for a moment in the doorway and glanced back. Halide was once more at the dressing chest, shaking something from a small bottle into her hand. Beyond her, behind the orange glow of the lamp, the bed was a towering obscurity. As she turned to mount the steps once more, something moved in the black shadows at the foot of the bed, something small and grey and quick moving. For one flesh-creeping moment I thought there were rats even in the bedroom, but then I saw the creature leap on the bed, and the large pale hand came from behind the curtain and stroked it. A half-grown cat.

Half wild as well. As Halide sat down on the edge of the bed the cat leaped aside and vanished. The girl, shimmering in her green silk, leaned forward towards the hidden figure of the old woman. She was offering her water in a tall, chased goblet. The scene looked like something remote and improbable, on a badly lighted stage. It could have nothing to do with me and Charles and daylight.

I turned and hurried out in the wake of John Lethman's torch.

The beam flicked upwards for a moment to light my face. "What is it? Are you cold?"

"No. It's nothing." I took a deep breath. "It's wonderful to get out into the air. You were right about that tobacco, it's a bit much."

"Was that all it was? I got the impression that the interview upset you."

"In a way, I suppose," I admitted. "I must say I found it all a bit odd, and she wasn't exactly easy to talk to."

"In what way?"

"Well, heavens—! Oh, but I suppose you're used to it . . . ! I meant inconsistent, and forgetful, and the way she tried to needle me at the beginning. And—well, she *looks* so outlandish, and then that pipe . . . ! I'm afraid I was a bit tactless once or twice, but I'd always heard she hadn't much time for yes-men, and I thought it was probably best to tell the truth, flat out. I thought I'd upset her, the time she started muttering at me, but I hadn't, had I?"

"It takes more than that. Take it from me, she meant it when she said she was enjoying the conversation."

He was, I thought, a bit curt. But any sour reflections I might have had about this were shaken as he went on: "I wish you'd told me earlier about this cousin Charles. I might have managed to persuade her."

"Yes, it was silly of me. I think I'd some idea of finding out first how the land lay. Is she likely to change her mind?"

"Heaven knows. Frankly, I've no idea. Once she's made a decision it's pretty hard to shift her. I sometimes feel she's obstinate just for the hell of it, if you know what I mean. I don't know why she suddenly stuck her toes in like that."

"Neither do I. She adored him, you know—he was the only one of us she'd any use for." I added, ruefully: 'Well, he's going to be furious with me for queering his pitch, which is what I seem to have done, goodness knows how! He's really pretty keen to see her—and not just out of curiosity like me. I don't know what he'll say. She must have talked of him to you, surely?"

"Oh, yes. If I'd only known he was here . . . Look out, mind that step. How long's he going to be in the Lebanon?"

"I've no idea."

"Well, if he has time to spare, tell him to leave it for a few days, will you, at least till after mid-week. I'll do what I can, and get in touch with you at the Phoenicia."

It seemed there wasn't much else I could do except trust to his good offices.

"Thank you," I said, "I'll tell him. When she's had time to think it over, I'm sure she'll change her mind."

"Stranger things have happened," said John Lethman, rather shortly.

Chapter Six

———✦———

Thy promises are like Adonis' gardens,
That one day bloom'd and fruitful were the next.
—SHAKESPEARE: *1 Henry VI*

IN THE NIGHT IT RAINED.

I had got back to my room at some time between half-past one and two in the morning. The night had been dry then, very black and perfectly still, with nothing to suggest a storm to follow. Mr Lethman saw me as far as my bedroom door, where I had left the oil lamp lit, said good night, and withdrew. I carried my lamp along to the hammam, washed as well as I could in a trickle of cold water, and then went back to my room again. There was no key, but I saw a heavy wooden bar on the inside of the door. I dropped this carefully into its sockets. Then I took off my outer clothing, turned my lamp down rather inexpertly and blew out the wicks, and climbed into bed.

Even though the hour was late, and I was tired, I lay awake for some little time turning the recent scene over and over in my head. I imagined myself telling Charles, telling my mother and father, and somehow none of the words seemed to fit or be right. "She seemed odd, she seemed ill, she's getting old, she's going to town a bit on this recluse thing—" none of these phrases seemed to fit the decidedly off-beat tone of the interview. And if she really was going to refuse to see Charles . . .

Well, that was Charles's problem, not mine. I slept.

I'm not sure whether it was the flash of lightning or the almost simultaneous crack of thunder that woke me, but as I stirred in bed and opened my eyes the sound of rain seemed to obliterate all else. I have never heard such rain. There was no wind with it, only the cracking of thunder and the vivid white rents in the black sky. I sat up in bed to watch. The window arches flickered dramatically against the storm outside, and the portcullis squares of the grille stamped themselves on the room over and over again with their violently angled perspectives of black and white. Through the window that I had opened the scents of flowers came almost storming in, vividly wakened by the rain. With the scents came, more palpably, a good deal of the rain itself, hitting the sill and splashing on the floor in great hammering drops.

Reluctantly, I got out of bed and padded in my bare feet across the chilly floor to shut the casement. Even while I groped in momentary darkness for the catch, my arm was soaked almost to the shoulder by the slashing downpour. I slammed the casement shut, and while I fought to fix the stiff and squeaking catch I heard, from the direction of the main gate, the sudden keening howl of a big dog.

It is one of the weirdest of all sounds, bringing with it, I suppose, race memories of wolves and jackals and such, overlaid by countless legends of death and grief. The first hound's voice rose in a throbbing wail, to be joined by the long tremolo of the other. The watchdogs, of course, upset by the storm; but I felt my hand instinctively clench stiff on the soaked iron of the window catch, while I listened with cold prickles running over my skin. Then I jammed the thing shut and reached for my towel to rub my arm dry.

No wonder a howling dog was supposed to foretell a death . . . As I scrubbed at my wet arm and shoulder I thought of the legend Charles had reminded me of, 'gabble ratchet', the Gabriel Hounds, Death's pack hunting through the sky . . . Certainly all hell seemed to be loose up there tonight, full cry. In the old days anyone in the palace might well have believed the hounds of the storm to be crying death.

In the old days. And you'd have been superstitious then, and believed in that kind of thing. Whereas now . . . oh, nonsense, there was nothing wrong . . .

I flung the towel down and padded back to bed.

About five seconds later I discovered something a good deal more disturbing than any Gabriel Hounds. The roof was leaking. Moreover, it was leaking in the corner right above my bed.

I discovered this—it being dark, in the simplest possible way, by getting back into bed straight into the middle of a soaking patch, and by receiving at the same moment a large gout of water squarely on the back of my neck. It was followed almost immediately by another, and another . . .

I hurled myself back onto the cold marble, and started a frantic hunt for my shoes. Perversely, the lightning had stopped almost as suddenly as it had begun, and it was now quite dark. I found one shoe eventually, and stumbled about looking for the other, but couldn't find it. I would have to light the lamp. This, of course, meant finding my handbag, and the matches I hoped I was carrying—and by the time I had done this another pint or so of water would have emptied itself into my bed. I suppose it would have been sensible to drag the bed straight away from the danger point before starting the hunt for my effects, but from what I had seen of the palace appointments, I wasn't prepared to manhandle any of their furniture about the floors in the dark. So I hopped about, blasphemously groping, until I had found my matches, and then it took me another five minutes or so to manage the lighting of the oil lamp.

Once the room was lit it was the work of moments to find my other shoe and throw something on over my near-nakedness. Then I recklessly dragged the bed away from the wall. It came across the cracked marble with a dot-and-carry-one screech of broken castors. With it out of the way, the water dripped steadily onto the floor. It was only after some moments that I realized how loud the dripping was. The rain had stopped.

I went back to the window. As suddenly as if a tap had been turned off the rain had ceased. Already I could see stars. I pulled open the casement to find that in the wake of the storm had come a small erratic breeze, which was clearing the clouds and whispering among the trees of the gorge. After the chill of the soaking storm the breeze was warm, so I left the casement wide. Then I turned back to deal with my problem.

Most of the bedcovers were still dry, having been pushed back out of the way when I got out of bed myself. I heaved these off the bed, put them gingerly on the dry part of the window seat, then, more gingerly still, turned the mattress. It was of thick horsehair, with a fresh cover of unbleached cotton, and I could only hope that it would last me the rest of the night before the wet soaked up through it. I discarded the sodden sheet, piled the dry bedcovers back on, put out the lamp and lay down, clothes and all, to pass what remained of the night.

But not yet in sleep. The steady dripping just beside me on the marble floor seemed as loud as a drum beat. I stood it for perhaps ten minutes, then realized I would get no sleep until I stopped it. So once more I rolled out of bed, groped for and found the crumpled and soaking sheet, and put it down under the drips. In the blessed quiet that followed, another sound from outside caught my ear, and I straightened up and stood listening.

No hounds of Death now; they were quiet. This was a bird singing in the garden, full and loud and echoing from the water and the enclosing walls. Another joined it. And then a third, waterfalls of song rinsing the clear air.

I unbarred the door and padded out across the arcade.

The surface of the lake was faintly shining, lighter than the dim starlight it reflected. Spatters of rain shook intermittently from the bushes as the breeze wandered. The nightingales' song filled the garden, welling out of the tangle of soaked and glittering creepers.

A pair of white pigeons rocketed out from their roost in the western arcade and vanished with a clap of wings over my head. Something—someone—moved in the darkness beneath the arches. A man, walking along under the arcade. He was moving very softly, and above the noise of the birds and the rustle of the leaves I couldn't hear him, but this was no white-robed Arab. It must be John Lethman. Probably he'd come along to see how I'd made out in the storm.

I waited a few moments longer, but he didn't come, and I saw nothing more. The garden, but for the song of the nightingales, was quiet and still.

I shivered suddenly. Five minutes' *Nachtmusik* was more than enough. I padded back into my room, crossly shut my door against the nightingales, and rolled back onto the bed.

*　　*　　*

I woke to blazing sunlight and a tapping on the door.

It was Halide with my breakfast, a plate of thin unleavened bread, some cream cheese, the inevitable apricot jam, and a big pot of coffee. The girl looked tired, and still eyed me sideways with that sulky glance, but made no comment on the disorder of the room, the sodden sheet on the floor, or even the bed shifted four feet out from the wall.

When I thanked her for the tray and said something about the wild night, she only nodded sullenly and went out.

But everything else was cheerful this morning, even the hammam, with sunlight pouring down through the blue and amber glass bells in the ceiling, and lighting the alabaster basins and pale marble walls in a swimming subaqueous light. The water trickled—colder than ever—out of a dolphin's mouth into a silver shell. I rinsed my face and hands, went back to my room and dressed, then carried the tray out into the blazing sunshine at the edge of the pool.

The golden heat, the high blue sky, made it difficult to remember last night's storm of pouring rain, but here and there on the path where the flagstones had sunk, or in the wells dug round the tree roots to catch the rain, the water still stood glittering, inches deep. The weeds between the stones looked already half as long again, the flowers brighter, the bushes glossy and refreshed. Even the water of the pool looked clearer, and beside it a peacock stood studying his reflection, with his tail fully spread, looking entirely artificial, like something from a picture book, or a jeweled bird by Fabergé. Some other bird, small and golden, flirted over a rose laurel. The little kiosk on the island, freshly washed, showed a gilded dome and a glimpse of bright blue tiling. One of the nightingales was doing overtime in the roses.

I wondered how John Lethman had got in and out last night, and why.

He came some half hour later. Whatever excursions he had undertaken during the night, they didn't seem to have affected him. He looked alert and wide awake, the blurred look gone from his eyes, which were clear grey, and very bright. He moved with energetic precision, and greeted me almost gaily. "Good morning."

"Oh, hullo. Nice timing." I emerged from my door with my luggage—a handbag—packed and ready. "I was just coming to look for you and hoping the dogs had been shut up."

"Always by day. Did they wake you last night? It was a bit rough, I'm afraid. Did you sleep through it?" Here his eyes went past me to the disorder of the room. "I say, rough was the right word, wasn't it? What happened? Don't tell me—the roof leaked?"

"It certainly did," I laughed. "Did you decide to rate me third class after all? No, I'm only joking, I shifted the bed and managed quite a bit of sleep in the end. But I'm afraid you'll find the mattress pretty wet."

"That doesn't matter, it'll dry in five minutes once it's put outside. I'm terribly sorry, the roof gutter must be blocked again. Nasirulla swore he'd cleaned it. Did you really sleep?"

"Fine, thanks, in the end. Don't worry, just think it's an ill wind that blows no good."

"Meaning?"

"If I hadn't come turning the household upside down, you'd have been the one under the waterspout."

"You've got something there. But believe me, you're no ill wind. Your aunt was quite set up last night after your visit."

"Was she really? I didn't tire her?"

"Not a bit. She kept me talking quite a time after you'd gone."

"No change about Charles, I suppose?"

"Not yet, I'm afraid, but give her time. You're ready, are you? Shall we go?" We moved towards the gate.

"Did she keep you very late?" I asked. "It seems hard, the way you burn the torch at both ends."

"Not very, no. I'd gone to bed before the storm broke."

"It woke you, I suppose?"

"Not a flicker." He laughed. "And don't think I'm neglecting my duty, will you? Your great-aunt thrives on disturbances like last night's. She tells me she enjoyed it. She'd have made a wonderful Katisha."

" 'But to him who's scientific There's nothing that's terrific In the falling of a flight of thunderbolts?' " I quoted, and heard him laugh again, softly, to himself. "Well, she's got a point, I rather enjoyed it myself. At least, I enjoyed the aftermath. The garden looked wonderful."

I caught a quick sideways glance. "You went out?"

"Only for a moment; I went out to listen to the nightingales. Oh, look at the flowers! Is that because of the storm? More good from the ill wind, would you say?"

We were crossing the small courtyard where Hamid and I had waited yesterday. Here, too, the rain had washed the place clean, and the marble pillars dazzled white in the sun. At their feet the carved troughs were a blaze of red anemones, wide open and shiny as fresh blood in the long grass.

"My Adonis Gardens," said Mr Lethman.

"Your what?"

"Adonis Gardens. I suppose you know the Adonis myth?"

"I know Aphrodite met him in the Lebanon and he died there, and that every spring his blood stains the river and it runs red to the sea. What is it, iron in the water?"

"Yes. It's one of the spring resurrection stories, like Persephone, or the Osiris myth. Adonis was a corn-god, a fertility god, and he dies to rise again. The 'Adonis Gardens' are—you might call them little personal symbols of death and resurrection; and they're sympathetic magic as well, because the people who planted them and forced the seeds and flowers to grow as quickly as they could, thought they were helping the year's harvest. The flowers and herbs sprang up and withered and died all in a few days, and then the 'gardens' with the images of the god were taken, with the women wailing and mad with grief, down to the sea and thrown in. See? It was all mixed up, here, with the Dionysiac cult, and Osiris, and the rites of Attis, and it still persists—only in nice, pure forms!— all over the world, believe it or not." He checked, with a glance at me. "Sorry, rather a lecture."

"I'm interested, no, go on. Why did you plant the gardens here?"

"No reason, except that this is the right time of the year, and it's quite interesting to see how quickly they do spring up and die, here in Adonis' own valley. Wouldn't you say so?"

"*I* would, sure. It's the kind of romantic notion that appeals to me like anything. But why to you? I mean, what have Adonis and Co. got to do with psychological medicine? Or is this Aunt Harriet's idea?"

"With—? Oh, didn't I tell you I was writing a paper? I was interested in the psychology of religious possession, and I'm touching on some aspects of the ecstatic religions of the near East—the Orphic myth and Dionysius and the Adonis story in its various forms. That's all. I've got some quite interesting stuff locally." He grinned, perhaps a little shamefacedly. "I haven't really let it slide, you know. Whenever I'm let off the chain I ride out and up into the hill villages. If you stay hereabouts for long you may—"

"Ride?"

We were in the *midan* now, the big entrance court. He nodded across it. "There's still a horse here. You know your great-aunt used to ride until only a couple of years ago? She really is remarkable—Hullo! The door's still shut. Nasirulla's not come over yet." He glanced at his watch. "He's late. Half a minute while I open it and give Kasha some air."

He pulled open the upper half-door, and latched it back to the wall with a rotten-looking wooden peg. In the dim interior a horse stood dozing, head down and ears relaxed. A chestnut Arab.

"Do you wear Arab dress when you ride?" I asked.

He looked surprised. "Usually, yes. It's cooler. Why? Wait a minute—didn't you say you'd gone to the Adonis Source yesterday? Did you see me up there?"

"Yes, at some village beyond the fall. I recognized the horse. You had the dogs with you." I smiled. "You looked terribly romantic, especially with the salukis. I may tell you, you made my day."

"And now I've spoiled the picture? Not an Arab Emir after all with his hawk and his hounds after gazelle, just a drifter who's found a lazy billet in the sun and will probably never have the *nous* to pull out of it."

I didn't answer, for the simple reason that I couldn't think how to. The words were bitter, but were spoken without a bitter tinge; and even if I had wanted to, there was no comforting reply to make. John Lethman must know as well as I did that his job, such as it was, would expire with Great-Aunt Harriet. Or would it? Was he actually playing for Dar Ibrahim itself, and a 'lazy billet in the sun' here eventually on his own? He had said it was a 'wonderful place to write in', and however I might disagree with him, I could think of worse places for an unambitious man to settle in, for a dilettante life in a delightful climate, and with a houri thrown in . . . It might be that the dilapidation of the place was due, not to lack of money, but to age and indifference. John Lethman might well be aware—none better—what means there would eventually be, not only to run part of the place comfortably, but to escape from it at need. Not a bad billet at all.

We were at the gate. There was no sign of Jassim, so Mr Lethman pulled back the heavy bolts and opened the bronze door. Outside, the sun blazed down white on the stony plateau. There was no one there.

"Your driver isn't here yet," he said. "If you'd rather come back in and wait—"

"Thanks very much, but I think I'll just walk down to meet him. And thank you for all you've done, Mr Lethman." I held out my hand and he took it, but when I would have gone on he protested very pleasantly that both he and Great-Aunt Harriet had enjoyed the visit very much.

"And I really will do what I can about your cousin, but if I can't—" he hesitated, and the light eyes met mine and slid away—"I hope you won't feel too badly about it."

"I? It's none of my business. How she lives is her own affair, and if Charles is really set on seeing her it's up to him to find a way. Good-bye then, and thanks again. And I hope the paper goes well."

"Good-bye."

The big door shut. The palace had sealed itself off once more behind me, silent walls of baked stone throwing back the glare from the white rock underfoot. In front of me the valley stretched in all the hard brilliance of morning.

The sun was behind me, and the cliff path was in shadow. Here, too, the effect of last night's rain was immediately apparent. Even the rock smelled fresher, and the dust had caked into mud which was drying rapidly into a million cracks. I could have sworn that on some of the fig trees that clung to the face of the rock there were fresh green buds. I wondered if, when I got down to the foot of the cliff, I would see Hamid crossing to meet me.

But there was no sign of him, and when I reached the Nahr el-Sal'q I saw why. The river was in spate.

The ill wind had been at work here, too, and this time to no good that I could see at all. There must have been, high up in the catchment area, as heavy a fall as, if not heavier, than that which we had had in the valley. It may even have combined with melting snow on the high tops to come pouring down now into the valley, for the Nahr el-Sal'q seemed to have risen at least two feet, and to be coming down very fast indeed. Where yesterday afternoon the pile of stone that had flanked the old Roman bridge had stood at least a foot clear of water, now there was nothing to be seen but the angry white of broken water as the river, streaked with red mud, cascaded down to meet the Adonis.

There is something in all of us which cannot quite accept so sudden a reversal of circumstance. It did not seem possible that I could really be cut off on the wrong side of the river. It should be still as it was yesterday, swift but clear, and easily to be crossed if one could find the place. I stood there on the rocky edge which, this morning, seemed barely to clear the rushing level of the water, and stared about me rather helplessly. This must be why Nasirulla hadn't turned up for work this morning. Even if Hamid did come for me—and there was as yet no sign of him—he couldn't cross the river any more than I could. I was nicely imprisoned here between the roaring stream of the Nahr el-Sal'q and the still bigger torrent of the Adonis. Unless I could make my way up the valley between the two, and cross somewhere where the stream was a good deal narrower, I was certainly marooned. I suppose that, once the spate began to subside, it would fall as quickly as it had risen, but I had no means of knowing how soon this might be.

Meanwhile Hamid would certainly come to seek me from the village, so there was nothing much to do but sit beside the stream and wait for his appearance. Behind me the palace, standing back from the head of the cliff, was invisible, but ahead I had a clear view of the village strung high along the valley's edge. I looked about me, found a flat boulder washed beautifully clean by the night's rain, and sat down to wait.

It was then that I saw the boy.

There had been no movement; that I could swear. One moment, it seemed to me, I had been gazing idly at the torrential water and beyond it a stony bank full in the sun and ornamented with a few harsh green shrubs. The next moment I found myself looking straight at a boy, sturdy and ragged in his rustic kaftan, who could have been anything from twelve to fifteen years old. He was barefooted, and unlike most of the Arab boys that one saw, his head also was bare, covered with a shock of wild dark hair. His skin was dark brown. He was standing stock-still beside a bush, leaning on a thick stick.

He seemed to be staring straight at me. After a moment's hesitation I got off my boulder and picked my way back to the river's edge. The boy didn't move.

"Hullo there! Do you speak English?" My voice whirled away and was drowned in the roar of the water between us, and I raised it and tried again. "Can you hear me?"

He nodded. It was a curiously dignified nod, the sort of gesture one might have expected from an actor, not from a herd-boy. That this is what he was I now saw; one or two of the goats that we had seen yesterday were moving slowly and at random down the slope behind him, cropping at the thin flowers as they came. Then with a movement that was all small boy, and not dignified at all, he thrust his stick into the stony earth, and pole-vaulted down towards his side of the stream. Now we were barely twenty feet apart, but with all the roaring of the Nahr el-Sal'q between us.

I tried again. "Where can I cross the water?"

This time he shook his head. "Tomorrow."

"I didn't say *when,* I said *where!*" But he had, in fact, answered my question. The implication was clear. The crossing place, probably the only crossing place, was here, and the river would take twenty-four hours to go down.

My dismay must have been obvious. He waved with the stick upstream towards the towering cliffs that barred the head of the valley, and then down to where the two rivers rushed together in a wrangle of white foam stained with red. "Bad," he shouted, "all bad! You stay there!" A sudden smile, very boyish, showing two gaps in the even white teeth. "You stay with the Lady, huh? Your father's father's sister?"

"My . . . ?" I worked it out yet again. He was right. And it was Nasirulla, of course, everyone in the village would know all about it by now. "Yes. You live in the village?"

A gesture, not to the village, but to the barren landscape and the goats. "I live here."

"Can you get a mule? A donkey?" I had thought of John Lethman's horse, but somehow that would be a last resort. "I would pay well!" I shouted.

That shake of the head again. "No mule. Donkey, too small. You all drown. This is a bad river." After some thought he added in explanation: "There was rain in the night."

"You must be kidding."

He got the meaning, even though he couldn't have heard me. The gap-toothed grin flashed again, and then he pointed towards the village. I hadn't seen him look that way, but when I looked myself I saw Hamid, a slim figure in dark blue trousers and steel-blue shirt, detach himself from the dense shadow under the retaining wall that held the village to the cliff top, and start on his way down the path.

I turned back to the boy.

The goats were there, still grazing; the river roared; the distant village wavered on the cliff top in the heat; but down here on the rocky bank there was no sign of any boy. Only the liquid rocks shimmering up in the heat, and where he had been standing, a shaggy black goat, staring at me with those cold yellow eyes.

A country where anything could happen.

"By all the gods at once," I said aloud, "I could do with your keeping that promise, cousin dear, here and now, and no kidding."

Some ten seconds later I realized that the small figure in the distance was not Hamid at all, but Charles himself, coming fast down the slope towards me.

Chapter Seven

While smooth Adonis from his native rock
Ran purple to the sea . . .

—MILTON: *Paradise Lost*

CERTAINLY a country where anything could happen. After my disturbed night among the storybook paraphernalia of the palace—peacocks, mute servants, harem gardens—no touch of magic would have surprised me. What did faintly surprise me was that I should so immediately have distinguished Charles at such a distance from Hamid, whom I had been expecting. So immediately—and with such a calm uprush of pleasure.

I sat still on my boulder in the sun, watching him.

When he was still some way off, he raised a hand to greet me, then something seemed to catch his attention, for he paused and turned, apparently to address a patch of shade under a dusty bush. As I watched, the patch of shade resolved into a black goat, and squatting down cross-legged beside it the herd-boy, his stick lying at his feet in the dust. The conversation lasted a minute or two, then the boy got to his feet, and the two of them came down together towards the river bank.

I walked down again to my side, and we stood surveying one another across the twenty feet of turbid, red-streaked water.

"Hi!" said Charles.

"Hi!" I shouted. Then, not very brilliantly: "We're stuck. It's in spate."

"So it seems. Serve you right. Stealing a march. How's Great-Aunt H?"

"Fine. You're early. How did you manage?"

"Made it this morning. Hotel told me. Saw your driver this morning, told him I'd fetch you."

"You did? Fine, you go right ahead and fetch me! . . . Oh, Charles, the boy says it'll be in spate till tomorrow. What are we going to do?"

"I'll come over," said my cousin,

"You can't! It's hellish deep. Did you get rain last night in Beirut?"

"Did I get what?"

"Rain?" I gestured to a flawless sky. "Rain?"

"I can't think why we're standing twenty feet apart talking about the weather," said Charles, starting to undo his shirt buttons.

I yelled in alarm: "Charles, you can't! And it wouldn't help if you did—"

"You can watch or not as you please," said my cousin. "Remember the good old days when we used to be dumped in the bath together? Don't worry, I'll manage this lot."

"I can hardly wait to watch you drown," I said tartly. "But if you'd only *listen—!*"

He stopped unbuttoning and turned a look of inquiry. "Yes?"

I threw a quick glance over my shoulder. It seemed all wrong to be standing yelling about our private affairs in the middle of the valley, but all I could see was the tangle of bushes and trees on the cliff behind me. The palace was out of sight, and nothing moved on the path.

I shouted: "It won't do you any good if you do get across. She says she won't see you."

"Won't see me?"

I nodded.

"Why not?"

I made a gesture. "Can't tell you here. But she won't."

"Well, then, when?"

"Never—she meant not at all. She won't see anyone at all. Charles, I'm sorry—"

"She actually told you that?"

"Yes, and she seemed a bit—" Here my throat, sore with yelling, made me stop and cough.

I saw Charles make a movement of intense irritation, then he turned to the boy who was standing just behind him, closely attended by the black goat. I had forgotten all about him. I somehow hadn't counted him as an audience to our conversation, any more than the goats, or the rocks and stones into which he could apparently melt at will.

From the boy's gestures, aided by his pointing stick, it seemed clear what Charles was asking him. And presently Charles turned back to me and raised his voice again.

"He says I can cross further up."

"He told me there wasn't anywhere."

"Still one or two things I can do that you can't," he retorted. "Anyway . . . hopeless . . . can't stand here yelling intimacies about Aunt H across twenty feet of flood water." A gesture indicated the palace, invisible above me at the cliff top. "Right underneath . . . hellish row . . . And I've got to talk to you. Ahmad says there's a place upstream. Can you make it your side?"

"I'll try."

I turned and began to make my way up my side of the

stream. There was no path, and here the water ran close under the cliff, so the going was rough, and complicated by a fairly thick growth of scrubby bushes and small trees. Soon I lost sight of Charles and his guide as I battled my way among bushes and rocks, intent on nothing but keeping my feet.

The Nahr el-Sal'q seemed to flow for most of this part of its length in a gully fairly thickly grown with trees. These, and the broken terrain, made it impossible to stay always within sight of the water. I caught one or two more glimpses of Charles and the boy, then they vanished, apparently following some winding goat track up into the thickets.

I clambered on along my side of the gully for some half mile, to find the stream then curving and its bed shelving steeply up into a narrower gorge where the water dropped from pool to pool in a series of rapids, running deep and fast. Charles and the boy reappeared here, their path apparently clinging close above the torrent, but though the stream was narrow here, and everywhere full of rocks, there was still no place where it seemed safe to cross. And the narrower the gully the faster and louder grew the water, so that any kind of communication, other than by gesture, was impossible.

The boy kept pointing upstream in an Excelsior kind of way. Charles spread his hands to me and jerked an encouraging thumb. We toiled on, separated by the loud white rush of water.

It must have been after a full mile of painful going that the stream bed took a sudden and final lift and curve, and ran, in a manner of speaking, right up against the cliff.

In fact, of course, the stream came straight out of the cliff. The spring which fed the Nahr el-Sal'q was almost a miniature of the Adonis Source, leaping suddenly into the sunlight from a gash in the dry rock face that blocked the upper end of the gully. It was much smaller, less dramatic, and much less haunted. The spring, a spout of ice-green water, jetted out of the cliff with a roar that the echoes magnified, tossed itself into a churning pool, then went tearing off down among the white boulders of the gully. A few hanging bushes, soaked and ragged with the spray, waved in the breeze of the fall. The sun drove against the cliff where the water gushed, lighting the cascade into glittering brilliance, but below, where we stood, the place was in shadow and the wind off the water struck chilly.

I stared about me with dismay. If communication had been difficult down at the ford, and worse in the gully, here it was impossible. The roar of the water, magnified a dozen times by its echoes, bellowed round from rock to rock so that, though Charles and I were here barely eight or nine feet apart, we could not have heard a word the other spoke. Moreover, I could still see no way across. To cross the torrent here would have been suicide, and above the cascade towered a seamed and sunlit crag as high as a cathedral.

It was at this that the boy was pointing, and presently, to my alarm, I saw Charles approaching it. My yell of protest, or perhaps my wild gesture, reached him, for he stopped, nodded his head at me, jerked a thumbs-up gesture, then with apparent confidence approached the cliff. Only then did I remember that rock-climbing had been another of the ploys with which (*vide* my father) my cousin had been wont to waste his time all over Europe. I relaxed. All I could do was hope that Charles had, as he usually did (*vide* my mother), wasted his time to good effect.

It seemed he had. I have no idea whether it was in fact an easy climb, or whether he simply made it seem so, but there was very little to it. He went carefully, because in places the rock was wet or loose, but it was not long before he had gained my side of the Nahr el-Sal'q. He came down the last pitch at no more than a scramble, to land safely beside me.

"Hullo, Aphrodite."

"Adonis, I presume? Nice to see you, but if you've any idea of guiding my tottering steps back across the north wall of the Eiger with you, you can have another think. It's not on."

"I wouldn't risk my own precious neck trying. No, I'm afraid you're stuck, sweet coz. It's beastly cold down here, isn't it, and there's still a hellish noise . . . Shall we get up into the sun where we can talk?"

"For goodness' sake, yes, let's. I must say it seems a lot of trouble to go to, just to have a little conversation."

"Ah, not with you," said my cousin. "Wait a moment, I'll tell the boy—where is he? Did you see him go?"

"Haven't you guessed? That's not a boy, that's a faun. He's invisible at will."

"Very likely," agreed Charles calmly. "Well, he'll turn up when he wants his tip."

I followed him out of the gully, and we soon emerged on a small stony plateau where the sun struck hotly.

Here, too, the resemblance to the Adonis Source was underlined, for on the plateau stood the tumbled ruins of some ancient temple. Nothing remained now but the steep steps of the portico, a stretch of broken floor, and two standing pillars. It must only have been a small place originally, perhaps a subordinate shrine of the greater Gods of Afka, built at the tributary source, and it was weedy, forgotten, and undramatic. Tufts of some yellow flower grew between the stones, and half way up one pillar where the masonry had fallen into a crumbling hole, a hawk had made an untidy nest liberally streaked with white droppings; but somehow the squared masculine-looking Roman stones, the honey-coloured pillars, the pitted steps where the thistles grew, fitted with a kind of beauty into that wild landscape.

The steps provided a seat for us in the shade of one of the pillars. The roar of the cascade was cut off by the sides of the gorge, and the silence was intense.

Charles got out cigarettes and offered one to me.

"No, thanks. Oh, Charles, I'm awfully glad you came! What am I going to do? I can't climb across that awful rock, and the faun told me the water wouldn't go down till tomorrow."

"So I gather. Actually there is another way. He tells me there's some kind of track going up into the heights near Afka, but it's a hell of a way, and if I was to take the car up by road to meet you, you'd have to go on your own, and you'd never find it. I suppose the boy might manage to cross and act as guide for you, but we'd still probably never manage an RV in a million years. The place is seamed with tracks."

"And probably creeping with wild boars and yelling tribes of Midian or whatever. Nothing," I said flatly, "will get me clambering up into the High Lebanon, boy or no boy."

"How I agree." My cousin leaned back lazily against the pillar and blew smoke at the sun. "If the water doesn't go down again before night there's only one thing to do, go back to the palace." He slanted a look at me, eyebrows raised. "That's certainly what I was hoping to do. What's all this about her not letting me in?"

"Just that she said she wouldn't, and as a matter of fact I'm not wild keen to go back there myself. I'll tell you about that in a minute . . . But look, I couldn't make out just what you were yelling at me down by the ford—you did say you'd seen Hamid, didn't you, my driver? He was to have come for me this morning."

"Yes, I saw him, and it's all right, I came instead. You knew Ben's father was delayed and couldn't get home till Sunday—yesterday? Well, he telephoned again last night to say he couldn't make it, had to go on to Aleppo and possibly Homs, and wasn't sure when he'd get home, so I told Ben I'd go back there later, but I wanted to come straight up to Beirut while you were here. I didn't try telephoning you last night because it was pretty late when he called, and I left first thing this morning—and I mean first thing, literally crack of dawn. There wasn't a thing on the road, and I came up the

Barada Valley at the speed of sound, and the frontier post let me through in twenty minutes, which must be an all-time record for them. I got to Beirut about eight o'clock. Your driver was in the hotel lobby when I checked in and asked about you, and he told me you were staying the night here and he'd promised to come and fetch you. So I told him not to bother, I'd come straight up myself."

"As long as he hasn't lost another contract by giving me the day."

"Not to worry, I paid him," said Charles. "I'm darned sure he'll get another contract anyway, the Phoenicia's always full of streams of people wanting cars. He seemed pretty pleased."

"That's all right, then. He's a very nice chap, as a matter of fact. I had a lovely day yesterday."

Charles tapped ash off into a clump of weeds. "That's what I've come to hear about. After all the trouble we've gone to to have a little conversation, it'd better be good. What the devil do you mean by stealing a march on me, young Christy? Was Aunt H so disgusted with you that she refused to see anybody else?"

"Probably." I sat up. "Oh, my dear, there's masses to tell you! Actually, I'd no real intention of calling at the palace, but when we got to the village Hamid stopped the car, and it looked so near, sort of weird and romantic, and of course it never occurred to me really that she'd refuse to see either of us. Look, away down there, see? You can actually see it from here, too. It looks rather gorgeous, doesn't it? I must say distance lends enchantment! Close to it's just about dropping to bits."

You could indeed, from this high eyrie, see the end of the promontory on which the palace stood. As the eagle flew, it cannot have been much more than three-quarters of a mile distant, and in that clean and brilliant air even the branches of the feathery trees were clearly visible.

We were looking down on the back of the palace. I could

see the high blank wall and inside it the flower-roofed arches enclosing the glint of the lake. Beyond the Seraglio sprawled the jumble of roofs and courtyards whose geography, even now, I couldn't guess at. From the distance the place looked completely deserted, like a ruin open to the sun.

"See the green courtyard and the lake?" I said. "That's the Seraglio where I slept."

"How appropriate," said Charles. "And Aunt H?"

"She has the Prince's Court."

"She would. Well, tell me all about it. Hamid told me you rather took them by surprise, but you got in in the end."

" 'In the end' is right, and I didn't get to Aunt H till about midnight."

I told him my story then, omitting nothing that I could remember.

He heard me out to the end without much interruption. Then he stirred, dropped the stub of his cigarette carefully beside his foot on the stone, and crushed it out. He regarded me frowningly.

"Quite a story, eh? Well, we expected a queer situation, didn't we? But it's queerer even than you think."

"Meaning?"

He asked flatly; "Did she strike you as sane?"

I have often read about moments of 'revelation'. These seemed to be sudden—blinding lights on the Damascus road, scales dropping from eyes, and so forth. I hadn't ever thought about it much, except to class it vaguely as a 'miracle', a thing that happened in the Bible or some other lofty context, and not normally—not in real life—at all. But in a minor and very personal way, I had a revelation now.

There was my cousin, the same boy I had known for twenty-two years, looking at me and asking a question. I had known him ever since I could remember. I had shared the bath with him. I had seen him smacked. I had jeered at him when he fell off the orchard wall and cried. I had discussed sex with him at the age when we had no physical secrets from one another. Later, when we had, I had regarded him with a tolerant and familiar indifference. Meeting him the other day in Straight Street I had been pleased, but not bowled over with delight.

And now, here, suddenly, he turned his head and looked at me and asked a question, and I saw, as if I had never seen them before, the grey long-lashed eyes, the well-cut dark hair growing thick and smooth, the faint hollow under the cheek bones, the slightly arrogant and wholly exciting cut of nostril and upper lip, the whole vivid intelligence and humour and force of the man's face.

"What's the matter?" he asked, irritably.

"Nothing. What did you say?"

"I asked you if Aunt H struck you as sane."

"Oh." I pulled myself together. "Yes, of course she did! I told you she was odd and woolly and said she forgot things, and she was really quite sharp and nasty in a way, but . . ." I hesitated. "I can't quite explain what I mean, but I do know she *looked* sane. However peculiar she was, and the way she was dressed and everything . . . Charles, her eyes were sane."

He nodded. "That's what I mean. No, wait, you haven't heard my side of it yet."

"Your side of it? You mean you've heard something more since we last met?"

"Indeed and indeed. I rang my people up on Friday evening to tell them I was leaving Damascus soon for Beirut. I told them I'd met you, and that we were going to spend two or three days together and we were coming up to see Great-Aunt H. I wondered if they had any messages to send, or anything like that. Well, my mother said they'd had a letter from her."

I looked at him, startled. "A letter? Do you mean another Will or something?"

"No, a letter. It came about three weeks ago, while I was in North Africa. Must have been just after you left. My mother had actually written to tell me about it, and when I phoned she told me her letter would be waiting for me care of Cook's in Beirut. What's more, she'd forwarded Aunt H's letter to me there." His hand went to his inside pocket.

"You've got it?"

"I picked it up this morning. Wait till you've read it and then tell me if it makes sense to you."

He handed me the letter. It as written on coarse-looking paper which could have been some sort of torn-off wrapping, and the handwriting was spidery and spluttery as though it had been written with a quill pen; which in fact it probably had. But it was perfectly legible.

My dear Nephew,

Last month I recd a letter from my dear Husband's friend and colleague Humphrey Ford who you will remember was with us in Resada in 1949 and again in '53 and '54. He tells me that he recently recd the news from a Friend that Henry's boy, Charles, yr son by adoption, is at present studying the languages of the East with a view (he thinks) to adopting my dear Husband's profession. Poor Humphrey cd not be clear over this as he is getting sadly absent, but he informed me that young Chas will be traveling this yr in Syria. If he wishes to call on me, I shld make a point of receiving him. As you know I do not approve of the freedom with wch young people are brought up nowadays, and yr son is what my dear Mother wd have called a Scapegrace, but a clever boy, and wd be amused to receive him. There is much to interest him here in the study of Eastern Life and Manners.

I do well enough here with my small Staff who are v. attentive and a man from the village who looks after the dogs. Samson cannot abide the Dr. Young Chas will remember him.

Regards to yr Wife also to my other Nephew and Wife—
the little girl must be well grown by now, a strange little
thing, but like enough the Boy to be called Handsome.

Yr. affec Aunt,
Harriet Boyd.

Post Scriptum—The Times continues flimsy so that I cannot
believe Yr. Representations were sufficiently decided.

Post Post Scriptum. I have purchased an excellent Tombstone locally.

I read through the letter once, then clean through again,
more slowly, and I think my mouth must have been wide open
all the time. Then I gaped up at my cousin. He was leaning
back against the pillar, head back, eyes narrowed under the
long lashes, watching me.

"Well?"

"But Charles . . . when did she—is it dated? There's a
squiggle at the top but I can't read it."

"Arabic," he said shortly. "Written in February. From the
postmark it looks as if she didn't get it mailed straight off,
and she didn't send it Air Mail, so it took nearly three weeks
on the way. But that's not the point. It was certainly written
after Christmas's Last Will and Testament. Would you or
would you not say that was an open invitation?"

"I certainly would. Two months ago? Well, obviously
something's happened to make her change her mind."

"John Lethman?"

"D'you think that's possible?" I asked.

"Not having seen the ménage, I wouldn't know. What's he
like?"

"Tallish and rather thin, and slouches a bit. Light eyes—"

"My dear girl, I'm reasonably indifferent to him physi-
cally. Would you say he was honest?"

"How do I know?"

" 'No art to find the mind's construction in the face?' Well, I agree, of course, but what was your impression?"

"Not a bad one. I told you he was a bit off-putting at first, but if Hamid's right he wasn't back on the beam properly, and in any case it's obvious he was only doing what Aunt H had told him to. After he'd seen her he was all right. She probably told him he'd nothing to fear from that strange little thing, however much she resembled the handsome boy."

He didn't smile. "Then you did think he might be feathering his nest?"

"The thought had crossed my mind," I admitted, "once Hamid put it there. We both agreed we had unpleasant natures. Does it matter?"

"Hardly, as long as it's her idea as well as his."

"I don't think you need worry about that. I got the impression that she did exactly as she liked about a hundred percent of the time. I doubt if he could stop her doing anything she'd set her heart on."

"So long as that's true . . ."

"I swear it. You know, there's no sense in trying to build up something out of nothing. She simply changed her mind since she wrote that letter. It's perfectly possible she really had forgotten how devastating you were. People do."

"You must tell me about it some time." He stirred. "Oh, God, I don't care what she's up to or how her mind's working, as long as things are going the way she wants them. It's just that she's as old as the seven hills, and alone except for this chap we know nothing about, and what you said about the hashish-smoking didn't sound too cheerful to me. He may be all right now, but he's on the road to nowhere, you must know that." He moved again, restlessly. "No doubt if she's lived here all this time she knows how many beans make five, and you say you got the impression she could deal with him—"

"Six of him."

"Yes. I'd have liked to see for myself, that's all. You have to admit that last night doesn't exactly chime in with this letter of hers."

"Would you expect it to? I wouldn't have thought consistency was her middle name."

"No, but—she gave no reason whatever for her embargo on me?"

"None whatever. I honestly did just get the impression that, having seen me, she'd satisfied her own curiosity, and now she wanted to get back to her own life, whatever it is. I told you, she seemed perfectly normal for long periods, then she'd suddenly look as if she were miles away and say the queerest things. I've never met anyone who was cuckoo before, so I wouldn't know how to tell, but I'd have said nothing worse than old and absent-minded. All I can tell you is, I quite like John Lethman, and Aunt H did seem perfectly happy and contented and not ill, apart from wheezing a bit. But as for knowing what she was thinking about, don't forget I hardly know her at all, and in any case at the time I wasn't feeling too good myself, what with that ghastly tobacco, and the stuffy room, and that rather revolting bubbling noise she made with her pipe. Oh, and Charles, I forgot completely— there was a cat in the room, and I didn't know it. It must have been behind the bed-curtains. I was feeling as queer as all-get-out, and thought it was just the stuffy room or something, but that must have been what it was."

"*Cat?*" His head jerked away from the pillar. His turn to stare. "Sweet Christ, was there?"

I was rather flattered than otherwise at the blasphemy. So Charles hadn't forgotten the thing I had about cats, or the real horror it was for me.

Now, a phobia can't be explained. And cat phobia—the genuine article—is something so grotesque as to be not quite believable. I admire cats; I love their looks; pictures of them

133

give me pleasure. But I cannot be in the same room with them, and on the rare occasions when I have tried to kill my fear and touch a cat, it has almost made me ill. Cats are my nightmare. When I was a child at school my dear little friends found out about this, and shut me into a room with the school kitten. I was rescued, a screaming jelly of hysteria, twenty minutes later. It is the one vulnerable thing about me that Charles, even at his most horrible stage as a boy, never tortured me with. He doesn't share the phobia, but he is close enough to me to understand it.

I smiled at him. "No, I haven't got over it, I don't know if one ever does. I saw it just as I was leaving the room. It sneaked out from behind the curtains and jumped on the bed beside her, and she started stroking it. It can't have been there all the time, or I'd have felt rotten earlier, and I'd have guessed. It occurred to me there must be another door into the room that I didn't notice. Stands to reason there would be, in a room that size."

He said nothing. I went back to studying the letter in my hand. "Who's Humphrey Ford?"

"Who? Oh, the letter, yes. He's Oriental Studies, Professor Emeritus. He's as old as the hills—was a friend of my grandfather's, my real grandfather, that is, not yours. 'Sadly absent' is the *mot juste,* I may say. He had the reputation of giving the first lecture of term, then sloping quietly off to Saudi Arabia for a sort of perpetual Sabbatical. Before my time, praise be to Allah, but he was still around the place, and had me to breakfast once or twice, and even occasionally recognized me in the street. A nice old chap."

"Why hadn't you told her yourself you were coming?"

"I wasn't sure when I'd get here, and I thought it might be better to play it by ear once I was in Beirut."

"And Samson? Is it Samson, there's a blot? The cat?"

"Dog. Tibetan terrier. She got him when she was home last—he used to belong to one of the Boyd cousins who died,

134

and she scooped him up and brought him back here as a mate for Delilah. He was originally called Wu or Pooh or something equally Tibetan, but she changed it to Samson, guess why."

"Too subtle for me." I handed the letter back. "I never saw the dogs, they were shut up except at night. John Lethman said they were dangerous."

"If Samson had taken a dislike to him, he was probably protecting himself, not you." He folded the letter and put it back in his pocket. I got the impression that he was talking slightly at random. "He was a savage little brute, as I remember, except with the family. You'd have been all right: don't they say there's some sort of family voice or smell or something that they recognize even if they've never seen you before?"

"Do they?" I laced my fingers round a knee and leaned back with my face lifted to the sun. "You know, Charles, that letter might work both ways . . . if she'd forgotten what she'd written in that letter when she saw me, she's probably forgotten now what she said about your not coming. See what I mean? In any case, I told you, John Lethman said he'd talk to her, and if his *bona fides* are okay, he will. Even if they're not—or is it 'it's'? . . . Even if it's not, he'll not dare just ignore you. It sounded as if he wasn't planning to; he talked about getting in touch with you. In that case you can produce Aunt H's letter and make him let you in."

"I suppose so." But his voice was absent, and he was making rather a business of lighting another cigarette.

"Or look, for goodness' sake, why don't you just come back with me here and now, because I am genuinely stuck here and *have* to go back? We can show John Lethman the letter now, and see if you can't bulldoze your way in to see Aunt Harriet tonight. He can hardly stop you if you're on the very doorstep . . . Charles, are you *listening?*"

135

I don't think he was. He was looking away from me, down the bright distance of the valley towards the palace.

"Look over there."

At first I could see nothing except the crumbling ruin sleeping in the heat, the fixed dazzling pattern of the rock seamed with violent shadows, the green of distant trees greyed by the heat haze. There were no clouds to move, or wind to move them. No sound.

Then I saw what he was watching. Some way from the palace, among the rocks and tangled bushes that marked the lip of the Adonis gorge, there was a movement which presently resolved itself into a man in Arab dress making his way slowly on foot towards the palace. He was almost indistinguishable from the countryside, for his dress was dust-coloured, and his headcloth brown, and if Charles and I had not both had abnormally long sight I doubt if we would have seen him at all. He moved very slowly, disappearing from time to time as his path took him behind rocky outcrops or through the thick overgrowth, but presently he emerged on the open rock of the plateau behind the palace. He carried a stick in one hand, and seemed to have some kind of bag over his shoulder.

"Looks like a pilgrim," I said. "Well, he's in for a disappointment if he's making for the palace, and I don't see where else he could be bound for. The faun must be right, there's a path there."

"There'd have to be, wouldn't there?" said my cousin. "Did it never occur to you to wonder how John Lethman got back to the palace before you did yesterday?"

"Silly of me, I never thought of it. Yes, and I remember now, there was something about the palace being on the old camel route down from the High Lebanon to the sea. In that case there must be a reasonable track." I grinned at him. "But not, Charles my love, not for me."

"On the contrary," said my cousin, "I'm beginning to think—Just a minute, keep your eye on that man."

The 'pilgrim' had reached the back wall of the palace, but instead of turning north to skirt the Seraglio wall, he went the other way, making for the corner where the walls literally grew out of the cliffs of the Adonis gorge. There was a clump of trees marking the drop, and into these he vanished.

"But he can't get round that way!" I exclaimed. "That's the way my bedroom looked. It's a sheer drop into the river."

"He's got a rendezvous," said Charles.

I narrowed my eyes against the brightness. Then I saw them among the trees, the Arab, and another man with him, this one in European dress. They came out slowly between the trees, obviously deep in talk, and stood there, tiny fore-shortened figures at the edge of the dappled shade.

"John Lethman?" asked Charles.

"Must be. Look there's someone else, I'm sure I saw someone else move among those trees. In white, this time."

"Yes, another Arab. That'll be your doorman, Jassim, I suppose."

"Or Nasirulla—oh, no, I'd forgotten, he couldn't get over today. Then it must be Jassim." I knitted my brows. "I don't understand, have they been waiting out there for him all this time? I haven't been watching, particularly, but if they'd come round from the front gate, you'd think we'd have seen them."

"There is a way round?"

"Yes, round the north side below the Seraglio arcade. The path goes through the trees above the Nahr el-Sal'q and skirts the palace wall."

"If they'd come that way we'd certainly have seen them. No, it's obvious there must be a back door. Stands to reason there would be. It must be hidden somewhere among those trees."

"Tradesman's entrance?" I said. "I suppose you're right.

Look, he's handed over his pack, whatever it is. He's going now. Will they see us if they look this way?"

"Not a hope. We're in the shadow of this pillar, and what's more, the sun will be in their eyes. I wish we had a pair of field glasses, I'd like to see your Mr Lethman. Yes, he's going. Watch the others. My bet is we'll never see them disappear."

Made tiny by distance, the little scene had a silent, curiously dreamlike quality. One moment there seemed to be three men standing beside the trees below the wall, then the next moment the traveling Arab had turned and was making his slow way back among the rocks, and the other two had vanished under the shade of the trees.

We waited in silence. The Arab had gone, the other two did not come out from the grove. There must indeed be another way into the palace. The distance was clear, the colours bright, but it still looked a very long way away. I thought with weariness, and then with irritation, of the long trek back down the gorge of the Nahr el-Sal'q.

I said suddenly: "I quite honestly don't want to go back there. Can't we scrub it?"

"Decided you'd rather try the pilgrims' way into the High Lebanon?"

"No, but couldn't you somehow convoy me across the Eiger after all? It looked terribly easy."

"Did it?" He grinned. No further comment.

"You couldn't?"

"No, love, I could not. What's more I wouldn't, even if I could. It's obviously the will of Allah that you should go back to Dar Ibrahim, and for once the will of Allah is perfectly timed. By which I mean that it coincides with mine. You're going back—and I'm coming with you."

"You are? You mean you're going to show John Lethman that letter now, and get him to let you in?"

"No. John Lethman has nothing to do with it. You're going to let me in yourself."

I sat up abruptly. "If you mean what I think you mean—"

"Probably. There's a back door, a postern."

"So?" I asked sharply.

"I've been thinking . . ." He spoke slowly, his eyes still on the distant sprawl of the palace. "The place where we met this morning, the ford . . . that was out of sight of the palace?"

"Yes. But Charles—"

"And you said that when you first saw me coming down the slope below the village, you thought I was your driver?"

"Yes, but Charles—"

"Now, they've seen your driver, but they've never seen me, and anyway they wouldn't be expecting me any more than you were. If they were looking out at all this morning, all they would see was you going down to the stream to meet your driver, who was walking down from the village. Fair enough?"

"Yes, but Charles, you can't! Are you really thinking—?"

"Of course I am. Now shut up and listen. I want to get into this place for myself and see exactly what's going on, and I want to get in now, not wait on Lethman's problematic goodwill. All right, it looks as if this flooding of the river has provided a heaven-sent chance; the will of Allah, plain and clear. Your part of it's perfectly simple and straightforward. You go back there now to the palace, ring for old Jassim again, and tell him what's more or less the truth. Tell him you couldn't cross the stream, and neither could your driver, but that you both went up the Nahr el-Sal'q as far as you could, to see if there was a place to cross. You got right up to the source, and there wasn't any place you could cross, even with the driver's help." He grinned. "Couldn't be truer so far. So you told your driver to go back to Beirut, and call for you again tomorrow when the stream had had a chance to go down. You also gave your driver a message for your cousin

139

Charles, to say you were staying here another night, and that you'd join him tomorrow at the Phoenicia."

"But, Charles—"

"They can hardly refuse to take you in. In fact, it sounded to me as if your Mr Lethman was quite glad of your company. Who could blame him? If you had to live in a place like that you'd welcome the Abominable Snowman."

"Thank you."

"You're welcome. So, you get back into the palace. You told me that you could explore anywhere you liked except the Prince's rooms. Well, do just that. You'll have hours of daylight this time. See if you can find this back door; you said it went from your end of the palace anyway."

"It must do. I told you about the man walking through the Seraglio Garden last night. Whoever it was, I'll swear he didn't come past my room to the main door, so he must have got in and out another way. But—you're serious? You're really planning to break in?"

"Why not? If you can find the door, see it's unlocked after dark tonight, and Mohammed will come to the mountain."

"And if I can't find it?"

"Then we'll have to think of some other way. No windows at all looking back on the plateau—no, I can see that from here; there aren't. Well, but you said there was an arcade of sorts on the north side facing the village, and a path underneath?"

"There is, but the windows are all barred. Don't forget it was a harem."

"You said the place was falling to bits; aren't any of the grilles broken? Or could they be broken?"

"Yes, I think so. But they're right up high in the wall, and—"

"Well, I can climb," said Charles. "If the wall's in bad repair there'll be plenty of footholds. I've always wanted to climb into a harem."

"I'll bet. But why not try the direct approach first? With me, I mean, at the main gate?"

"Because if it doesn't work you mightn't get in either, and then there'd be no chance even of a break-in. And I'd sooner by-pass Lethman in any case."

I started to ask why, saw my cousin's face, and decided to save time and energy. I know Charles. I asked instead: "Well, once you're in, what then? What if you're caught?"

"All that'll happen is a bit of a row, or at worst a turn-up with John Lethman, and I'll risk that. It won't worry me, and at least I'll get to see Aunt H, if only to have her tear a strip off me."

I regarded him. "This I just don't get. I mean, curiosity is one thing, but this sudden outburst of devotion . . . No, Charles, it simply isn't on. It's all very fine and large, but you just can't do this sort of thing."

"Can't I? Look at it this way. You've got to go back tonight. You don't want to. Wouldn't you rather I was there, too?"

"Under the circumstances," I said, "I'd be glad of the Abominable Snowman."

"Thank you. Well then, sweet Christabel—"

Of course I protested further, and of course he won in the end, as he always had. Besides, his last argument was the most cogent of the lot. However 'romantic' my last night at Dar Ibrahim had been, I had no desire to repeat it alone.

"Then that's settled." He got decisively to his feet. "I'll climb back across now, and in due course, if they're interested, they'll see me going back towards the village. Now, you said you'd finished supper by about ten, and Aunt H didn't send for you until about twelve. Just in case she decides to receive you again, we'd better say that I'll be at the back of the palace any time from ten-thirty on. If you can't get the postern unlocked, I'll give a couple of barks like a hill fox under the wall, and if it's all clear for me to climb up, hang a towel out, or something light coloured that I can see. Soap-opera stuff, I know, but simple ideas usually work out best. In fact, if it's climbable, I'd prefer the window, if the hounds get the run of the place at night."

"Lord, yes, I'd forgotten that . . . I don't know if I could do anything about them. If he does take me to see Aunt H again, there's a chance he may shut them up, but other-wise—"

"Have to chance it, don't worry. It's a big place. Let's get back, shall we?"

"What about the faun?"

"I dare say I could buy his silence, wouldn't you say?"

"I'm darned sure you could," I said.

"And there's no one in the village going to be able to cross the Nahr el-Sal'q to report that a white Porsche has been standing in the village street all day. Incidentally, I'll wait for a bit till I've made sure they've let you back into the palace. If they don't, come down again to the ford, and we'll think again. But I'm certain they will."

"It's all very well for you. I don't want to have to spend another night without even a nightie."

"That's not my fault, that's the will of Allah. I'll bring you a toothbrush tonight, but I'm damned if I'll climb back across the cascade carrying a nightie. You could always bor-row a djibbah from Great-Aunt Harriet."

And on this note of unfeeling comfort he led the way back towards the cascade and the gully.

Chapter Eight

—◦◦◦◦—

But who shall teach thee what the night-comer is?
—THE KORAN: *Sura* LXXXVI

IT ALL WENT exactly as Charles would have wished. It seemed almost too easy. Jassim may have imagined it was Nasirulla who was ringing for entry, for he opened the gate immediately, and when he saw who it was, let me in with not much more than a bit of sulky muttering, and in a moment or two I was explaining the circumstances to John Lethman.

If he was put out he concealed it very well. "How stupid of me not to have expected this, especially when Nasirulla didn't turn up. It's happened before after heavy rain when the snows are still melting. Of course you must stay. Did you really go the whole way up the river to try and find a way across?"

"Yes, right up to the source, at least I suppose it's the source, it's a sort of cascade coming out of the cliff. The driver thought there might be a way over if he helped me, but it would have taken a rock climber, and I jolly well wasn't going to risk it. So we gave up, and I came back."

"He's gone back to Beirut?"

I nodded. "He said there'd be no chance of its going down before tomorrow. So I gave him a message for my cousin Charles not to come up here, because Great-Aunt Harriet wasn't well enough to see him." I added: "That's how I put it, anyway. I'll explain better when I see him myself. Are you going to tell her I've come back?"

He hesitated, then turned up a hand, smiling. "I'm not sure. Let's defer the decision until she wakes up, shall we?"

"You play by ear, do you?"

"Exactly that. Come back to your garden, Miss Mansel. You're just in time for lunch."

Whether Jassim had managed to convey the news to Halide, or whether she would normally have shared the meal with John Lethman herself, I had no way of telling. Only a few minutes after he had shown me back to the room in the Seraglio Court, the girl arrived with a tray set for two, which she thumped down with patent resentment on the table, and then stood smouldering at me and directing a rapid stream of Arabic at John Lethman which sounded like nothing more nor less than the spitting of an angry cat.

He took it calmly, only once interrupting with slight irritation, and finally, with a glance at his watch, making some statement that seemed to satisfy her. At any rate it silenced her and sent her away, with another look at me and a flouncing swirl of black skirts. No pretty silks this morning, I noticed, and no paint; just a working dress of rusty black, and none too clean at that. I thought with half-irritated amusement that if it was competition she was worrying about, she need hardly count me; I hadn't seen hot water or a hairbrush for more than twenty-four hours, and must look the worse for my long, hot trek up the Nahr el-Sal'q and back; but it wasn't exactly possible to explain that I wasn't entering the competition anyway.

Lethman was looking embarrassed. "I'm sorry about that. Have a drink."

He brought a glass of wine and handed it to me. As I took it our hands touched. His was reddish-brown, mine pale brown; but both what you would call white. Perhaps she had reason after all.

"Poor Halide," I said, and sipped wine. It was the same cool golden stuff of yesterday. I added quickly: "It isn't fair when she has so much to do. Would she be offended if I left her something? I didn't this morning because I wasn't quite sure."

"Offended?" There was the slightest edge on his voice. "You can't offend an Arab with money."

"How very sensible," I said, and helped myself from a dish of *kefta,* savoury meat balls on a mound of rice. "This water-fall I saw at the top of the Nahr el-Sal'q, does it have any part in the Adonis cult you were telling me about?"

"Not really, though there's a minor site nearby which was supposed to be a subsidiary of the temple of Venus at Afka. You wouldn't see it unless you climbed up out of the gorge . . . no? Well, it's hardly worth a special trip . . ."

The rest of luncheon passed pleasantly, and it was easy enough to keep him on impersonal subjects. This much to my relief. I didn't want to strain my talent for deception too far, and my recent meeting with Charles was just a little too vivid in my mind. Any further discussion of family affairs was better avoided, and I wasn't anxious to press for another interview with Great-Aunt Harriet. And here it seemed probable that John Lethman's interests coincided with my own.

As soon as lunch was over he got to his feet. If I didn't mind . . . ? He had things he must see to . . . If I would excuse him now . . . ? I reassured him quickly, almost too eagerly. The garden was drowsy with the afternoon's heat, and I would sit there, I told him, and doze over a book. And if I might do a bit of exploring later on? Not the Prince's Court, of course, but elsewhere? So fascinating . . . a chance

I might never have again . . . and of course I wouldn't dream of disturbing Great-Aunt Harriet . . . no earthly need for her even to *know* . . .

We parted on a mutual note of restrained relief. After he had gone, taking the tray with him, I collected some cushions off the window seat and took them out into the garden, where I settled myself at the edge of the pool in the shade of a tamarisk tree.

It was very quiet. The trees hung still, the water was a flat, flashing glass, the flowers drooped in the heat. Near me on the stone a lizard slept motionless, not even moving when a quail shuffled past to settle in the dust, wings outspread. On the broken bridge the peacock displayed half-heartedly to a mate who wasn't even watching. Somewhere among the blazing magenta flowers of the bougainvillea which covered the arcade a bird sang, and I recognized last night's king, the nightingale. Somehow, he didn't sound the same as he had with the trappings of storm and starlight. Some finches and a turtledove started up in opposition, and the nightingale, with a trill that sounded like a yawn, gave up. I didn't blame him. I slept.

It was about an hour later that I woke, and the sleepy heat seemed to have overtaken the whole place. Now, there was no sound at all. When I got up from my cushions the lizard flicked out of sight, but the quail never moved its head from under its wing. I set out to explore.

There is little point in describing here in detail my wanderings of that afternoon. It wasn't likely that any outer gate would open straight into the women's quarters, but the 'postern' had been at the back, and since the Seraglio Court, with its rooms and enormous garden, stretched the full width of the palace at the rear, my search had obviously to start there. Now, the postern had apparently been hidden in the trees at the southeastern corner. When I looked out of my bedroom window I could just see the tops of these trees where they projected beyond the corner. They were level with my windowsill. The Seraglio was, in fact, a story and a half above the level of the plateau. The postern must open on some corridor below it, or at the foot of a flight of steps.

A hunt along the eastern arcade and into the recesses of the hammam on the corner convinced me that there was no staircase there, nor a door that could lead to one, so after a while I abandoned the Seraglio, and set out to investigate the untidy sprawl of the palace buildings.

I am sure that the place was not as vast as I imagined it to be, but there were so many twisting stairs, narrow dark corridors, small rooms opening apparently at haphazard one out of the other—many of them in half darkness and all untidy with the clutter and decay of years—that I very soon lost all sense of direction, and simply wandered at random. Every time I came to a window I looked through it to get my bearings, but many of the rooms were lit only by skylights, or by narrow windows giving on corridors. Here and there a window would look over the countryside; one small court, indeed, had an open arcade giving straight out over the Adonis Gorge, with a magnificent view of snow-clad peaks beyond, and a sheer drop to the river below. One ground floor window, I remember, looked north from the end of a black corridor, towards the village; but this window was barred, and beside it were two heavy doors with grilles inset, giving on what I had no difficulty in recognizing as prison cells.

After wandering for nearly two hours, getting my hands grimy and my shoes grey with dust, I was no nearer finding any door that could be the postern, or any staircase that took me down to it. Certainly during my wanderings I had come across several locked doors. The most promising of these was on the east side of the *midan*, a high door with a barred ventilator. But when (the place being apparently deserted for the afternoon) I pulled myself up for a quick glance through, I could see nothing except a yard or two of roughly cobbled flooring leading into darkness, apparently on the level and in the wrong direction. No sign of stairs—and in any case the door was fast locked. There were, of course, stairways in plenty that led crazily and seemingly at random from one level to another, but I found nothing that could definitely be called a basement or lower story. The longest flight of steps counted only twelve, and led up to a gallery surrounding some echoing chamber big enough for a ballroom, where swallows nested in the roof, and the bougainvillea had come in through the unglazed window arches. These, running along the gallery at knee height, lighted the two long sides of the chamber, one row looking out to the south, the other inwards over an otherwise unlighted corridor. Hot buttresses of sunlight thrust diagonally in through the outer arches; round them the magenta flowers hung limp and still; the sound of the water from the gorge below came as little more than a murmur.

Quarter to five. I moved to the shady inner side of the gallery and sat down rather wearily on a deep sill to rest. Either the 'postern' was a mirage after all, or it was irrevocably hidden from me by one of the locked doors. My search could not have been anything but perfunctory, but I dared not take it further. The chance simply hadn't come off. Charles would have to climb in after all. And (I thought irritably, brushing dust from my slacks) serve him right.

In one respect my luck had been in; I had met no one all afternoon, though under the complex of watching windows I had been careful to preserve the air of an innocent and random explorer. I did wonder several times if the hounds were loose, and if the fact that they had seen me in John Lethman's company would make them friendly; but I need not have worried, I saw nothing of them. If they were still shut in the small court, they made no sign. Doubtless they, too, slept in the heat of the afternoon.

I was roused by the sound of a door opening somewhere below me on the far side of the corridor. The siesta was over, the place was waking up. I had better get back to my room in case someone thought of bringing tea.

Light steps on stone, and the gleam of scarlet silk. Halide paused in the doorway, looking back to speak softly to someone still in the room, her slim brown hands languidly adjusting the gilded belt at her waist. She had discarded her working clothes; this time the dress was scarlet over pale green, and her gilt sandals had high heels and curved Persian toes. The bird had its plumage on again, and prettier than ever.

Mating plumage, at that. It was John Lethman's voice that answered her from the room, and a moment later he followed her to the door. He was wearing a long Arab robe of white silk, open to the waist, and his feet were bare. He looked as if he had just woken up.

It was too late to move now without being seen: I kept still.

The girl said something more, and laughed, and he pulled her towards him, still half sleepily, and made some reply against her hair.

I edged back from the window, hoping they were too absorbed to catch the movement and look up. But almost immediately a sound, familiar by now but almost shocking in the drowsy silence, froze me to my windowsill. The bell from the Prince's Divan. And after it, inevitably, the clamour of the hounds.

I don't know what I had expected to happen then—some reaction from Halide, perhaps, like the fear she had shown last night; certainly a rush to answer that arrogant summons. But no such thing happened. The two of them raised their heads, but stayed where they were, Halide (I thought) looking slightly startled, and throwing a question at John Lethman. He answered shortly, and then she laughed. A stream of Arabic from her, punctuated by laughter, then he was laughing too, and the hounds stopped their noise and fell quiet. Then the man pushed the girl away from him, with a gesture and a jerk of the head which obviously meant "You'd better go," and, still laughing, she put a hand up to push the tumbled hair back from his brow, kissed him, and went, not hurrying.

I made no attempt to move. I stayed where I was, staring after her. And for the first time since Charles had made his fantastic proposal for tonight's break-in, I was whole-heartedly glad of it. I could hardly wait to tell him what I had seen.

Halide had been wearing Great-Aunt Harriet's ruby ring.

There was no mistake about it. As she had lifted her hand to John Lethman's hair, the light, falling from some source in the room behind him, had lit the jewel unmistakably. And she had laughed when the bell had rung, and gone, but not hurrying.

I stared after her, chewing my lip. I had a sudden picture of the lamplit room last night; the old woman wrapped up, huddled in the welter of wool and silk on her bed in the corner; Halide beside her, watching all the time with that wary look; and behind me John Lethman . . .

He went back into the room and shut the door.

I gave it three minutes, then went quietly downstairs from the gallery, and made my way back to the Seraglio Court.

* * *

At first I thought that Charles's alternative plan—the 'soap-opera' one—was also doomed to failure. In the last brief hour between daylight and darkness—between six and seven o'clock—I explored the arcade on the north side of the lake. Still carefully looking as if I was interested only in the view outside, I wandered from window to window examining the metal grilles and the state of the stone that held them. All were sound enough—too sound for me to be able to do anything about it, and the only one that wasn't barred had been boarded up with heavy shutters. Here and there, it is true, a bar was broken or bent, or the edge of the grille had rusted out of the rotten stone; but the grille was in heavy six-inch squares, and only a gap of half the window would have served to let a body through. There was no such gap, nothing that would have let anything in larger than a cat or a small and agile dog.

And if there had been, I thought bitterly, surprised at my own furious disappointment, it would have been blocked up somehow. Charles and I had been too sanguine. This was after all a lonely place, and Great-Aunt Harriet had had the reputation of being rich. It was only reasonable, whatever the interior of the building was like, that the guards on the only accessible windows should be kept in good repair.

I am ashamed to say that I had stood there for a full five minutes staring at the barred windows and wondering what in the world to do next, before the thought hit me with all the beautiful simplicity and force of the apple dropping on Newton's head. One of the windows *had* been blocked. The end one. By a shutter.

And a shutter that was put up from inside could presumably be taken down from inside.

I ran along the arcade and peered anxiously at it in the now fading light.

At first sight it looked horribly permanent. Stout wooden shutters with nails as big as rivets were closed tightly over from either side like double doors, and across these a heavy bar, or rather plank, was nailed to hold them together. But when I examined this more closely, fingering the nails that held it in place, I found to my joy that they were not nails, but screws, two to each end, big-headed screws that I thought I might be able to manage. Surely among the assorted junk that I had seen lying around, there would be something that would do the job?

I didn't have far to look; most of the rooms were empty, some even open to the air with doors broken or left standing wide; but three doors down from the corner I remembered a room that—when I had literally pushed my way in to find a way to the postern—had looked like an abandoned junk shop.

It had been at some time a bedroom, but would have rated a poor fourth class in the tattiest hotel guide. The sagging bed, the broken table, every inch of the dusty floor was covered with a clutter of the most useless-looking objects. I picked my way over a camel saddle, an old sewing machine and a couple of swords, to a chest of drawers where I remembered seeing, beside a pile of dusty books, a paper knife.

It was good and heavy and should do the job admirably. I carried it to the door and blew the dust off, to find it was no paper knife after all, but a quite genuine dagger, an affair with an elaborately inlaid handle and a workmanlike steel blade. I ran back to the shuttered window.

The screw I tackled first was rusty and had bitten deeply into the wood, so after a few minutes' struggle I abandoned it and attacked the other one. This, though stiff at first, came out eventually. I went to the other end. The bar was lying on a slant, and I had to stand on tiptoe to deal with the other two screws, but after some difficulty got one of them out, and the other moving fairly easily. I left it there. There was no point in opening the shutters yet, before John Lethman had been and gone. I didn't bother with the rusted screw; if I freed one end of the bar I could pull it down using the rusted screw as a hinge, and leave it hanging there.

No one was likely to miss the dagger. I hid it under the cushions of the window seat in my room, went along to the hammam to wash, and regained my room just in time to meet Jassim carrying a lighted lamp, a bottle of arak, and a note from John Lethman to say that he himself had to dine with

Great-Aunt Harriet, but food would be brought to me at nine and he would come along at ten to make sure I had everything I wanted for the night.

The note concluded: *"I didn't tell her you'd come back. It didn't seem quite the time. I'm sure you'll understand."*

I thought I understood very well. I put the note into my handbag, and regarded the bottle of arak with loathing. I'd have given an awful lot for a nice cup of tea.

*   *   *

He came as he had promised, staying chatting for half an hour, and went shortly after ten-thirty taking my supper tray with him. At something just after eleven I heard again the furious peal of Great-Aunt Harriet's bell, and somewhere in the palace the sound of a slamming door. Thereafter, silence. I turned out my lamp, sat for a little while to let my eyes get used to the darkness, then opened the door of my room and went out into the garden.

The night was warm and scented, the sky black, with that clear blackness that one imagines in outer space. Hanging in it, the clustered stars seemed as large as dog-daisies, and there was a crescent moon. Here and there its light struck a gleam from the surface of the lake. A couple of nightingales sang one against the other in a sort of wild angelic counterpoint, punctuated from the water with rude noises from the frogs. In the shadow of a pillar I nearly fell over a sleeping peahen, which went blundering off with loud expostulations between the pillars, disturbing a covey of rock partridges which exploded in their turn, grumbling, through the bushes. A few frogs dived with a noise like the popping of champagne corks.

Altogether it was a fairly public progress, and by the time I reached the shuttered window I was waiting, with every nerve jumping, for the hounds to add their warning to the rest. But they made no sign. I gave it a minute or two, then tackled the window.

The screw answered easily to the dagger, and I lowered the bar.

I had been afraid that the shutters might prove to be fixed in some way, but the right-hand one shifted when I pulled at it, and finally came open with a shriek of rusty hinges that seemed to fill the night. Recklessly I shoved it back to the wall and waited, straining my ears. Nothing, not even from the nightingales, which had apparently been shocked into silence.

So much the better. I pulled the other side open and leaned out.

And I could lean out. I had been right about the reason for the shutters. Except for a few inches of crumbling iron sticking out of the stone here and there, the grille had gone completely. I hung over the sill and strained my eyes to see.

The window was about thirty feet from the ground, and directly below it ran the path which skirted the north wall of the palace. Beyond the path the rocky ground fell away in a gentle bank covered with bushes, scrubby trees, and a few thin poplars which clung at the edge of the drop to the Nahr el-Sal'q. Off to the left I could see the sizable grove of sycamores which shaded the top of the cliff path down to the ford.

Nothing of any height grew near, except the thin un-climbable poplars, and there were no creepers on the walls; but Charles, I thought, might be right, and the decaying state of the palace be in his favour. I couldn't see much in the moonlight, but here and there below me something furred or broke the line of the masonry, indicating that ferns and plants had thrust the mortar from between the stones, and the rock below that, though sheer, looked rough enough to provide holds for a clever climber.

Well, that was up to my cousin. I strained my eyes to see if I could see any movement, or even possibly the brief flash of a torch, but saw nothing. Beyond the near shapes of the trees

154

all was darkness, a wide still darkness where blacker shapes loomed, but nothing was clear to the eye except the strung lights of the village and the distant glint of snows under the young moon. He would have had to make the climb across the top of the Nahr el-Sal'q by moon or torchlight, and even that climb was probably simple compared with this sheer wall below me, where he wouldn't dare use his torch at all. It occurred to me suddenly to wonder if there were a rope in the junk room, or anywhere else in the court. If so, one of the projecting pieces of iron might be strong enough to hold it. I hung my white towel over the windowsill as a signal that the way was clear, and turned to hurry back along the arcade.

Something moved in the bushes near the end of the broken bridge. Not one of the peacocks; this was too big, and moved too purposefully. I stood still, my heart suddenly thumping. It forged through the crackling thicket, and a thousand scents came with it, as sharp as spice from the crushed leaves. Then it came slowly out onto the flagway in the moonlight, and stood staring at me. It was one of the hounds. Almost immediately I heard a splashing sound, followed by the swift scrabble of paws on stone, and the other came racing round the edge of the lake towards me.

I stayed where I was, frozen. I don't think it occurred to me straight away to be afraid of the dogs themselves; I assumed John Lethman to be with them, approaching through the garden. What was frightening me was the thought of the telltale window behind me, with my All Clear hanging in it inviting Charles to begin his climb . . .

The second dog had stopped beside the first, and the pair stood shoulder to shoulder, rigid, heads high and ears pricked. They looked very big, and very alert. They were between me and my bedroom. Charles or no Charles, I'd have given a lot at that moment to have heard John Lethman's tread and his voice calling them in.

But nothing moved—they must be patrolling on their own.

I wondered fleetingly how they had got into the Seraglio; Lethman must have left the main door open when he went with my supper tray, and like a fool I hadn't checked. Of course, if they did give tongue, Charles would hear them and be warned. Or if they attacked me, and I screamed for John Lethman . . .

The only thing to do was to stand perfectly still and stare back at them. The moonlight caught their eyes, reflecting back brilliantly. Their ears were cocked high, their long narrow heads making them look predatory, like foxes.

"Good dogs," I said falsely, putting out a reluctant hand.

There was a horrible pause. Then one of them, the bigger of the two, gave a sudden little whine, and I saw the ears flatten. In a sort of dazed relief I realized that the plumed tail was stirring. The smaller hound seemed to take a cue from this. Her ears went back, her head down, and she crept forward towards me, wagging her tail.

Relief made me feel weak at the knees. I sat down on the edge of a stone tub containing tobacco flowers, and said, on a breathless gasp; "Good dog, oh good *dog!* Here, chaps, here— and keep quiet for pete's sake . . ." What the blazes were their names? Soupy? Soapy? Softy? Surely not . . . ! Sofi, that was it, and Star. "Star!" I said, "Sofi! Come on now—here— that's right . . . Keep quiet, you great dollops, you great soft idiots . . . Watchdogs my foot . . . ! Oh, you horrible dog, you're wet . . . . "

And the hounds were delighted. We made a rather confused, damp, and reasonably quiet fuss of one another, till I felt absolutely certain they were safe to handle, then I got to my feet, feeling for their collars, ready to put them out and clear the field for Charles.

"Come along now, chaps. You'd better get back on the job, you dangerous brutes, you. We've got a burglar coming any minute now, and I want you out of here."

At that precise moment, from directly below the north

wall, I heard Charles's signal, the sharp double bark of a hill fox.

The salukis, naturally, heard it too. Their heads went up, and I felt the bigger one—the dog—stiffen. But it must have sounded to them a fairly unconvincing fox—and a foreign one at that—for when I grabbed for their collars again, murmuring soothingly, they allowed me to pull them away towards the gate.

They were so tall that I didn't even have to stoop, but hurried along the flagged path with a hand hooked in each collar. That is, I tried to hurry, but whatever sounds they were hearing from the far end of the garden so intrigued them that they hung heavily against their collars, looking back now and again with little whining noises deep in their throats, so that I expected at any moment the outcry to begin. But there was no outcry, and at length I got them to the gate—to find it, against all expectation, firmly shut.

No time to stop and wonder how on earth they had found their way in; there were probably a dozen decaying holes in the walls that they knew perfectly well. I concentrated on getting them shut out. It was a bit of a struggle to hold both dogs and get the door undone at the same time, but eventually I managed, and with a final pat pushed both hounds outside, shut the gate firmly on them, and dropped the latch into place.

For a moment all was stillness again. The sounds from the end of the garden had stopped, though, straining my eyes, I thought I saw movement in the far shadows. A moment later I heard the soft footstep. He was in.

I had started to meet him, when to my horror I heard the dogs begin to whine and bark just outside the gate; the eager scrabbling of paws on wood as loud as a charge of galloping horses. They still sounded absurdly friendly—too damned friendly; it seemed that even the burglar from outside rated a noisy welcome on the mat. I could see him fairly clearly now, coming rapidly along in front of the pillars of the eastern arcade.

I ran to meet him. "I'm sorry, but it's the dogs, the blasted dogs! They got in somehow and they're making a ghastly noise, and I don't know what to do with them!"

I stopped abruptly. The shadowy figure had come up to me.

"I'm fearfully sorry," he said, "did they frighten you? That idiot Jassim left a door open and they got through."

The newcomer wasn't Charles at all. It was John Lethman.

Chapter Nine

Of my Base Metal may be filed a Key,
That shall unlock the Door . . .
—E. FITZGERALD: *The Rubáiyát of*
Omar Khayyám

IT WAS PROBABLY a very good thing that the dark was hiding
my expression. There was a long, ghastly pause, while I could
think of nothing whatever to say. I did a desperate mental
recap of the way I had greeted him, decided it couldn't have
given much away or he wouldn't have sounded so unsur-
prised, thanked Allah I hadn't actually called him 'Charles',
and settled on attack as the best form of defense.

"How in the world did you get in?"

I thought he hesitated for a moment. Then I saw the
movement of his head. "There's a door over in the far corner.
Hadn't you found it in your wanderings?"

"No. Was it open?"

"I'm afraid so. It's not a door we usually use at all, it only
gives on a warren of empty rooms between here and the
Prince's Court. Probably his suite and personal slaves were
kept there once." He gave a short laugh. "It isn't even fit for

the slaves now, nothing there but the rats. That's probably why the dogs went ramping through—they're not allowed near the Prince's rooms normally, but Jassim must have left a door open somewhere. Did they frighten you?"

He was speaking softly, as I suppose one does instinctively in a quiet night. I was only half attending to what he said. I was wondering if the sounds I had heard before had in fact been sounds of Charles's climb, or only of John Lethman's approach. If the latter, had Charles heard him too, and waited at the foot of the wall, or was he likely to erupt at any minute from the window?

I raised my own voice to normal pitch. "They did rather. Why in the world did you tell me they were savage? They're actually terribly friendly."

He laughed again, a bit too easily. "They can be sometimes. I see you managed to put them out, anyway."

"They probably recognized me as one of the family—or else they saw me with you yesterday, so they know I'm allowed in. Are there only the two? Didn't she have some small dogs—pets?"

"She used to have a pack of spaniels, then some terriers. The last of them died just last month. You mightn't have got away with it if he'd still been around." Again the abrupt laugh. " 'Pet' was hardly the word, really . . . Look, I really am terribly sorry about this. You weren't in bed, I take it?"

"No. I was just thinking of going. I'd just put the lamp out, and I came out to look at the garden. Can you smell the jasmine and tobacco flowers? And don't the roses ever go to sleep?" I moved determinedly towards the gate as I spoke, and he came with me. "If it comes to that, don't you? Were you doing the rounds, or just trying to find the dogs?"

"Both. I was wondering whether you'd been counting on seeing your great-aunt again."

"No. I wasn't staying up for that, honestly. I was just on

my way to bed. Don't give it a thought, Mr Lethman, I quite understand. Good night."

"Good night. And don't worry you'll be disturbed again, I've locked the other door, and I'll see this one's safe."

"I'll lock it myself," I promised.

The gate closed behind him. There were strangled yelps of welcome from the dogs, and then the sounds receded into the labyrinth of the palace. At least the disconcerting little interlude had given me a watertight excuse for locking the Seraglio gate on the inside. The key turned with a satisfying *clunk*, and I fled back towards the open window.

It was my night for shocks. I'd got two-thirds of the way back along the water-side when a soft "Christy" brought me up short, and a shadow detached itself from a dark doorway, and materialized as my cousin.

I gasped, and turned on him furiously, and quite unjustly. "You high-powered nit, you scared me silly! I thought—when did you get *in*?"

"Just before he did."

"Oh, you saw him then?"

"I'll say. Lethman?"

"Yes. He got in by a door in the far corner. The dogs must have—"

"Like hell he did. He came from the island," said Charles curtly.

"From the *island*? He couldn't have!"

"I tell you I saw him. I heard some queer noises when I was half way up the wall, so I went pretty cautiously, and took a quiet little gander over the sill before I climbed in. I saw you and the dogs making off down the path. I let you get down to the far end, then I couldn't hang on much longer, so I heaved myself in through the window. Next thing was, I saw him coming across the bridge."

"But—you're sure?"

"Are you joking? He went past within feet of me. I'm permanently crippled through jack-knifing down too near a prickly pear. After he'd gone by I went back into one of the rooms and hid."

"But if he's been on the island all the time, he must have seen me open the window. Those shutters made the most awful noise. He must have guessed why I was opening them up, so why didn't he tackle me, or wait a bit longer to see what I was up to? Charles, I don't like it! It's all very well saying that even if you were caught there wouldn't be much trouble, but this is just the kind of place they'd loose off a shotgun at you or something, on spec. *And why didn't he wait*? What's he gone to do?"

"Dear girl, don't get so steamed up. If he had seen you at the window he'd obviously have asked what the blazes you thought you were doing, and whatever guess he made, he'd have stopped you. So obviously he didn't see you. *Quod erat.*"

"I suppose so . . ." I added quickly: "Now I come to think about it—yes, the dogs could have been on the island. I saw Star—that's the big one—by the bridge, and when Sofi came there was a lot of splashing, and she was wet. Perhaps John Lethman heard them over there and went across to get them . . . ? No, that won't do, because then he'd have seen me. But he'd have seen me too if he'd come by a door in the far corner. He'd have passed me when I was at the window. Oh, I give up! Charles, what on earth's it all about? Why should he lie?"

"I don't know. But when we know how we know why. Is there really a door in the corner?"

"I don't know, I didn't see one. But it's terribly overgrown and I didn't really search, because it wasn't the right place for the postern."

"Supposing we look, then? He got in somehow, didn't he, and not by the main door. And if he was on the island all the time, and didn't ask you what the blazes you were up to, I could bear to know why. Does the main door lock, by any chance?"

"I locked it."

"And bonny sweet Christy was all my joy. What the sweet hell's that?"

"A peacock. Do be careful, Charles, they're all asleep."

"With cat-like thump upon our way we steal. Can you see in the dark, love?"

"Just about, by this time," I said, "And incidentally, so can John Lethman. You'd think if he was doing his rounds in this boneyard of a place he'd show a torch, wouldn't you? I suppose it didn't enter your head to bring one?"

"You wrong me every way; you wrong me, Brutus. But we'll do without as long as we can."

"You're very high tonight, aren't you?"

"The intoxication of your presence. Besides, I'm enjoying myself."

"As a matter of fact, so am I, now you're here."

"Watch it," said my cousin, "there's a prickly pear on your near bumper." He pulled back a bough for me, and dropped a casual arm round my shoulders to steer me through. "There's your door, I think?"

"Where?"

He pointed. "Under the luxuriant herb, whatever it is."

"You ignorant peasant, that's jasmine. It's terribly dark here, could we use the torch? That's it . . . aha!"

"What d'you mean, aha?"

"Look," I said.

Charles looked. He could hardly avoid seeing what I had meant. There was certainly a door, and it was certainly decayed, but nothing—neither dogs nor man—had been through it for a very long time. The weeds grew a foot high in front of it, and the hinges looked like spindles of wool, so thickly were they cocooned with cobwebs.

"Aha, indeed," said my cousin. "And a beautiful web right across it, too, just in case we thought it might have been opened the other way. But how corny, no clichés spared . . . but then things only become clichés because they're the slickest way of saying something. No, this door hasn't been opened since the last time the old Emir tottered along to the harem in 1875. *Videlicet*—if that's the word I want, which seems doubtful—the spiders. So he didn't come in this way, our John Lethman. Well, I hardly thought so. Come back, come back, Horatius."

I said blankly: "But there *can't* be a way in from the island!"

"We can but look," said Charles reasonably. "Hullo!" The beam of the torch, narrow and bright and concentrated, speared down through the weeds at the foot of the wall, to light a tombstone, a small flat slab let into the masonry, and carrying a name deeply tooled: JAZID.

"A graveyard, no less," said Charles, and sent the torch-light skidding along a couple of feet. Another stone, another legend: OMAR.

"For goodness' sake, turn it up!" I exclaimed. "D'you mean it really is a graveyard? In here? But why on earth . . .? And anyway, they're men's names. They can't be—"

I stopped. The light had caught another one: ERNIE.

"Charles—"

"So that's it. I remember Ernie quite well."

I said, exasperated: "Be serious, for goodness' sake! You know perfectly well that Great-Uncle Ernest—"

"No, no, the dog. He was one of the King Charles spaniels she had when she first came out here. Don't you remember Ernie? She always said he was called after Great-Uncle Ernest because he was absent over everything but meals." He sounded pretty absent himself, as if he was thinking hard, but not about what he was saying. The torchlight moved on. "It's the pets' graveyard, hadn't you guessed? NELL, MINETTE,

JAMIE, still the spaniels . . . HAYDEE, LALOUK, those sound more Eastern . . . Ah, here she is. DELILAH . . . Alas, poor Delilah. That's the lot."

"They can't have got round to him yet."

"Who?"

"Samson. John Lethman says he died last month. Look, must we spend the whole night in a dogs' graveyard? What are you looking for?"

The torchlight drifted along the wall, met nothing but a tangle of creepers and the ghostly pale faces of flowers. "Nothing," said Charles.

"Then let's get out of here."

"I am coming, my own, my sweet." He snapped the light out, and swung back an armful of stems to let me through. "I suppose that's a nightingale singing its ducky little heart out up there? Damn these roses, my sweater must look like a yak's pelt by now."

"What does it take to make you romantic?"

"I'll tell you some day. Can you manage this?"

'This' was the bridge. The faint moonlight reflecting back from the water below made the broken gap clearly visible; it wasn't as far as I had thought, perhaps five feet. Charles jumped it first, light-footed, and more or less caught me as I jumped after him. And soon, with a hand in his, I was treading carefully off the bridge onto the rocky shore of the island.

This was very small, being nothing more than an artistically placed tumble of rocks, planted with bushes and shrubs long gone wild, but designed to lead the eye up to the grove of shade trees (of a kind I didn't recognize) which overhung the kiosk. This, as I have said, was a small summer pavilion, a circular building with slender pillars supporting a gilded dome. The door was an open archway, and to the sides, between the pillars, fretted lattices of stone made fantastic patterns where the moonlight fell. Wide shallow steps led up from the shore, and a tumble of creepers hung half across the doorway, darkening the interior. My cousin let go my hand, pulled some of the tangle aside, and flashed his torch on. With a clap and flurry of wings two pigeons hurtled out over his head, making him duck and swear, then he led the way in.

The interior was empty except for a small hexagonal basin in the center of the floor where there must once have been a fountain playing. A green fish, solid verdigris, gaped dry-mouthed over dead water which hardly reflected back the torchlight. On two sides the floor was bracketed with wide semi-circular couches, cushionless and filthy with twigs and birds' droppings. The wall opposite the doorway was solid, and painted all over. Charles shone the torch on this.

The painting was done in the Persian, rather than the Arab style, for I could see trees with fruit and flowers, and figures seated under them clad in rich blue and green robes, and something that might have been a hunting leopard leaping after a gazelle on a golden ground. I supposed that in daylight, like everything else in the place, it would be faded and dirty, but in the fleeting rich yellow of the torchlight it looked enchantingly pretty.

The scene was in three panels, a triptych divided by painted tree trunks, stiff and formal, following the line of the pillars that framed the section of wall. At one edge of the center panel, all down the side of the trunk, a dark line showed.

"Here we go," said Charles, approaching it.

"You mean it's a door?"

He made no reply. He was playing the light slowly over the picture, his hand following the probing beam, sliding and patting over the surface of the wall. Then he gave a grunt of satisfaction. From the middle of a painted orange tree a section of the leaves seemed to detach themselves into his hand; the ringbolt of a door. He turned it and pulled. The painted panel opened on quiet, accustomed hinges, showing a gap of blackness behind.

I found my heart beating faster. A secret door can't fail to be exciting, and in this setting . . . "Where can it possibly go?" Then, as he made a gesture of quiet, and jerked a thumb downwards, I said on a whisper that threatened to choke itself with sudden excitement: "You can't mean an underground passage?"

"What else? You notice this wall's flat, but if we looked round the back of this place, in the grove, we'd find the outer wall followed the curve of the rest, and the building was circular. There's room in the segment for the head of the shaft." He laughed at my expression. "Not so very surprising; these old palaces had as many doors and passages and secret exits as they had wormholes—all the go in the good old days when you slept with armed guards round the bed and ate with a couple of slaves tasting for poison." He added: "This is the harem. The Emir would have his private stairway, one would think."

"My God, it's all it needed! Now all we want's a magic carpet or a genie in a bottle."

He grinned. "Hope on, hope ever, we may get one yet." The light played over the door. "This must be how he got in, and the dogs. In that case it probably pushes open quite easily from the inside, but I don't trust it, and I don't want to be locked down there for ever like the Mistletoe Bough. Let's find something to wedge it open with, shall we?"

"Down there?" I asked in alarm. "You're not going down?"

"Why not? Can you resist it?"

"Easily . . . No, actually, Charles dear, this is all very exciting, but we shouldn't. It feels all wrong."

"That's just the setting. If this was the back stairs at home you'd think nothing of it. It's all this Arabian Nights' stuff that's getting you."

"I suppose that's true. Can you see?" This as he shone the torchbeam into the gap and stepped over the sill.

"Perfectly. There's a steep flight of steps here, in good repair, and even reasonably clean."

"I don't believe it," I said, as I took his outstretched hand, and stepped carefully over the sill after him.

But it was true. From just inside the painted door the steps went steeply downwards, spiraling round a central column. This seemed to be richly carved, and on the curved outer wall there were more paintings, similar to the one on the door. Dimly I could see the trunks of trees, and green interlacing boughs, and a pale flower-dotted ground where a racing camel, curiously elongated by the curve of the wall, carried a moustachioed warrior waving a saber, and a lady unconcernedly playing a zither. Fastened to this wall was a handrail of some blackened metal that could have been brass, held at intervals by elaborate lizards or small dragons which clung riveted to the stones. Certainly an important staircase, a royal staircase, the Prince's own way to the women's quarters. It would be his regular and by no means secret way; merely his private stair, as richly decorated and attractive as his own apartments. The pavilion was in fact the top story of a circular tower or stone shaft which was let down through the center of the lake into the solid rock on which the garden had been built.

"Coming?" said Charles.

"No—no, wait—" I hung back against his hand. "Haven't you realized—if this is the Seraglio stair from the Prince's rooms, that means Great-Aunt Harriet's, and she'll be wide awake, probably with John Lethman reading aloud to her out of the twenty-seventh Sura of the Koran."

He stopped. "You've got a point there. But it must go somewhere else as well."

"Must it?"

"The dogs came this way. I doubt if they're allowed to

roam the old lady's bedroom at night, so they must have got through from elsewhere. And what's more, doesn't it occur to you that this might be a way to the postern?"

"Of course! It was on a lower level! But oughtn't we to wait a bit? If we met someone . . ."

"I must admit I'd sooner not," said Charles. "You're right, we'd better leave it for a bit." He followed me back into the pavilion, and behind him the painted door shut silently on a cushion of dead air. Back in the latticed moonlight it was comparatively easy to see the way. He switched off the torch. "What time does she settle down?"

"I've no idea," I said, "but John Lethman'll probably be around for a bit yet. Are you going to try and see her when he's gone?"

"I don't think so. Unless it were urgent, I wouldn't do it this way. It'd be enough to frighten an elderly person into fits, bursting in on her in the middle of the night. No, if I see her at all it'll be the legit way, daylight and front gate and one clear call for me. But you know, on what's happened up to now I'm damned if I'll clear quietly out without taking a good look round. Would you?"

"Probably not. Anyway, if I've got to spend the rest of the night here I'd rather you spent it with me than not."

"Such passion," said my cousin tranquilly. We were at the bridge now, and he paused and cocked his head to listen. Stillness held the place. No shadow moved. He started softly across the bridge, and I followed him.

"You're not going out of this court?" I whispered quickly. "The dogs'll make an awful row—"

"No. I'm not interested in the part of the palace they let you loose in, only the part they didn't. The gap looks wider from this side, doesn't it? Think you can jump it if I catch you?"

"I can try. Charles, you said 'they'? Are you making a bit of mystery out of all this? There's really no reason to suppose—"

"Probably not. I'm probably wrong anyway. Tell you later, alligator. Now jump." I jumped, slipped on landing, and was caught and held. Ridiculous that I hadn't realized until this minute how strong he was. We climbed down off the bridge and pushed our way through the rustling bushes.

He said over his shoulder: "Just in case we don't find the postern down there, we'll go now and take a look at my other line of retreat, shall we? I saw a rope in that room full of junk along here—at least I think I did. It would make life easier on the downward trail."

"I thought there might be one there. I was just on my way to look when the dogs caught me. Do you suppose John Lethman got in via the island last night, too?"

"You can bet your boots he did," said Charles shortly.

"But why not say so? Why lie? Did it matter?"

"Only if he wanted to stop you knowing there was a way under the lake."

"You mean he was afraid I'd by-pass him and go straight to Aunt H on my own?"

"Possibly. But it seems a lot of trouble to go to for something that wouldn't have mattered very much, wouldn't you say?"

"I suppose so. And after all, I might have found it by myself. He didn't stop me wandering around exploring in here."

We had gained the flagged pathway. After the darkness of the pavilion and the overhanging bushes, it seemed light here. Something shuffled rustling into the undergrowth, clucking to itself. I saw Charles slant a look at me. "Why didn't you go over to the island before? I'd have thought that'd be the first thing. It's dead romantic."

"I meant to, but when I got to the bridge . . ." I paused. "Yes, I see, you mean that's what he counted on? I probably could have got across the broken bridge by myself, but it didn't seem worth the bother."

"There you are. Unless you were wild keen, which you'd no particular reason to be, he could reckon you wouldn't be likely to bother. And even if you had jumped over you'd probably never have realized the painted wall was a doorway."

"But if it was all that important that I shouldn't find the staircase, why put me in this court at all? I know it's probably the only reasonable bedroom, but if it *mattered*—"

"Simply because it is the Seraglio, and was designed as a sort of five-star gaol. There's probably a million ways in and out of every other corner of the palace, so he had to put you here and spin you the story about the savage dogs to keep you in. What's more," he added, not sounding worried about it all, "we'll almost certainly find there's another door at the foot of the spiral stairway—the one Jassim left open for the dogs—and it'll equally certainly be locked now."

I glanced at him, but he hadn't got the torch on, and I couldn't see his face. "And if we do?"

"Well . . ." said my cousin, and left it at that.

I asked sharply: "You don't mean that you could pick the lock?"

He laughed. "That's the first note of honest admiration I've heard from you since the time I blew the apple-loft door open with carbide. Christy, my sweet, you were born to be a banker's moll. Take it from me, lock picking is practically required study in Mansels."

"Well, naturally. But—" I paused, then went on slowly: "What this amounts to is that there really is something wrong going on . . . I haven't had time to tell you yet, but this afternoon I saw Halide wearing Great-Aunt Harriet's ruby ring—you remember the one?—and she and John Lethman are certainly having an affair, and not paying very much attention to Aunt H, either, from the look of things—which seemed odd, after last night, when they were so attentive in front of me."

I told him then, very quickly, about the little scene I had glimpsed this afternoon. He had stopped to listen, and against the moonlight I could see the attentive slant of his head, but when I had finished he made no comment, merely moving on along the arcade.

I followed. "And why did he lie to me?" I persisted. "There must be some reason for the lies about the way he got in, and the hounds, too . . . Oh, he passed it off tonight, but he really did make a lot of it before, how savage they were, and how unsafe it would be for me to wander about. He made rather a thing about their being loose at night."

"Probably wanted you contained in your own court while he carried on his affair with the girl."

"Come off it," I said curtly. "He was carrying that on with me wandering about the place all afternoon. Anyway, the palace is big enough, heaven knows. Charles, she really was wearing that ring, and if you ask me—"

"Hush a minute, I want to put the light on. Can you hear anything?"

"No."

"Then stay out here and keep your ears open while I go in and look for a rope."

He vanished through the doorway of the junk room.

I looked after him thoughtfully. I might not have seen him for four years, but I still knew every tone of his voice as well as I knew my own. For some reason he had suddenly clammed up on me. There was something he knew, or something he thought, that he didn't propose to share with me. He had been stalling very well, but still he had been stalling.

"Ah," he said, from inside the room.

"Found one?"

"Not so long as a cur's tail, nor so strong as a cobweb, but 'twill serve. Hold the torch while I test it, will you . . . ? Good grief, it's filthy . . . well, I wouldn't exactly climb the west face of the Dru with it, but it should help me down the wall if we don't find the back door."

He emerged from the room, wiping the dirt off his hands. "And now a wash, and a wait. We'll give it an hour, shall we? As long as I can get out of here and away by first light . . . It's even possible the Nahr el-Sal'q may have gone down dramatically by morning, and I can save myself a lot of trouble by cutting straight across it and away before anyone sees me."

"Where's your car this time?"

"I left it about half a mile below the village. There's a small quarry where I could get it off the road and pretty well out of sight. I did play with the idea of spending the rest of the night in the car and coming across for you myself in the morning, but there's always the risk that someone might see it standing there in the small hours and Nasirulla bring the news over before you're clear of the place. And if I ever do want to see Aunt H, I don't fancy having to talk my way out of that one . . . So I left a message for Hamid to come up for you at half past nine tomorrow, and I'll go down to Beirut and wait for you there. And now show me your bathroom, Christy mine, and we'll listen to the nightingales while I get my picklocks sorted out."

Chapter Ten

———————•∞•———————

O softly tread, said Christabel.

—S. T. COLERIDGE: *Christabel*

BUT THEY WEREN'T NEEDED AFTER ALL.

When we set out again the thin moon had drifted higher, clear of the island trees, and by her faint light we negotiated the bridge once more, and made our way up into the pavilion. The painted door swung out silently, and Charles wedged it open with a stone. Torchlight speared ahead of us into the black gap as we stepped delicately inside and started down the spiral stair.

The paintings slid past us, spectral in the moving light. Domes and minarets, cypresses like spearheads, gazelles, hawks, Arabian stallions, fruit trees and singing birds . . . and at the bottom a door.

Shut, of course. It looked massive and impassable in that frail light, but to my surprise, when Charles put a hand to it and pulled cautiously, it came easily, and with the same well-oiled silence as the one above. I saw then that the latch was gone, and where the original lock had been was a splintered panel of wood. Part of the place's history, no doubt, that smashed lock . . . The door had been secured again in more recent times—by a stout hasp and staple and a padlock— but a lock is only as strong as its moorings, and these, like the rest of the palace appointments, were rotten. The padlock was still in place, and locked, but on one side the hasp had been pulled away from the crumbling jamb, and hung there with one socket still holding the useless screw, the other empty.

This, then, was how the dogs had got through. It seemed probable that they had broken the lock themselves, and tonight, since otherwise it would surely have been mended again. And the damage was obviously recent, for splinters and sawdust showed on the floor, and when Charles shone the torch down I caught the gleam of the fallen screw.

"Luck," he said softly.

"Good for the Gabriel Hounds," I breathed.

He smiled, and beckoned. I soft-shoed after him through the door.

It was very dark, a great arched passage with ribbed and vaulted ceiling where the torchlight seemed little more than an impertinent gleam. We were at the end of a sort of underground T-junction, under a vault made by crossed arches. Our door closed one end of the top shaft of the T. A few yards along from us on the left, an open archway led off into blackness, some sort of passageway down which came a draught of air. Straight ahead, and closing the top bar of the T was another door. Like the main gate of the palace, this door was of bronze, its panels elaborately worked and its surface—in spite of age and damage—retaining the silky beauty of hand-hammered metal. To either side of it were ornate iron brackets which must once have held torches, and beneath these we saw recesses in the wall, man high like sentry boxes. The archway itself was carved, and held traces of peeling paint.

"Must be the Prince's Door," I whispered. "You were right, it's the low road to the Seraglio. See if it's locked."

But he shook his head and sent the light shifting from the door towards the passageway on the left.

"Line of retreat first," he said softly. "This way to the postern, what do you bet? Shall we go see?"

The tunnel was long and curved, not quite level, and very dark. Our progress was slow. As far as I could see the walls were of rough stone—no paintings here—and at intervals bore rusty iron brackets for lights. The floor was rough, too, big slabs of paving with a border of crude cobbles, all worn, filthy, and treacherous with holes. Once a scuffle in the blackness made me stop and clutch at Charles's arm, but the rat or whatever it was made off without my seeing it. The passage bent to the left, turned uphill a little, and met another at right angles.

We paused at the junction. Our passage was the main stem of another T, this time with a bigger passage crossing the head of it. Charles put the torch out, and we stood for a moment listening. The air was fresher here, and it was an easy guess that this corridor was open to the upper air. Then from somewhere away to the right I heard, faintly, the snuffle and whine of the hounds.

Charles flashed the light that way momentarily, to show the rough floor of the tunnel mounting in wide and very shallow steps. "That probably goes up to the gate you saw in the *midan,* which means, unless I'm wrong—" He turned the beam to the left, and almost immediately it seemed to focus on something lying in the middle of the sloping way. A scattered trail of droppings, horse or mule. "I'm not wrong," he said. "This way."

A minute or two later we were looking out through the grove of trees at the edge of the Adonis Gorge.

The postern gate was built into the solid rock, recessed deeply into it, and below the level of the plateau behind the palace. A steep ramp cut from the rock led down to it through the grove, and the roots of the sycamores, level with the lintel, reached bare and twisted like mangroves half across the top of the doorway. A buttress protected it on the landward side, and weeds and creepers grew profusely among the tree roots and overhung the cutting from above. Anyone approaching from the plateau would have seen merely a buttress jutting out into the grove, and beyond this the drop to the Adonis Gorge. The ramp was just wide enough for a laden beast, and the gate was a heavy studded affair in excellent repair, both locked and barred.

"You see?" said my cousin. "Just big enough to take a mule or horse—an emergency door—and then the long passage leading under the Seraglio and up to the *midan*. Well this'll save me a climb, praise be to Allah. Nice of them to leave the key in the lock, wasn't it? Come back in—no, don't shoot the bolts again, I think we'll leave it unlocked." Inside the shut gate again he glanced at his watch. "After two. They can't stay up all night, surely?"

"If anyone's still awake, it'll only be Aunt Harriet."

"Yes," said my cousin. "Well . . . "

He was looking at the ground, fiddling with the button of the flashlight. As it came on again, I caught his expression. This was abstracted, even bleak. He glanced up suddenly. "Shall we go back now?"

"Back? To the Prince's Door? That'll be locked, too, I expect." There must have been something in the ancient secrecies of the place that were making themselves felt; I found myself almost speaking with relief, and I saw him give me another quick glance.

"Possibly, though I doubt if they'd have the place sealed up internally, so to speak. Christy—"

"Yes?"

"Do you want to go on?"

"On?" We had reached the first T-fork and turned into the home run. "Back here, you mean? Where else can we go?"

"I mean on to the Prince's Door. Would you rather just go back to the Seraglio?"

"Would you?"

"No, not now. But if you'd rather get out from under and leave it to me—"

"Do me a favour, will you? I'm not afraid of John Lethman, even if you are."

He started to say something, apparently thought better of it, then grinned and said merely: *"En avant, mes braves."* We went on.

And the Prince's Door wasn't locked. It opened silently, and beyond it was a long, vaulted corridor, pitch black and very still and quite empty. Charles paused. The torchlight seemed almost to be lost in the blackness ahead of us. I thought he hesitated a moment, then he went forward. I followed.

The corridor, like the spiral stair, had once been richly decorated, but though it was swept and reasonably clean underfoot it was in bad repair, and the painted landscapes on the walls were faded and peeling, and even in the torchlight could be seen to be very dirty. The floor was of marble, overlaid with some drab and tattered matting, on which our footsteps made no sound. The air was still and dead and smelled of dust.

To either side, at intervals, were doorways of the kind familiar to me from my wanderings in the palace, most of them gaps of darkness where broken doors hung open on emptiness or confusion. Charles shone the light into the first of these, which seemed to contain nothing but large earthenware jars.

"Nothing there but forty thieves," he commented.

"What did you expect?"

"Heaven knows . . . And here's Aladdin's cave. Half a minute, let's look."

At first I couldn't see what had caught his attention. The room seemed to contain much the same jumble as the 'junk room' in the Seraglio; furniture, ornaments, cobwebs—the same dreary and neglected clutter of years. On a rickety chest of drawers was a pile of books, rather less dusty than the rest.

The torchlight probed along the pile, and after it went Charles's fastidious fingers. He turned the thickest volume spine upwards. "I thought so."

"What is it?"

"Chambers's Dictionary."

It had fallen open in his hand. I peered at it in the torchlight. "So useful. Did you know what a cusk was? It says it's a torsk or a burbot. What d'you know? Crosswords, Charles."

"As you say." He shut the book on a puff of dust, and picked up another.

This was smaller than the dictionary, but had a more important look, with thick leather covers which, under their fine greying of dust, seemed to be elaborately tooled. He handled this gently, and when he blew the dust off I caught the gleam of gilding.

"What is it?"

"It's a copy of the Koran, and a rather gorgeous copy at that. Take a look."

The paper was thick and felt expensive, and the Arabic script, beautiful in itself, was enhanced by the ornate designs which headed the Suras, or chapters. It was certainly not the kind of book I would have imagined anyone would throw out into a dusty room to be forgotten.

He laid it down without comment, and the light was sent straying further over the debris. It halted suddenly.

"See what I see?"

At first, among the grey anonymous rubbish, all I could

distinguish was the shape of a battered violin, something that might have been a pair of roller skates, and a tangle of leather thongs and buckles and tassels which resolved itself eventually into a couple of bridles. Behind these and half hidden by them were two dusty objects that looked like ornaments. China dogs.

Even so, I stared at them for a good five seconds, I suppose, before I got there.

"Charles! Not your Gabriel Hounds?"

"Indeed and indeed." He knelt down in the dust beside the tangle of leather. "Hold the torch, will you?"

I watched him as he carefully lifted the bridles aside and took one of the china ornaments in his hands. I noticed with some wonder how gently, reverently almost, he handled the thing. He took a handkerchief out of his pocket, and began to wipe the dust away.

Slowly, under the gentle ministrations of the handkerchief, the thing emerged. It was a creature which might have been a dog or lion, about six inches high, made in vivid yellow porcelain with a glowing glaze. It was sitting back on its haunches with one paw down, and the other poised delicately on a fretted ball. The head was turned over one shoulder, at gaze, ears back, wide mouth grinning as dogs grin. It had a thick, waving mane, and its plumed tail curled over its back. Its air was one of gay watchfulness, a kind of playful ferocity. Its mate on the floor, her bright coat fogged with dust, had a plume-tailed pup under her paw instead of a ball.

"Well, my God, who'd have thought it?" said Charles softly. "What do you think of them?"

"Heavens, don't ask me, I'm not up in these things. Are they really meant to be dogs?"

"They're what are known as Dogs of Fo, or Buddhist lions. Nobody seems sure exactly what kind of creatures they were."

"Who was Fo?"

"The Buddha himself. These are the only creatures in the

Buddhist mythology that are allowed to kill, and then only in the Lord Buddha's defense. They're officially the guardians of his temple." He turned the glowing creatures over in his hands. The wrinkled pansy-face grinned like a Pekinese over the pretty ball.

"Do you know," I said, "I've a feeling I do remember them. But why do you suppose they've been shoved out here? I mean, I'd have thought—"

"Yes," said Charles. He set the dog down again on the floor, straightened up abruptly, and took the torch out of my hand. I got the impression he hadn't heard a word I'd said. "Shall we get on with the programme?"

Without waiting for an answer, and without another glance at the contents of the room, he led the way quickly back into the corridor.

Here was silence and darkness, and the still smell of unused, dusty air. The trees of the faded, painted landscape slid past, punctuated by the dark cave-mouths of empty rooms. Then ahead of us the corridor curved slightly to the left, and on the outside of the curve the torch picked out another doorway, the same arched shape as the rest, but very different. Here was no empty cave, no sagging and rotten timber. The arch was blocked with a door of oak, brand new and solid as a ship, and it was not only shut fast, but locked with a new brass padlock.

The light paused on this for a moment, then moved on to the next door. Here again a new lock winked.

I said under my breath: "The real treasure chambers, huh?"

My cousin didn't answer. The light slowly raked up the door to the barred ventilator above it, and down again, to fix on what stood beside it. He walked over to look, and I followed him.

Between the two doors, stacked against the wall, were a dozen or so cans, the size of small petrol cans, bright yellow with some sort of design on them. As the torchlight caught them I saw on the nearest, in bold black lettering: FINEST COOKING OIL. *Ideal for Frying, Mayonnaise, Salads.* And below this, something else. I stopped.

The light came back to me swiftly. "What is it?"

"On the tins," I said, blinking in the beam, which swept down from my face again to the pile by the door. "I just noticed—I can't remember where I saw it before. Oh, yes, now I've got it! It's nothing, Charles, only that design on the cans in red, the running dog."

"Yes? What about it?"

"Nothing, I suppose. It's not important. Just that I've seen it before."

"Where?" I looked at him in surprise. He sounded interested, even sharp.

"Sunday afternoon, up at the village Hamid took me to. I told you, didn't I? The sunflower field with the little sign on the tree trunk, the red dog that I thought looked like a saluki."

"This is the same?"

"I think so."

We stooped closer, and now under the drawing of the running dog I could see in smaller black lettering: *Hunting Dog Brand. Best quality, beware immitations.*

"Sal'q," said my cousin, half to himself. The torchlight was full on the tin. He looked absorbed.

"What?"

"That's what 'Hunting Dog' is, did you know? The word 'saluki' is the Arabic *seluqi* or *slughi* and means 'hound'. I imagine the Nahr el-Sal'q is some sort of corruption meaning 'Hound River'. Local produce, in other words. This is the same as you saw in the field?"

"Exactly the same." I straightened up. "Local produce it will be—sunflower oil, I suppose, and what I saw was a marker for the field. I think I read somewhere that the peasants use markers like that for their crops—I suppose it's sense, when a lot of them can't read. Heavens, this must be about ten years' supply! What on earth do you suppose they use it all for?"

He lifted one of the cans and put it down again. "Empty," he said shortly, and turned away.

I looked at him curiously. "Why so interested?"

"Not here," he said," not now. Let's finish this, shall we? And we'd better stop talking."

When we rounded the curve of the corridor, going warily, we saw some thirty yards ahead of us a stairway, a wide sweep leading up to a landing and another elaborate arch. The door was standing open, back to the wall, but in its place a heavy curtain hung across the arch. And at one edge of the curtain a line of light showed. We stopped still, listening. Even our own breathing sounded loud to me in the dead air. But nothing moved; no sound came from beyond the curtain.

Carefully shielding the torch with his fingers, so that only a rosy crack of light showed to dance like a glowworm towards the curtain, Charles mounted the stairs and inched his way forward across the landing to the doorway. He paused beside the curtain, with me at his elbow. The torch was out now, the only light the streak at the curtain's edge.

Still no sound. But now I could smell the curiously pungent scent of Great-Aunt Harriet's tobacco. This must be the Prince's Divan. She might be very near us. She must have been reading, I thought, and have fallen asleep over her book. I couldn't hear her breathing, but then the room was so vast, and if she had drawn the bed curtains before she slept . . .

My cousin put out a stealthy hand and drew the edge of the curtain back a couple of inches. He laid an eye to the crack, and I stooped to look

It was certainly the Prince's bedchamber. And this was actually the curtain at the back of Great-Aunt Harriet's bed.

There was very little light in the room; the streak at the curtain's edge had only seemed bright in comparison with the outer darkness where we stood. The lamp stood on the table, its flame turned low, the smallest slug of light. But knowing the room, I could see fairly clearly. It was exactly as last night; the red lacquer chair, the unwashed dishes on the table, the hypochondriac clutter on the dressing chest, the dish on the floor with DOG now half-hidden with milk for the cat, and on the bed . . .

For one breathless moment I thought Great-Aunt Harriet was there too, within a yard of us, sitting where she had sat last night in her welter of shawls and silks; then I saw the room was empty. The dark corner at the bedhead held only the tumble of blankets, and the red of her discarded jacket and the fleecy pile of the shawl.

A moment later it hit me again, the cold wave of sickness and the shiver over the flesh, as the cat lifted its head and eyed us from the tumbled bed. Charles saw it at the same moment as I did, and as I backed sharply away he let the curtain fall and came with me. His arms went round me.

"Okay, okay, it's not coming."

"Sure?"

"Of course. You're all right, love, relax."

I was shivering, and the arms tightened. The top of my head came just up to his cheekbone. "Give it a minute," he whispered, "then we'll go."

He held me like that for a while, till the shivering quietened, and I felt the cold leave my body. It was very dark and still. I knew from the sound of his breathing that he had turned his head away, and was watching and listening. He turned back, and I felt him draw breath to speak, then with an abrupt but stealthy movement his cheek came down against my hair.

"Christy—"

"Yes?"

A tiny pause. The breath went out like a light sigh, stirring my hair. "Nothing. All right now?"

"Yes."

"Come along then."

"You—you really didn't want to wait and see her? I don't think somehow—"

"No. Forget it, we'll go back."

"I'm sorry, Charles."

"So you should be." His whisper mocked me gently. "Brace up, love, it can't get you. Be a big brave girl. Charles'll fight the nasty cat for you."

The terror receded. I laughed. "Big brave Charles," I said. "What if we meet the dogs? I'm fine now, thank you."

"Really? Then we'll call it a night, I think. Back to your harem, my girl."

* * *

The painted door was still wedged open, and the air outside in the pavilion was wonderfully fresh and sweet. We crossed the bridge to the gap, and I jumped it after him. He didn't let me go straight away.

"Christy . . . " He spoke softly, quickly. "There's something I've got to tell you."

"I knew it. I knew you were holding something back. Well?"

"Not quite that. I don't *know* anything. I've been making a few wild guesses, let's say. And I know that there's one thing very wrong, and it makes me smell a hell of a big rat. But—and I want you to take this if you will—I'm not going to tell you here and now."

"Why not?"

"For the simple reason that you've got to stay in this place until morning, and I haven't. No, listen, Christy . . . you've got to meet John Lethman and be civil and normal to him, and you never know, Great-Aunt Harriet may take it into her head to see you again, and—"

" 'Civil and normal' to John Lethman? Then there *is* something wrong about John Lethman?"

"I told you I was only guessing. Most of it's only a guess. But you have got to stay here."

"So the less I know the better?" I said derisively. "Corny, Chas darling, corny! Blast you, I can *act* innocence, can't I? I'm doing it all the time. Don't be so maddening! If it comes to that, it's me that's in the middle of this, and not you! Come on, you've got to tell me! Is John Lethman Aunt Harriet's lover or something?"

"Heavens," said Charles, "if that were all . . . "

I argued, of course, but he wouldn't be moved. Eventually he let me go, and prepared to jump back across the gap. I said: "Why do you have to go back that way? Why don't you just shin down now from the window with the rope?"

He shook his head. "It's easier this way. Close the shutters now, will you, so there's nothing to catch the eye? Don't put the bar back yet, just in case. I'll go now. You get yourself to bed, I'll see you at the hotel in the morning." He seemed to hesitate "You're not scared, are you?"

"Scared? Why on earth should I be scared?"

"Well, as long as you're not," said Charles, and left me.

Chapter Eleven

So free from danger, free from fear,
They crossed the court: right glad they were.
                                    —S. T. COLERIDGE: *Christabel*

I THOUGHT I wouldn't have slept well, but I went out like a light for the five hours or so until my breakfast came, and woke to a glorious morning, and the sunlit peace of the Seraglio garden with the ripple of water where a light breeze touched it, and the singing birds.

All the same, I remember that I came back to consciousness not of the romantic peace of the place, but of the incipience of something cloudy, the faintest shadow of apprehension colouring the day ahead. Even when I realized that this was probably only the result of Charles's hints about John Lethman, whom I would have to meet again this morning, and that the rest of the day would be shared with Charles himself, I still found that the Seraglio Court, the whole palace locked in its hot valley, afflicted me with a sort of claustrophobia, and I got up quickly and swallowed my coffee, restlessly eager now to get out of the place and back to the hotel and the life and colour and vulgar bustle of Beirut. And to Charles.

Hamid had been told to come for me at half past nine, but it was barely half past eight when I finished the coffee that Nasirulla had brought me, lingered for a few minutes for a last look at the garden with the sun on the pavilion's golden dome, then let myself—by the orthodox route—out of the Seraglio.

My first apprehension had been removed by Nasirulla's appearance with my breakfast. If he was here, the river must be passable this morning. I decided to go immediately, and walk up to the village to meet Hamid there. I had tried to indicate to Nasirulla by signs that I wanted to leave early, and though he had merely stared at me in his unsmiling way without a hint of understanding, he must have told John Lethman, for I met the latter coming to meet me in the second courtyard, where the anemones of the Adonis Gardens had already, in the one day's heat, withered and died.

I thought he looked the worse for wear this morning, and wondered if the same could be said of me.

"You're up early," he said.

"I suppose I must have been worrying about the ford. I gather it's all right and I'll be able to get across?"

"Oh, yes. Did you sleep all right in the end after the alarums and excursions?"

"After the—? Oh, the dogs. Yes, thanks. Did you shut the poor things up? I admit I was a bit scared at first, but they were rather pets, and it's just another romantic episode to think about later on. But they're not like that with everybody, are they?"

"By no means. You must have something special." A smile that didn't reach his eyes. "I wouldn't say they're exactly savage, but they make good guard dogs, simply because they make a hell of a row if they hear anything out of the ordinary. I did shut them up, and it may have been a mistake."

I didn't want to ask him why, but he had paused as if he expected it, and it was certainly the natural question. At least the pause gave me time to get my face in order. I asked: "Why?"

"I should have left them on patrol. We found the side gate open. Anyone could have got in during the night."

"The side gate? Is there another gate, then?"

"There's one opening out on the plateau at the back. What with that, and letting the hounds into the Seraglio, Jassim seems to have had himself a ball yesterday."

I said, as casually as I could: "But would anyone break in? You don't mean you've found signs of something?"

"Oh, no. It's just that universal trust isn't a habit of mine, particularly since I came to live in this country. What time's your driver coming?"

"Nine," I said, lying, "but I thought I might as well take myself straight off, and walk over to meet him in the village. You've been terribly good to put up with me for so long. I know I said it all to you yesterday, but you can take it today that it's easily doubled."

"It's been a pleasure. Well, I'll see you out."

He didn't even try to sound, today, as if he meant it. Yesterday's calm had vanished, he seemed harassed and edgy. He hurried me through the smaller court with quick, nervous strides, a hand going to his face in that gesture I had noticed the first day, as if the skin was tender. He was sweating a little, and his eyes were inflamed. I noticed that he didn't look at me, but kept his face turned away, as if conscious or ashamed. I wondered if he were being hagridden by the need for a smoke, and looked away, embarrassed.

"Your Adonis Gardens are dying."

"Yes, well, they're meant to."

"Of course. She doesn't know I came back?"

"No."

"Well, I didn't expect you'd tell her, it's all right. I just wondered if she'd said anything more about my cousin."

"Not a word."

Short, sharp, and to the point. Well, he owed me nothing but my escape. And far from preventing that, he was as eager to get rid of me as I was to get out. He walked out of the main gate with me, and right to the edge of the plateau, and stood there to watch me start down the path. When I reached the ford I looked back, and saw him still there, watching as if to make sure I really went.

I turned my back on Dar Ibrahim for the second time, and trod carefully out over the stepping stones.

These were clear now, and already dry, but the water that swirled round them was higher than the last time I had crossed, and ran iron red, blood red for the dead Adonis. Twigs, leaves, scarlet flowers, had been rushed down the stream and strewed in debris on the banks. Two of the goats browsed desultorily among the jetsam, but I could see no sign of the boy. As I gained the far side of the stream and picked my way up the stony bank I saw Hamid—this time unmistakably Hamid—coming down the path towards me.

We met in the shade of a fig tree where three more of the goats were sleeping in a dusty heap. When our greetings were over I asked him the question that had been simmering on the surface of my mind ever since Nasirulla had brought me my coffee.

"Have you seen my cousin this morning?"

"No." He smiled. "He is very like you, that one, is he not? I should have thought brother and sister."

"He's actually a second cousin, but we used to be taken for twins. Family likeness runs pretty strong with the Mansels. You didn't meet a white sports car on your way up from Beirut? Or see one parked?"

"This morning? I saw nothing on the road at all except one car—a black one with an Arab driver—and a Land-Rover with three Maronite fathers." He eyed me curiously. "I know

190

your cousin's car, I saw it yesterday. You mean he has also been for the night at the palace?"

I nodded. "This means he probably got away all right before he was seen. That's a relief . . . Hamid, you mustn't tell anyone, promise. Actually, my great-aunt doesn't even know he was there. She did see me on Sunday night—I'll tell you about it later—but she said she wouldn't receive my cousin Charles, and he needn't even bother to come up to Dar Ibrahim. Well, you know how he drove up yesterday morning from Damascus, and came up to meet me, but the stream was flooded, so I had to stay another night anyway. It was partly because of that, that my cousin hatched up a plan to get inside the palace and take a look round for himself." I went on to tell him rapidly the main facts: the meeting at the temple and the plans for the 'break-in'. "So I let him in and we explored a bit. We didn't see my great-aunt again, and my cousin didn't think it right to force himself on her like that, so I went back to bed and he went to let himself out by the back entrance. I was just hoping he'd got his car away before anyone saw it."

"I certainly didn't see it." Hamid, though obviously intrigued by my story, contented himself with reassuring me. "It's a Porsche, isn't it? I don't think you need worry. I know the quarry you mean, and I think I'd have noticed if the car was still there when I went by."

We had been climbing as we talked. Now I saw what I had been looking for, a patch of shadow under a tree thirty feet away, where half a dozen goats stood or lay, chewing and eyeing us with supercilious boredom. Among them the faun, shock-headed, grinning, squatted cross-legged in the dust and chewed a leaf with the same kind of disenchanted thoroughness as the goats.

"There you are!" I said.

"I am always here." It was said with a sort of cosmic simplicity that one could readily believe.

"It's all right," I said to Hamid, who had looked slightly startled. "It's only the goatherd."

"I never saw him." He regarded the boy doubtfully. "If he saw your cousin, Miss Mansel, the whole village will know by now that he spent the night at Dar Ibrahim."

"I don't think so. I've a feeling this boy isn't exactly an idle gossip . . . In any case if Nasirulla had known, you can bet Mr Lethman would have had something to say this morning." I called to the faun. "Ahmad, did you see the Englishman leave Dar Ibrahim this morning?"

"Yes."

"At what time?"

"Just after daylight."

"About four o'clock, that would be," said Hamid.

"He must have stayed on for a bit after we parted, then. I wonder what for? However . . . " I turned back to the boy. "He went up this way to the village?"

"Yes. He went to get the white car which was in the quarry by the road."

Hamid's eyes met mine. I laughed, and he shrugged, turning down his mouth.

"You heard him go?" I asked, and the boy nodded briefly, and waved a hand towards Beirut.

I was surprised at my own feeling of relief. "Did he speak to you?"

"No. I was over there." A jerk of the head seemed to indicate some inaccessible tumble of rocks a quarter of a mile away. "He came from the gate at the back of the palace."

There was no curiosity in his voice, but he was watching me intently. I regarded him thoughtfully. "And this was very early? Before anyone else was about?"

A nod.

"No one else saw him?"

"No one, only me."

"And I am sure that you have already forgotten that you saw him, Ahmad? Or that there was a car?"

A brief flash of the white teeth, clenched on the chewed green leaf. "I have forgotten everything."

I fished some notes out of my handbag, but though the black eyes watched me unwaveringly, the boy made no move. I hesitated. I had no wish to offend his dignity. I laid the notes on the rock beside me, and put a stone on them to hold them down. "Thank you very much," I said. "May Allah be with you."

Before I had got more than two steps away there was a flash of brown limbs and a swirl of dust, and the notes had disappeared into the dirty kaftan. Dignity, it seemed, took second place to common sense. "The goats would eat it," explained the boy carefully, and then, in a rush of Arabic which Hamid laughingly translated for me as we moved off up the path: "And the blessing of Allah be upon you and your children and your children's children and upon your children's children's children and upon all the increase of your house . . . "

*   *   *

It was strange to find the hotel looking the same: I seemed to have been away for ever, like Sleeping Beauty, in a storybook world. It was even the same desk clerk on duty, and he smiled and lifted a hand and said something, but I said, "Later, please," and went straight past him to the lift with only two thoughts in my mind, to get out of these clothes and into a gorgeous hot bath before I spoke to a single soul, or even thought once about Charles.

It was heaven to be back in my airy, modern, characterless and superbly comfortable room, throw my horrible clothes on the bathroom floor and climb into the bath. The telephone rang twice while I was there, and once there was a knock at the outer door of the lobby, but I ignored the calls without effort, broiled myself happily for a dangerously long time in a concentrated solution of bath oils, then climbed languidly out, dried myself, and dressed carefully in the coolest frock I had—white and yellow and about as far-out as a daisy—then rang down for coffee, and put a call through to my cousin.

But here at last the desk clerk caught up with me, slightly aggrieved and perhaps in consequence just a little pleased that he could disappoint me. Mr Mansel was not there. Yes, he certainly had suite fifty, but he was not in the hotel. The clerk had tried to tell me; he had tried to give me Mr Mansel's letter, but I hadn't waited . . . Then he had telephoned twice, but had not been answered. A letter? Yes, Mr Mansel had left me a letter, he had left it this morning, to be delivered to me as soon as I arrived . . . Yes, of course, Miss Mansel, it had already been sent up to my room; when I had not answered the telephone, he himself had sent a page up with the letter. I hadn't answered the door, either, so the boy had pushed the letter underneath it . . .

It was lying out in the lobby, white on the blue carpet, startling as an alarm signal. I pounced on it and carried it back to the light.

I'm not sure what I had expected. Even after last night I couldn't see the situation vis-à-vis Great-Aunt Harriet as anything more than highly bizarre, but my disappointment at not seeing my cousin straight away was such that I tore open the envelope in a fury of irritation, and eyed the letter as if I expected it to be an anonymous obscenity, or at least a forgery.

But it was, unmistakably, my cousin's hand. And unequivocally ordinary, unexciting and infuriating. It said:

Dear Coz,

I'm fearfully sorry about this, as there's nothing I'd have liked better than to forgather this morning once you'd got out of purdah, and hear all about it. Am particularly interested to know if J.L. let you see Aunt H again. Was nearly caught just after I left you. Aunt H came down the underground corridor with the girl, just as I was letting myself out at the foot of the spiral stair. I dodged back in time, but managed to get a glimpse of her. As you say, a weirdie nowadays, but she seemed active enough and was talking nineteen to the dozen to the girl. I was very tempted to pop out and have a word then and there, but it might have scared the daylights out of them, so I stayed where I was till they went in through the Prince's door, then I let myself out. No trouble. Picked up the car and got down here without seeing a soul. Didn't want to walk into the hotel at crack of dawn, so had breakfast at a café and rang Aleppo to see if I could catch Ben's father. Was told he'd left for Homs and is due home today.

This is where you're going to be blazing mad at me, especially after all my dark hints last night. I may have been wrong about that—something I heard her say to Halide explained quite a bit to me. Tell you when I see you. But there's still a bit of a problem, and the only person I can take it to usefully is Ben's father, and I gather he'll be leaving home again for Medina almost straight away. So I've gone down to Damascus to catch him. Sorry about this, I know you'll be mad at me, but bear up, I'll be back as soon as I can, tomorrow, possibly, or Thursday morning. Wait for me till then, and sharpen your claws. But don't, please don't, do anything else, there's a maiden—except extend your booking, and when I get back we'll have fun. And I think—if my idea works out—that I'll get to see Aunt H after all.

Love and one kiss
C.

I read the letter twice, decided that my claws would do perfectly well as they were, and Charles was lucky he was half way to Damascus right now, then poured out my coffee, and sat down and reached for the telephone. One was, of course, completely independent, and had run one's own affairs for years. One was twenty-two, and came of a family that declared itself indifferent. One certainly didn't need help or advice, and one didn't particularly like Great-Aunt Harriet . . .

But it would be very nice to tell Daddy all about it. Just for a laugh, of course. I put a call through to Christopher Mansel at Mansels of London, and then sat down to wait for it, drinking coffee and pretending to read Hachette's *Moyen-Orient* and watching the unchanging blue of the sky above the concrete skyscrapers of the changing East.

*　*　*

Daddy's advice was short and to the point. "Wait for Charles."

"But, Daddy—"

"Well, what did you want to do?"

"I don't know. It's not that, I suppose, it's just that I'm furious with him; he *might* have waited for me! It's so exactly like him to play it the selfish way."

"Certainly," said my father. "But if he was anxious to catch Ben's father he couldn't afford to wait for you, could he?"

"But why should he be? What's with Ben's father? I'd have thought if he wanted a useful contact he could get hold of some of our people in Beirut."

There was a short pause. "I've no doubt he has his reasons," said my father. "Do you know if he has actually made any contacts there yet?"

"Not unless he did some quick telephoning this morning. I suppose he could have talked to someone yesterday after his first trip up to see me, but he never mentioned it."

"I see."

"Shall I get in touch with our people?"

"If you want to . . . But I'd leave family matters to Charles for the moment, I think."

"Head of the family stuff? Big deal."

"It's as good a reason as any," said my father equably.

"Well, all right," I said. "For one thing, I haven't a clue why he's gone rushing off like this, specially if his 'dark hints' last night haven't come to anything."

"Did you tell me all he'd said in his letter?"

"Yes."

"Then I'd have said the sensible thing was to stop thinking about it. The boy seems to know what he's about, and he's certainly quite clear on one point."

"Meaning?"

"Meaning, my child, don't go doing anything fat-headed just because Charles is getting on your wick," said my parent frankly. "Forget him, and get on with your sight-seeing, and telephone him tonight to find out what he's up to. Don't dream of going up to the palace again without him . . . Christy?"

"I'm still here."

"Did you get that?"

I said: "I got it. Blast you, Daddy, men are all the same, you're still in the Stone Age. I can look after myself perfectly well and you know it. In any case, what's *wrong?* Why shouldn't I go up again if I want to?"

"Do you want to?"

"Well, no."

"Then try not to be more of an idiot than Nature made you," said my father crisply. "How are you for money?"

"Okay, thanks. But, Daddy, you don't really think—?"

The operator intervened, in that smooth mechanical voice. "Your time is up. Do you wish an extension?"

"Yes," I said promptly.

"No," said my father, across me. "Now go and enjoy yourself, my child, and wait for your cousin. Nothing's wrong as far as I can see, but I'd rather you were with Charles, that's all. He's got a lot of sense."

197

"I thought he was spoiled rotten and lived for nothing but pleasure."

"If that doesn't show sense I don't know what does."

"And don't I?"

"Lord, no, you take after your mother," said my father.

"Well, thank goodness for that," I said acidly, and he laughed and rang off.

For some absurd reason relieved and immensely cheered, I put my own receiver down and turned to the serious business of doing my face and hair and thinking about lunch.

* * *

I had planned originally to see Beirut at leisure and alone, and it was indeed idiotic to be annoyed that I had been left alone to do so. In any case there was nothing else to do with the afternoon. I went out to explore.

The Beirut souks are dirty and crowded and about as dramatic as Woolworths. Though my recent sojourn at Dar Ibrahim, and a lot that I had read about Beirut, had conditioned me to expect romance and excitement here, I have to report that nothing whatever happened except that I trod in a pile of rotten fish and ruined a sandal for good, and when I asked the name of some exotic blue powder in a sack, expecting it to be hashish or crude opium to say the least, I was told it was Omo. The Souk of the Goldsmiths was best, and I fell heavily for a necklace of huge turquoises, and almost decided to start a bank account like Halide's—so lovely, and so cheap, were the thin gold bracelets tinkling and glittering in their hundreds along the rods that spanned the windows. But I resisted them, and eventually found myself emerging from the souk into Martyrs' Square with nothing to show for the afternoon but a tube of hand cream and a gold-mounted turquoise bead that I had bought as a charm for Charles's Porsche before I remembered that I was furious with him and the sooner the Evil Eye got him the better I'd be pleased, and that if I never heard from him again it would not be a moment too soon.

It was dusk now, soon to be dark. Perhaps he had arrived in Damascus. Perhaps he had already telephoned . . . I got into one of the service taxis, and soon was set down within a few yards of my hotel.

The first person I saw was Hamid, leaning gracefully against the counter talking to the desk clerk. It was a different clerk this time, but Hamid smiled across the foyer at me and said something to the man, and before I had crossed to the desk the clerk had checked my pigeonhole and was shaking his head. No messages.

I suppose my face must have given me away, for Hamid asked quickly: "Were you expecting something important?"

"Only my cousin. I haven't seen him since last night."

"Oh? He wasn't here when we got back this morning?"

"He'd already left for Damascus," I said.

"For Damascus?"

I nodded. "There was a letter waiting for me when I checked back in this morning. He'd had to go early. I thought he might have been there by now, and phoned me . . . Yes?"

This to the clerk, who had been attending to some query from a sad-faced Arab gentleman in a red tarboosh, and who was now claiming my attention.

"I'm sorry, Miss Mansel, I heard what you were saying, and I wonder if perhaps there has been a mistake. There was a call from Damascus earlier. I understood it was for Mr Mansel, but it might have been 'Miss Mansel'." He spread his hands. "I am so sorry."

"Oh. Well, even if it was for me," I said reasonably, "I'd have missed it. I've only just come in. What time was this?"

"Not long ago, perhaps an hour. I had just come on duty."

"I see. Well, thanks very much, that may have been the one. Don't worry, it's not important—and if it is he'll call again. I suppose he didn't leave a number?"

"I don't think so, but I can check."

He reached a chit down from Charles's pigeonhole and handed it to me. It said merely that a call had been made from Damascus at 5:05. No name. No number.

I handed it back. "Well, I shan't be going out of the hotel again tonight, so if he does call again, you'll have me paged, won't you?"

"Of course. I'll tell the switchboard right away." He picked up the telephone and began to talk into it in Arabic.

"If you knew where he was staying," said Hamid, "you could ring him up yourself, now."

"That's just it, I'm afraid I don't. He's gone to see a friend, and it's only just occurred to me, I've forgotten the surname completely—can't even remember if I ever heard it, but I suppose I must have done. I've even visited the house, but haven't a clue what the address is." I laughed. "I could find out easily enough if I rang around a bit . . . they've connections in Beirut, and there's a brother-in-law who's something in the Cabinet—Minister of the Interior, whatever that may be."

"Among other things, the police," said Hamid cheerfully, "which should make him very easy to trace. Do you wish me to ask—?"

"No, no, don't bother, really. I'd much rather not disturb them. My cousin will ring again."

"Is he coming back to Beirut?"

"On Wednesday or Thursday, he wasn't sure."

"Miss Mansel." It was the clerk. "Here is some luck. The call came again while I was talking to the switchboard. It is for Mr Mansel, but when the caller heard that he was not here, he asked for you. He is on the line now."

"Then it's not my cousin? All right, where do I take it?"

"In the booth just there, if you please."

The booth was one of those open stalls which are supposed to be soundproof if you lean far enough forward into them, but which in fact broadcast just about as well as the Whispering Gallery of St. Paul's. Just beside it, two Englishwomen were discussing the ruins of Byblos, a group of Americans were talking about food, and a French youth twiddled the knobs of a transistor, and in the booth next to mine the sadfaced Arab was apparently failing in sullen Arabic to get the connection he wanted. I put a hand over my free ear, and tried to get on with it.

It was Ben who was on the line, and in the general hubbub it was some time before we could sort ourselves out, and then he was decisive and a little surprised.

"Charles? Here? Not yet, at any rate. What time did he leave?"

"I've no idea, but early. He didn't telephone?"

"No. Not that it won't be very nice to see him again. He couldn't have waited and brought you along with him?"

"It would have been lovely, but I gather there was something fairly urgent he wanted to talk to your father about, and he wanted to be sure of catching him."

"That's what I was calling him about. My father's due home tomorrow from Homs. We expect him for dinner. I promised I'd let Charles know."

I said puzzled: "But he said, he definitely said . . . Oh, well, he must have got it wrong."

"What's that?"

"Nothing, I'm sorry, I'm in the foyer of the hotel, and there's a frightful row going on just behind me here. It's just that Charles seems to have got his days mixed—he thinks your father's due home today. Then he could have waited, after all, instead of walking out on me! Look, I wonder—I'm sorry to bother you, but could you please ask him to ring when he does arrive?"

"Of course I'll tell him. You're not worried, are you?"

"Not a bit," I said, "only mad as fire."

He laughed. "Well, look, I've had an idea. I've been longing to meet you myself, and I know my father would like to, so why don't you come down and join Charles here anyway—join the conference, whatever it is? Stay two or three days and I'll show you Damascus myself, and if Charles never does turn up, so much the better; How about that?"

"It sounds very tempting."

"Well, why not? Temptation's no use if it's resistible. Do come. Have you got a car?"

"I—no, I haven't. I've been using a hired one . . ." I hesitated. "Do you know," I added slowly, "I think I'd like to, very much. If you're sure . . . ?"

"Of course I'm sure." He certainly sounded it, he sounded warmly welcoming. "It would be lovely to have you. I was sorry I missed you before, and I know my father will be pleased. That's settled, then! We'll expect you. Did you get to see the Lady of the Lebanon?"

"The—? Oh, I forgot you knew about that. Yes, I did, but Charles didn't. To tell you the truth, he's a bit needled about it, and there are one or two complications and I gather that's what he wants to talk your father about. He's making a bit of a mystery about it all. We had quite a turn-up there, Charles and I, but I'd better not tell you over the telephone."

"You intrigue me. I hope you don't mean there was trouble?"

"Oh, no, but he seemed to think there was something a bit off-key. He got all mysterious about it, and now he's belted off without telling me a word, and that's why I'm so mad with him."

He laughed. "I'll warn him."

"As if he'd care!"

"Well, we'll get it out of him between us. I'd certainly like to hear all about Dar Ibrahim! Then I'll see you tomorrow? Have you got the address?"

"Lord, no, I haven't! What must you think of me? Half a minute, I've got a pencil here, if you could spell it out . . . ? Mr Who? Thank you . . . And the telephone number, just in case? Yes, I've got it. I'll read it back, shall I . . . ? Okay? Fine, my driver will find it. It's really marvelous of you, I shall love it. Does it matter what time I arrive?"

"Not a bit. We'll look forward to seeing you, and we'll show you the real Damascus this time."

The line—roaring and crackling and certainly bugged at the frontier—went dead. Behind me, the English ladies had switched to the ruins of Krak des Chevaliers, the Americans were still talking about food, and the Arab in the next booth, clinging to his receiver, regarded me with sour envy. I looked at him sympathetically, and emerged from my booth.

Hamid was still at the desk. The clerk looked up. "It was not the right call?"

"In a way it was. It was the people my cousin was going to see in Damascus. They say he isn't there yet. He may ring later when he does arrive."

"I'll have you called," he promised.

"Thank you." I turned to Hamid. "Are you booked for tomorrow?"

"Not yet. You want me?"

"Will you take me to Damascus, please? I'm going to see them myself. The name's Sifara, and there's the address. You'll be able to find it?"

"Certainly."

"I won't be coming back the same day, but of course I'll pay you for the return trip."

"You have already paid me for a lot I haven't done. No, don't trouble yourself, I'll arrange to bring back another one-way fare from Damascus to Beirut. It's a perfectly normal arrangement and we do it every week. What hour shall I call for you in the morning?"

"Ten, please."

"And if the cousin rings?"

"Let him ring," I said. "We still go to Damascus."

But there was no telephone call from Charles that night.

Chapter Twelve

But shall be overtaken unaware.
> —E. FITZGERALD: *The Rubáiyát of*
> *Omar Khayyám*

AND NO TELEPHONE CALL IN THE MORNING.

Three times I picked up the paper where I had scribbled the number, and three times put a hand to the receiver. And three times dropped it. If he wanted to ring me, he would ring me. If he didn't, then I certainly wasn't going to bother him. The days of trailing after my cousin Charles were over, but definitely over.

Besides, I was going to Damascus anyway.

I left the silent telephone and went down to the foyer.

The morning was hot and cloudless. The familiar big car slid to the door at ten, and I slipped into the seat beside the driver. Hamid, immaculate as usual in his whiter-than-white shirt, gave me a cheerful greeting and swung the car away from the curb and up through the traffic of Bab-Edriss and the narrow streets behind the Great Mosque, to gain the long curve of the Route de Damas and climb away from the coast and through the summer gardens of the rich to the foothills of the Lebanon. Just beyond Bar Elias the road divides, north for Baalbek, and southeast for the junction whose left fork takes you to Wadi el Harrir and the pass between Mount Hermon and the Djebel of Sheikh Mandour where the frontier lies.

I had crossed this frontier before in the reverse direction, traveling from Damascus to Beirut with the group, so I was prepared for the long wait, the crawl from point to point, the four tedious halts and the frenzy of suspicion that the almost domestic frontiers of the Arab countries demand. We were fourth in line at the Lebanese side, but two hundred yards away, across no-man's-land, I could see quite a queue of north-bound vehicles, including a bus, waiting in the hot dust to be free of the Syrian border.

Hamid took the car's papers and my passport, and vanished into the concrete hutments which did duty as a frontier post. Time passed, crawling. The first car went through the barrier, stopped again for the car-check and the bribe to the gatekeeper, and crept across to repeat the performance on the other side. Fifteen minutes later the second car followed it. Only one in front of us now.

It was hot in the stationary car. I got out and climbed the roadside bank and found a boulder slightly less dusty than the rest, where I sat down. The hotel had provided a picnic, and I sat munching a sandwich, till I met the eyes of a thin dog which had crept to the edge of the road below me and was eyeing me wistfully, just out of stick distance. I held out the remains of the sandwich. He looked at it with his soul in his eyes, and came no nearer. I made to throw it down to him, but at the first movement of my hand he flinched violently away. I got up slowly, took two steps down to the road, leaned over and placed the bread and meat carefully in the dust, then retreated the few paces back towards the car. Watching me, the dog inched forward, every bone eloquent through his dirty skin, and took the food. The faintest movement of his tail thanked me.

"Was it nice?" I said gently, through my anger, and the dog's eyes rolled up whitely to me as the tail wagged again. It was so closely clamped to his body that only the tip of it moved, and I suspected it was the first time he had wagged it for years. The next sandwich, I saw, was chicken, a fresh roll full of luscious meat. I put it in the dust. He snatched it, more confidently this time, but even in the act of bolting it, turned and fled. I looked round. Hamid had left the frontier buildings and was approaching the car.

I had my door half open when I saw he was shaking his head. "I'm afraid there's something wrong. They say we cannot pass."

"Can't pass? Why on earth not?"

"Apparently your passport is not in order."

"But that's nonsense! Of course it's in order! What's supposed to be wrong with it?"

He was apologetic and unhappy. "There's no entry visa for the Lebanon . . . in fact he says that there isn't an exit from Syria, so you're not officially in the country at all, and he can't give you an exit now."

I stared. I hadn't quite taken it in yet. "Not officially in the—well, how the blazes does he think I got here? Tunneled?"

"I don't think he's worked that out. He realizes there's some mistake, of course, but he can't do much about it here and now."

I said angrily: "Well, isn't that nice? Have you got the passport there? May I see? Damn it, I came through this very frontier on Friday, there *must* be a stamp . . . Hamid, why do you have such a terrible alphabet? Have you looked through this yourself?"

"Yes, I did, and I'm afraid he's right, Miss Mansel. There isn't a stamp."

There weren't all that many stamps in my passport, so my hasty search didn't take long, and it did, indeed, seem as if he was right. I looked up, not prepared to admit even yet that the mistake, whatever it was, could actually prevent me from going to Damascus. "But I tell you, I came through here on Friday. They must have stamped it then, surely? If they didn't stamp it, it's their mistake. I certainly handed the passport over, and they let me through . . . Did you tell the man I'd been through here on Friday?"

"I told him you'd come from Damascus recently. I was not sure which day."

"I came with the group, five cars—twenty-two people and an English courier. It was Friday at about midday. If it's the same man on duty, he may remember passing us all through, and anyway, they'll have records, won't they? And the courier had a list; it would have my name on it. Would you please go back and tell him this?"

"Certainly I'll tell him. But you know, I think this may be the trouble; if you came through with a group your name was no doubt on the group passport—the 'list' your couriers showed. They do not always stamp the individual passports of these groups unless you ask them specially. You did not ask them for a stamp, no?"

"Of course I didn't, I never thought of it. I suppose our courier should have realized—he knew I was supposed to be staying on in Lebanon . . . But look, Hamid, this is nonsense! They surely must *know* I couldn't be here illegally! Surely they know you and your car? You must come this way often."

"Every week. Oh, yes, they know me . . . I can pass, and my car; our papers are in order. But not you, I'm afraid. The rules are very strict."

Another car, it seemed mockingly, revved up and moved off through the barrier. From the other side the bus arrived, shaking and roaring and churning up dust. I moved back out of the cloud to the road's edge. People were staring, but not much interested. This must happen every day. The rules, as Hamid had said, were very strict.

I said angrily: "It seems so stupid! It's like having this hooha between England and Scotland. It seems to me these days that the smaller the country the more silly fuss it makes . . . I'm sorry, Hamid, I didn't mean to be rude. It's just so *infuriating* . . . and it's beastly hot. I'm sorry."

"You're welcome," said Hamid, meaning it generously. His look was troubled and sympathetic. "But he will be coming back tomorrow, no?"

"Who will?"

"The cousin."

"I wasn't even thinking about the cousin," I snapped. But I was, of course, and Hamid had known I was before I did. I felt somehow vulnerable, a feeling which was new to me, and entirely unpleasant.

He was saying gently: "I know these frontiers are annoying to foreigners, but we have problems here, I'm afraid, big problems. Among other things a good deal of smuggling goes on . . . Do not mistake me, I do not say that anyone thinks you are taking part in this, but the rules have to be made and kept, and unhappily you have fallen wrong of them."

"Foul."

"Pardon?"

"I have fallen foul of them. Fallen wrong means something different. Smuggling? What sort of smuggling, for pity's sake? Do we look as if we were loaded down with guns or brandy or whatever?"

"Not brandy, no, not here. But you could easily be carrying drugs."

I raised my eyebrows. "Drugs? I suppose I could. I was forgetting where I was. One of my cousin's books called it 'the hashish run'."

He laughed. "Is that the phrase? Yes, I'm afraid that Beirut has—shall we say it has certain reputations? And it isn't only hashish, I'm afraid—there's still opium grown in Turkey and Iran, and smuggled through to the sea. I told you the controls were tight now, and getting tighter. The National Assembly of the U.A.R. has been making representations to the governments, and the penalties are being made more severe, and as you see, things are a little fierce at the frontiers."

"I can see they have to be, I suppose. But surely they needn't bother tourists about this?"

"A few tourists have even been guilty. Quite recently two English students were arrested, and found guilty. Didn't you see it in the papers?"

I shook my head. "What happened to them? What's the penalty?"

"For them, imprisonment. They're still in Beirut. It used to be only about three years, but now it's a long term of hard labour. For a Lebanese national, besides the sentence, it would mean being deprived of his civil rights and registered in the police files as a trafficker—is that the word?—in drugs. And in other countries, much worse penalties. In Turkey, for instance, the penalty is death—and in Egypt now, and I think also in Iran. You see how seriously it is taken."

"But I thought you said the other day that it wasn't taken seriously in the Middle East? At least, you implied that nobody thought it very wrong to smoke hashish."

"Whenever a government takes anything seriously you will find that it is not a moral problem but an economic one," said Hamid cynically. "In Egypt, for instance, the problem is very serious—your addict is pretty useless as a worker, you know—and the Government has been getting badly worried about its illegal imports from the Lebanon, so it makes representations to the National Assembly, and unhappily at present we all have to take a lot of notice of what Egypt thinks and wants." He smiled. "So you see why things are difficult? They are also, I may say, difficult for the Customs men. Do you see the bus?"

This had, mercifully, switched off its engine, and was immobilized at the Lebanese barrier. The passengers had alighted, and were standing about while their papers were checked. They all had the fatalistic air of people prepared to wait about all day, and one could see why, for on top of the bus, piled up like a refugee's cart or a poor man's removal van, were what looked like the household goods of every person on board. There even seemed to be overstuffed arm-chairs and mattresses, along with rugs, bundles of clothing, filthy canvas bags which had once been labeled Air France or B.O.A.C., and a wicker cage full of unhappy-looking hens.

"They have to search all that," explained Hamid.

"For a few packets of powder?" I exclaimed. "Not really?"

He laughed. "But yes. Sometimes more than a few packets. And there are hundreds of ways in which the hashish can be disguised and carried. Only last week a man was stopped, a cobbler he called himself, and with his cobbler's kit there was a large suitcase full of leather soles for shoes. But these were hashish, powdered very finely, and then stamped into this shape. Sometimes it looks like gum, or jam, or sheeps' droppings."

"Well," I said, "I imagine that anyone caught carrying a suitcase full of sheeps' droppings through a frontier ought to be locked up anyway."

"That is very true," said Hamid gravely. "Well, if you like I will go and explain about the group passport. Will you wait here?"

"I'll come in with you if you don't mind, and talk to them myself. Does anyone speak English in there?"

"I doubt it, but I will translate for you."

The room inside the hut was small and stiflingly hot, and rather too full of stout olive-coloured men all talking at once. The talk broke off as I went in with Hamid, and the uni-formed man—stout and olive-coloured—behind the office counter raised his eyes despairingly and shook his head. I explained, and Hamid translated, and the official listened as well as he could, while other cars piled up outside and the drivers shoved their way to the counter with their dog-eared papers, and the flies droned in the heat, and the smell of sweat and ink and Turkish tobacco was almost visible in the air.

But it was no use. The official was civil but firm. He nodded understandingly when I explained, he even commiserated with me, but that was as far as he would go. And the matter was clear. There was no entry stamp; how then could he affix an exit? He was sorry, but it was not possible; he had his orders. He was very sorry, but a rule was a rule.

It was obvious enough that he wasn't being obstructive, and he had been patiently civil in the face of considerable odds. I gave up at last, before my own temper frayed in the sticky heat, thanked him, and fought my way back out of the shed.

After the sweaty crowded room the hot air outside seemed almost fresh. I walked over to the car, wondering crossly what to do now. Go back, of course, that was obligatory; all I could do was salvage the day somehow and get Hamid to take me somewhere for a run. Baalbek, I supposed . . . I had seen Baalbek already, with the group, but it had been a crowded sort of day; perhaps if we went up the Bk'aa valley, taking it slowly, saw Baalbek again, then went back into Beirut by the road through the mountains . . . I could telephone Ben when I got back, there was no hurry for that, and tell him what had happened. It was disappointing, even infuriating, but it really didn't matter.

But by the pricking of my thumbs, it did.

I met Hamid's eye. I said suddenly, abruptly: "I know I'll probably be seeing him tomorrow, but I wanted to see him today, now, as soon as possible. Don't ask me why, I can't tell you, not in any words that make sense, but . . ." I lifted my shoulders, and spread my hands in a very un-English gesture, but one which must have been as familiar as every day to the Arab.

He said quickly: "You mean you think he is in trouble?"

"Oh, no, no, nothing like that. How could he be? I told you I couldn't explain. Well, if we can't get through, we can't get through, and there's not much point in staying here talking about it, is there? We'll just have to go back, and I'll ring up Damascus when I get to the hotel again. Thanks for being so patient with me, Hamid—it's terribly good of you to take such a lot of trouble for me. Oh Lord, wait a minute . . . I forgot! Did you fix up a return job in Damascus? What'll happen if you can't get there in time to pick them up?"

"It doesn't matter. I wasn't due to come back until to-morrow in any case. I can telephone, and someone else can do it." He opened the car door for me. "Don't give it a thought, today is yours. Where else can I take you? You've seen Baalbek?"

I hesitated. "I suppose it's too late in the day to start now for Homs?"

"Not really, but there's a frontier there, too."

"Hell's teeth, I suppose there is. We're nicely stuck, aren't we? Well, if you're sure it's all right about your Damascus job, I certainly wouldn't mind seeing Baalbek again on my own, with time to spare." But in the act of getting into the car another thought struck me, and I paused. "You know, I really think we'll have to call it a day and go back to Beirut. I've just thought—what's going to happen when I want to leave the country for London? Will I have to get a new visa, or go to the Consul and make inquiries about this wretched exit stamp, or something? If there are going to be difficulties, it might take time. I'd better do it straight away."

"I think you're right, but I don't think it will concern your Consul, I think we'll have to go and see the Chef de Sûreté in Beirut and get another visa. If you'll wait a moment longer

I'll go back and ask the official here what we should do. And who knows, it may not take so very long. We might even be able to come back and get through to Damascus by nightfall."

Even I was not expecting the surge of pleasure and relief that this gave me. I smiled at him. "Oh, yes, that would be marvelous, and you could do your return job, too! Thanks a million, Hamid, you're very good!"

"For a smile like that," said Hamid, "I would be prepared to be very bad. The cousin is lucky."

And he disappeared into the buildings.

The car was like an oven, so I waited outside in the road. The bus—it was labeled Baalbek—had been unloaded, and the dirty baggage was lying in the dust and being prodded over by sweaty, sullen-looking men. People hung around, staring, smoking, spitting. One or two youths lounged nearer, eyeing me.

I glanced across at the office buildings. Through the open door I could see the shoving, vociferous crowd round the counter. Hamid might be some time. I left the car and climbed the bank again above the road.

This time I went higher, out of the dust and the petrol fumes, but still keeping the car in sight and directly below me. The road here was in a shallow cutting, and almost immediately as I climbed I found myself in cooler air and treading on grass and flowers.

There wasn't the profusion of flowers that I had seen along the Afka road, but the hillside was green enough, with sparse grass moving in the breeze, and the grey whorls of thistles, and drifts of some small white flowers that looked from the distance like frost. Over this in violent contrast, blinding over grey stone, went the blazing, cascading gold of the broom; and everywhere, thrusting up boldly from the hoarfrost veils of the white flowers, were hollyhocks—the simple familiar hollyhock of the English cottage garden, red and yellow and white, crowding wild among the rocks of a mountainside in Lebanon.

And a quarter of a mile away, where the same hollyhocks and the same broom flowered above the same rocks, that was Syria.

I had climbed, I suppose, about a hundred feet, and from this height I could see away beyond the no-man's-land, beyond the Syrian frontier post, to where the road curved round underneath a rocky bluff and dropped down to cross the water at the bottom of the valley.

As always in this thirsty country, the green of the trees and cultivation followed the water, and the river wound its way south in a thick sash of trees and corn and vines which crowded along the valley bottom. Here and there, like green veins threading a dry leaf, the small tributary valleys ran down to join the main stream. I could see—perhaps a quarter of a mile beyond the Syrian frontier—one such tributary, curling down through the bare hillside with its ribbon of green, its few patches of growing corn, the bone-white stems of poplars with young leaves whitening in the breeze, and the dusty track where a donkey plodded with a woman beside it carrying a jar on her head. I was watching her idly, when I suddenly stiffened and stared, all attention now, at the point where that distant dusty track met the main road.

Just off the road was a small thicket of trees. And under those trees, something white, metallic. A car. A familiar car, parked there in the shade, nose to the south.

I think I have mentioned before that I am very long-sighted. It did not take me more than a minute or two's staring to convince me that this was indeed Charles's Porsche. The screen of leaves prevented me from seeing if he was in the car, but soon I was almost sure I had caught a glimpse of movement beyond the bushes.

I turned and began to make my hasty way down to the

road, arriving with a thump in the dust beside the car just as Hamid came out of the buildings.

He started without preliminary. "I think it will be all right. It is the Sûreté we must go to, so if we go back now—Is something the matter?"

Excitement and the sharp scramble had made me breathless. "I've just seen his car—Charles's—my cousin's! It's parked about a quarter of a mile past the other frontier. I went up there," pointing, "and you can see over that bluff down towards the river, and it's there, parked behind some trees. You don't suppose Ben's told him I'm coming, and he came to wait for me?"

"Perhaps, but it doesn't make much sense to me," said Hamid. "You're sure it's his car?"

"Pretty sure. At any rate it's a white Porsche, and they can't be all that common hereabouts. It must be his!"

"Which way is it facing?"

"South." Near us the barrier shut with a bang behind a south-bound car, and the Arab guarding it squatted down by the roadside and lit another cigarette. Beyond the further frontier the sun dazzled on the waiting windscreens. I frowned into the glare. "But you're right, it doesn't make sense. If he was all that eager to see me, he'd have waited for me yesterday, or else telephoned, not left it to a chancy pickup. But then what *is* he doing here? If he did get to Damascus last night, he'd hardly come straight up again before Mr Sifara gets home, and Ben'll have told him I'm expected. Anyway, he was facing south."

Hamid said slowly: "I've been thinking . . . he may be going south from Homs. Did you not say that this friend, this Mr Sifara, would be coming from Homs? It is possible that when your cousin telephoned Damascus he found this out, so he went to Homs instead."

"And spent last night there? I suppose so . . . but then why didn't he come back to Beirut this morning? You'd have thought, even if he still had business in Damascus, he'd have come for me, or at least telephoned."

"He probably did. If he rang up from Homs this morning and heard you had gone, he may have decided to drive down this way instead of the desert road, and catch you at the frontier. If they told him you hadn't yet passed here, then he would perhaps get himself through, and settle down to wait for you."

"I suppose so . . . or it may be pure chance, and he's just come this way to avoid the desert road. And now this happens!" I glared at the dusty road in an agony of frustration. "He may be gone at any moment, and I can't even get through to tell him!"

"No," said Hamid, "but I can." He smiled reassuringly. "Don't distress yourself, Miss Mansel, it's very simple. I will go through now and see your cousin."

"You? Would you?"

"Well, of course. I'll tell him you're here and can't get through the frontier. He may want to come back and take you to the Sûreté in Beirut himself, and if he does, I'll go straight on to Damascus and pick up my return job there. If not, I'll come back for you. You don't mind being left here?"

"Of course not. I'm terribly grateful. Yes, you're right, let's hurry in case he goes. I'll take the rest of my lunch packet up the hill and wait."

"And your handbag—and the jacket in case you need it—" He was already fishing for them in the car. "The coffee, yes? And fruit . . . so. If there is a crowd at the frontier, it may be a long wait."

"Please don't worry about me. In any case I'll be able to see from up there."

"Does he drive fast?"

"Sometimes," I said. "Why?"

"Only that if he doesn't know you're here, if it is just chance that he stopped there—he may be gone."

"Would you try to catch him?"

"If it seemed possible. Now, can you carry these yourself? I think I should go straight away."

"Of course I can. Don't wait for me, you go."

He got into his car and started the engine. "You said he was parked behind trees? Can I see him from the road, do you think? Exactly where?"

"A quarter of a mile past the other frontier, some trees on the right, and just beyond them a humped-backed bridge. You can't miss it. There, the way's clear, you can get through. And thank you, Hamid, thank you—"

"Please . . . at your service . . ." A smile, a quick disclaiming wave of the hand, and he was off. I panted back to my perch above the road.

The Porsche was still there. I dumped my things among the flowers and shaded my eyes to watch. Since he had not already gone, my fear that this was just a brief 'comfort stop' must be unfounded. He must either have paused to eat, or in fact be waiting for me.

I peered down at the stretch of road immediately below me. The second Lebanese barrier was lifting to Hamid's bribe, and the big car sailed, windows flashing, through the stretch of no-man's-land. It checked at the Syrian barrier, and I saw Hamid jump out and hurry across to the buildings to show his papers. Since he was alone, and went this way frequently, they would surely let him go without more than a moment's checking.

I looked the other way at the Porsche.

Just in time to see the white car break out of the trees like a greyhound out of the slips, wheel right-handed in a swirl of dust, and shoot off down the road towards Damascus. Seconds later I heard the snarl of a racing change as he whipped over the bridge.

But by the time the sound reached me, the car was already out of sight.

Chapter Thirteen

------------◆◆◆◆◆◆------------

As sure as heaven shall rescue me
I have no thought what men they be . . .
—s. t. coleridge: *Christabel*

I DON'T KNOW how long I must have stood there on the breezy hillside, staring at the empty stretch of road where the white car had been. It was as if I had been lifted up into the vacuum of its wake, and then dropped, dazed, into its dust.

I pulled myself together, and looked to see how far Hamid had got.

He was already at the second Syrian barrier, and showing papers—the car's papers presumably—at the car window. The man on duty took them, glanced, and gave them back. A bribe passed. A few moments later the barrier was pulled open, and the car was through and had gathered speed down the road till it disappeared from my view behind the bluff.

I suppose he cannot have missed the Porsche by much more than four minutes. In a matter of seconds he had reappeared on the stretch of road leading to the bridge, and I saw the dust mushroom up as he braked and brought the big car in to the verge by the clump of trees. He got out, must have seen straight away that the cover was not thick enough to hide the Porsche completely, and turned, hand to eyes, to stare south down the valley. He stood like that for only a second or two before he whipped back into the car, slammed the door, and was gone in his turn over the bridge and out of sight down the twisting road.

It was a safe guess that he had glimpsed the white car on the road ahead. And it was anybody's guess how long it would take for him to catch it. I reflected that a professional driver who must know the road like the palm of his hand might well be able to cancel out Charles's start, and even the difference in performance between the town car and the Porsche. Four minutes is a long time on the road, but if Charles had really been in a hurry he would hardly have spent so much time in the grove. The racing start could only have been due to high spirits; by now Charles was probably idling happily along admiring the wild hollyhocks on the slopes of the Djebel Ech Sheikh Mandour.

I sat down beside a patch of broom that smelled of wild honey, and ate my lunch. They had given me (besides the rolls stuffed with meat) a paper of black olives and some creamy white cheese and some little ravioli-like pastry envelopes filled with a kind of sausage mixed with herbs. By the time I had eaten as much as I wanted and started on a peach, the road below me was clear of traffic except for another bus—southbound this time—and the gatekeeper was obviously well away on his afternoon snooze. I glanced at my watch. Half past one. And the road still empty either of Hamid or the returning Charles.

And at two o'clock it was still empty. And at half past two.

Nor was there any question, even on the flowery hillside, of a peaceful siesta for me. Two of the Arab youths who had been lounging idly at the corner of the customs buildings had decided at length, after a grinning, nudging conference which I had pretended not to notice, to come up and talk to me. It was probably nothing more than curiosity which drove them, but they had only three or four words of American English, and I had no Arabic at all, so they hung around grinning and staring till my nerve broke and in sheer irritation I got to my feet and began to pick up my things.

I thought I knew what must have happened. Hamid, misled by my outburst of exasperation at the delay, had construed it as acute anxiety for Charles, and imagined trouble where I only saw annoyance. Either he was still determinedly pursuing the Porsche, or there had been some sort of mishap delaying whichever car was on its way back to me. And if I waited much longer and neither of them came, there would be no possibility of my getting to Beirut in time to visit the Sûreté office about a visa, and that would be that.

So when one of the Arab youths, leering, sat down a yard from me on a dusty boulder and said for the dozenth time, "New York? London? Miss?" and then made some remark in Arabic which sent his companion off into fits of mirth, and at the same moment a bus labeled Baalbek ground to a halt below me, I picked up the last of my things, said "Good-bye" politely and finally, and walked downhill to the road.

The thin dog was lying in the shadow of a parked car. He watched me with recognition, but (I thought) without much hope. I dropped the last of the meat rolls beside him as I passed, and saw him snatch it and bolt out of the way of the youths who were following me downhill. The crowd of passengers from the bus were standing about in the heat, apathetically watching as the customs men rifled the household goods of what looked like the entire Exodus. Someone was half-heartedly checking their papers. The gatekeeper let another car through, then relapsed into sleep. Nobody was bothering very much about anything. Even the two youths had abandoned the chase.

I went into the buildings, to be met by the slightly glazed

and wholly unwelcoming stare of the olive-coloured gentleman behind the counter. It took a few minutes before I could find someone in the crowd with sufficient English to pass on what I wanted to ask, but I managed eventually.

"The bus," I said, "what time does it get to Baalbek?"

"Half past three."

"Is there one that goes from here to Beirut?"

"Oh, yes."

"At what time?"

"Five." A shrug. "Perhaps a little later. It gets there at six."

I thought for a moment. Baalbek was well off the direct road home, but there would be a good chance of getting a car there, and taking the shorter route back to Beirut through the mountains. That way I should be there long before the problematic five o'clock bus. In any case I had no desire to sit here for another two hours or so. Even the bus would be preferable.

"Will there be a taxi to hire, or a self-drive car, in Baalbek?"

"Surely." But he qualified it with a shrug. "Well, you must understand, it is late in the day, but possibly . . ."

"Where do I find the taxis?"

"At the temples, or in the main street. Or ask at the Adonis Hotel, just where the bus stops."

I remembered the Adonis Hotel. It was where the group had gone for lunch on Friday, and the manager, I remembered, had spoken reasonably good English.

I asked, "Where is the Sûreté in Beirut?"

"In the Rue Badaro."

"What time does it close?"

But here we stuck. "One o'clock" was the first dismaying answer. Then, from someone else, "Five o'clock." Then again, "It opens again at five o'clock till eight." "No, no, till seven." Then, with shrugs all round, "Who knows?"

Since the last guess was obviously the most accurate of the

lot, I abandoned the questions, to add my postscript. "If my
driver, or anyone else, comes back asking about me, tell him
I've gone back to the Sûreté office in the Rue Badaro in
Beirut, and then to my hotel, the Phoenicia. I'll wait there.
Compris?"

They admitted it was *compris,* so I left them to it, said a
thank you all round, and went out.

The bus's engine was roaring, and a cloud of black smoke
poured from the exhaust. There was no time to do more than
look quickly up the road for a white Porsche or a black taxi
and to get in. Six seconds later, with a horrible shaking roar
and a smell of soot, we were heading for Bar Elias and the
Bk'aa road to Baalbek.

It was a horrible journey, and it ended perforce where the
bus finished its run, in some dirty hot street within shouting
distance of the ruined temples, and just in front of the portals
of the Adonis Hotel.

I got out of the bus, shaking the creases from my skirt with
a strong feeling that I was dislodging fleas from it in clouds.
The bus went off to turn, the other passengers dispersed, and
the filthy black fumes slowly cleared from the air. The street
was empty except for a big, sleek black car parked at the
curb, and just beyond it, incongruously, a white camel with a
ragged Arab holding the headrope.

He bore down on me now, with a shrill stream of Arabic
interspersed with a few English words, from which I gathered
that I was being offered a ride on his camel for the paltry sum
of five English pounds or more. I beat him off with some
difficulty, parried his offer to pose for a snapshot for only ten
shillings, and ran up the steps into the hotel.

I was lucky to find the manager himself was still around,
and not absent, as might have been expected, on siesta. I
found him in the little graveled court that did duty as a
restaurant garden, sitting with a companion at one of the
small tables under the pines, drinking beer. He was a small-

ish round-faced Arab with a thin line of moustache and various chunks of Beiruti gold about his person. His companion, whom at first I barely noticed, looked English.

The manager rose and came hurrying to meet me. "Madame—mademoiselle? You are back again? But I thought your party had left the Lebanon?"

"Good heavens, you recognized me?" I exclaimed. He was bowing over my hand with every appearance of joy. You'd have thought I'd spent a month in the hotel's best suite with all found, not merely bought a drink to take with the group's packed lunch a few days ago. "What a memory you've got! I'd have thought you had so many tourists here that you wouldn't even see them any more!"

"How could I forget you, mademoiselle?" The bow, the gallant look, assured me without a hint of offense that he meant it. He added, frankly, "As to that, I have only been here since the beginning of this season. So far, I remember all my guests. Please—will you sit down? Will you join us, it will be a pleasure?"

But I hung back. "No, thank you very much—there was something I wanted to ask you. I'm here on my own today, and I wanted some help, so I thought I would come to you."

"Of course. Please tell me. Anything. Of course."

He obviously meant it, but to my dismay, as soon as I began to explain my difficulty and mentioned a car, he made a *moue* of doubt, and spread his hands.

"I will do all I can, naturally . . . but at this time of day most of the local cars are already hired and gone. It is possible you may find one at the temples—do you speak Arabic?"

"No."

"Then I will send someone with you to help you. There may be a car still there. If not—perhaps I can find one— perhaps one of my friends, even . . . It is urgent?"

"Well, I do rather want to get to Beirut as soon as possible."

"Then please do not worry, mademoiselle. Of course I will do for you whatever I can. I am glad that you felt you could come here for help. I would offer to telephone for you now, but as it happens I had to get a car only ten minutes ago for one of my guests, and I had difficulty. But in another twenty minutes, perhaps, or half an hour, it will be worth trying again."

"Forgive me." It was his companion who spoke. I had forgotten all about him, and turned in surprise as he set down his beer glass and rose. "I couldn't help overhearing. If you really are anxious to get to Beirut, and there's any difficulty at all, I'm going that way and would be delighted to offer you a lift."

"Why, thank you—" I was slightly taken aback, but the manager intervened quickly, sounding relieved and pleased.

"Of course, that would be excellent! An excellent idea! May I perhaps introduce you? This is Mr Lovell, mademoiselle. I'm afraid I don't know your name."

"Mansel. Miss Mansel. How do you do, Mr Lovell?"

"How do you do?" His voice was English and cultured. He was a man of rather less than middle height, somewhere in his forties, with a face made Arab-olive by the sun, and dark hair receding from a high forehead. He was well dressed in a light-weight grey suit and silk shirt, and wore heavy-rimmed dark glasses. Something about him was faintly familiar, and I thought I must have met him somewhere before.

Even as the thought crossed my mind he smiled and confirmed it. "As a matter of fact we've met before, though without an introduction, and I don't suppose you remember it."

"I'm afraid I don't, but I did have a feeling I'd met you. Where?"

"In Damascus, last week. Was it Wednesday—or perhaps Thursday? Yes, it was Thursday, in the morning in the Great Mosque. You were with a group then, weren't you? I'd been

225

talking to your guide while you ladies were admiring the carpets, and then he had to intervene in some minor international incident, and we exchanged a word or two while it was going on. You wouldn't remember, why should you? But do tell me, did the stout lady allow herself to be parted from her shoes in the end?"

I laughed. "Oh, that's what you meant by an 'international incident'! Yes, she did, and even admitted she wouldn't have wanted all that crowd walking on *her* carpets in outdoor shoes. There was a bit of a scene, wasn't there? I thought I knew your voice. That's it, then."

"You're on your own today?"

"Yes. In fact, I won't make a story of it now, but that's the reason why I'm stranded here today looking for a car. Do you mean you're really going straight to Beirut?"

"Certainly." He moved one square, well-kept hand to indicate the car parked at the edge of the road below the garden wall. I saw now that it was a black Renault with an Arab impassive at the wheel in native dress and white kaffiyeh. "If I can be of any help to you, I'll be delighted. I was intending to leave within a few minutes anyway. Of course, if you want to stay and see the sights here first, then you might prefer to take a chance of getting a taxi later, and Mr. Najjar will probably be able to help you." He smiled. "Any other day I'd have been delighted to show you the place myself, but as it happens I have an engagement in the city that I daren't cry off, so I'm driving straight down now."

"It's terribly good of you, and I'd love to come with you," I said. "I've seen Baalbek before—I was here with the group on Friday—but in any case I'm anxious to get back to the city as soon as I can."

"Then shall we go?"

The manager came with us to the car, the Arab driver whipped round to open the rear door, and Mr Lovell handed me in, spoke to the man in Arabic, and settled beside me. We said our good-byes to the manager, and the car moved off.

We threaded the narrow streets quickly and skilfully, then gathered speed along the road to Beirut. In a few minutes we had passed the last of the houses crouching among their gardens, and on our right the great sweep of hill and valley stretched brilliant in the afternoon sun. The air through the open window was fresh and cool. I leaned back gratefully.

"Oh, this is heaven after that bus! Have you ever been in one of the local buses?"

He laughed. "No, praise be to Allah, I have not."

"I should have warned you to keep right away from me until I've had a bath."

"I'll take the risk. Where are you staying in Beirut?"

"The Phoenicia. But don't you bother about that, I can get a taxi from anywhere it suits you to throw me out."

"It's no trouble, we'll be passing it."

"Thanks all the same, but as a matter of fact I've a call to make first, in the Rue Badaro. I don't know where it is, but perhaps you do?"

"Yes, of course. Well, that's even simpler, it's practically on the way. The Rue Badaro joins this one just before the *place* where the National Museum is. If we cut through the side streets when we get to the city we can go in that way, and I'll drop you."

"Thank you very much."

His voice betrayed no curiosity. He had given me a brief glance—unreadable because of the dark glasses—when I had mentioned the Rue Badaro, and I thought he must surely know that the Sûreté Générale was there, but he was either too indifferent or too well-bred to question me about my affairs. He asked merely; "What happened to your group?"

"Oh, I didn't break away from them today! I'm only stranded and thrown on your mercy because I hadn't a proper visa and my own car went on . . . that is, there were reasons why I had to send my driver on to Damascus, even if it meant my finding my own way home to Beirut. The group actually left on Saturday, and in a way, that's the cause of the trouble." I explained briefly what had happened about the visa.

"I see. But how extraordinarily awkward. I suppose you have to get a new visa? Then do I gather it's the Sûreté you want in the Rue Badaro?"

"Yes." In spite of myself I cast a worried glance at my watch. "Have you any idea what their hours are?"

He didn't answer immediately, but I saw him give a quick glance at his own wrist, then he leaned forward and said something in Arabic to the driver. The big car surged forward smoothly at an increased pace. Mr Lovell smiled at me. "You should be all right. In any case, I might be able to help you. Stop worrying."

"You? You mean you know someone there?"

"You might say so. I can see how the mistake occurred, it's no one's fault, and I doubt if there will be any difficulty in getting you a new visa. You'll have to pay another half crown, I'm afraid, and wait while they fill in a form or two in triplicate, but that's all it will take. So relax now till we get there. I promise you it'll be all right. And if you like, I'll come in with you and see you through it."

"Oh—would you really? I mean—if you've time? It's terribly good of you!" I found myself stammering in a sort of confusion of relief.

"Think nothing of it," he said calmly. "Do you smoke?"

"No, well, sometimes I do. Thank you, I think I will. Oh, are they Turkish?"

"No, Latakia—it's the best Syrian tobacco. Go on, try it."

I took one, and he lit it for me. The driver, who all this time had said nothing, was smoking already. Mr Lovell lit a cigarette for himself, and leaned back beside me. His lighter I saw, was a gold Flaminia, and the cigarette case had been gold, too. The cuff links in the silk cuffs were of heavy gold with a beautiful, deliberately 'roughed' surface. A man of substance, and certainly a man of easy self-assurance. Someone of importance, perhaps? He had that air. I began to wonder if quite by chance I had found the 'useful contact' in Beirut that I had talked of to Daddy. It certainly seemed as if I could stop worrying about the Sûreté and the visa.

He was silent, half turned away to look out of his window. We sat for a while smoking in silence, while the big car sped silently south and west, then took the High Lebanon pass in its stride and began to nose downhill towards the distant sprawl of Beirut. I was content to sit back in silence and stop thinking. This was an interval, a gap in time, a moment to free-wheel before the next effort. And the next effort would be eased for me by the pleasant and competent Mr Lovell.

It was only then, as I found myself relaxing, brittle tension melting like toffee into a sweet goo of softened bone and nerve and sleepy muscle, that I realized how taut and tight-strung I must have been, how senselessly, uselessly keyed up to meet something which could have been no more than a challenge of my own imagination. Something I had let Hamid see and feel, and which, because he had over-interpreted me, I had been left to sort out on my own. Well, I seemed to be doing just that . . . and meanwhile the car sailed on at speed, and the sun beat warm and heavy through the window, and the breeze stirred the ash in grey dust from my cigarette and feathered the smoke away in veils of blue nylon, and I was content to lift a lazy hand to wave it away from my eyes, then drop the hand, palm up, into my lap while I leaned back, tranquil, without thought.

My companion, seemingly as relaxed as I, was turned away from me gazing out at the view on his side of the car. Here the steep hillside fell away from the road in an abrupt sweep of rock-strewn green to the dark sprawl of forest and the gleam of running water. Beyond the forested stream the land rose again through terraced fields of gold and green and dark-gold to more stony heights, and the grey seams of snow. The poplars along the road's edge flashed and winked past like telegraph posts, bare and lacy against the far snow and the hot blue sky.

"Good Lord!"

Mr Lovell, who had been gazing out almost dreamily, now stiffened to attention, whipped off his dark glasses, craned his neck further, and shaded his eyes to stare down the mountainside.

"What is it?"

"Nothing, really—rather a pretty sight, that's all. And not quite so out of place here as one might think." He gave a short laugh. "It still goes on, of course, the high romance— Haroun Al Raschid and the perfumes of Arabia and blood on the roses. It's an Arab riding down there with a pair of Persian greyhounds, you know them?—salukis, beautiful things. How very dramatic."

I didn't for the moment take in what he was saying. I was fiddling with the ashtray in the back of the seat in front of me, trying to stub out my cigarette.

He added: "He ought to have a hawk on his wrist, probably has, but it's too far away for me to see."

I looked up quickly. "Did you say a rider with two salukis? *Here?*"

It must be pure coincidence, of course. We must be miles on the wrong side of Beirut, and Dar Ibrahim was a long way away. It couldn't be John Lethman and the salukis. But it was enough of a strange coincidence to make me sit up straighter and say: "Where? Can I see?"

I had to lean right across him to see down the hill. He sat back to let me do so, indicating a point well below us and some way off.

The car was sliding smoothly round the outside of a bend. The road was bounded by neither wall nor fence, its verge only a yard of dried clay where thistles grew between the poplars, and beyond this the steep mountain-side. I peered down.

"I can't see anything. What's the colour of the horse?"

"Bright chestnut." He pointed again. "There, look, just going into the trees. Quick. The man's in white. See?"

I strained to see where his right hand pointed. As I leaned close across him his left arm came quietly round me and held me fast.

For a moment I thought he was supporting me against the swing of the car on the bend. Then—incredulously, as his arm tightened—that this was a heavy pass; and I stiffened against it and tried to pull away. He held me, the arm like iron, his hand now gripping my left arm and holding it helpless. With my body pressed to his my right arm was imprisoned against him.

"If you keep still you won't be hurt."

The voice, whispering now, was recognizable. The eyes, too, uncovered and staring into mine. The long nose, the olive face that would look pale in lamplight . . .

But it was mad. If it was mad to suppose John Lethman was riding out here forty miles from Dar Ibrahim it was still madder to suppose that my Great-Aunt Harriet, disguised as a man of forty-odd, was holding me with this ferocious strength with one hand, while the other came up holding something that gleamed . . .

I screamed. The Arab driver drove smoothly on without even turning his head. He took a hand off the wheel to tap ash into the tray under the fascia-board.

"What are you doing? Who are you?" Gasping and twisting in his grip, I fought as hard as I could, and the car rocked, swinging wide on the next bend. But there was nothing coming. There was nothing on the road.

The dizzy swoop of the car round the bends, cliff on one side, open sky on the other, like the flight of a fulmar through an empty bright afternoon; the flicking pulse of shadow as the poplars whipped by; the unheeding silence of the Arab driver . . . all these combined in some curiously merciful way to insulate me from the nightmare of what could not—could not possibly—be happening.

He was grinning. From a few inches away, his teeth looked obscene, like something in a horror film. Great-Aunt Harriet's eyes blinked and glittered as he fought to hold me.

"Who are you?" It was a last gasp on the edge of hysteria, and I saw him recognize the fact. His voice was smooth. He had me still now, boneless, dumb.

"You remember now, of course. I told you we'd met before, but we weren't introduced properly. Henry Lovell Grafton, if you want it in full . . . Mean anything to you? Yes, I thought it might. And now hold still, or I'll hurt you."

On the phrase his right hand flashed down at my bare arm. Something pricked, clung stinging, was withdrawn. He dropped the hypodermic into his pocket and smiled again, holding me tightly.

"Pentothal," he said. "Being a doctor has its uses. You have ten seconds, Miss Mansel."

Chapter Fourteen

. . . Nor do I know how long it is
(For I have lain entranced I wis.)
                    —S. T. COLERIDGE: *Christabel*

I WAS TO FIND that Dr Henry Grafton had a habit of overestimating. It took about seven seconds to put me under, and when I woke it was to near-darkness, the thick closeness of a shut and windowless room lit only by the faint light from a small barred opening high in the wall above the door.

At first, of course, the waking seemed normal. I opened blurred eyes on a dark wall where shadows moved slightly like rags in a draught. It was warm and very quiet, a heavy airless quiet that slowly conveyed to me the sense of being shut in. A small fluttering, like that of a moth against a pane, pattered into my consciousness through the layers of drugged sleep. It worried me. I must move and let the poor creature out. I must open the window and let in the air . . .

But not yet; I wouldn't move just yet. My body felt slack and heavy, my head was aching, and I was cold. This last had its own compensations, for when I put a hand to my throbbing forehead the hand was damply cool, and comforting. I was, I found, lying on blankets. I scruffled a couple of these over myself, and turned on my face, cold hands against cheeks and forehead. The heavy lassitude of the drug still possessed me, and in a vague way—nothing was other than vague—I was thankful for it. I had an idea that something large, dark, and terrifying loomed and gibbered just out of reach; but something in me refused to face it yet. I checked my groping mind, shut my eyes against the blankets, and thought of sleep . . .

I have no idea how long it was before I came back to consciousness the second time: I imagine it was no great while. This time the return was final, sharp, and altogether frightening. I was suddenly wide awake, and fully aware of all that had happened. I even knew where I was. I was back at Dar Ibrahim. The smell told me, seconds before my brain caught up with my senses—dead air and dust and lamp-oil, and the indefinable sharp smell of Great-Aunt Harriet's tobacco. I was in one of the storerooms under the Seraglio lake, behind one of those massively locked doors in the underground passage where Charles and I had gone exploring to find the Prince's Divan . . .

That was it. That was the gibbering thought that had lain in wait for my return from the dead; the thought I had been refusing to face.

The interview in the Prince's Divan. Great-Aunt Harriet. Henry Grafton . . . I could only think of one reason for Henry Grafton's grotesque masquerade to fob off my persistence, for the dusty abandonment of the Chinese treasures and the beloved books, even for the glimpse I had had of the ruby ring on Halide's hand. Something had happened to my Great-Aunt Harriet which this gang had been at pains to hide. Not just ill, or even crazy—they must have known they needn't fear her family when it came to Will-making, and wherever Lethman and Halide might stand, I didn't think this was Henry Grafton's concern. And surely the risks were

234

too great for the rewards? Nor could she be a prisoner, like me; there had been no attempt to stop me wandering where I wished through the palace by daylight.

Well, then, she was dead. And for some reason the death had had to be concealed. At the moment, my skin crawling with cold in that warm airless dungeon, I could only think of one reason for that. But whatever it was that had necessitated the masquerade and the midnight prowling, and now the elaborate operation that had hauled me back into the net, I was soon going to find out—the hard way.

And Charles who had apparently, heaven knows how, suspected the truth—Charles was miles away, heading for Damascus with Hamid after him. Even if Hamid caught him up and persuaded him to come back for me, it would be some time before they would find my trail. No one would miss me at the Phoenicia; and Ben had said "Come when you can . . ."

Christy Mansel, sunk without trace.

Like Great-Aunt Harriet and her little dog Samson. Or like the Gabriel Hounds, locked away in the dust of the rotting palace for ever . . .

This was sheer crying stupidity, the drug reducing me when I could afford it least to a useless contraption of slack nerves and jellied bone. I slapped the nerves down hard, sat up, and tried to look about me.

Gradually, the place took shape. A few feet of dusty floor near the bed where the dim light fell, a low ceiling hung with webs, a stretch of rough stone wall where a tumble of leather and metal—harness, perhaps?—hung from a rusty hook. The tiny flickering sound came again from outside, the fluttering of a wick in an oil lamp. The weak light wavered through the tiny grating to drown within a yard or two in thick darkness where, faintly, could be seen stacked shapes of crates, boxes, tins like small petrol cans . . .

I had certainly been right about where I was. The ventilator must look out on lamplight in the underground corridor, and the door below it would be one of those massively barred affairs with the uncompromising locks that Charles and I had seen. There would be no questioning that door. And there was, of course, no window.

The silence was intense, thick and suffocating like the stillness one finds in caves, the silence of underground. I held myself still, listening. My body felt stiff and sore here and there, as if there were bruises, but the headache was gone, to be followed by an awareness which at that moment was worse and more painful, a feeling of quickness, a light aliveness and nerve-end vulnerability, like a snail that has been torn from its shell and wants nothing better than to creep back inside.

The silence was complete. There was no way of telling if anyone else was still about in the palace. You would think I had been buried alive.

The cliché slipped through my mind without thought, then struck home like a poisoned dart, as with it came the quick vision of the rock above me, the tons of rock and earth with the heavy sheet of water lying over it. Man-made; fallible; rotten, probably, as the rest of the place was rotten. The weight must be terrific. If there was the slightest flaw in the rock above me, the slightest movement of earth—

Then with the rush of cold prickling over my skin, I heard it through the dead silence, the tick of settling earth.

I was on my feet, rigid and sweating, before commonsense broke over me like a breath of sweet air. The ticking was merely my watch. I stretched up on tiptoe near the door, holding my wrist high towards the ventilator. I could just see it. The little familiar face was like a friend, the familiar tick brought sanity and the knowledge that it was a few minutes short of six o'clock. It had been just on four in the afternoon when I had accepted the lift from Henry Grafton. I had been unconscious for more than twelve hours.

I put a hand down to the door and, for what it was worth, tried it. The latch lifted silk-smooth, but the door never budged a millimeter. This was so much a foregone conclusion that I hardly registered it with any emotion at all. I was conscious all the time of the positive effort involved in keeping at bay the image of the tons of rock and water pressing down over my head.

The sound which a little while ago I had been dreading came now like the lifting of a nightmare. A key in the lock.

When the door opened smoothly, in that accustomed, well-oiled silence, I was sitting, I hoped composedly, on the bed, trying to conceal with a straight back and poker face that I couldn't have trusted my legs to let me stand. My lips were dry and my heart thumping. What I expected I have no idea. But I was afraid.

It was John Lethman, carrying a lamp, and behind him Halide, as ever with a tray. I smelled soup and coffee as soon as the door opened. If I had thought about it, I'd have expected to be ravenously hungry, but I wasn't. He put the lamp up in a wall niche, and the girl came past him to set the tray down on a packing case. She let her big kohl-rimmed eyes slide sideways to look at me, and I saw pleasure there. The smile reached the corners of her mouth in a malicious little curl. The silk of her dress shimmered, bordered with gold, and I was sharply reminded of what my own state must be, crumpled from the blankets and with my hair all anyhow. I ignored her stonily, and said abruptly to Lethman:

"What's happened to her?"

"To whom?"

"To Great-Aunt Harriet, of course. Don't try to keep the charade up, I know your beastly pal was masquerading. Where's my aunt?"

"She died."

"Died?" I said sharply. "Was murdered, do you mean?"

From the corner of my eye I saw Halide's silks shimmer as she started, and Lethman turned quickly to look down at me. His back was to the lamp, and I couldn't see him clearly, but his voice was edged with nerves. "Don't be melodramatic. Naturally I meant no such thing. She died of natural causes."

"Melodramatic! Look who's talking, what with your underground prisons and your sloe-eyed charmer there and your dear little pantomime dame upstairs with his White Slaver techniques. Natural causes my foot," I said angrily, "be precise. What did she die of and when?"

He said stiffly: "I'm not going to answer questions. Dr Grafton was her doctor, he'll explain."

"By God he will," I said.

He had been moving towards the door, but my tone brought him round again to face me. The light was on him now. I saw in his face a sort of startled reappraisement, even a kind of alarm, and he opened his mouth to say something, then shut it again without speaking. I thought he looked as edgy as his voice, a down-drawn look, with pouched flesh under the eyes that betrayed lack of sleep, and lines which I had not noticed before and which had no business to be there. What had certainly not been there before was the swollen bruise at the corner of his mouth and a nasty-looking mark like a weal from the cheekbone to the ear. I was just taking this in when Halide said, quickly and venomously:

"Don't let her talk to you like that. You are the master here."

I laughed. "It looks like it, doesn't it? For a start, who's been knocking you about? And you think I'm the one who's in trouble? Well, you'll learn. And I do assure you it'll pay you to listen to me and get me out of here. I should like to go now. At once, please."

He drew a sharp little breath, either of anger or effort. His voice was deliberately braced. "I'm sure you would. But you'll stay here just the same. Dr Grafton will see you later."

"He'll see me now. After I've had a wash. And what's more, I should like my handbag back."

"It's there by the bed. Now stop being stupid, you must see

you've got to do as you're told. There's some food. We'll leave you now, and if you've got any sense you'll take it quietly. If you behave yourself you'll come to no harm. All right, Halide."

"I don't want the blasted food!" I said angrily. "Will you stop behaving like Oddjob and take me to the bathroom?"

"Later." Halide was going, sliding out past him with a final gleam at me which made me want to slap her face. John Lethman was going too, closing the door.

I stood up and said sharply: "Don't be such a clot, Mr Lethman. I want to go to the loo. You know—the loo, the lavatory, W. C. . . . do I really have to spell it out?"

"Oh." He paused, and I saw with pleasure that he looked once more disconcerted. It seemed obvious that he had expected, possibly even braced himself for, a scene along set lines of outrage and perhaps fear, and that this intrusion of commonplace reality into his thriller-situation had thrown him completely. He said at length, lamely: "Oh, well, you'd better come along, I suppose. But don't try anything. And it won't do you any good—"

" 'And it won't do you any good to scream for help, because I have a hundred Nubian guards within call?' " I finished the threat with a derision that got him right between the eyes, and sent my own morale rocketing. "Come off it and take me to the lavatory, Commander of the Faithful."

He made no reply. I laughed again, and went out past him. My exit was spoiled by the fact that I stumbled in the dim light over a broken flagstone, and my head swam dizzily with the aftermath of the drug. He took my arm, and I controlled the impulse to shake him off. For one thing, I needed the help; for another, he was probably determined to hang on to me, and I might as well go on turning the tables by treating the gesture as one of solicitude. So I thanked him and allowed him to escort me from the room. I don't know whether Halide followed: I didn't glance her way.

I had been right. This was the corridor under the lake, and my door one of the locked storerooms. There was the pile of tins still outside it. John Lethman led me up the stairs towards Great-Aunt Harriet's room. As we reached the heavy curtain and he drew it aside to disclose the bed, I gave an exclamation of surprise.

"Don't pretend you didn't know the way," he said sourly.

"I'm not pretending anything," I said. This was the truth; what had amazed me was the light. It was not early morning, as I had expected, but golden afternoon, six o'clock of a blazing day. And it must be the same blazing day on which I had set out for Damascus or my watch would have stopped by now. The pentothal had laid me out for barely two hours.

John Lethman stepped carefully through onto the dais, and handed me after him. I added: "I'm just surprised it's daylight still. It feels like a month since I was out in the open air and in pleasant company. Tell me one thing, Mr Lethman, how did you get me here? Don't tell me you carried me over from the village in broad daylight."

"The car didn't touch Beirut at all, or Sal'q. There's a road off past Zahle, and after that a quite negotiable track up behind the head of the valley. You only had to be brought down a couple of kilometers or so from the car."

"Down the path behind the palace? I suppose that's why I'm as stiff as a board. What did you bring me on, a mule?"

Absurd though it may seem, I think I was angrier at that moment then I had been almost through the whole affair, angry and ashamed. There was humiliation in the knowledge of how these men had manhandled my unconscious and helpless body. So far, the thought made me want to run away and hide; but perhaps later on the anger would help.

He said: "The bathroom's this way."

It was the next door opening off the Prince's Garden. I escaped into the labyrinth of the hammam like a rabbit scuttling down a safe burrow.

It had in its day been a grander hammam than the women's quarters had boasted. The walls were alabaster, and the light came from overhead in all the rooms from lozenges of stained glass which threw jewels of amber and jade and lapis onto the rosy floors. The sunshine, muted by this, glowed among the labyrinth of peach-coloured columns like light through a transparent shell, and the murmur of water trickling through the shallow channels and dripping into marble basins echoed like the sea in the corridors of a cave.

The cool touch of the water, the light, the blinding glimpse of the little garden as I had crossed to the hammam, dispelled immediately the claustrophobic nightmare of my prison. I threaded my way through the complex of rooms to the center of the cool stone maze. Here water splashed and glittered into a blackened shell that had once been silver, and a stone faun leaned out with a cup of wafer-thin alabaster. I took it from him, filled it, and drank, then took off everything but pants and bra and washed deliciously in the cool water, drying myself on my slip. The sunlight swimming down in its shafts of amber and amethyst seemed to soak into my body like oil, smoothing away the stiffness of the bruises. I shook my frock out and put it on, did my face and hair, and last of all dried my feet and put my sandals on again. I dropped the soaked slip in a corner, took another drink of water, rinsed the cup for the faun, then went out to meet John Lethman.

He was sitting on the edge of the dry fountain. I had only previously seen this garden at night, and now I got no more than a brief impression of a maze of yellow roses and a tumble of honeysuckle over broken pillars. John Lethman got quickly to his feet and started to speak but I cut across it abruptly.

"You needn't think you're going to get me back into that foul little room again. If this Dr Grafton wants to see me, he can see me here. What's more he can see me now, in daylight. He needn't pretend any more that he likes staying up half the night, so he can leave his turban and his nightie off." I marched past him into Great-Aunt Harriet's bedroom, flinging over my shoulder: "And if you want me to eat anything you can make that girl bring it in here."

He hesitated, and I thought he was going to insist. But he said merely: "As long as you realize that this part of the palace is locked right away. If you do try to bolt you won't go far, and even if you hid, the dogs would find you."

I laughed. "And tear me limb from limb? Big deal!"

I crossed to the red lacquer chair, and sat down with as much of the grand manner as I could muster, while Lethman, with a look of acute dislike at me, mounted the dais to pull the bell.

The familiar jangling peal bounced and ricocheted through the stillness, and, inevitably, the clamour from the hounds tore the afternoon to shreds. Somehow, the noise was comforting; they were on my side, the 'Gabriel Hounds', Aunt H's dogs who had known my voice and my cousin's step, and who (I saw it now as the thought lit my mind like a sudden flare) perhaps disliked 'the Dr' as much as Samson had done, and so were kept shut away except when on guard at night to keep the nosy Miss Mansel within bounds.

Before the echoes of the bell had died the bed curtains were pulled violently back and Henry Grafton came through the private door like a genie erupting from the lamp, and said furiously: "What the hell's happened to that girl? The door's wide open, and if she gets as far as the main gate that idiot's probably forgotten his orders by now, and he'll see her on her way with an illuminated address."

"It's all right," said Lethman, "she's here."

Dr Grafton came up short like someone running into a wire, and swung round on me where I sat in the high-backed chair. For a nasty moment I thought he was going to come and grab, but he seemed to hold himself in with an effort, and gave me instead a long summing-up look that I by no means liked.

"What's she doing here?" He spoke to John Lethman without taking his eyes off me.

"She asked for the bathroom."

"Oh." The simple demand of nature seemed to disconcert Henry Grafton as much as it had Lethman himself. He teetered there on the edge of the dais, seemingly at a loss, while I sat poker-spined on my chair, trying to look several degrees cooler than an ice cube, and preparing to fight every step of the way should they decide to force me back into my dungeon.

"You rang?" said Halide, at the garden door. At least I suppose that's what she said, it was in Arabic. She was wearing Great-Aunt Harriet's ring.

She was looking at Grafton, but I answered in English. "Yes, we rang. Not for you, but since you're here you might as well bring the tray in here for me. I don't want the soup, thank you, but I'll eat the bread and cheese, and I wouldn't mind a cup of coffee while I'm talking to him."

She spat something at me—no pretenses now—and whirled furiously on the men:

"You're not going to leave her out here? Why don't you put her back in the room and shut her up again? Why do you let her sit there like that and give orders? Who does she think she is? She is nobody, I tell you, nobody, and very soon she will know it! When we get her—"

"Look, Halide—" It was John Lethman, feebly, but she ignored him, blazing at Grafton.

"*You* are afraid of her too? Why? Dare you not leave her there? Then why not give her some more of the drug and put her in the other prison? Or tie her up? I would do it, me!"

"Oh, belt up," I said wearily. "Never mind about the tray, I can last out, just stop yelling and making me feel like an extra in *Kismet*, will you? And I'd still like the coffee. You

243

can heat it up again before you bring it. I dislike lukewarm coffee."

The look she gave me this time was pure bastinados and boiling oil and I was glad to have deserved it. She swung back to Grafton, simmering like a kettle, but he cut her short. "Shut up and do as you're told. John, for God's sake can't you clout some sense into her? It won't be long now." He added something in Arabic to Halide, more conciliatory in tone, and there was a brief exchange which seemed to mollify her. After a while she went, scowling.

John Lethman gave a sigh, half of relief, half of exasperation. "Sorry about that. She's been like a snake with the jitters for days. She'll come to heel when the time comes." He dabbed at his face, winced, and dabbed again. "Shall I take the Mansel girl back?"

"Not for the moment. You can get on. I'll talk to her here. And afterwards—" he finished the sentence in Arabic, and John Lethman nodded. His reply was wordless and quite horrible. He merely drew the edge of his hand across his throat in a murderous little gesture, and Henry Grafton laughed.

"If you can," he said in English. "All right, *ruh*."

Lethman went out. I wanted to keep what miserable initiative I could, so I spoke immediately. My voice came out harsh and high with nerves, and surprisingly formidable.

"Well, supposing you start, Dr Grafton. You've got quite a bit of explaining to do, haven't you?"

Chapter Fifteen

---◈---

So bury me by some sweet Garden-side.
> —E. FITZGERALD: *The Rubáiyát of*
> *Omar Khayyám*

HE DIDN'T ANSWER FOR A MOMENT. He stood there eyeing me
under dropped lids, still with that appraising, almost clinical
look. His eyes were dark and shiny as treacle, and in contrast
the heavy lids looked thick and waxen. The skin all round
the eyes was brownish, like overripe plums.

"Well?" I said curtly.

He smiled. "You're a fighter, aren't you? I admire you for
it."

"You excite me beyond words. Sit down and get on with
it." He stepped down from the dais and crossed the room to
get a chair which stood against the wall. He had changed his
neat businessman's suit for dark trousers and a high-necked
Russian shirt in olive green which made him look sallower,
and did nothing to flatter his thick build. He looked very
strong, with strength in the back of his neck, like a bull. My
rudeness didn't even ruffle him. His manner was perfectly
civil, pleasant even, as he brought the chair over and sat
himself opposite me.

"Cigarette?"

"No, thank you."

"It'll help compose your nerves."

"Who said they needed composing?"

"Oh, come, Miss Mansel, I thought you were a realist."

"I hope I am. All right. There, my hand's shaking. Please you?"

"Not at all." He lit my cigarette, and waved out the match. "I'm sorry I had to do what I did. Please be sure I don't mean you any harm. I just had to get you back here and talk to you."

"You had to—?" I opened my eyes at him. "Oh, come off it, Dr Grafton! You could have talked to me in the car. Or you could have talked to me before I left Dar Ibrahim, if you were going to drop the disguise anyway." I leaned back, drawing on my cigarette. The gesture helped to give me the extra touch of confidence I needed, and I felt my nerves beginning to relax. "I must say, I liked you a lot better in that neat little number you were wearing the other night. I quite see why you only interviewed guests at midnight. You and the room looked a lot better in the dark."

As far as the room was concerned this was certainly true. What could have passed in the lamplight for romantic shabbiness was shown up by daylight as plain dirt and neglect. The bed hangings were tattered and filthy, and the table beside me was sordid in the extreme with used cups and plates and a saucer half-full of cigarette stubs. "Well, all right," I said, still aggressively, "let's have it. And start at the beginning, please. What happened to Aunt Harriet?"

He looked at me frankly and showed an apologetic hand. "Be sure I'm only too willing to tell you everything. I admit you've every ground for suspicion and anger, but believe me it's only on your own account, and I'll explain that in a moment. As far as your great-aunt is concerned there's nothing to worry you, nothing at all. She died quite peacefully.

You know of course that I was her doctor: I was with her all the time, and so was John."

"When did she die?"

"A fortnight ago."

"What of?"

"Miss Mansel, she was over eighty."

"I dare say she was, but there has to be a cause. What was it, heart? This asthma of hers? Plain neglect?"

I saw him compress his lips slightly, but he answered with the same pleasant appearance of frankness. "The asthma was a fiction, Miss Mansel. The most difficult thing for me to disguise was my voice. When John told me how persistent you were, and we realized you might be impossible to fob off, we concocted a story that would allow me to speak in a whisper. And, as you must realize now, the picture I had to give you of a forgetful and very strange old lady was far from the truth. Your aunt was very fully in possession of her faculties right up to the time of her death."

"What was it, then?"

"Primarily her heart. She had a very slight coronary last autumn, and another in late February—after I had come to live with her here. Then, as you may know, she was difficult about food, and latterly had periodic sickness and stomach trouble which added to the strain. She had one of these gastric attacks three weeks ago, a bad one, and her heart wouldn't take it. That's the story, as simply as I can put it. She was, I repeat, over eighty. One would hardly have expected her to get through."

I said nothing for a moment, drawing on my cigarette and staring at him. Then I said abruptly: "Death certificates? Do you have them here?"

"Yes, I signed one, for the record. You can see it any time you wish."

"I wouldn't believe a word of it. You concealed her death,

you and John Lethman and the girl. One might even say you went to pretty fair lengths to conceal it. Why?"

He turned up a hand. "Heaven knows I don't blame you, in the circumstances I wouldn't believe a word of it myself; but the plain fact is that, far from wanting your great-aunt out of the way, I'd have done a lot—in fact I did do a lot—to keep her alive. I don't ask you to believe me when I tell you that I liked her, but you may believe me when I tell you that her death was damned inconvenient, coming when it did, and could have cost me a fortune. So I had a base motive for keeping her alive as well." He tapped ash on the floor. "Hence the mystery and the masquerade, which I'll explain in a moment. It didn't suit me to have lawyers or family invading the place, so I didn't report her death, and we've allowed the local people to think she's still alive."

"And then my cousin and I turned up, just at the wrong moment. I see. But the wrong moment for what, Dr Grafton? You really had better start from the beginning, hadn't you?"

He leaned back in the chair. "Very well. I was your great-aunt's doctor for about six years, and for the last three or four of them I came up here once a fortnight, sometimes oftener. She was very fit and active for her age, but she was something of a *malade imaginaire,* and besides, she was old, and I think, in spite of her fanatical independence, a bit lonely. And living alone as she did with the Arab servants I think she must have had some dread of illness or accident that would leave her completely at their—in their charge."

I thought he had been going to say "at their mercy." I thought of Halide wearing the big ruby, of Nasirulla thick-set and tough and sullen, of the idiotically mouthing Jassim. "Yes?" I said.

"So I paid her a regular call, and this set her mind at rest—and besides, she enjoyed the company of a countryman. I may say I enjoyed the visits, too. She could be very entertaining when she was on form."

"And John Lethman? He gave me a version of how he got taken on here, but I don't know if it was true."

"Ah, yes, one of the few occasions where John managed a bit of lightning thinking. You may have guessed that he knows about as much as you do yourself about psychological medicine. He's an archaeologist."

"I . . . see. Hence my great-aunt's interest. Yes. I remember feeling a bit surprised when he talked about a 'loony-bin' . . . They don't, if they know what they're talking about. But the Adonis Gardens?"

"They're genuine enough. You could say they were his premise. The paper he was working on was on the Adonis cult, and I suppose that's what suggested the exercise in morbid psychology—the 'ecstatic religions' nonsense he gave you when he was cornered. Not bad, eh? Apart from that, I believe he told you the truth. He was traveling around doing research for his paper, and camping up near the little temple above the palace, and got caught by a storm one day—just as you were—and came to Dar Ibrahim. Your great-aunt took a fancy to him, and asked him to stay on while he did his work, and without anything much being said on either side he settled down and started looking after the place for her. I must say I was thankful when he decided to settle here. It made my job a lot easier." There was the ghost of a smile I didn't quite like. He tapped ash off his cigarette again, delicately. "A nice boy."

"And useful?"

"Oh, certainly. He made a great deal of difference here. The Lady thought the world of him."

"I'm sure. But I meant to you. Useful to you."

The heavy lids lifted. He gave a tiny shrug. "Oh, yes, to me. I find him an excellent partner in my—business."

"Yes, well, let's come to that now. Your business. You've been at Dar Ibrahim ever since you left Beirut? Yes, it figures. You were the 'resident physician', not John Lethman.

You were 'the doctor' Jassim was talking about when Hamid and I came to the gate . . . John Lethman certainly made a quick recovery from that one! But I was puzzled, because the Gab—the dogs liked him."

"The dogs?"

"Oh, nothing to matter. She sent a letter home in February, did you know? She said her dog 'couldn't abide the doctor'."

"Oh yes, that was the wretched little brute that I—that died. . . . Yes, indeed, I was the 'resident physician'. That was part of the Stanhope legend, as you'll probably know; your great-aunt rather fancied having her own 'Dr Meryon' in attendance." He looked not unamused. "It was a small price to pay. She was entitled to her own legend, even though I didn't quite see myself in the role of that unfortunate man ministering to that monstrous egoism day and night."

"Don't tell me that poor Aunt Harriet made you minister to her monstrous egoism day and night? Even if she had it, which seems likely, since she was a Mansel, she had a sense of humour too."

"Don't try and find motives for me. I told you I liked her." He gave a little twist of a smile. "Though I must admit that she was pushing it a bit the last year or two. On occasions the impersonation could get to be a little trying."

I glanced above the bed to where the stick and the rifle hung. "It'd be too much to hope that she really used them on Halide?"

He laughed, quite genuinely. "She did occasionally throw things at Jassim, but that's about as far as it went. And you mustn't be too hard on Halide. She's working very hard for what she wants."

"John Lethman? Or Dar Ibrahim? Both sacred, I assure you." I leaned forward to stub out my cigarette on the saucer. Then I regarded him for a moment. "You know, I think I do believe you about my great-aunt . . . I mean, I doubt if you

250

meant her any harm. For one thing you don't seem worried about what she may have written in her letters . . . unless you censored all her letters, and I doubt if you did, since I gather she was free to speak to the village people and to the carriers who brought supplies across. You obviously never saw her last letter inviting Charles to visit her, or Humphrey Ford's letter, either."

I half expected him to ask what I was talking about, but he didn't. He was watching me steadily.

"And I'm inclined to pass John Lethman," I said, "but what about the servants? Are you quite sure that Halide didn't have a good reason for wanting the old lady out of the way?"

"No, no, that's nonsense. Your aunt used to be pretty fierce sometimes with the servants—they tend to do nothing at all unless one stands over them—but she liked the girl."

"That wasn't quite what I suggested."

"And Halide looked after her devotedly. I told you your aunt could be difficult, and the late-night sessions really were a fact. The girl was sometimes run off her feet." He waved a hand. "These rooms—they've only been neglected since her death, you must realize that. We cleared them a bit roughly of some of the worst clutter because we wanted to use them— they were naturally the best kept and most central rooms— but there simply wasn't time to clean them up properly before you saw them." A look. "We were glad of the darkness for more reasons than one. Oh, the place was always shabby, and she liked to live in a clutter, but the rooms were kept clean when she was alive . . . my God, they had to be! But to suggest that Halide hated your great-aunt enough to . . . No, Miss Mansel."

He broke off as Halide came in with the tray. She set it down near me on the table with no more than a bit of a rattle, then, without looking at either of us or speaking a word, went straight out of the room. She had taken me at my word and just brought coffee. It was a bit weak, but it was hot and fresh. I poured a cup, and drank some, and felt better.

"What's more," said Henry Grafton, "the same applies to John and Halide as applied to me. They had more reasons to wish the Lady Harriet alive than dead."

"Meaning that they're in your racket with you?"

"You could put it like that."

"Did my great-aunt leave a Will?" I asked bluntly.

He grinned. "She made them every week. Apart from crossword puzzles it was her favourite amusement."

"I knew that. We sometimes got copies. What happened to them all?"

"They'll be somewhere about." He sounded unconcerned. "She used to hide them away in odd corners. I'm afraid this isn't exactly an easy place to search, but you're welcome to try."

I must have looked surprised. "You mean you'll let me look around?"

"Naturally. In fact it's possible that the property now belongs to you—or more probably to your cousin."

"Or to John Lethman?"

He shot me a look. "As you say. She was very fond of him."

"Another of her eccentricities?"

"A very common one. But I'm afraid that there'll be little left of any value. There may be one or two personal souvenirs you may care to unearth from the general chaos, and as I say you're welcome to try."

"Such as the ring that Halide's wearing?"

He looked surprised. "The garnet? You would have liked that? It was certainly your aunt's favourite, she always wore it, but I understood she gave it to Halide . . . well, of course . . . probably Halide wouldn't mind . . ."

"Dr Grafton, please don't think I'm standing with one foot in my aunt's grave, but the ring has what they call 'sentimental value', and I'm pretty sure that the family will fight to get it back. Besides, she meant me to have it. If she did give it to Halide then she must really have been round the bend, and no court would allot it to her."

"Is it so very valuable?"

"I know nothing at all about the value of garnets," I said, momentarily truthful, "but you can take it from me it's not just a keepsake for the maid, however devoted. It belonged to my great-grandmother and I want it back."

"Then you must certainly have it. I'll speak to Halide."

"Tell her I'll get her something to take its place, or there may be something else left she'd like to have."

I put down my cup. There was a pause. Some big insect, a beetle, hurtled in through the bright doorway, blundered around the room for a moment or two, and went out. I felt suddenly very tired, as if the conversation were slipping away from me. I believed him . . . and if I believed him surely the rest didn't make any sense?

"All right," I said at length, "so we come to what's happened since her death. But before we go on, will you show me where she is?"

He got to his feet. "Of course. She's out here in the Prince's Garden, as she wished to be."

He led the way out into the little court, past the dry fountain, through diagonals of sun and shadow and between beds of baked earth where in early spring there would be irises and Persian tulips. Over the high outer wall fell a tangle of white jasmine, and beside it a cascade of yellow roses made a blinding curtain. The scent was wonderful. In the shade thrown by the flowers was a flat white stone, uncarved, and at its head stood the stone turban of the Moslem dead.

I looked at this in silence for a moment. "Is this her grave?"

"Yes."

"No name?"

"There hasn't been time."

"You must know as well as I do that this is a man's grave."

He made a sudden movement, quickly suppressed, but I felt a jerk of apprehension as my body tightened back into wariness. This was still the man who had savaged me in the car, who was playing some nasty game or other where he had a lot at stake. . . . Somewhere, not far below the surface— just under the sweating skin, behind the oil-black eyes—was something not as calm, as pleasant, as Dr Henry Grafton would like me to believe.

But he said with what sounded like gentle amusement: "No, really, I can't have you suspecting me of anything else! You know—of course you do!—that she liked to dress as a man, and indeed behaved like one. I suppose it gave her a kind of freedom in Arab countries that a woman couldn't have normally. When she was younger the Arabs called her 'the Prince' because of the way she rode, and the horses and state she liked to keep. She had this planned"—a gesture to the gravestone—"some time before she died. It was surely part of the same conceit."

I stared in silence at the slender column with its carved turban. Somehow of all that I had seen this was the most alien, the most foreign symbol. I thought of the leaning lichened stones in the old churchyard at home, the big elms, the yews by the lych gate, the rooks blown past the tower in the evening winds. A shower of yellow petals drifted down on the blank hot stones, and a lizard flashed out, palpitated for an instant there, watching us, then vanished.

" 'I have purchased an excellent Tombstone locally'."

"What?" asked Henry Grafton.

"I'm sorry, I didn't realize I'd spoken aloud. You're right, this is what she wanted. And at least she's with friends."

"Friends?"

"In the next garden. The dogs, I saw the graves."

I turned away. The tired feeling persisted. The heavy scented heat, the sound of bees, perhaps still the effects of the injection and the strain of the day, were weighing on me.

"Come back in out of the sun." His dark eyes were peering at me. They looked very intent. "Are you all right?"

"Perfectly. Floating, rather, but it's not unpleasant. Was that only pentothal?"

"That's all. You weren't out for long, and it's quite harmless. Come along."

The room seemed comparatively cool after the trapped heat of the garden. I sat down with relief in the lacquer chair and leaned back. The corners of the room were swimming in shadow. Henry Grafton picked up a glass from the table and poured water into it.

"Drink this. Better? Here, have another cigarette. It'll help you."

I took it automatically, and he lit it for me and then moved away to hitch his chair out of the shaft of sunlight which slanted low now from a window, and sat down again.

I flattened my hands on the carved lacquer of the chair arms. Somehow the little, practiced touch of solicitude had changed the tone of the interview; the doctor-patient gesture had put him back, subtly, on top. I made an effort, through the invading fatigue, to resume the cool accusing tone of attack.

"All right, Dr Grafton. That's the first part of the inquisition over. For the time being I'll accept that my great-aunt's death was a natural one, and that you did all you could. Now we come to why you had to conceal it, what you called the 'mystery and the masquerade' . . . and what you've done to me. You've an awful lot of explaining still to do. Go on."

He regarded his hands for a minute, clasped in his lap. Then he looked up.

"When you rang up my house and were told I was gone, did they tell you anything about me?"

"Not exactly, but they played hell with the silences. I gather you're in trouble."

"True, I was in trouble, so I got out while the going was good. I can think of a lot of places I'd rather be in than a Lebanese prison."

"As bad as that?"

"Oh, quite. A little matter of getting and selling medical supplies illegally. You can get away with murder here more easily."

"You wouldn't just have been deported?"

"That would hardly have helped. As it happens, I'm a Turkish national, and the penalties there are even worse. Take it from me, I had to get out, and fast, before they caught up with me. But I had assets in the country, and I was damned if I left without realizing them. Naturally, I'd been afraid this might happen one day, so I'd made arrangements. Dar Ibrahim had been my center and—shall we call it storeroom?—for some time, and over the past few months I had managed to—" a flick of the brown eyelids and a tiny pause—"engage John's interest. So the actual getaway went smoothly enough. I was driven to the airport and checked in, then someone else took over my ticket and boarded the flight. If you know the airport here you'll know it can be done. John was waiting outside the airport and drove me up here by the back road—the way I brought you today—and I walked down to Dar Ibrahim. Your great-aunt expected me. Naturally I hadn't told her the truth; I spun her some story about an abortion and procuring drugs without charge for certain poorer class patients. Like the Stanhope woman, she had the highest disregard for the laws of this country, so she took me in and kept it secret. She was too delighted to have her doctor here as a permanency to ask many questions, and she talked too much herself to be over-curious about other people. As for the servants—Halide had her eye on John as a one-way ticket out of Sal'q, and her brother was employed by me already. Jassim's silence one hardly has to buy; it takes practice to understand more than one word in twelve, and in any case he's too stupid to know what's going on. So here I was, sitting pretty, with a good base to work from and John's help as outside agent to start cashing in on my assets. It went like a dream, no suspicions, winding up as smoothly as clockwork, cash due to come in, myself due to check out finally at the end of the summer . . ."

He paused. I leaned forward to flick ash into the saucer. It missed, and went on to the table to add to the patina of dust.

He went on: "Then just a fortnight ago came your great-aunt's death. My God, for you to think I'd killed her! I spent nine hours solid at her bedside—right there—fighting for her life like a mother tiger. . . ." He wiped his upper lip. "Well, there you are. She died—and her death could have thrown the doors wide open, and me to the lions. In the end we decided to play it cool—I believe that's the expression nowadays?—and keep her death quiet. We thought we might just get away with it for the couple of weeks that were needed to complete the current operation. I couldn't hope to keep it quiet much longer than that, and the risks were too big. We had to cut our losses and plan a complete get-out in a big hurry—but we did it. What we didn't reckon with was you. Nothing your great-aunt had ever said led us to think we'd have a devoted family hammering at the door within a day or two. But—and just at the wrong moment—you came."

The sun had almost gone, and its last light sloped in a low bright shaft across my feet. Dust motes swirled in it. I watched them half idly. Beyond their quick dazzle the man in the other chair seemed oddly remote.

"We thought at first you'd be easy to fob off," he said, "but you're a persistent young woman, and a tough one. You managed to put the wind up John, and we were afraid you were in a position, if you really got worried, to whistle up all sorts of help and come back armed with lawyers and writs of habeas corpus and God knows what else; so we thought we hadn't much to lose by trying the masquerade, and if it seemed to satisfy you you might keep quiet for the few days' grace we needed. It was a desperate sort of idea, but I thought I might get away with it for a few minutes in semi-darkness, especially with the male clothes she used. In fact it was that habit of hers that gave me the idea in the first place. If we'd refused to let you see your aunt at all, you'd have been convinced she was ill, or that John was keeping you out for his own ends, and if you'd got suspicious enough to bring the doctor or a lawyer from Beirut, we'd have been sunk. So we tried it, and it worked."

I nodded, thinking back over the interview; the hoarse whisper disguising the man's voice, the grotesque glimpses of the balding skull under the turban, the sunken mouth from which presumably he had removed his lower teeth, the alert black eyes. Halide's nervousness and John Lethman's watchful, edgy look had been for none of the reasons I had imagined.

"I get it now," I said. "All that chat of John Lethman's at supper—he was finding out all he could about the family so as to fill you in on things Aunt H didn't tell you. You knew I hadn't seen her since I was a kid, so you thought you'd probably fool me easily enough, but Charles had seen her recently, so naturally 'Great-Aunt Harriet' wouldn't receive him. Oh, yes, clever enough, Dr Grafton." I blew a long cloud of smoke into the air between us. "And as a matter of fact you rather enjoyed it, didn't you? John Lethman tried to hurry me out, and heaven knows I'd have gone, but you wouldn't let me, you were enjoying yourself too much making a fool of me."

He was grinning. Grotesquely, it was Great-Aunt Harriet's face as I had thought of her, vaguely seen through the smoke and the dusty shaft of sunlight, remote as something glimpsed down the wrong end of a telescope.

I said: "Yes, all right, so it worked. You fooled me, and you fobbed Charles off quite successfully, and surely after I'd left the place you were in the clear, so why drag me back? I'd gone, hadn't I, quite satisfied? Why drag me back here like this?"

"Because we hadn't fobbed your cousin off, and you know it. Oh, don't give me that great big innocent look, it doesn't suit you. Shall I tell you what happened? The first time you left here it wasn't your driver who met you, it was your cousin, and between you you hatched the plan to let him in on Monday night. He came, and you explored the place together. Yes, my dear, that stare's a bit more genuine."

"How do you know all this?"

"Your precious cousin told me all about it himself."

I don't think I spoke. I just stared. I couldn't quite take in what he was saying. The room seemed to be swirling round me, smoke and dusty sunlight dazzling like fog.

"After you'd gone back to your room that evening, he was to have left by the back gate—the mountain gate, wasn't he?" Grafton's voice was smooth as cream. "Well, he didn't. John and I came across him in the passageway below here, trying to force one of the padlocked doors. It wasn't much use denying who he was—you're very like one another, aren't you? So we—er, we took him in. He's been safely locked away in the palace prison ever since. It won't surprise you to know the palace has its own gaol? Unhappily there was only one cell serviceable, so when we caught you as well, we had to use the storeroom for you."

"Here? Charles here? I don't believe you. He can't be!" My brain seemed to be groping, like someone feeling through a roomful of smoke, not sure of the direction of the door or the distance to the window. I think I had a hand to my forehead, "You're lying. You know you're lying. He wrote me a letter, and left it for me in Beirut. He went to Damascus to see Ben's father . . . no, to Aleppo. And we saw him—yes we saw him on the way. . . ."

"He certainly wrote you a letter. He suggested doing that himself. If he hadn't done it to ensure you kept away from Dar Ibrahim and didn't start hunting for him when he failed to turn up at the Phoenicia, we couldn't have let you go in the morning."

"Why did you?"

"Your driver," he said shortly, "and your hotel. Your cousin pointed out that it was easier to let you go than to risk someone starting to ask questions. Besides, as he told us, you thought you'd seen your great-aunt alive and well, and could help spread the belief that all was normal."

"So he wrote the letter—all those elaborate lies—he even pretended he'd seen her himself and recognized her . . . I've been wondering about that, I thought he must have seen you and made the same mistake as I did . . . You mean—that letter—it was all quite deliberate? Just to keep me out?"

"Exactly that."

I said nothing. The conversation no longer seemed to have much to do with me. He was still smiling, and as I stared at him, bemused, I saw the grin widen. The top teeth were his own; the incisors were yellowish and long. He was talking again, fragments of information drifting like torn paper to lie in a crazy pattern: John Lethman—no doubt the 'Englishman' seen in the distance by the faun—had driven the Porsche down to Beirut in the early morning, hidden it in someone's backyard, woken the someone whose name seemed to be Yusuf and given him the letter, then been driven back by Yusuf, who later got the letter delivered to the hotel, and went himself to ride herd on me . . .

"But you, my dear, didn't stay out of the line of fire. You made it fairly obvious that you were going to ask some damned awkward questions and make some damned awkward contacts. You even telephoned England. And from what our man heard of your telephone conversation with Damascus, we decided to remove you."

"The Arab in the red tarboosh. He was in the next booth." I said it to myself, not to him.

"Certainly. Well, since you'd made your plans public, and that damned driver was already there with you, and we didn't want any eyes turning to Dar Ibrahim, we decided to get you the wrong side of the frontier and then let you disappear. All very simple, no great harm done—your car stopped, yourselves robbed, your papers taken and the car wrecked . . . somewhere beyond the Antilebanon, we thought, or even off towards Qatana. Yusuf was confident he could immobilize you for long enough. So he got the Porsche out and drove it through to wait. It was the bait, of course. You'd have followed it—"

"Hamid! If you've harmed Hamid—!"

"Not if he's sensible. Most Arabs are, if you make it worth their while." He laughed. "I thought at first your being stopped at the frontier was going to bitch all our plans, but it worked out like a dream. You didn't see me, but I was there, and I saw what happened. My driver followed yours into the frontier buildings and heard the whole thing, so I sent him through to tell Yusuf to go on south and get rid of your cousin's car, but as luck would have it you'd seen it yourself from above the road, and came running down to tell your driver to go through after it. My own car came straight back, and reported he'd crossed yours at the frontier. Since neither your driver nor the Porsche came back, one gathers Yusuf made him listen to reason, or else simply carried out the original plan and left him somewhere to cool off till tomorrow. We can't afford to let him near a telephone, you must see that." A little grunt of amused satisfaction. "After that it was so easy it was hardly true. You told everyone within hearing that you were going to the Adonis Hotel to get a car for Beirut, so I simply went there first and waited for you to come. The manager's new, so there was no fear of his recognizing me, but I'm damned sure that by the time you turned up he was sure he'd known me all his life. You'd never have accepted a lift from someone picking you up on the road, but someone you met in the hotel, someone you were introduced to by name . . ." That smile again. "I hope you appreciated the touch about the Great Mosque? You remember telling your 'great-aunt' all about it?"

"Very clever. You're so very clever. Quite a little empire you've got, haven't you, with all your spies and drivers and cars. Something's paying pretty well. Don't grin at me like that, you snag-toothed little viper. What have you done with Charles?"

"I told you. He's in the lock-up." The grin had vanished.

"Have you hurt him?"

"There was a bit of a rough-up last night."

"You tried to rough Charles up? No wonder John looks the worse for wear. I thought his face was hurting him yesterday, and now I come to think of it, he kept that side turned away. It's come up lovely now, hasn't it? Good old Charles! And oh, my poor auntie! Did he hurt you much?"

The smile had certainly vanished. He had flushed darkly, and I saw the vein in his temple begin to beat. "He didn't touch me. I had a gun. I admit John isn't much use, but then he drugs."

"Drugs?" I don't think I managed to speak the question, I only looked it. He had gone far away from me again. The room was all shadows now. I found myself straining forward, peering to see where he had gone. Dimly, I knew I should be frantic with worry about Charles, with fear for myself. But I couldn't tie my brain down. It wouldn't work for me. It spun high and light. It floated, lifting me with it out of the chair, up towards the high dim corners of the room.

He was suddenly close, gigantic. He was out of his chair

and standing over me. His voice was vicious. "Yes, drugs, you silly spoiled little bitch. Drugs. I said 'medical supplies', didn't I? There's a fortune in Indian hemp lying there in the cellars waiting for collection tonight, and another fortune growing in the fields above Laklouk if your great-aunt hadn't died, and I'd been able to hang on till harvest." He drew in his breath. "And not only hemp. They grow opium in Turkey and Iran, didn't you know? That's the real stuff. Opium, morphine, heroin—and I've a pipeline across Syria that's been working like a dream, and all it needs for the processing is a bit of time and the kind of privacy we get here at Dar Ibrahim . . ."

I'd been meaning to stub my cigarette out in the saucer, but the saucer was too far away, and the effort was too much. The stub fell through my fingers to the floor. It seemed to fall in slow motion, and I made no attempt to retrieve it, but just sat there, looking down at my own hand, which seemed a long way away and not attached to my body at all.

". . . And that's just what we had, till you came. The room next to the storeroom where we put you, that's our lab. We've been working like slaves putting the stuff through since the last lot came down. Oh, we'd have had to pack it in this year, no doubt of that, and move our base—those bastards at the Narcotics Division of the U.N. have been putting the screws on, and the National Assembly's promising to make it hotter than ever in this country next year . . . and of course since the old lady went Dar Ibrahim was due to shut down anyway. Phased withdrawal, don't they call it? The caravan comes through tonight . . ." His voice trailed off, and I heard him laugh again. He stooped and picked up the stub, and dropped it in the saucer. His face swam near mine. "Feeling a bit far away, are you? Not exactly fit to cope? That was a reefer you had in the car, and you've just smoked two more, my pretty, and now you're going back to your nice little room to sleep them off . . . till tonight's over."

I wished I could care. I ought to care. Fragments of pictures were there in smoky darkness, like dreams edged with light. John Lethman's slack body and defeated young face with the sunken grey eyes. The Arab girl watching him fiercely. The patch of hemp with the label of the racing dog. The crates in the cellar. But they dislimned and the light beat in a steady echoing rhythm that was somehow my own heart beating, and someone's voice was coming and going in the throbbing air like the pulse of a drum, and I was out of it all, safe and high and floating as scatheless and beautiful and powerful as an angel among the cobwebs on the ceiling, while down there below in the dimming room sat a girl in a red lacquer chair, her body slack and drowsy in its plain expensive frock, her face pale, the cheekbones highlighted with a film of damp, her mouth vaguely smiling. Her hair was dark and smooth and fashionably cut. Her arms were sunburned, the hands long and slender, one wrist weighted down with a gold bracelet that had cost all of eighty pounds. . . . A spoiled silly bitch, he had called her. She was blinking at him now. She had very big eyes, dark-fringed, made bigger by the make-up she affected, and now by the drug . . . Poor silly bitch, she was in danger, and I couldn't do a thing for her, not that I cared. And she didn't even look afraid . . .

Not even when John Lethman came quietly in, floating like another shadow in slow motion across the dim floor, to stand over her and ask of Henry Grafton, as if it hardly mattered:

"She's out, is she?"

"Two cigarettes. Well taken care of. And the boy?"

"Blocked. Cell blue with smoke and himself out cold. No trouble there."

Henry Grafton laughed. "No trouble anywhere. Safe under our hands till it's over. And you, young John, will stick to your ration and stay with it. You've just had your fix, by the look of you? Well, that's the last you'll get. Oh, you can smoke if you want to, but don't come asking me for more of the hard stuff because you won't get it till that cargo's safely through Beirut. D'you hear me? Right. Take her back."

The younger man stooped over the chair. The girl moved her head dreamily and smiled at him, eyes misty. She seemed to be trying to speak, but couldn't manage it. Her head lolled back.

"I must say," said John Lethman, "I like her better this way."

"Meaning she's too pretty to have a tongue like a wasp's backside? I agree. My God, what a family! She reminds me of the old lady on her bad days. Well, she's asked for all she's getting. Take her away. I'm afraid you'll have to carry her."

Lethman leaned over the lacquer chair. At his touch, some of the fumes of the drug must have lifted for a second. I came down from where I had been floating, into the body on the chair, as he pulled me forward to slide an arm round me and lift me. I managed to say slowly and with what I thought was immense dignity: "Can manage qui' well, thank you."

He said with impatience: "Of course you can't. Come along, I won't hurt you. Don't be afraid."

"Of you?" I said. "Don't make me laugh."

He bit his lip, yanked me out of the chair, and heaved me over his shoulder in the he-man lift. I'm ashamed to say I spoiled the heroic scene by laughing like an idiot upside down all the way back to my dungeon.

Chapter Sixteen

———— ∞ ————

Truly we have been at cost, yet we are forbidden harvest.
—THE KORAN: *Sura* LVI

AN EMPIRE I had called it, and I hadn't been far wrong.
Heaven knows the clues had been there if I had only had the
knowledge to work from; and heaven knows I had all the
pieces now.

It was hours later. My watch said eleven, within a minute
or two. The time had gone like a dream, literally like a
dream, passed like smoke from the cigarettes that had sent me
floating. I felt firmly enough based now—too firmly. I was
back on the bed in my prison, sitting on top of the tumbled
blankets holding an aching head, no longer the slack-boned,
don't-careish girl hopped up with bhang, but a young woman
with a crashing hangover, still in reasonably full possession of
her five wits, and every one of them scared, with all the
evidence literally under her eyes.

They had left me a light this time. Up in its niche the
three-branched lamp held up its buds of flame. Beside the
bed was a jug of water and a glass. I drank, and my mouth
felt a little less as if someone had been cleaning it out with an
abrasive cleaner. I tried putting my legs down, and my feet to

the floor. I could feel the floor, which was probably something. I didn't try anything violent, like standing up, but sat there, holding my head on to my body, and gently, as gently as possible, allowing my eyes to look here and there in the swimming light . . .

The room was far bigger than I had thought, stretching away back into the shadow. Behind the clutter of broken-down furniture and the piled rugs and harness that would be all one could see from the corridor, I now saw that the place was stacked, literally stacked, with wooden boxes and cardboard cartons and small tins. Some of them, I thought, would probably be 'blinds'—genuine consignments of whatever article (like the cooking oil) was used to disguise the drugs, but if even a fraction of these held hashish or the opium derivatives, the room would have bought up Aladdin's cave four times over. I thought of Hamid's sheeps' droppings, but somehow it wasn't funny any more.

On the cartons nearest me the device of the running dog stood out clear and damning, with its misspelled warning carefully stenciled below: "Best quality, beware immitations." It shook the last piece into place, and Henry Grafton's sketchy story, with all its gaps and evasions, became, with this gloss added, very clear indeed. The hashish, grown copiously in the high hills; John Lethman crop-watching, or bargaining with the growers, or arranging for the piecemeal ferrying of the stuff down by the peasants—perhaps one of them the very man whom Charles and I had seen approaching the back gate of the palace. Dar Ibrahim must have been used as the center of the filthy trade for some time, might even have been so used long before the old lady moved in. It was the perfect clearing house, and also the perfect retreat for anyone in Henry Grafton's situation—the lonely hilltop fortress kept by the strong-minded old woman who refused to receive visitors, and who had (like her prototype Lady Hester) once or twice defied the law and would presumably defy it again on a friend's behalf. I couldn't believe that my great-aunt would have concealed Henry Grafton had she known what trade he was engaged in, but no doubt his story had been plausible enough, and equally plausible the account of whatever 'experiments' he and John Lethman were conducting in the underground storeroom. And John Lethman's own role in the business became pathetically clear. He had probably started innocently enough, being persuaded by the unscrupulous Grafton that the occasional 'smoke' would do him no harm; then quietly, inevitably, hooked on the hard drugs that would ensure his dependence and continued help. It was not my Great-Aunt Harriet who was the victim of this affair— for every reason I was now convinced that Grafton would never have wished her out of the way—but John Lethman.

And I was very much afraid that there were going to be two more victims. Henry Grafton might keep insisting that he meant me and my cousin no real harm, but people have been murdered for a lot less than a fortune in drugs and a possible death sentence (since Grafton was a Turkish national) if they went astray. He could hardly imagine that Charles or I would fail to report all we knew the moment we were able to, yet I—and probably my cousin as well—had been handed both information and evidence with a carelessness that terrified me. Whether he had got round to realizing it yet or not, he would have to kill us both if he wanted to save his skin.

The door must have been very thick. I had heard no movement out in the passageway, but the door swung open suddenly to reveal Halide standing there with—as ever—a tray in her hands. There was nobody with her, and she managed the tray one-handed while she opened the door, so I supposed that my captors knew the condition their drugs would reduce me to. She now stood propping the door open with one shoulder, and eyeing me with her usual contempt and hostility.

"So, you are awake. Here is your food. And do not think that you can push past me and get away, because the one way is only to the back gate, which is locked this time, and the key out of it, and Jassim is in the outer court, and the men are in the Lady's room."

I eyed her sourly. "If you knew how funny that sounds in English."

"*Quoi?*"

"Never mind." Confronted with her shimmering grace—it was the green silk again—I felt terrible. And I didn't think the bathroom gambit would work again. I made no attempt to get to my feet, but watched her as she came gracefully away from the door and set the tray down on a box with a rap which made the crockery rattle.

"Halide—"

"Yes?"

"I suppose you know what they—the men—are doing, why they have locked me up, me and my cousin?"

"Oh, yes, John—" she brought the name out with a kind of flourish—"tells me everything."

"You lucky girl. Did he tell you what the penalties were for running drugs in this neck of the woods?"

"*Quoi?*"

"Even in this dirty corner of the dirty world? Even in Beirut? Didn't John warn you what the police would do, to you and your brother as well, if they discovered what was happening here at Dar Ibrahim?"

"Oh, yes." She smiled. "Everybody knows this. Everybody does it, here in the Lebanon. For many years before the doctor came here, my brother used to bring the hashish down from the hills. It is only the brave men who are the carriers from the hills to the sea."

I supposed it was too much to hope that the primitive mind would see it as anything other than a sort of Robin Hood gesture of bravery. To the peasant, the hashish brought pleasure, and money. If an unreasonable government chose to forbid its growth for private purposes, why then the government must be fooled. It was as simple as that. It was the same mentality which, in more sophisticated societies, assumes that the tax and speed laws are made to be broken.

"You need not be so afraid," said Halide to me, with contempt, "I think they do not mean to kill you."

"I'm not afraid." I met her derisive look as steadily as I could. "But I think you had better be, Halide. No, listen, I don't think you quite realize what is happening here, and I'm not quite sure if John knows, either, just what he's got himself into. It isn't just a case of you and your friends having a quiet smoke now and then and your brother shooting it out with a few local police on his way to the sea. Not any more. It's big business, and the governments of every responsible country are wild keen to stop it. Are you hoping to clear out with your John when this lot's been shifted and he's got his share of the money? Where d'you think you can go? Not into Syria—they'd catch you up in no time. Not into Turkey—there's a death penalty there. The same applies to Iran, Egypt, where you like. Believe me, Halide, there's no future in this for you or for John. Don't think he can take you to England, either, because you'll be picked up there as soon as I or my cousin open our mouths."

"Perhaps you will not get out of here for a long time."

"That's silly talk," I said. "You know as well as I do that any minute now the Damascus police will start looking for us, and where would the trail lead them first if not to Dar Ibrahim? Dr. Grafton'll be lucky if he gets the stuff away at all."

"He will get it away. I think you do not realize what time it is, or what day? It is nearly midnight, Wednesday. The caravan is already on its way here. The palace will be empty by daylight."

"I . . . suppose it will," I said slowly. I had lost count of time. I put a hand to my forehead, pressing the heel of it against my temple as if that would clear my thoughts. At least the headache had gone. "Listen, Halide, listen to what I have to say. And take that look off your face, I'm not pleading for anything, I'm offering you something, you and John Lethman, because he's nothing much worse than weak and stupid, and you've had no chance to know better. My family—my cousin's family—we're wealthy, what you'd call important people. I obviously can't offer you the kind of money you'll get by helping Grafton with this operation, but I can offer you some help which believe me you're going to need, and badly. I don't know your laws, but if you let me and my cousin go now, and if you and your John were to give evidence against Dr Grafton, and the police stopped the cargo of drugs, I think you'd find they wouldn't prosecute you or your brother, or even John Lethman."

I had been watching her as I spoke, but her face was turned away from the lamplight and I couldn't see if my words were having any effect. I hesitated. It would certainly be no use beginning to talk about rights and wrongs, or why I should have any interest not strictly personal in stopping the cargo from reaching the sea. I added, flatly: "I don't know whether or not your Government would give a reward for information, but in any case I'd see that my family gave you money."

"You!" The blazing contempt in her voice made it an expletive in its own right. "I do not listen to you! All this talk of police and governments and laws. You are only a stupid woman, too stupid to get a man! Who are you?" And she spat on the floor at my feet.

It was all it needed. My head cleared miraculously, as the adrenalin came coursing out of the booster pumps. I laughed. "As a matter of fact I have got a man, I've had one for twenty-two years, and he's the grandson of your Lady's eldest brother, and therefore probably at the moment owner or part owner of this palace and its contents. So for a start, my nasty little Arab maiden—because in spite of your efforts I wouldn't back John Lethman ever to have got past first base—you can hand over my great-aunt's ring. And I may warn you that your precious Dr Grafton will make you give it up even if I can't. Hand it over, poppet."

It was obvious that Grafton had already spoken to her. Her face darkened, and for a moment I saw her hand clench and hide itself in a fold of her silk robe. Then with a gesture she drew the ring off.

"Take it. Only because I wish. It is nothing. Take it, daughter of a bitch."

And she threw it at me with the gesture of an empress flinging a groat to a beggar. It landed with an accuracy she could never voluntarily have achieved in a dozen years, slap in the bowl of soup.

"Well," I said cheerfully, "that should sterilise it. Or should it? I've never seen the kitchens here, but when I was a guest I had to take them on trust. Now I'm only a prisoner I don't need to eat what I don't fancy, do I?"

I leaned over and picked up the fork from the tray, fished Great-Aunt Harriet's ruby out of the soup, dunked it in the glass of water, and dried it on the napkin provided. Then I noticed the silence. I looked up.

When she spoke I knew something had put her out considerably. "You do not wish the meal?"

"Oh, I'm quite glad of something, and it's a wise gaolbird that lets nothing slip. I'll eat the bread and cheese. Thanks for the ring." And I slipped it onto my finger.

"Not the soup? The ring was clean . . . it . . ."

"I'm sure it was. I wouldn't have been rude about it if you, my proud beauty, had not just called me the daughter of a bitch. Not that I mind, I like dogs, but Mummy might be a bit narked. No, Halide, not the soup."

She had obviously not followed anything except the first and last statements. "Then let me bring you more—please."

I looked at her in surprise, then the surprise slid into a stare. To begin with it had only seemed odd that she had offered to oblige me at all, but the last request had carried an urgent, almost pleading note.

"Of course I will bring more. It is no trouble. Any minute now they will come to start loading the boxes and you will be taken out of here and put with the man, so you must eat while you can. Please allow me!" There was an abject quality in the eagerness, the automatic bending of the shoulders and thrusting of the chin and opening of hands, palms up, that suddenly spoke more clearly than any documentary could have done, of generations of slavery and the whip.

"It's good of you, but there's not the slightest need." My own reaction, I noticed with sour self-contempt, was also predictable. While she was insolent I was angry and unpleasant; as soon as she crept into her place, I could afford a cold civility. I made an effort. "I don't want the soup, thank you. The bread and cheese will do very well."

"I will take it back, then, just in case—"

"No, no, don't bother. But I'd be glad if you'd go straight to Dr Grafton—"

I never finished the sentence. We had both reached forward together, she to lift the bowl from the tray, and I to stop her, and for a moment, inches apart, our eyes met.

Then I shot out a hand and took hold of her wrist before she could take the bowl. Her expression, and the tiny intake of breath, told me that—incredibly—I had been right.

"What's in it?" I demanded.

"Let me go!"

"What's in it?"

"Nothing! It is good soup, I made it myself . . ."

"I'm dead sure you did. What did you put in it? More of your *cannabis indica* to keep me quiet, or something worse?"

"I don't know what you're talking about! I put nothing in

273

it, I tell you! Chicken and herbs and vegetables and a little *zafaran* and—"

"And a drop or two of poison to top it up?"

She drew back sharply, and I let her go and stood up. We were much of a height, but I felt inches the taller of the two and ice-cold with contemptuous rage. There is something infuriating, rather than frightening, about this kind of attack. That one is there to react to it at all means that the attempt has failed and the danger is over, and I suppose one's very relief at that failure explodes in contempt for the poisoner and blazing anger at the filthy method used.

"Well?" I said, quite softly.

"No, it was not! No! How can you be so foolish as to think so? Poison? Where would I find poison?"

The words were bitten off with a gasp as Henry Grafton said from the doorway behind her:

"What's this? Who's talking about poison?"

She swung round to face him, hands out as if to ward him off, her body still curved in that lovely windblown bow that one sees in the carved ivory ladies of Japan. Her mouth opened, and her tongue licked across her lips, but she said nothing. His eyes went past her to me.

"I was," I said. "The sweet creature seems to have put something in my soup that she doesn't care to talk about. Would this by any chance be by your orders?"

"Don't be a fool."

I raised my eyebrows. "Dope, yes, but poison, never? You and your Hypocritic Oath . . . Perhaps she'll tell you what it is, and why? Or would you like to take it away and analyze it in your little lab next door?"

He stared at me only briefly, then his eyes went to the tray.

"Did you take any of the soup?" he asked eventually.

"No, or I've no doubt I'd be writhing on the floor."

"Then how do you know there's anything wrong with it?"

"I don't, it's an inspired guess. But she was too anxious by half for me to drink it, and she hasn't cared terribly for my welfare up till now. She threw the ring into it by mistake, and when I said I didn't want it after that she was upset. Then I knew. Don't ask me how, but I'd take a twenty to one bet on it now, and don't tell me you don't think the same. Look at her. And as for where she got it, hasn't she got a whole roomful at her disposal, all that stuff of Great-Aunt Harriet's? Ask her," I nodded at the silent girl, "ask little Miss Borgia here. Perhaps she'll admit it to you."

Long before I had finished speaking his attention had switched back to Halide, the black eyes bright and deadly as an oil-slick. I had a moment's sharp relief that under this night's various pressures he should take time to handle this so seriously; it must only mean that he intended no real harm to Charles or myself. But the expression in his eyes as he looked at her, and the girl's obvious terror, surprised me. Her hands were tightly clasped at the base of her throat, clutching the lovely silk of the robe together as if for warmth.

"Is this true?"

She shook her head, then found her voice. "It's all lies, lies. Why should I poison her? There is nothing in the soup—only the meat, and the herbs, and onions and *zafaran* . . ."

"Then," said Henry Grafton, "you wouldn't object to drinking it yourself?"

And before I knew what he was about, he had whipped the bowl up from the tray, and was advancing on the girl with it held up to the level of her mouth.

I think I gave a gasp, and then said weakly: "Oh, no!" It was somehow too much, so absurdly the stock situation from a thousand and one Arabian Nights, an Eastern melodrama come ludicrously to life. "For God's sake," I said, "why not just call in the dogs and try it on them? That's the form, isn't it? For pity's sake call the scene off, I withdraw the complaint!"

Then I stopped as I realized, not amused any more, that the melodrama was taking Dr Grafton away from the door of the room as the girl backed in front of him . . . and there was a gun on the wall above the Prince's bed, if I could grab it before they got me . . .

Neither of them took the slightest notice of me. She had retreated until she was backed right up against a stack of crates beyond the bed, and her hands came up in front of her to push the bowl away. He drew back quickly to prevent its being spilled.

"Well, why don't you? Am I to believe this nonsense is true?"

"No, no, of course it isn't true! She only says this because she hates me! I swear it! I will swear it if you like on my father's head! Where would I get poison?"

"Considering my great-aunt's room is like remnant day at the chemist's," I said drily, "I'd have thought one could lay hands on almost anything."

He didn't look round when I spoke; all his attention was fixed on the girl, who stared back at him like a mesmerised rabbit which might at any minute burrow its way backwards through the stacked boxes. I edged a bit nearer the doorway.

"Why don't you call her bluff?" I asked.

I didn't see a movement, but she must have sensed that he was planning to do just that, for she gave in suddenly. "All right, if you won't believe me! I did put something in it, and I did want her to drink it, but it is not poison, it is only a purge, to give her pains and make her sick. She's a bitch and the daughter of a bitch, and you have made me give back the ring when she is rich already, and of course I do not try to kill her, but I hate her and I put the oil in the soup only to make her suffer a little . . . just a little . . ." Her voice faltered and seemed to strangle itself for a moment, defeated somehow by the heavy musty silence of the dungeon.

"Charming, my God, charming!" I was within two jumps

of the door now. "Then you lock me in with Charles and leave me to it?"

Neither of them took the slightest notice of me. She finished in a rush: "And if I must drink it I will, to prove to you that it is true . . . but tonight you will need me to help you, you and John, so we will give it to a dog, or to Jassim, or to someone who does not matter, so that you will see . . ."

Grafton's face was suffused, and that ugly vein was beating again. Neither of them was concerned with me any more; whatever was between them shut me out completely, and I stood rooted there watching, afraid now to move and direct that raging concentration back to myself.

"Where did you get it?" He spoke quite evenly.

"I forget. From her room, perhaps . . . I've had it a long time . . . all those bottles . . ."

"There were no purges in her room, I know that. Don't give me that, you never got it from there. I saw to it that there was nothing harmful lying about, and after she'd had her sick turns I checked to see if she'd been dosing herself. Come on, what was it? Did you get it from the village, or was it some filthy brew you made yourself?"

"No . . . I tell you it was nothing. It was something John had. I took it from his room."

"From John? Why should he have that kind of thing? You said 'oil'. Do you mean castor oil?"

"No, no, no, I tell you I don't know what it was! It was a black bottle. Why don't you ask John? He will tell you it was harmless! He said it tasted strong, so I used to put in extra herbs, and pepper—"

"When did you use it first? The time I was away near Chiba?"

"Yes, yes, but why do you look like that? It was nothing, a drop or two, and then a little sickness—the pain was not bad— and afterwards she was always so quiet and good . . ."

I wouldn't have moved now for worlds, open door or not.

The bowl had begun to shake in his hands, and his voice had that stretched, even thinness of a wire about to snap, but the girl didn't seem to recognize the signals. She had ceased to look alarmed, and had dropped her hands to twist them in the skirt of her dress, glowering back at him, sullen and defiant. I don't know just at what point through the swift, unemphatic exchange I had realized that that they were no longer talking about me, but about Great-Aunt Harriet.

"Quiet and good!" He repeated the words with no expression at all. "I see. My God, I wondered. Now I begin to see . . . Did this happen whenever I went away?"

"Not always. Sometimes when she'd been too difficult. Oh, why the fuss, it did her no harm! You know how well I nursed her! You know how I had worked and cared for her all those months, and how she would ring her bell night and day, and never must we be tired, always ready to run for this thing and that thing, and cook special food . . . But I wouldn't have harmed her, you know that! Only one or two drops I gave her, and then I would nurse her through it, and afterwards there would be peace for a few days."

"And she would be grateful. Yes, of course. Clever girl, Halide. Is that when she gave you the ring? Yes? What else did she give you?"

"Many things! And she meant me to have them! She said so! She gave me these things herself because I had cared for her! You shall not take them from me . . . indeed you dare not, because I gave them to my father and brother who will keep them! And then when I become an English lady—"

He spoke between his teeth. "You killed the old woman. Do you not realize that even now, you stupid bitch?"

"I did not!" Her voice was shrill with rage. "How can you say this? It was only medicine, I tell you, and I took it from the chest that John keeps in his room—you know the old medicine box that the Lady's husband took on his expeditions—"

"That prehistoric collection? God knows what was in it! Do you mean to tell me John knew about this?"

"No, I tell you I took it! But I asked him what it was before I used it. I would not have used it unless I knew it was safe! It was not poison! He said it was a purge, made from the seed of some plant . . . yes, a spurge plant—I remember that because the words were the same, and—"

He had been sniffing at the bowl he held. Now he gave a great gasp as though he needed air. "So that's it! Spurge plant, my God! It's croton oil, and I doubt if even old Boyd used the stuff in the last fifty years except for the camels! 'One or two drops,' indeed! Twenty drops and you'd kill a healthy horse! And you gave that stuff to an old woman, a sick woman—"

"It did her no harm! You know it did her no harm! Three times I gave it to her, and she got better—"

"And the last time," said Henry Grafton very softly, with the wire in his voice beginning to shake, "she'd had a coronary just three weeks before. And so she died . . . and if you'd kept your stupid fingers out of the pie she'd be alive today and we wouldn't have these damned people round our necks, and the whole job done as smoothly as kiss your hand and away with one fortune and time to collect another at harvest. But you—you—"

And he dashed the soup, bowl and all, in her face in an access of blinding rage.

The stuff was no longer hot, but it was greasy and it took her full across the eyes. And the bowl smashed. It must have been of fine china, because it didn't smash against the boxes behind her, but right across her cheekbone. There was a still second before she screamed, and the scream choked because some of the slimy stuff went into her mouth and throat and gagged her, then she doubled up, retching and choking, and the blood came welling in a slabby stream on her cheek and mixed with the greensick slime of the soup.

279

Grafton swung his arm as if to strike her. I gave a cry of protest and jumped forward and grabbed it.

"That'll do! For pity's sake!"

He wrenched away to disengage himself. The movement was violent, and—thrust by his shoulder—I went reeling back, sent the tray flying, and almost fell against the door. His face was that curious dark red, and his breath snorted in his throat. I don't know if he would have hit her again, but there was a flash in her hand, and she came away from the wall of crates like a leaping cat, claws and knife, and went for his face.

He was quick on his feet as many shortish men are, and I think it was purely reflex, too quick even for his thought, which made him leap back clear of those raking claws and the knife she had whipped from somewhere, Damascus-bright. She was on him. The knife flashed. He had no weapon—who would need it against me?—and he snatched up from the clutter the first thing that came to hand. I think even then what he snatched for was the whip that lay on the pile of camel harness, but his hand missed it by centimeters, and what he lifted and lashed down with was not the flexible whip, but the heavy, cruel goad.

It caught the girl full across the temple. She seemed to slacken in the middle, as if a spring had broken. She still lurched forward, but the claws slid loose and harmless down the man's neck, and the stabbing knife missed his throat by inches as her body pitched against him and slithered, joint by joint, into a slack and thudding collapse at his feet. The knife fell just before the final drop of the body, with a little tinkling sound on the floor. Then the upper part of her body slumped, and the head hit the stone with a small, and quite final little crack.

In the silence, I heard the lamp fluttering again like a caught moth.

My knees felt as if they didn't belong. I was back in the

smoke, helpless, floating. I remember that I had to push myself away from the door, to go to Halide.

I had forgotten he was a doctor. Before I had done more than decide I must move, he was down beside her on one knee.

I took a step. I croaked somehow: "Is she dead?"

What he was doing took no more than a moment, then he got to his feet. He didn't speak. He didn't need to. I'd never seen a dead body before, only people shamming dead on stage or screen, and I can tell you, no one could ever mistake death for anything but death, not once they'd seen it.

Whatever I was trying to say, choking on it through bile in my throat, never got said. Henry Grafton turned round on me now. He still had the goad in his hand.

Of course he had never meant to kill her. But she was dead, and I had seen it. And something else, I believe, got through to me—how, I don't know, except that just at that moment in the horrible little room reeking with soup and the oil lamp and something else that may have been death, all nerves were stripped raw and felt as if they were exposed like white roots all over the skin. He had never killed before, and maybe he didn't quite believe it even yet, or believe how simple it had been. Whatever soothing lies he had been telling himself about Charles and me, now he knew. Now the decision had made itself. He had taken the first step on a very easy slide . . . And behind those dilated black eyes, for all I knew, he could be smoked as high as an Assassin with the damned drug himself.

I shall never be sure if what I did then was the stupidest thing I could have done. Perhaps I should have stayed where I was and spoken calmly, till the dark-red look went from his face and the suffused eyes cleared.

But all I could see was that the doorway was clear, and that I was nearer to it than he was.

I didn't stop to argue. I turned and ran.

Chapter Seventeen

———◆◆◆◆———

The Stars are setting and the Caravan
Starts for the Dawn of Nothing—Oh, make haste!
—E. FITZGERALD: *The Rubáiyát of
Omar Khayyám*

THE PASSAGE was well enough lighted; someone had put oil
lamps in one or two of the old torch-brackets—probably in
preparation for the night's work—and these showed me the
stairway to the Prince's Divan.

It was the only way to go. There was no point in making
for the Seraglio, since I couldn't hope to get down from the
window alone; the postern was locked, and Jassim was guarding the main door. Besides, there was Charles. My only hope
was the Prince's Divan and the rifle.

I was about a third of the way up the stairs when the arras
at the top was swept aside and John Lethman came through
like a pea from a catapult, shouting, "Grafton! Grafton!" and
hurtled downstairs three at a time. Before I could stop
myself, I had run straight into him.

He gave a grunt of surprise and held me fast. What must
have surprised him even more was that I made no attempt to

get away. I suppose if I had been in a fit condition to think I might have expected Halide's murder to put him on my side against Grafton, but I wasn't thinking, and it was only instinct that made me see him almost as a rescuer, as corruptible rather than yet corrupt, a man who could surely not stand aside and watch me killed.

"How did you get out?" he snapped. Then—"What's happened?"

I couldn't speak, but as I clung to him, pointing back at the storeroom door, Henry Grafton erupted into the corridor below us with the goad in his hand.

At the sight of us he stopped dead, and the goad slowly sank until its iron tip rested on the floor. There was a little pause, during which nobody said anything, then Lethman, gripping me by the arm, dragged me after him down the staircase and back towards the door.

I didn't look. I think I shut my eyes. Lethman didn't go in, he stopped just short of the doorway.

Henry Grafton cleared his throat and spoke. "It was an accident. She went for me." Then as no one said anything, suddenly savage, to me: "Tell him it was an accident, you little fool! Tell him what happened!"

I didn't look at either of them. "Oh, yes, it was an accident. He never meant to kill her, I'm sure of that. He threw the soup at her in a temper and she went for him and he grabbed for something—the whip, I think—and got hold of that thing. I don't suppose he noticed in the mad rush that it was made of iron." I added, in a tight voice that was unfamiliar even to me: "And as a matter of fact I can't even pretend I'm sorry. I gather from what they were saying that she killed Great-Aunt Harriet."

That brought him up sharply. He still kept his grip on my wrist, but he seemed to have forgotten about me. He swung on Grafton.

"She what? Halide killed the old lady? What's this?"

283

"It's true." Grafton was staring down at the thing in his hand as if he'd never seen it before. "She'd apparently been treating her off and on to doses of croton oil."

"Doses of—Good grief, so *that* was it? I remember her asking about the stuff." His hand went to his head. He looked sick and shaken. "But why? I don't get it. That stuff—good God—what could she hope to gain?"

"A dowry," said Grafton drily, "Oh, she didn't mean to kill her, that was ignorance. She was just clever enough to choose the times when I was away. I admit it never entered my head—it was one of those simple, stupid schemes one might expect from that mentality—she wanted the old lady periodically ill and helpless so that she could nurse her through it with the sort of devotion that sticks out a mile and gets its due reward. Which it did."

He was watching the younger man as he spoke. Lethman said nothing. You can always tell when someone is thinking back, remembering. He was biting his lip, his face still shocked and sick-looking. Behind the slack lines and pin-pupiled eyes of the addict I thought I could see the ghost of the pleasant-faced boy who had been pulled into Henry Grafton's orbit. And I thought I saw, too, the ghost—hastily suppressed with shame—of a boy relieved of a burden.

Grafton saw it too. "Oh, yes, there were rewards. You know how lavish the Lady could be at times. I gather that most of her pickings are being kept for her by her family in the village. As I said, a dowry."

"For heaven's sake," I broke in, "cover her face and let's get out of here before I'm sick."

Grafton gave me a look, and then obeyed me, stooping over the thing on the floor to pull a greasy, merciful fold of the pretty silk across. John Lethman turned abruptly away, dragging me with him towards the stairs. I went, only too willingly. As we reached the top and he pulled the arras back, Grafton came out of the storeroom below, shutting the door behind him, then as an afterthought pushed it open again, and flung the goad back inside. I heard it go clattering down on the floor, then the door slammed again, finally, on the dreadful little room.

The Prince's Divan was brilliantly lit tonight. The usual lamp stood on the covered fountain which served as a table in the middle of the lower room, other lamps burned in niches by the door, and from a bracket high in the wall a double cresset gave a smoky red light. As Grafton followed us through and the arras swung shut behind him, the cresset blew and guttered in the draught, sending grotesque shadows reeling up the walls.

"For Christ's sake hang on to the girl." His voice was harsh but controlled. It seemed he was back in charge. "If you let her go we'll both be in the can. God knows I'm sorry about what happened, John—it's perfectly true that Halide killed the old woman and landed us both in this, but do you seriously imagine I'd have hit her if she hadn't gone for me with a knife? The way I see it, we'd better get out of the jam we're in before we start calling the odds over this. So snap out of it, and let's get back on the job. One thing, I suppose you know what'll happen if Nasirulla gets wind of it? We'll have to shift the body now, and think up some way of stalling him off if he asks where she is. Christ!—" He sounded suddenly, viciously irritable—"Stop gawping at me! What's done's done, and you can't pretend you won't be damned grateful to me when you're free as air and with money to burn and no dusky charmer wound round your neck like a god-damned snake! And for a start, you can get that girl under lock and key—and hurry up, she looks as if she's going to pass out on us. Shove her in the lock-up with the boy, there isn't long to go."

It was quite true that I wasn't feeling too good. Still held by John Lethman, I had got as far as the red lacquer chair, but as soon as he let go of my arm I felt my knees give way, and collapsed into it, fighting back the feeling of icy nausea that splashed over me again and again, alternating with drenching heat. Through the waves of goose-pimpling sickness I was aware of a sharp and urgent exchange of words going on over my head. I didn't catch what John Lethman said, but Grafton's reaction was violent.

"*What?* What the devil do you mean?"

"I was coming to tell you. The boy's out."

"That's not possible!"

"It's true. He's out. Gone. No sign."

I surfaced for a moment. "Bully for Charles," I said.

"And," said John Lethman, "he'll be back here in an hour or two with every damned flic he can drum up."

"Back here?" Grafton took him up like lightning. "You mean *out*—he's right outside?"

"He must be. I found Jassim knocked out, and the main gate open. Of course he didn't know we had the girl here, or—"

"You bloody fool! And you've been wasting time!" This, it seemed, was how Halide's death could now be classed. "How long has he been gone?"

"Not long, I guess. He'd knocked over his water jug, and the footprints he'd left from treading in it were still wet when I came to find you."

"Get the dogs out," snapped Grafton. "Go on, get them now. He'll be making for the village, he won't have got far. They'll catch him easily enough, and you can tell Nasirulla it doesn't matter how they pull him down as long as they do it."

"They probably won't touch him. Don't you remember I told you—?"

"What the hell does that matter? Can't you see, the point is, kill two birds with one stone—get Nasirulla away from the place with the hounds, while we clear up down below. The dogs'll find the boy all right, and if Nasirulla takes a gun

. . . He's to be stopped, do you hear me? I suppose Jassim's back on his feet again? Go on, man, hurry, leave this silly bitch, I'll deal with her. And get back here as fast as you can and help me with the job below stairs."

I made a grab at John Lethman's sleeve as he turned to go.

"Don't leave me with that little swine, for goodness' sake! Can't you see he's gone overboard? Halide, and now Charles . . . and you—can't you see you haven't a chance?" I gripped his arm, shaking it. It was like pleading with a zombie. "Look, I know you've only been doing as he made you! You'd nothing to do with Halide's death! If you let Charles go, and get me out of here, I swear I'll stand up for you and tell them—"

"Get," said Grafton, and John Lethman pulled himself free and went.

Grafton jerked his head at me. "Come on. Get going."

"Where to?"

"Back to your cage, my girl."

I gripped the arms of my chair until the lacquer scored my palms. "Not back in there with her?"

"By no means, we'll be busy there, didn't you hear? You can have the official dungeon this time, but don't think you'll get out of it, even if your cousin did."

I began to get slowly to my feet, helping myself by the chair arms. The swimming nausea had cleared and I was steady enough, but I still can't have looked much to reckon with, for he had obviously dismissed me from a mind leaping ahead to the next—and major—move.

"Come on, don't waste my time. Get moving."

I got moving. I shoved myself suddenly upright, and the heavy chair away from me with a jerk that sent it skating across the marble tiles between Grafton and myself. I ran the other way, towards the bed. Up the steps, across the dais, then

I jumped onto the foot of the bed itself and yanked the rifle down from the wall.

I swung round, unsteady on the soft bed, bracing my shoulders against the wall, and had the thing leveled at his midriff before he had done more than take three strides after me.

I had no idea if the gun were loaded. I thought it probably wasn't, but Henry Grafton might not be sure. And you have to be very sure indeed to risk outfacing a gun. You only call a gun's bluff once.

He checked, as I had known he would. "Put the damned thing down, it isn't loaded."

"Are you sure?"

"Quite sure."

Outside, suddenly, the hounds bayed wildly from the court where Nasirulla was presumably loosing them in the fond hope that they would pull Charles down. I laughed in Henry Grafton's face.

"Then come and get me," I invited.

He didn't move. I laughed again, and keeping the rifle at the ready, put out a hand to the wall to steady myself as I stepped down from the bed.

And suddenly there it was again, the wave of heat, the choking nausea, the sweat and the stopped breathing. I groped for a fold of the arras and hung on, dimly aware of the rifle sinking forgotten to the trail, of Grafton hesitating momentarily before taking a step towards me, of the baying of the dogs wild and loud, of someone shouting.

I pulled myself upright. But it was too late. He was on me. He snatched the rifle from my slack hands, checked the empty magazine, kicked it under the bed, and with a vicious swing of the hand to the side of my head sent me sprawling across the bed just as the grey cat, spitting furiously, erupted from the blankets like a rocket on blastoff, and cleared me with a centimeter to spare and every hair on its body brushing my face.

I screamed. Grafton shouted something and I think he made a grab for me, but I had gone beyond fear or even thought of him. Caught up in my own private nightmare, fighting not the cat but my own terror, I struck out at him with feet and hands as I jack-knifed away towards the far side of the bed.

From the garden outside came a sudden volley of noise, a hoarse shout, a scrabble of racing paws, then the inhuman yell of a terrified cat, drowned in the wild exciting tumult of hounds sighting a kill. The cat shot back into the room, a hissing grey streak, and after it the salukis, full cry, with a broken leash trailing from one collar, and Nasirulla in loud pursuit.

The cat leaped for the bed hangings. The hounds saw it, and hurled themselves after it. The heavy chair went flying, crashed into the table, and toppled, smashing the lamp in a sprayed arc of oil. The flame ran along it like ball-lightning. Grafton yelled something, dragged a blanket from the bed, jumped clear down the dais steps, dodging the dogs, slipped in the burning oil and went down, striking his head hard on the stone edge of the table. Over my head the cat leaped like a silver bird for the high windowsill, and was gone.

It all seemed to happen in seconds. The flames ran, clawed out, rippled, caught the bed hangings, and went licking up them in great lapping gulps of flame. I rolled off the bed, fighting clear of the curtains, and hurled myself into the quiet dimness of the corridor beyond. The last thing I saw as the arras swung back behind me was the Arab bending to drag Grafton clear towards the other door.

The hounds came with me. Sofi, whining with fear, scrambled through the arras and went tumbling anyhow down the steps. The dog was at the foot of the staircase already. I slammed the door and raced down after them.

289

"Here!" I called breathlessly. "This way! Here!" And we ran on, down the curved corridor, past the room where poor Halide lay, through the still air already sharp with smoke—and there was the Prince's Door.

My hands were shaking, and twice the dogs, leaping in eager fear, shoved me aside before I could lift the heavy latch. Then I had it open, and we were through. It swung easily, massive and silent. It might make a lock on that dead air, and check the fire. I slammed it shut and drove the latch home. Then turned, to find that there was fire outside as well . . .

Or so I thought, for one heart-stopping moment, as I saw the outer passage lit and flickering before me. Then I saw why. This, too, had been illuminated for the night's work. The ancient brackets to either side of the Prince's Door held makeshift torches which flared sullenly, red and smoking. It must have been this smoke I had smelled in the corridor as I ran.

I hung there, irresolute, gasping, while the hounds whined and shivered and stayed close. The caravan was due soon, and presumably by the postern. But I had heard Halide say that the postern was locked, and the key out of it. It would have to be the main gate, and chance it.

I ran up the passage to my right, and had stumbled perhaps some twenty yards on the rough and ill-lit cobbles when Sofi whined again and I heard, clearly ahead of me, a turmoil of shouts from the main court. I stopped dead. Of course they would all be there: Grafton, Lethman, Nasirulla, Jassim—go that way, and I would run into them all. What was more, if they had any hopes of salvaging their precious cargo, this was the way they would come at any moment now. And even with the whole rotten place going up like tinder round them I wouldn't have betted a pin on any of them doing other than throw me straight back into the flames.

I ran back to the door for the Seraglio stairs.

It opened, and we tumbled through. Darkness dropped

over us like a velvet drape, stifling, silent, terrifying. I shut the door behind me and took two hesitating steps forward, then stumbled over the bottom stair and fell, hurting my shin. One of the dogs whimpered, pressing close. Under the silky coat the hot skin shivered. On my other side a narrow head nudged me, and I felt for the beast's collar and got to my feet. With one hand on the collar, and the other groping for the handrail on the outer wall of the staircase, I began to fumble my way up the spiral.

"Show me the way, mates," I whispered.

The dogs thrust upwards so eagerly that I realized they could see even here. I wondered if they smelled water. I could almost smell it myself. The thought of that great sheet of water lying above our heads was no longer terrifying; it was the bright, cool promise of safety. With the big hound pulling me, and my left hand groping past the invisible minarets, the cypresses, the singing birds, I stumbled and panted up the spiral stair. Then the bitch, leaping ahead, pushed open the painted doorway, and the three of us ran out into the night air, and the light.

But the night air smelled of smoke, and the light was red and gold and leaping. I ran with the dogs down the pavilion steps, and paused at the edge of the water.

Through all the buildings to the west of the lake, it seemed, ran the fire. The old rotten wood, crumbling dry, had caught like tinder in the night breeze, and as I stood there, afraid and dismayed, a stream of sparks like a comet's tail blew clear across the lake and scattered along the arcade to the east, near Charles's window, and began to burn.

Chapter Eighteen

———⚬◦∞◦⚬———

But not against the flame shall they shade or help you.

—THE KORAN: *Sura* LXXVII

ONE THING THE FIRE DID; the place was as bright as day. There was still a chance I could get into the junk room under the eastern arcade, find the rope, and sling it down from the window before the flames took hold. As for the dogs—as far as I could afford to think about them at all—I certainly couldn't lower them from the window, rope or no rope, but they were in the safest place in the palace. They had only to take to the water.

I ran onto the bridge, the dogs pressing close to me—so close indeed that when we got to the broken span Sofi jumped first, and Star, pushing forward to follow, shoved against my legs and threw me off balance. I slipped, tried to recover, cried out as I trod on some stone not quite secure, and went into the water.

I suppose it was about four feet deep. I went right in, down under the lilies and the shiny lily pads and the floating weeds, before I struggled to the surface and stood again, ankle deep in mud and breast deep in water, with my hair streaming like weed across my face, and the hounds gazing at me, curious and excited, from the bridge.

Then Sofi, with a little yelp of excitement, plunged in beside me. Star, inevitably, followed. They swam round and round, with little whining barks, splashing and clawing, avid to be near me, and completely ignoring my distracted croaks of command as I tried to push them away among the creaking irises, and began myself to flap and struggle out through the clotted lily leaves.

But not to the arcade. The few minutes I had lost through my accident had cost me access to the junk room. Flakes of blazing stuff—straw or rags—had blown across the water and ignited the roof at several more points. Most of it was wooden shingles bleached dry for generations, and covered with creepers already brittle with coming summer heat. The honeysuckle went up like straw, and all along the arcade burning fragments fell or were blown like fire-arrows to start fresh buds of flame. A veil of smoke wavered across the junk-room door.

Even the garden was burning now. Here and there patches of the drier scrub smouldered, and at the tip of one young cypress, where some flying tinder had lodged, a brush of flame hovered like St. Elmo's fire. The smoke was aromatic with blazing herbs.

The northern arcade was still clear, but without the rope I knew the window was useless to me. Useless, too, the gate out into the buildings. There was only one thing for me to do, what the dogs had already made me do, take to the water. But I didn't think I needed to do it yet. The island was safe enough for the time being, most of its plants too moist with the abundant water to catch fire easily. And I, thanks to the dogs, was in the same case. I reached the built-up shore and clambered out. The hounds, dripping, scrambled after me. They shook themselves over me straight away, of course, and the water flew from them like showers of liquid fire, so fierce now was the light.

I pushed my way up through the tangle of cool green bushes, and reached the pavilion steps. Smoke swirled in a sudden eddy, making me cough, but then it fanned away and the air was clear. I ran up the last steps into the comparative shelter of the pavilion, then my legs gave way at last, and I sat down on the top step, with the dogs crouched close to me for comfort, and we had time to be afraid.

*   *   *

The hounds were really scared now, and huddled close, one on either side of me, shivering. I had an arm round each of them. Now and again some stream of sparks blew across the lake. The sky all around was ringed with fire, vivid tongues and spires and meteors of fire, so that the stars which swarmed thick and glittering overhead seemed cold and infinitely distant. Through the bright heart of the flames shot flashing pulses of blue and purple and green, and the noise they made was like the galloping of wild horses with the wind in their manes. There was very little smoke, and what there was streamed mercifully away in the light winds that fanned the blaze. The lake was a sheet of melted copper, so bright that it hurt the eye, with red and gold and silver flying through the stiff black spears of the irises, till the very water seemed alive, rippling and beating with flame like the sky.

I rubbed my stinging eyes to dispel the illusion. But when I looked again I saw that it was true. The water was moving, and not with the wind. This garden was a pocket of calm overleapt by the winds, but in it the water was moving, alive with spearhead ripples as the creatures of the garden, driven by the fire, came arrowing towards the island.

The peacocks came first. The two hens flew, clumsily and in panic, from stone to stone of the broken bridge, but the cock, weighted by the magnificence of his springtime tail, came noisily yelling across the open lake, half paddling, half flying, his great useless wings flailing the golden water, his streaming train bedraggled with mud and damp and laying a wake like a VC. 10; then the three big birds, oblivious of me and the hounds, raced with hunched and staring feathers up the rocky shore, and clucked to an uneasy roost near us on the marble steps.

The little rock partridges flew more easily. There were seven of them round my feet, fluffy with fear, their bright eyes winking like rubies as they stared at the flames that ringed the garden. In the flashing scarlet light their feathers shone like chased metal. One of them quivered warm against my ankle.

I didn't even see the squirrels till one slid up the steps beside me and sat bolt upright, chittering and bedraggled, within six inches of Star. Then I realized that the water was full of heads, little black arrow tips heading for the island. I suppose there were voles and shrews and housemice; I saw shadows galore, darting and squeaking under the evergreens. Rats I certainly saw, big beasts of every shade of grey and black and brown, who eyed us askance with bright intelligent eyes as they shimmied ashore and then streaked for the safety of the shadows. Lizards darted and weaved up the stones like something in an alcoholic's dream, and I saw two snakes within a handspan of my shoes; they lowered their beautiful deadly heads and went past like smoke, and the dogs never moved, and nor did I. I hadn't room for fear of them, or they of me; the only thing that mattered was the fire. All of us, rats, birds, snakes, dogs and girl, had a right to that island until the danger was past. The hounds never even moved when one rat went clean across my feet and brushed its way through the silk of Sofi's tail.

A dove fell, out of the sky. The birds of the air were safe enough, they had been blown away on the first hot draught of air. But one grey dove fell, a wing damaged or slightly singed, almost into my hands. It came down like a badly made paper dart, sidelong and drifting, to flutter between my feet, and I leaned forward between the hounds and lifted it, then sat holding it gently. Below my feet I thought that even the water nearest the island boiled and bulged with fish, as the carp crowded away from the bright edges of the lake towards the quiet center. I could see them just under the surface, bright darts and gleams of gilt and silver and glowing firecoal red.

And above the noise of the galloping flames was the noise of the animals. The dogs whined, the peacocks vented their harsh, scared cry, the partridges crooned in panic, the rats and squirrels chittered and squealed, and I said at distressingly frequent intervals, as I hugged Sofi and Star close to me: "Oh, Charles . . . Oh, Charles . . . Oh, for heaven's sake, *Charles* . . ."

We hardly even noticed the heavy splash from the northeast corner of the lake, or saw the violent run and ripple of the melted-gold wake as the black head speared straight for the island. I sat and rocked and crooned comfort and held the grey dove and put my cheek down to Star's damp head and wondered how soon I would have to crawl down to the water's edge and plunge myself in again among the jostling fish.

The creature, whatever it was, had reached the island. It broke from the water, tossed a black lock of hair, and heaved itself ashore. Then it stood upright, and resolved itself into my cousin, dripping and plastered with weed, and dressed in the sodden drapes of what could only be a pair of baggy Arab cotton trousers girded up with a gilt belt, a pair of soggy Arab sandals, and nothing else at all.

He advanced to the bottom of the steps, and regarded me and the menagerie.

"Eve in the Garden of Eden. Hullo, love. But did you have to set the bloody place on fire to fetch me back?"

"Charles." It was all I could say. The dogs whined and wriggled and stayed close to me, and Sofi waved her wet tail. Half a dozen lizards whipped out of the way as he ran up the steps, and when he stopped in front of us a quail moved a couple of inches aside to get out of the drips. I looked up at him. "It wasn't me," I said rather waveringly, "the dogs did it. They knocked a lamp over. And I thought you'd gone, they said you'd escaped. They—they had me locked up . . . oh, Charles, darling . . ."

"Christy."

I don't remember his moving, but one moment he was there in front of me, with the firelight sliding in lovely slabs of rose and violet over his wet skin; the next he was down beside me on the marble floor, and Star was elbowed out of the way, and Charles's arms were round me and he was kissing me in an intense starving, furious way that somehow seemed part of the fire, as I suppose it was. They say that this is how fear and relief can take you. I know I went down to him like wax.

We were thrust apart by the wet jealous head of Star, and then Charles, with a laughing curse, rolled aside from Sofi's eager paws and tongue.

"Hey, pax, that's enough—hell's teeth, will you call your beastly dogs off? Why do you have to hole up with a zoo? Oh, dear heaven, and that peacock's filthy, and I've rolled all over its tail . . . Shove over, mate, will you? I've only known the girl twenty-two years, you might give me a chance. When did I last kiss you, Christabel?"

"You'd be about ten. You've changed."

"You must tell me some time . . ."

It was a lizard, dropping from the dome, that shook us apart this time. He swore, swiped at it as it shot away unhurt, and sat up.

"Christy, I love you, and I could spend the rest of my life

297

making love to you and probably will, but if we're going, the sooner we go the better, *nicht war?*"

"What? What did you say?"

"I said we ought to go."

"Yes. I love you, too. Did I say?"

"You made it plain," he said. "Oh Christy, love . . . *Christy!*"

"What?"

His grip on me changed, as it were, and it was no longer my lover, but my cousin Charles who took me by the shoulders and shook me. "Pull yourself together! Darling, are you doped, or what?"

"I'm all right."

"We've got to get out of here while there's still a chance!"

"Oh . . . Yes, let's." I sat up and blinked at the leaping flames. "But how? Unless you can fly? Oh, the sadist you are, you've nearly squashed my pigeon . . . No, there it goes, thank goodness, it must only have been doped with smoke." I started to get up. "Mind the squirrel, won't you?"

He laughed. "Is that what it is? Oh, and look at all the dear little rats. Come on!" He jumped up and pulled me to my feet and held me for a moment, steadying me. "Don't look so scared. We'd be safe enough here, probably, if we had to stay, but it might get a bit hot and uncomfortable before it dies down, so we'll have a bash at getting out straight away. There's only one possible way out, and we'd best be quick about it."

"What way? We'll never get down from the window now, because we'd never get at the rope, and I couldn't make it without one, I really couldn't—"

"It's all right, darling, I didn't mean the window. I meant the postern."

"But the corridor'll be going like a torch! The fire started in the Prince's room, you know.

"Even so, I doubt if it will. The shaft back there—"

nodding at the painted door—"would act as a chimney if the underground passage really were going up, and it shows no sign of it. Come and let's look."

He pulled the door open cautiously. The smell of smoke was no stronger here than elsewhere, and the spiral shaft was pitch dark. Behind me, Sofi whined deep in her throat, and I made a comforting sound and touched her. "You'll come too. Don't worry."

My cousin turned his head. "Was the big door shut, the bronze one to the Prince's corridor?"

"Yes, I shut it. I came that way. I thought it would seal off the draught."

"You have your moments, don't you? And the air in there was so dead that it may only be burning slowly down from the Prince's room. We'll have to try it, anyway."

"But even if the passage is all right, we can't get to the main court—the fire's there too by now—you can see it! And it's no good trying the postern, Charles, it's locked, and the key's out, they said so. And even you surely can't pick locks in the dark?"

"Not to worry, I've got the key." He grinned at my look, fishing somewhere in the tatty off-white trousers, and producing a ring with keys that gleamed and rattled. "What do you bet it's one of these? I snitched it off poor old Jassim when I made a break for it. They were no use for getting back in with, because they bolt the gates as well here, but if one of these fits the postern we'll get out." He stopped short with his hand on the door. "Look, before we go down you'd better dip a hankie or something in the lake to hold over your mouth if the smoke's bad. Come on, it won't take a moment."

"Have you got something?"

"Half a trouser leg will do for me if I can tear the things."

We ran down the steps. "Where did you get that Carnaby Street rig anyway?" I asked.

"Oh, it's quite a saga, I'll tell you about it later. I suppose they're Jassim's, but never mind, they've had a dip now and only smell of weeds and water-mint and lovely mud. I only hope I can tear the beastly things, they're still damp and as tough as hell . . . There, that's it. What the well-dressed refugee is wearing. While you're about it I'd splash a bit more water over yourself, too . . ."

It was like kneeling by a lake of liquid fire, but the water was cool and sharply restorative. Its flickering reflection caught Charles's laughing face and brilliant eyes. I laughed back at him. It was impossible to be afraid. A light, almost wild exhilaration seemed to possess me, something sharp and positive and clear, the aftermath of a far more powerful drug than any Grafton had given me.

He jumped to his feet. "That's better, shall we go?" We ran up the steps. Most of the small animals and birds seemed to have dispersed into the cool shadows of the bushes, or among the wet growth at the water's edge. "This way, my lovely lady Christabel; give me your wet little hand. If anyone had told me when I had to share the bath with you twenty years ago . . ." A pause while we negotiated the threshold of the painted door. This was made no easier by the fact that he held me all the time, and I him . . . "Though as a matter of fact I don't think I had any doubt even then. It's just been a case of taking the air here and there for a few years till the true north pulled, and here we are. D'you feel like that?"

"Always did. When I saw you in Straight Street, the bells went off like a burglar alarm and I thought 'Well, really, here he is at last.' "

"As easy as that. Are you all right? There is a bit of smoke after all."

There was in fact a good deal. If it had been possible to feel fear any more, I might have felt it then. As we crept down the spiral stair—slowly because we had no light and even a twisted ankle might have meant disaster—the heat grew palpable, and smoke met us, the real thing, acrid and heavy and scraping the lungs like a hot file. The dogs whined at our heels. Nothing else had followed us.

"Will they be all right—the animals?" I asked, coughing.

"Should be. There's always the water if things get desperate. Once the fire's out and the place is cool again, the birds will be able to get out into the valley, and I'm afraid I'm not just terribly concerned about the rats and mice. Hold it, here's the door. Let's see what's cooking outside."

He pulled it open cautiously. More smoke came wreathing in, and with it a red and sullen light, that flickered. He shut it quickly.

"Hell's delight! It looks as though we may have to try the window after all. We can—"

"Perhaps it's only the torches they lit for the fun and games tonight," I said quickly. "They frightened me to death when I came this way before. There's one just outside."

He inched the door open again and craned through, and I heard his grunt of relief. "You're right, praise be to Allah, that's all it is. Our luck's in. The smoke's seeping under the Prince's door like floodwater, but no fire." He pulled me through and let the door swing shut after the dogs. "Come on, darling, we'll run for it. Thank God to be able to see. Can you make it?"

"Of course. Let's just hope we don't run smack into the caravan."

"The camels are coming yoho, yoho . . . Don't worry about that, love, I tell you our luck's in—and it's going to hold."

And it did. Two minutes later, after a terrifying run along a passageway hot and choking and blind with smoke, we reached the postern, and while Charles fumbled with the lock I felt for and dragged back the heavy bolts. Then the key clicked sweetly in the oiled wards, and he pulled the door open.

The hounds brushed past us. Ahead was clear air, and the cool rustle of trees. My cousin's arm came round me and more or less scooped me up the rocky ramp and onto the clean rock under the trees. The postern door clanged to behind us, and shut us out of Dar Ibrahim.

Chapter Nineteen

. . . A charm
For thee, my gentle-hearted Charles . . .
—S. T. COLERIDGE: *This Lime-Tree
Bower my Prison*

ONLY THEN did I notice the shouting. Not the noise from the direction of the *midan,* of which I had been vaguely conscious all the time, but a new uproar, as of an excited crowd, which came from beyond the west wall where the main gate stood.

With the hounds trotting, sober now, beside us, we picked our way through the dancing shadows of the trees and along under the rear wall. The shade it cast was inky black, the night sky above it fierce as a red dawn.

At the corner of the Seraglio, below Charles's window, we paused to reconnoitre. There seemed to be no one about. We ran across the path and into the belt of trees which overhung the Nahr el-Sal'q. High above us I could hear the cry of some wheeling birds, jackdaws, I think, flushed from the burning walls. Far down at the foot of the cliff I saw, through the stems of the trees, the red gleam of the river, this time dyed by the fire.

We paused in the darkness of the sycamore grove. There was smoke, thin and stinging, in the air, but it smelled fresh after the garden. Charles held me close.

"You're shivering. Are you cold?"

"Not a bit, not yet, there hasn't been time—and you must admit it was warm enough in there! Charles, the shouting. Ought we to go and help?"

"Not the slightest need," he said shortly. "Apart from the fact that I don't give a damn if Grafton and Lethman are both crisped to a cinder, half the village is there already by the sound of it, and with the place going up like a torch, any minute now they'll be running sight-seeing buses from Beirut. And there's the little fact that nobody came to look for you. Let them burn. But for heaven's sake, what were you doing back in there? You were supposed to be miles away and as innocent as the day. What happened?"

"They brought me back." As briefly as I could I told him my story, cutting through his shocked comments with a quick: "But you? What made you come back for me? How did you know I was there?"

"Darling, I heard you, screeching like a diesel train just before the place went up in smoke."

"You'd have screeched if you'd been me, let me tell you! But never mind that now—how did you get in? They said you'd escaped by the main gate."

"I had. They tried to dope me with their filthy pot, and I filled the place with smoke and pretended to be stoned, and poor old Jassim fell for it and I clobbered him and got out. The only trouble was that when they laid me out first and locked me up they took my clothes . . . I can't imagine why Lethman thought that would stop me from getting out if I could find a way, but it seems he did."

"He probably wanted them to wear. He went up to drive your car away, you know, and he'd want to look like you if anyone saw him."

"I suppose so. He might in that case have left me with something more than an old blanket for the duration. And I rather cared for that shirt, blast him. Well, I took Jassim's keys off him and hurtled out of my little pad in a state of nature, and grabbed a few dreary-looking garments that were lying about in the gatehouse. Don't you like them? I took what you might laughingly call the bare minimum, and ran for it. I knew if anyone followed me they'd go straight down by the ford, so I doubled round the back, this way, under the Seraglio windows. Big deal. There went our hero, stark naked, with his pants in his hand, and leaping like a grasshopper every time he trod on a thistle."

"My poor lamb. Still, you wouldn't be the first."

"What? Oh, storming the Seraglio. Sure . . . Well, I stopped under the trees to put the pants on. As a matter of fact there was a shirt and a kaffiyeh as well, if only I could find them . . . then I heard you scream. Did that so-and-so hurt you?"

"Not really. It was the cat I was screaming at, not him. Go on, I want to hear about you. How did you get back in?"

He had been casting about under the trees while we talked, and now pounced on something with a soft exclamation of satisfaction. "Here they are . . . I suppose I shall be thankful of this shirt, such as it is, before the night's out . . . Where was I? Oh, under the Seraglio windows—just about here, in fact—when I heard you scream. I tore into the pants and shoes and belted back to the main gate, but they'd barred it again. While I was trying it, all hell broke loose inside the palace, and then I smelled the smoke. I imagined that if the fire was bad they'd open the gate, but even so I didn't fancy our chances, so I ran round here again. I knew the postern had been bolted again after they caught me, so I didn't waste time trying it; I simply ran round to that window and climbed in. It's not a bad climb at all."

"Not bad!" It was the first time I had seen it from outside. I stared up at the sheer black wall. "It looks impossible!"

"Not for your big brave cousin. Anyway, I knew you were in the garden, because when I was half-way up I heard you swearing at the dogs, and as soon as I got in I saw the Noah's Ark act on the island. That's all . . . I wish Jassim's wardrobe ran to socks—there's nothing more disgusting than wet sandals. Look, why don't you put the headcloth round your shoulders? It's not too filthy, and at least it's dry. Let me tie it . . . What's this round your neck?"

"Oh, I forgot I'd put it on. It's a charm I got for you against the Evil Eye. You wanted one for your car, you said."

"For my love, I said. You'd better keep it, it seems to work . . . There. Now you're almost up to my standards."

"Flattery will get you nowhere."

"I'm not flattering, you look wonderful. There's some weed in your hair, and that frock looks as if it had been poured over you out of a dirty jug, and your eyes are as big as mill wheels and as black as outer space."

"I've been smoking their filthy pot, that's why."

"*Du vrai?*" he asked. "I thought as much. Nice?"

"Hellish. You think it's rather pleasant and you stop worrying about things, and then suddenly you find your bones have sort of rotted from inside and your brain's made from old rags and you can't even think. Oh, Charles, it was so awful, they're dealing in the stuff . . . they've been planning for months—"

"Darling, I know. Lethman told me quite a lot, probably more than he realized. Did you know he was a junkie?"

"Grafton told me. I ought to have guessed from the way he looks sometimes, but I never thought about it. Did he tell you Great-Aunt H was dead?"

"I knew that."

I stared. "You mean you knew it all along? Was that what you were making all the mystery about?"

"I'm afraid so."

"How did you find out?"

"Guessed, to begin with. Didn't you ever know that she had your cat phobia? Full blast and all the stops out?"

"*Did* she? I don't think I ever knew that. We never had a cat at home, of course, so when she stayed with us the subject wouldn't come up. Yes, I see now. I suppose as soon as I told you 'she' had a cat in her room you knew there must be something wrong. But Grafton would know, surely?"

"He can't have realized the cat was in the room that night. More likely he never even thought about it. They may have always had stableyard cats—must have, now that I think of the rat population of the Seraglio—but in Aunt H's day they'd never have invaded that room."

"Because of the dogs?"

"One imagines so. From the way these terrifying brutes behave with you and me—" he indicated Star and Sofi, who grinned amiably, feathering their tails—"they were probably treated as pets with the run of the place, and I know Samson always slept on her bed, and he was death on cats. If 'the doctor' was scared of the dogs and shut them up, then the inevitable would happen . . . Let's get somewhere where we can see, shall we?"

We began to pick our way along the stony cliff top through the thickest part of the grove.

"Yes, go on."

"Well, the cat business made me think there was something decidedly off-key somewhere, so I made up my mind to get in and look around and find out what, if anything, had happened to the real Aunt H. The fact that Lethman and Co. had let you wander around the place indicated that she wasn't hidden there. I thought she must be dead. Then when I got in and saw the way her things were left lying about derelict—the Koran and the Dogs of Fo—and that Samson had died and apparently not been buried properly with benefit of clergy along with the other dogs, I was sure of it. So after you'd gone off to bed that night I went snooping back, and you know what happened; I got caught and knocked out and locked up and that was that. Here we are, steady, hang on to those dogs and don't let anyone see you. My God!"

We had reached the corner now, and we could see.

The scene was like something from a coloured film of epic proportions. The walls towered black and jagged against the leaping flames behind them, and one high roof, burning fiercely, was now nothing but a crumbling grid of beams. Windows pulsed with light. With every gust of the breeze great clouds of pale smoke, filled with sparks, rolled down and burst over the crowd which besieged the main gate, and the Arabs scattered, shouting and cursing and laughing with excitement, only to bunch again nearer the gate as the cloud dispersed. The gate was open; both the tall double leaves stood wide, and there was a coming and going of men through the general mêlée which indicated that some salvage work was going on—and also that Grafton would be lucky if he saw any of the salvaged goods again.

It was to be presumed that the remaining inmates of the palace were safe: the mules had certainly been got out; here and there among the crowd I saw the wicked heads tossing, the firelight bright on teeth and eyeballs, as the loot piled up on the glossy backs, and yelling Arabs fought for the head-ropes. Then I saw the chestnut horse, its coat as bright as fire, and someone who could only be John Lethman at its head.

He was dragging something—some cloth or blanket—from the beast's head. He must have had to muffle its eyes and nostrils to get it out of the burning stable. It was fighting him, jibbing and terrified, as he tried to pull it clear of the crowd.

I clutched Charles's arm. "Lethman's there! He's got the horse out. Charles, he's mounting! He'll get away!"

"Let him go. We can't do a thing. Grafton's the one—hello, look, they're stopping him."

Lethman, astride the chestnut, was fighting with knees, whip and head-rope to turn it for the corner where we stood hidden, and the track past the Seraglio wall to the open hillside and freedom. The animal, its ears laid flat back on its skull, whirled plunging in the dust, and the crowd scattered in front of it—all but one man, and he ran in under the vicious hooves and jumped for the headrope and held it fast. He was shouting something at John Lethman. I saw the latter throw out an arm, pointing back to the blazing building, and he yelled something, his voice suddenly clear and powerful above the excited roar of the crowd. Faces turned to him like leaves when the wind blows through them. He brought his whip slashing down at the man below him, and drove the chestnut forward at full gallop towards the grove where we stood.

The Arab, struck by the beast's shoulder, was sent flying. As he rolled clean over, and came unhurt in one swift bunching movement to his feet, I saw that it was Nasirulla. Two or three other men had started, vainly, to run after John Lethman. One of them, yelling like a dervish, waved a shotgun. Nasirulla snatched it from him, whirled, leveled it, and shot.

But the chestnut was already out of range round the palace wall. It went by within a few feet of us. I never even saw John Lethman's face; he was just a crouching shadow against the bright mane, gone with a crash and sparkle of hooves and the horse's snorting terror.

Nor did I notice at what moment Star and Sofi left us. I thought I saw two shadows, swifter than the horse and far more silent, whip through the trees to vanish in its dust, and when I looked round the hounds had gone.

The shot harmlessly chipped the masonry at the corner of

the palace. The men who were running our way hesitated, saw it was no use, and milled aimlessly about, shouting.

"I think that's our cue to go, my love," said Charles in my ear. "Any minute now and they'll all be coming to look for a way round the back."

"Wait . . . look!"

What happened next was almost too quick to understand, and certainly too quick to describe.

Nasirulla had hardly paused to see if his shot had gone home. While plaster still scaled from the bullet marks on the wall he turned and shoved his way back towards the gate. The others crowded back with him.

Then we saw Henry Grafton. The knock on the head had obviously not incapacitated him for long, and apparently he had been organizing the salvage operations. As the crowd by the gate eddied and momentarily thinned I saw him, just emerging past the gatehouse, his arms full.

One or two men ran forward, presumably to help him. Another tugged one of the mules nearer. Then Nasirulla yelled something, high and clear, and I saw the crowd check again, and men turning. There must have been women there; I heard one screaming something that sounded like invective. Grafton paused, staggering a little as the man who had taken half his load abandoned it suddenly and left him. Nasirulla ran forward, still yelling, and as Grafton turned to face him, flung the gun up at a range of perhaps ten yards, and fired again.

Grafton fell. As he dropped the load and went slowly, how slowly, forward over it, the Arab swung the gun butt uppermost, and ran forward, and the crowd with him.

Charles pulled me back under the trees.

"No. No. There's nothing you can do. He's dead, quite certainly. We'll get the hell out of here, Christy my girl, before that bunch of J. Arthur Rank extras really gets going."

I was shaking so much that for a moment I could only cling, and say through chattering teeth: "It was Nasirulla. I suppose—was it because of Halide?"

"Sure to be. Nasirulla may have tried to salvage the stockpile before Grafton could stop him, and found the body. Or he may simply have been asking Lethman if she'd got out, and what we just saw was Lethman passing the buck. Hold up, sweetheart, I think we can get down to the ford this way. Can you make it? Let's get the hell out, shall we? Arab mobs are not exactly my thing at the best of times, and I doubt if this lot found us here if they'd stop to listen to my elegant literary Arabic. It's all right for you, they'd only rape you, but I don't want to be castrated the day I get engaged."

"That's my big brave cousin." The little spurt of laughter I gave was more than half hysterical, but it steadied me. He took my hand, and together, by the light of the now dwindling fire, we made our way down the cliff path, across the river still running scarlet for Adonis, and gained the safe shadows of the far valley side.

Chapter Twenty

My dog brought by Kings from Saluq.

—ANCIENT ARABIAN POEM

IT WAS NOON NEXT DAY. The high hot sun poured into the village street. We sat on the low wall that bordered the graveyard, waiting for the car to take us to Beirut.

It was already difficult to remember clearly what had happened last night after we had left the scene of the fire. I had no recollection of the climb up the path to the village. I must have accomplished it on some emergency high-octane mixture of reaction, love, and residual hashish fumes. The only memory I retain to this day is some queer detached nightmare of staring eyes and neat hooves pattering like rain and the smell of goat, as (Charles tells me) we disturbed the sleeping flock, and from some invisible corner the faun tore himself from a fascinated grandstand view of the fire to offer his entirely practical help as escort up to the village.

It was he who piloted us at length through the deserted street to a house near the far end, set slightly apart behind a terrace of apple trees. No light showed, but a woman was awake and peering half fearfully out of the door at the fire which still spurted among the smoking ruins across the valley.

The boy shouted a greeting, and then a flood of what must have been explanation. I was too dazed by now and too tired to care what was said or what happened, just so that I could get out of my damp and filthy clothes, and lie down somewhere and sleep.

Charles's arms half lifted me up the steep rough steps of the terrace. He must have been as tired as I, because I seem to remember that he paused to collect himself before trying to speak to the woman in Arabic. Some minutes later, after an exchange helped out (from somewhere out of sight) by the faun, we were taken into the house; and there, behind the curtain which divided the single room, I undressed by the light of a small yellowish candle which spluttered as it burned, wrapped myself in some loose cotton garment which came from a box in the corner and which smelled clean, lay down on a bed of blankets which did not, and was almost immediately asleep. The last thing I remember was my cousin's voice, softly talking in his slow Arabic, and waiting—as I found out later—for the headman, the woman's husband, to come home from the fire.

*　　*　　*

So all the explanations had been made. Henry Grafton was dead—had died mercifully enough from the shot—and Lethman had vanished clear away into the High Lebanon. I never heard or cared overmuch what happened to him. He had gone, faceless and shadowy as the night hunter with his horse and his Gabriel Hounds, as much a victim as poor Halide of Grafton's single-minded greed. The girl's body had been recovered. Some freak of breeze and fire had left the underground corridor more or less undamaged, and with it the contents of the storeroom, which the police, arriving with the dawn light, found mysteriously depleted but still well worth impounding and investigating.

Our turn came next. We had answered the first round of questions this morning, and now the police were down on the plateau where the palace ruins stuck up on their crag like a blackened tooth, still idly smoking. From the height where we sat we could just see the gleam of the lake, calm and jewel-like, with its unburned frame of green. The plateau and the charred ruins scurried with movement, like a corpse full of maggots, where—presumably dodging the police with some ease—looters prodded about the wreckage.

At length I stirred. "I wonder if she'd have liked to know we were here?"

"From what I remember of the old dear," said Charles crisply, "she'd have been delighted to know she'd taken the whole place up with her—and laughed like a banshee to see you and me scurrying about in the lake with the rats and mice. Well, at least those hounds of hers put a nice flourish on the end of her legend. Talk about a funeral pyre. Nobody in the Lebanon will ever forget her now."

"It certainly looks as if most of the local households will have a souvenir or two," I said drily. "And your own 'Gabriel Hounds', Charles? If the storerooms didn't burn they may still be there."

"They'd hardly survive that." He nodded at the scene below us. "Anyway, I'm damned if I'll compete with those jackals and go raking among the ruins. Some day I'll find another pair, and buy them in memory of her. Ah, well . . ."

Some children, too small to be in the schoolroom or the looting party, came running by, kicking a tin, and stopped to play in the dirt under the graveyard wall. Two or three thin dogs skulked by, sniffing for scraps. A three-year old boy threw a stone at the smallest of them, and it swerved automatically and dodged behind a rusty oil drum. A dirty white cockerel padded past, intent on a tattered brown hen.

"Love is everywhere," said Charles. "Which reminds me, Christy love—"

What it reminded him of I never knew, and have never asked him. With a gush of diesel smoke and a squeal of brakes, a tourist coach drew up not fifty yards from where we sat, and the driver turned in his seat to point across to the ruins of Dar Ibrahim before he killed the engine and dismounted to open the door. The passengers piled out, English, a party who knew one another and who talked and laughed as they trod forward in twos and threes to the edge of the valley and stared down at the smoking ruins. Cameras clicked. I could hear the driver telling someone a version of last night's story. The legend was on its way.

Charles and I sat still. The children, retreating from the strangers, backed till they stood right beside us. The small dog, its long hair filthy and tousled like a wilting chrysanthemum, crept out from behind the oil drum and watched with bright avid eyes a biscuit which one of the women was eating.

Her friend, a stout lady in a wide straw hat and sensible jersey suit, lowered her camera and looked about her.

"A pity it's not a more appetizing village." She had a splendidly carrying middle-class voice. "The mosque's quite pretty, though. I wonder if they'd mind if I took a photograph?"

"Offer them something."

"Oh, it's not worth it. You remember how horrible that man was in Baalbek, the old chap with the camel? *He* looks as if he could make himself quite unpleasant, too. Look at the way he's staring."

"Layabouts, the lot of them. It's a wonder she isn't slaving in the fields to keep the children. Look at them all, and hardly a year between them. Rather revolting. He'd be quite good looking, too, if he were clean."

It was only then, as I felt Charles quiver beside me, that I realized who they were talking about. Actually he was as

315

38 I

clean as cold water and a gourd full of Omo could make him; but he hadn't shaved for two days, and he still only wore the grubby cotton trousers girdled with a cheap and cracking gilt belt, and a shirt which exposed more than it covered of his brown chest. My frock had dried remarkably filthy, and my bare legs were scratched and bruised and hadn't answered terribly well to the Omo. The dip in the lake had done my sandals no good at all. The red checked kaffiyeh Charles had given me last night covered what was left of my very Western hairdo, and Great-Aunt Harriet's ruby looked like Woolworth's last word on my hand.

I felt my mouth drop open, but Charles said under his breath, "Don't spoil it," and the women were already turning away.

"It's not worth it anyway," the thin one was saying, "there'll be better places. Oh, look, they're going. Well, what a stroke of luck seeing that! What did you say the place was called?"

She put the last of the biscuit into her mouth and wiped her fingers on a handkerchief. The children looked disappointed, and the small dog's ears sank, but she never noticed. The coach drove off. The children threw a few stones after it, then turned on the small dog again, till Charles clicked his fingers and said something to it in Arabic, and it came slinking to hide behind his legs.

"And they were dead right," I said indignantly. "Layabout's the word. Sitting there laughing! You might at least have *begged* or something! We could do with some cash! If the police don't give us a lift after all—"

"Then we'll walk, you trailing suitably in my wake with your children. Hullo, here's another car coming. More police, do you suppose? It can't be for us, it must be top brass, a car like that."

"It looks like a taxi. Do you suppose they'd take us on credit if we told them we were staying at the Phoenicia?"

"Not a chance. The way we look they wouldn't let us set foot in it."

"Oh, I don't know, you'd be quite good looking if you were clean."

"My God." Charles, who had been in the act of rising, sank back on the wall. At the far end of the village street the big glossy car had slid to a stop behind a gaggle of police vehicles. The driver dismounted to open the rear door, and a man got out, a tall man, unmistakably English as to tailoring, and unmistakably self-assured as to bearing.

"Father!" exclaimed Charles.

"Daddy!" I cried at the same moment.

"It's my father," said my cousin, "not yours. After I telephoned home from Damascus he must have decided—"

"It's not your father, it's mine. I telephoned from Beirut, and he must have caught last night's plane. D'you think I don't know my own father when I see him?"

"Want to bet? Hullo, Father!"

"Hullo, Daddy!"

The newcomer, for his part, had identified us even at that distance with unerring eye. He came our way, not hurrying.

"Give you twenty to one?" said Charles in my ear.

"N—no." Whichever it was, he had come. It was absurd and unadult to feel such a pleased rush of relief and pleasure.

He stopped in front of us, surveying us. If he felt the same way, he concealed it very well. "My poor children. Well, I'm very glad to see you. I won't say it's a relief to see how well you've brushed through what happened, because I have never seen you look worse, but I take it it's nothing that a bath won't put right? No?" His eyes went beyond us, to Dar Ibrahim across the valley. "So that's the place?" He watched the distant scene for perhaps a half a minute, without comment. Then he turned back to us. "All right, you can tell me the whole thing later on, but I'll get you back to Beirut now, and into those baths before I do anything else. I've squared the police, they say you can come, and they'll see you again later."

"I suppose you know what's happened?" said Charles.

"Roughly. Nobody's talking about anything else in Beirut. I gather you two young idiots got into some nasty doings up to your necks. What the devil were you about to let Christy in for that, Charles?"

"Unjust, unjust," said Charles, without heat. "The stupid girl got herself into a jam and I rescued her. Wait till her own father hears the story, I'm demanding a hero's welcome and his half of the kingdom. Incidentally, you might settle a bet for us, and tell her it's only you."

"It's a wise child." He smiled down at me, lifting an eyebrow. "Actually, I don't think I particularly want to lay claim to either of you at the moment."

My cousin uncurled from the wall. "You're going to have to lay claim to both. One of us wants your consent and the other your welcome or blessing or whatever, you can take your pick which."

"So? I'm very glad. Welcome, darling." He put an arm round me and hugged me to him, reaching the other hand to my cousin. "Congratulations, boy, we were beginning to think you'd never make it. Certainly far more than you deserve." And he kissed us both in turn.

My cousin grinned at me. "Well?"

"You win, of course. You always do. Oh, Uncle Chas, it's wonderful to see you!" I hugged him again. "Thank you for coming! Couldn't Daddy make it?"

"Afraid not. He sent me as deputy. You look a bit battered, child, are you sure you're all right?"

"Oh, yes, truly! And it's true Charles looked after me. Real hero stuff, too, wait till you hear!"

"This seems the right moment to tell you," said Charles, "that I lost the Porsche."

"So I gather. It's at the Phoenicia."

"Efficient devil you are," said his son admiringly. "How did you do that?"

"Christy's driver brought it back."

"Hamid!" I cried. "Oh, thank goodness! What happened to him?"

"The man who had stolen Charles's car was a bit too zealous with it, and ran it off the road at a bend. No, Charles, it's all right, a scratch or two, that's all; it simply went wide into the shale and bogged down. Hamid was right on its tail, and managed to lay the man out before he'd quite realized what had happened. You'll be able to thank him yourself—he's here, he drove me up."

"Is that his taxi?" I asked. "They all look alike, I didn't recognize it. Oh, that's marvelous! Do you think we could go now?"

"Why not?" He turned to look again, a longer look this time, at Dar Ibrahim. There was a pause. It was very quiet. The children had long since abandoned us to go and talk to Hamid, and now the little dog, perhaps encouraged by the silence, ventured out of hiding and crept across the space of dust to my uncle's feet. At length the latter turned. "Well . . . that's the end of a long story. When you're both rested you can tell me all about it, and Charles can come back with me when the excitement's died down a bit. For the moment, you two had certainly better try to forget it. Leave it to me." He stretched out a hand to me. "Come along, child, you look tired out . . . What in the world—?" As he turned to go, he had almost tripped over the little dog, tangled and shapeless as a dirty mop, crouching flat at his feet in the dust. Through the filthy hair an eye shone out eagerly. An apology for a tail wagged furiously. "Not yours, surely?"

"Good grief, no," said Charles. "It's one of these miserable village dogs."

"Then do you mind discouraging the poor little beast? I'm

319

afraid we can't—what is it?" This as Charles, who had stooped obediently to pull the dog aside, let out an exclamation.

"Believe it or not, it's got a collar on—" I peered over my cousin's shoulder as he disentangled the collar from the dirty hair— "and a label. Thy life hath had some snatch of honour in it . . . Yes, there's something printed. If there's an address, then it's genuinely lost, poor little beast, and perhaps we can return it. Any dog in this country that achieves a collar must be one of the aristoc——" He stopped dead.

"One of the what?"

Then I saw the name printed on the collar. SAMSON.

Charles looked up. "He knew our voices." His voice was so dry that I knew he felt, as I did, absurdly moved. "He recognized us, me and Father. Some smatch of honour, by heck. He must have run away after she died, or more likely that little swine threw him out to starve."

"Do you know the dog after all?" asked his father.

"Indeed, yes." Charles had swung the little creature up, and now tucked him under one arm. "And quarantine'll seem like the Phoenicia to him after this."

"Quarantine? You're surely never thinking of taking that living mophead home?"

"Mophead nothing," said my cousin. "Don't you remember Samson? This is Great-Aunt Harriet's wedding present to me, Father. My personal Gabriel Hound. We can hardly leave him here to fend for himself; he's one of the family."

Hamid, all smiles, was at the door of the car. I got into the back seat between the two men. Charles's arm held me close and my head went down on his shoulder.

The little dog and I were both fast asleep before the car had covered the first mile to Beirut.

RECENT SELECTIONS
and other fine books

In addition to the editors' alternate described on the previous page, you may order any book described in **Preview** in place of or in addition to the featured selection. All of these count toward your purchase agreement and give bonus credit. If you wish to order any of these books, please list the title(s) on the back of the enclosed statement card. These special editions for Literary Guild members always represent substantial savings from the price of the publisher's editions.

NICHOLAS AND ALEXANDRA *by Robert K. Massie*

Brilliantly recreating the majesty, splendor and final downfall of Imperial Russia, this superb biography is the tragic, moving story of the last of the Romanovs—of Nicholas and Alexandra—their passionate love, their parental sorrow, and their fall from the pinnacle of earthly power to a butcher's grave. Presented with scrupulous historical accuracy and fascinating detail, here too are the others—Rasputin, the lecherous "holy man," Lenin and Kerensky, the revolutionaries—who made this one of the most decisive eras in history. *With 24 pages of photographs.*

#1089   *Publisher's Edition $10.00* • **MEMBERS' EDITION $3.95**

ALL THE LITTLE LIVE THINGS *by Wallace Stegner*

A "beautiful novel" *(Publishers' Weekly)* concerned with the clash between two misunderstanding generations—between the Joseph Allstons, a retired couple seeking peace on their secluded hillside, and Jim Peck, the radical free-thinker who camps on their property and invites his hipster friends in.

#1002   *Publisher's Edition $5.75* • **MEMBERS' EDITION $2.95**

A NIGHT OF WATCHING *by Elliott Arnold*

A suspenseful, gripping novel of heroism and courage—of Adolf Hitler's order that all Danish Jews be deported in World War II, and of the Danish Underground's subsequent smuggling of those Jews to neutral Sweden and safety.

#1024   *Publisher's Edition $5.95* • **MEMBERS' EDITION $2.95**

"Mary Stewart is magic..."

—ANTHONY BOUCHER,
The New York Times

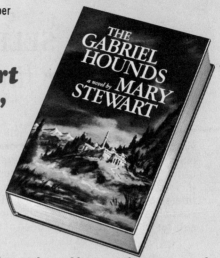

THEY MET in a street called Straight, and because they were youthful, impetuous and slightly spoiled, Charles and Christy Mansel decided to enliven their tour of the Middle East by calling on their Great Aunt Harriet.

This was not only breaking the family rule of non-interference, but also their Great Aunt's ban on visitors, for the "Lady Harriet," as she chose to call herself, was an eccentric recluse living in a crumbling, menacing Arabian Nights palace, Dar Ibrahim, in the High Lebanon, with her beloved hounds and a handful of Arab servants.

Dar Ibrahim proved difficult to get into . . . and almost impossible to get out of alive. The young cousins discovered that the "Lady Harriet" had very good reasons for not wanting witnesses to what was going on in the underground rooms below the Seraglio—reasons made even more ominous by the presence of John Lethman, the mysterious English "researcher". . . the exotic Arab servant girl who is wearing Aunt Harriet's ruby ring . . . and Aunt Harriet's former doctor whose "medicine" is quite deadly.

The title of this magnificent thriller comes from an English legend about a pack of ghostly hounds that hunt through the sky with Death and clamor over the house at night — when someone is going to die. It is pertinent to the story, one written with all the atmosphere, suspense and flavor of foreign lands that have made a new novel by Mary Stewart an international event.

Purchase Counts Toward Bonus Books

#1084   *Publisher's Edition $5.95* • **MEMBERS' EDITION $2.95**